KNIGHT
EVERLASTING

little ◄ ······

free

······ ► *library*

NORTHERN LIGHTS LIBRARY SYSTEM

Scan me

Books by Jackie Ivie

Knight Everlasting

A Knight and White Satin

Once Upon a Knight

A Knight Well Spent

Heat of the Knight

The Knight Before Christmas

Tender Is the Knight

Lady of the Knight

"A Knight Beyond Black" in *Highland Hunger*

Published by Kensington Publishing Corporation

KNIGHT EVERLASTING

Jackie Ivie

ZEBRA BOOKS
KENSINGTON PUBLISHING CORP.
http://www.kensingtonbooks.com

ZEBRA BOOKS are published by

Kensington Publishing Corp.
119 West 40th Street
New York, NY 10018

All Kensington titles, imprints and distributed lines are available at special quantity discounts for bulk purchases for
sales promotion, premiums, fund-raising, educational or insti-
tutional use.

Special book excerpts or customized printings can also be created to fit specific needs. For details, write or phone the office
of the Kensington Special Sales Manager: Attn. Special Sales
Department. Kensington Publishing Corp., 119 West 40th
Street, New York, NY 10018. Phone: 1-800-221-2647.

Zebra and the Z logo Reg. U.S. Pat. & TM Off.

ISBN-13: 978-1-4201-0885-9
ISBN-10: 1-4201-0885-9

First Printing: October 2011

10 9 8 7 6 5 4 3 2 1

Printed in the United States of America

To Jolene Amy,
who never fails to warm my heart

Chapter 1

"Run!"

The shout came through the ground-swell of mist, became a blurred man, and then more of them. They were running . . . directly at her.

"Hide!"

Juliana dropped her apron, scattering berries at her feet.

The thumping of horses' hooves penetrated the remnants of fog next. And then the first indistinct outline of a mounted man appeared. Armed and charging . . . with drawn sword.

The first runner reached her, swooped, and without even breaking stride, tossed her up and over his shoulder, as if she weren't the size and heft of a grown woman paralyzed in place. Not much on her moved. He had her legs locked with an arm, her belly atop his shoulder, her arms dangling uselessly, and everything else on her upper body slamming against his back.

A backward glance showed her man to be one of the strongest or most agile, since he was outdistancing the others, and then losing them in the fog.

Juliana dropped her head and wrapped her arms about his

lower back. The man carrying sensed her new position, for he increased his pace, making the upside-down view of forest meld into a blur, while her arms expanded and contracted with the filling and emptying of air from his chest.

There was nothing else she could do. Agonized cries and shrieks filled the opacity all about them, mingling with thudding noises and crashing sounds of what might be branches, but could be bodies just as easily. And through all the sounds of pounding hooves, ringing steel, and bloodcurdling cries was the heart-pounding overhang of fear.

Juliana swallowed and her ears popped. Fear was always about and risked, especially in a predawn forest. The villagers believed the devil haunted these woods, spawning gremlins and goblins and banshees. The man carrying her could be one of the devil's demons. He could also be a clansman from a Northern clan: barbaric, primitive, illiterate, and unclean. It was possible. His sett was an unfamiliar plaid . . . black and red with a gray-cast smaller stripe.

It didn't truly matter to Juliana. She'd have clung anyway. There was something these Scots feared more: the Sassenach scourge that was King Edward II and his soldiers. King Edward had already defeated and quashed the Welsh clans back when she was a child. Now he wanted the same of Scotland. Juliana hadn't known how King Edward warred and hadn't cared.

Until now.

She'd just begun to grasp her luck when her man jumped a fallen log, bouncing her viciously with the motion, and then he leapt over another one. Sounds of pursuit were everywhere . . . getting close, fading. Louder. Farther. A shout came from the spot to their left. Leaves and branches reached out, slapping them with dew. The man ran on, dodging things that rarely slowed his stride, feinting to one side as she swayed the exact span over the other.

Then, without warning, he launched forward, going airborne more than a body length before reaching and rolling over a fallen log, pulling her up and over his shoulder with the roll, and bringing the back of his *feile breacan* with her, since that was what she grabbed. He had her smashed against him with the tumble and then he had her slammed onto her back. The impact took all her air, before it worsened with his body weight landing atop her, locking her arms and legs in place.

Black and red plaid settled over them, covering everything. But when that didn't prove sufficient to him, Juliana got hammered with the hard humps of his chest muscles as he burrowed with both hands, digging them into the rotting leaves and tree mash beneath the log. The back of her thigh met a rock, her knee a root, her buttocks settled onto what was probably damp ground, her shoulder hit another rock, and all the while she was getting flattened with his weight.

Then he stilled completely, halting even his breath, although the heavy pounding of his heart made up the difference. Juliana tried sucking for air. She tried moving her arms to lift him. She was going to suffocate, held beneath a Highland devil and not one person would ever know of it.

Heave off!

She tipped her chin and mouthed the words at him since he wouldn't move, and then everything went ice-cold with shock and fear. A sword tip spliced through the area directly between their noses, glinting wickedly as it nicked the log beside her cheek before being pulled back out.

Eyes as wide as hers bored into her, and for a moment she didn't think her heart would continue beating. He seemed to have the same issue, as not one pulse beat sounded anywhere from either one of them. And then it got harder to bear as every bit of him that was pressed to her went rigid and tense, making him even thicker and heavier. She knew why. He was preparing for the next jab of the sword . . . and what it might hit.

A thump of the wood echoed through her forehead, showing the soldier had moved farther up the log. Then there was another thump, even farther away and more dull-sounding. And then . . . nothing.

The sound of her man's renewed heartbeat was loud through where her cheek was pressed against his neck. Relief washed through her, sending such bliss it made her giddy. Or maybe it was the odd grouping of dots dancing through the air between them. Juliana watched as the dots combined to a gray shade that meshed with the dark material about them, before it grew larger, sucking at her . . . taking her down to oblivion with it.

The man shifted, pushing his legs and groin into hers. Juliana barely felt it. Then his upper arms hardened against her head. She didn't realize it was to pull up from her until he did it, granting her air with the gap.

Nothing had ever felt so sweet!

He shushed her with a huff of breath that barely trembled with sound. Juliana didn't comply. She couldn't help it. He didn't give much space and she filled it with gasps that pushed her chest and belly into his over and over, making a harsh sigh of sound in their enclosure.

He did the hush sound again, and this time tightened the arms beside her head more.

If it killed her, she wouldn't give them up! Juliana swallowed and held each small breath before easing it out, until they were calm and silent. Her reward was a slight lift of his mouth at one side, drawing her eye.

It wasn't a far move to look from his mouth at the rest of him, and that was when everything changed. Shifted. Warped. Spun. She'd been taught to fear the Highland clans. Fear them and run from them. They meant trouble. Spawned by the Norsemen and weaned at a witch's teat, everyone knew to avoid them. But nobody had warned her of locking gazes with one of them. Juliana's bottom lip dropped open. She couldn't stop it.

This Highlander had to be the handsomest man birthed,

or the lack of air had altered her vision. Handsomeness like his wasn't possible. It also wasn't fair. Or just. Or right. And she had no preparation! Thick dark hair fell forward all about him since he hadn't tied it back, or he'd lost his tie in the chase. He had dark eyes of an indecipherable shade, thick lashes, and all of that was graced by a face that lasses had probably sighed over long before she did.

Right then. And without one bit of forewarning.

Juliana's heart decided to curse her as well when it stumbled, restarting with a thud that sent heat to each cheek, and there was nothing to temper or hide it. She didn't know where her wits had gone. Each ragged beat of her heart accompanied a jolt of movement from her own body. Right against him. It was instinctive and involuntary. And horrible. All of it was being observed, noted, and evaluated. She could tell. One dark brow lifted, the smile moved to encompass his entire mouth, and then it got worse, as the heavy bulk of his loins tickled into volume and heft against her.

Juliana's eyes got even wider. Soldiers had to be still about hunting them, clansmen were probably being captured or worse, and this man was showing every sign that he desired *that*? Now?

Juliana sent the command to her eyes to narrow, to show him the disdain and disgust she felt. It didn't work. Nothing seemed to. Every bit of her body was tingling and alert where it pressed against him. Her stance was vile and did worse things to him. Juliana felt him enlarge and harden further, going to a size that forced her legs apart before settling between her skirt-covered thighs.

Nothing on her worked as it should. Nothing. She didn't know a near-death experience heightened things to such an extent it took one's will away at the same time. She'd never felt so vibrant, aware, and ready and primed.

Primed . . .

The exact description flit through her mind. She did feel

primed . . . and with that came willing, pliant, desirous . . .
and lax. And wicked. She was alive with them. Each breath
was pushing them together, especially since his breathing
tempo had quickened to match hers. There wasn't any way to
avoid him. Or move from him. Or do anything other than experience what he was doing to her.

There couldn't be much worse.

Then, she knew exactly what was worse as his slight smile
faded, replaced by a pout of kissable shape, while the wealth
of eyelashes dipped, covering his eyes. He tipped his head.
Juliana had a bare instant of time before receiving his lips
against hers. She used her moment to turn her head, barely
avoiding this kind of trouble. It was instinct, self-preservation,
and fear. And it was massive. Shaking was overtaking her as
he nuzzled what had to be his lips against her cheek and then
along her jaw. Rivulets of goose bumps went everywhere,
leaving his touch to trill along her shoulders, creep over her
scalp and to her toes, before flowing back and finding a
center at each breast tip. Those offending bits pushed right
into his chest, making things even more unfair. She already
knew how sturdy he felt . . . especially shirtless, and without
most of his sett since it was atop them. Every caress gave her
more to experience of the sweat-dampened, overheated, and
thick feel of him, and it combined with a sensation that slithered right from where her nipples were squashed against him
down to the bottom of her belly . . . and then even lower than
that. Unbidden wantonness joined the feeling of liquid heat
that slid together all the way to where her loins were jammed
against the rock-hard flesh of his lower belly.

She almost wished she'd fainted.

Then her body gave a nearly imperceptible upward movement, thrusting her pelvic area against him. It was completely
against her volition. And will. And experience. Nothing was
fair. She didn't even know where her cloak had gone to, and
the linen of her shift left little to mute any of it. The touch of

what had to be a tongue grazed her chin next, earning him a quick thrust with that against his mouth. And that brought her right back into eye contact with him.

He looked as surprised by her movement as she was, but for differing reasons. She was amazed something on her body had actually obeyed while his was probably due to any lass declining his favors. She still couldn't tell his eye shade. That was all well and good. She didn't want to know anything more about him. And she definitely didn't need further description of him. Or further demonstration of what he could do to her. And with her.

Juliana managed to hold his gaze for more than eight heartbeats, each one gaining in volume as she counted. Then she dropped her eyes to his chin. He had a perfectly sculpted jaw that matched the rest of him. If he'd grown a beard like every other Scot, she wouldn't have to be looking at every facet of a lower face and lush full lips that were still pursed slightly. Nor would she be suffering the reaction of it. Her body gave the horrid pulsing motion again, shoving all of her against all of him. Involuntarily. Horribly.

"Jesu'." He breathed it, although she was saying a curse word very like it in her mind in tandem with him. He'd also lifted his head, denting the tent of plaid atop them and making their enclosure lighten the moment he did.

"Heave—" Juliana whispered back.

"Hush!" he interrupted her with a hiss of sound. Everything on him went taut and rigid and heavy again as he held himself immobile.

"Why?"

His downward glance didn't have anything but fear in it, regardless of how dark his eyes still appeared. And then he scrunched them closed and started praying. Whispering the words. She knew then why. Their hiding spot was lighter because the foliage atop them had slid away when he'd moved. He'd given away their position.

Juliana was watching when he finished. Something was different when he opened his eyes and she couldn't quite figure it. His body was also relaxing, getting heavier as it did. She locked gazes with him again, pulsed against him, and hoped she didn't die of the embarrassment rather than a Sassenach sword.

"Aidan." He whispered it.

"What?"

He dipped his head slightly and repeated it. Slower. Drawing her eye to his lips with the way he split it into two words.

"Ai . . . dan."

"Aidan," Juliana repeated.

"Aye."

He smiled, stealing her voice while her throat closed off, and if she didn't look elsewhere, she was going to be back in the same trouble she'd just avoided. She settled on moving to the fabric beyond his head.

"What?" she asked.

"Aidan MacKetryck. Aidan Niall MacKetryck. 'Tis my name."

"Oh," Juliana replied. She'd been right. He was a Highlander from Clan MacKetryck. She played the name through her mind. She'd heard of them, but didn't know much more than that.

He blew a sigh over her, gaining her attention back. She didn't need to know how that felt either!

"Is that all?" he asked.

"Aye," she answered.

He must have finished maneuvering himself back into place atop her, because she was supporting a massive amount of his brawn and volume, and other things she wasn't going to acknowledge. She watched the plaid material fan back out with his movement.

"What if I want to hear . . . more?" He'd added a slight bit of voice to his whisper, making the last word a deep throb of sound.

"The soldiers . . ." She didn't know what the rest of her sentence would be as it just trailed off, taking her wits with it.

He huffed what was probably amusement. "They've gone."

Juliana narrowed her eyes and moved her glance back to him, settling on the spot between his eyebrows. It was safer. "How do you know?"

He adjusted a shoulder up and then back against her, moving her shift with it. "I gave our position away. I still have my head. Simple."

"Then, heave off."

He wasn't just smiling this time. It had to be a grin if the way his eyebrows lifted was an indication. She didn't dare check. With his visage and what happened to her every time she looked, it was safer this way.

"Na' yet."

She flitted her eyes to his, cursed the impulse in the same instant, and did her best to ignore how her heart stumbled. "Why not?" she tried to command, but it sounded more like a plea. She decided the roof of plaid atop his head was safer and moved her eyes there again.

"I deserve a reward," he said finally.

"Reward? You near got me killed," Juliana replied.

"Oh nae. I just rescued you," he countered.

"Near got me killed. Along with you," she replied.

He shook his head, dragging locks of hair along her face. Juliana had to close her eyes for a moment while she forced the horrid tingling sensation down.

"I saved you. Along with me."

He was waiting until she opened her eyes and looked at him again. It was getting slightly easier to ignore the reaction to him, including the way his belly shoved against her with every breath, the length of him weighing her down, as well as how all of her tingled with the prolonged contact. His argumentative nature made it a bit easier, but not by much.

"Do you always argue?" she asked.

His lips twisted as if considering it. Then he shook his head. And then he grinned. She'd been right. It was devastating. Her vision flew back to the plaid.

"Nae need, lass. I always win."

The words were said close to skin if his breath was any indication. And then she knew how close he was as a quick jerk of her head had his lips hovering above her nose rather than her mouth, where he'd aimed.

"Not this again." She sighed, and if she could get her hands freed from where he'd pinioned them at her side, she'd be putting up more of a struggle than simply moving her head side to side in denial.

"Why na'?" He'd lifted from her enough to ask it and watch her while she answered at the same time. It was too much of an impact and she was exactly certain that he knew it.

"You haven't . . . asked." The words limped out. Juliana was breathless. She hoped it wasn't apparent in her voice, although it was probably visual everywhere else. This Aidan fellow knew very well the effect he had on her. He probably had it on every lass. He was used to wielding it. All of which was clear and apparent, and making her squirm with what she hoped was embarrassment.

"Verra well. I'm asking." His voice dropped, as did his head. Juliana managed a gasp before he had his nose lined up against hers and was running it up and down, and tickling the tip of her lip with the slight growth of whiskers on his upper lip each time.

"No." The word didn't make much sound as she opened her lips slightly for air and received just a bit of space dividing his mouth from hers. She was still wondering how she managed to say something that was so patently different from everywhere else as his neck flexed, lowering his mouth to hers. Everything about her reacted, and not just where his kiss touched, sparked, flashed, and sent a burst of effervescent prickling roving about her that nobody had warned her of. Everywhere.

"Aidan! MacKetryck!"

He lifted his head at the dim shout, pulling her lips awry at the move. Juliana hadn't time to gasp before he'd gone to a full-length push-up, and then shoved from it to his feet. If she hadn't just seen him move that quickly, she'd have had trouble believing it.

The morn had lengthened as they'd lain hidden, although she had no concept of how. Or how long. Or anything. Juliana blinked up at the image of this MacKetryck fellow, flipping his kilt band over his shoulder as he adjusted his *feile breacan* back into place. Then he was rolling his head about on his shoulders and doing twists of motion that had cracking sounds happening throughout his body. Then he stopped and stretched. His entire frame was encased in morning sunlight that dappled every nuance of him into masculine strength and prowess, showing that God had been heavy-handed with those blessings as well. This Aidan was beautifully formed . . . and brawny. All of it was displayed perfectly in the sun, before getting shadowed. Dark fingers blocked the sun. The fog was gone. And then the smell reached her.

"Something . . . burns? What?"

Aidan ignored her question just as he did her move to sit up. He didn't bother to assist her. Juliana set her lips and swallowed the scorn away. He was a MacKetryck and a Highlander. A barbarian. They probably didn't know of chivalry and honor and valor. It didn't truly matter. The battle for the Scot throne had taken it all away anyway.

It took some time to feel her lower legs and feet since they were just coming alive from where he'd lain atop her. That hurt, and made getting to her knees difficult. Her cloak was on the ground beneath her, while the ribbon tie of her hair covering was askew. Her skirts looked like she'd taken a tumble into a loch and just let them dry wrinkled, except they weren't faded nor were they clean. There were spots of mud and mulch and more than one rotten leaf attached to her attire. She picked at them as she surreptitiously watched him. He didn't look at her again nor did he help her reach her feet and stand beside him, waiting.

The man was just as immense as he'd felt while atop her. Juliana stood at midchest height to him. She stood a bit taller. Maybe she reached his brooch clip.

She'd just decided it when he lifted his jaw and sniffed.

"Aidan! There you are. Thank the saints! Unharmed? And safe."

Two large-sized, redheaded men shoved through forest greenery and took giant-sized steps to reach them. Only one of them was speaking.

"Will you look there, Kerr MacGorrick. The laird's safe, unharmed . . . and he's found a bonny lass to attend. And here we thought him in danger."

Juliana looked to the ground, bit her tongue, and longed for deafness.

"How he manages such, I canna' fathom. Nor do I wish to try. Aidan."

The men were slapping shoulders in turn and ignoring her. S*hortly, Juliana,* she counseled herself. Soon now, these two brawny Highlanders and this Aidan fellow would leave her life exactly as they'd entered—without warning. After that, she'd make her way back to the croft. Then she was going to put him where he belonged . . . in her memory.

"It's na' how it looks," Aidan told them, sounding slightly sheepish.

Juliana slanted a glance up at him and then colored when she caught his wink.

"Well, it looks plenty. But we've nae time to hear it. We canna' stand about, waiting for our own cleaving."

The one who'd spoken turned away. The other man followed suit. Juliana wasn't given the choice as the Mac-Ketryck grabbed her arm and started pulling her along with him.

"I'm not going with you." She hissed it, but it didn't seem to do much.

"You are," he countered.

Fallen, marshy ground muck was getting dragged before her boots since she wasn't walking and he didn't seem to care.

"Am not." She tried again.

"You're na' safe here!"

"I live here," Juliana informed him.

"See that?" He gestured to the black cloud moving in chunks of shadow into the sky. "That's the village. There's naught left. You ken?"

"No." Juliana shook her head. He was wrong.

"Ewan!" MacKetryck turned from her and said it to the farther redhead, the one who'd been talking.

"Aye?"

"Where's Beathan?"

"With his maker," the man announced grimly.

"Gavin?"

"Dead."

"Iain?"

"Dead."

Juliana's eyes got wider, her belly got heavier, and the listing just kept going.

"Rory?"

"Aye. Rory, too. And looks to be Filib and Duff as well. Dead. Unburied. We only found parts of them."

The green all about them was melting, turning into a wash with black and red at the center. There was the loudest, most

prolonged humming note in her ears as well, throbbing into
a cacophony of sound that should have muffled the men's
words. She put her attention to stopping it and swayed a bit
while she pondered the green mash of ground at their feet.
She might have fallen without the grip on her arm. The gray
was back in her vision, but with it came a strange numb sensation about her nose. Juliana fought it. She'd never fainted.
She refused to faint now. Not in the grip of a MacKetryck
and with two more Highlanders between her and safety.

"How many are left?" The man holding her asked it.

"Counting us?" Both redheads stopped and turned to
face him.

"Aye." There wasn't a bit of joviality anywhere about any
of them.

"Three. If we tarry more, they'll be adding us to the dirt
as well. Now come. Bring the wench if you must, but come."

The branches slapped back into place as they turned and
disappeared into them. Juliana quit fighting it and welcomed
the bite of tension in Aidan's fingers about her arm. She kept
blinking, and breathing, and walking as she followed him.
She didn't faint.

Chapter 2

Aidan Niall MacKetryck was rash and reckless. Always. He'd been cursed with it at birth by the clan seer, Lileth Fallaine-Dumphat. Despite the teachings and warnings and years spent practicing at patience, he'd done nothing to alter it. He wasn't just rash, he was also thoughtless, just as the seer had predicted before the laird MacKetryck had her silenced with a stay in his dungeon.

His father hadn't done it soon enough, Aidan decided, shoving his way through a last thicket and receiving more scratches for his trouble. They'd finally reached a meadow, making the walk easier. It was about time. Aidan sneered at the waist-high grasses, tipping to one side with wind that didn't cease. If he wasn't mistaken, the breeze coming toward them had a bite to it, too. It wasn't raining, but it probably would soon enough. To punish him even more.

Aidan sucked in a breath and let it out, doing his best to ignore the ache that had started with the slaughter this morn and just kept growing. It made his chest heavy and tight and that made his frown deepen. Anyone looking at him would probably dub him the "Black MacKetryck," although that title belonged to his uncle, Dugald. Seer Lileth Fallaine-Dumphat hadn't cursed the laird's firstborn with foul moods and a sour disposition. Those were an aftereffect of rash actions he continually suffered.

Dead clansmen and a morn of walking did nothing to change anything, including his mood. The sidelong glances the lass gave him occasionally didn't help either. Aidan consciously avoided meeting any of her looks. He practiced at ignoring her, except to guarantee she stayed between him and Ewan Blaine's back.

Saving the lass had been another impulsive act. Attempting ravishment of her during the rescue was another. For the life of him, he didn't know why either. She may be bonny and have a lush woman-shape that she'd swaddled in a dark cloak, but she was also an encumbrance. A responsibility. And from the looks of her, he probably wouldn't gain any ransom—if there was anyone left to send the demand to. He didn't know her name, her clan, or even her station in life. She could be a serf with the manners of a swineherd for all he knew.

Aidan sighed, ignored how she looked over at him, since he'd nearly overtaken her with his strides. He'd rather look at the backside of Kerr MacGorrick, who'd assumed the lead.

Aidan didn't dare look to her. It invited thoughts and actions and impulses that no MacKetryck laird in the midst of battle ought to have to deal with. He pulled in another deep breath and barely escaped it being labeled a sigh. The lass had bottomless, clear bluish-green eyes, the color of Loch Buchyn in sunlight. Meeting her gaze had stunned him. It probably still would . . . if he allowed himself to look.

"You should na' have camped so far away . . . nor left the horses."

It was Kerr MacGorrick, turning and walking backward across the meadow as he announced it over Ewan's head.

Aidan ignored him. Ewan wasn't as smart.

"He already kens it," the other redhead answered.

MacGorrick grunted. "It dinna' do what it was set to."

"He kens that as well."

Ewan was still answering for him. It was just as well. Aidan was practicing at keeping his words in check. MacGorrick's taunts meant little. Any fool was granted perfect hindsight about what should have been done.

"Does he now?" MacGorrick mused. He was directing his words to Ewan, but his attention was fully on Aidan.

"Reaving requires sneaking about. You canna' go reaving with horses. They'll give it away."

"Well, we should have hobbled them closer, then. Horses would have helped with the odds. Barring that, they'd have helped with this walk."

"How was the laird to ken Sassenach murderers were about?"

MacGorrick swore. They were still heading into a breeze heralding an oncoming storm. Aidan started hoping for it. Rainfall might muffle their words.

"Any man knows better than to take on English soldiers without assist . . . especially when they're mounted on horseback and fully armed. Laird MacKetryck knew it. Everyone does."

"They were doing the devil's work! You saw it! You heard the screams."

"I saw and heard MacKetryck clan getting killed. That's what I witnessed!"

"You heard the screams. You know why he did it."

"Aye, I ken. Aidan MacKetryck decided to take on more mounted Englishmen than any man should. And for what? To stop them from their devil work and save those villagers? Fool's bane. No one can stop a Sassenach horde bent on destruction."

"You only say that because we hid our sorry arses in the bushes. 'Twas a coward's move, MacGorrick."

"Cowardly? I'll have your tongue, you whelp!"

The leading man shoved at the younger, but missed since Ewan Blaine was the quicker of the two and sidestepped it.

Aidan sucked in on his cheeks as he considered it. They'd both been hiding. That explained how they'd survived.

"'Twas cowardly."

"You're alive, are na' you?"

"Aye, I'm alive. And now I'm a coward. My thanks."

Ewan flipped a hand through the taller stalks beside him, scattering seeds and particles into the air. Aidan squinted his eyes against the onslaught as it passed by.

"Nae, man. You're alive. There is nae such thing as a brave dead man."

"What of the laird? Look at him! Just look. He's alive. Unharmed. And he even saved one of them. He's brave."

"Nae, Ewan," Aidan interrupted their banter. "Your laird was na' brave. I was lucky."

Kerr MacGorrick met his eye and nodded. "Aye," he replied. "That you were." He swiveled back around.

The lass was plucking at the plants they were walking through. She didn't slow them or break stride to do it. She'd tied her skirt front into a basket shape and was busy filling it with the grass. That was interesting and took his mind from his clansmen's words.

"What is it you do?" He moved a half-step forward to ask it.

"I'm hungry." She glanced at him, interrupted a breath again with the impact of her eyes, and then looked away. She also continued her gathering. Aidan was left with walking beside her and waiting for her to make eye contact with him again. That wasn't typical. Most lasses found him pleasing to look at and tried to catch his eye. At least, that was what they'd always told him.

"This grass . . . 'tis good to eat?"

She put the end of one to her mouth, bit off the bulb at the tip, and chewed. Then she handed him one.

"What is it?" he asked.

She waited until she'd swallowed to reply, giving some

answer to his question about her manners. "Millet," she told him.

Aidan grunted, twirled the stalk in his fingers before gesturing to the forest at the end of the meadow where the shadow of cloud cover made it a faint gray color about the trunks. "See there? Those trees?"

She nodded.

"That's where we left our horses. Afore eve, we'll be at camp. My camp."

She shrugged. "So?" she replied.

Aidan pulled his head back at her insolent tone. "We pulled down a deer yesterday. There's food a-plenty."

"Well . . . there isn't any here now. Is there?"

She ate another plant tip. Aidan bit at his to mute the instant ire and stay his retort. He wasn't used to being treated with what sounded and felt like disdain and contempt. He didn't like it. The millet stalk was hard to chew and not worth the effort. He spit it out.

"You'll find venison far tastier," he informed her. He might as well be talking to the wind, since she ignored him and added more grasses to her pile. "Dinna' you hear me?"

She shrugged again. He felt the heat from a flush overtaking his chest and neck and sucked on both cheeks as he forced the reaction down. The lass needed a birch taken to her. That was what she needed. That shrug gesture of hers was offensive and dismissive and meant to be.

"Well?"

"I'm your captive. What makes me think you'll see me fed?"

If she hadn't flashed a look up toward him as she asked it, he'd have an easier time replying. And arguing. Aidan had to look aside while he calmed another rush of heat to his face. None of this was normal. He didn't know what was wrong with him.

"You're nae captive," he replied finally. "I rescued you."

"Stole me."

Aidan turned back to her. He'd never met a more argumentative wench. "I rescued you. It was na' an easy feat. And then I kept you safe. I still do."

A slight dimple puckered her cheek and then she sobered. "You stole me," she replied finally.

"Rescued you."

"Took me captive," she replied as if he hadn't even spoken.

"You dare argue it?" Aidan asked.

"And then you make me go hungry," she informed him.

"Chew more of your horse fodder. I've better things to warrant my time than bandying words with a disagreeable wench."

"Such as . . . ?" she asked, drawing the last word out in order to force a reply. It was definitely a smile toying about her lips, he noted.

Aidan barely stopped the answering quirk on his own lips. "Such as pondering the why of a wench that loses her kin and her home . . . and yet shows naught in sorrow."

"You wish me lamenting?" she asked, raising her brows with the question. "Perhaps a loud wailing while I drag my feet?"

"You've a fast tongue, haven't you?" Aidan replied.

She didn't answer him for a bit. He watched as she chewed on her bit of millet. "Perhaps you're looking for tears," she said.

Aidan shook his head. "I'm na' looking for anything, lass."

"Good. Keep it that way," she replied.

Aidan's feet stopped and his bottom lip went slack while he waited for the surprise to dissipate. The wench dared give orders? What madness was this? He had to double his steps to a trot to catch up to her. He also had to bend and duck branches since they'd reached the tree line again and started climbing.

"Now, listen here, wench," he said through gritted teeth as he went.

She cocked her head to one side but didn't slow her steps. She was still chewing her little bud, too. That was probably due to the hard and tasteless texture of them. They'd have to be sucked into an edible state before swallowing.

"Hear what?" she replied once he'd reached where she was standing, holding a branch aside in order to pass.

"I'll na' take brazen words from a wench I rescued."

"Stole," she argued.

He sighed heavily. "A wench I saved. And then rescued. And then continue to keep safe . . . regardless of her argumentative and strange nature."

"Argumentative? Me?" she asked and actually pretended to be surprised.

"And strange."

"I've no experience with how a captive acts. You call me strange and give no reason. You wish me fighting? Screaming? Wailing? What?"

The smile was gone from her face. Aidan's frown deepened, and a pounding in his head decided to join in. "Nae," he replied.

"Good thing. I'm not certain I can affect them."

"What?"

"To your . . . satisfaction, that is," she amended.

"Your silence would be to my satisfaction," he snapped.

She sighed. "You are a dense one, aren't you?"

Aidan pulled back, and the limb she'd been holding smacked him full in the chest, scattering more dust and seed and leaves about him, as well as stopping him again. His eyes were wide and nostrils were flared as he sucked for breath and forced the instant anger down. He didn't have to guess it. He could see it. He was called the Red MacKetryck for a reason.

Then Ewan Blaine added to the humiliation by chuckling.

"You find something amusing?" Aidan asked it after shoving through the branch and catching up to where the other three were standing, as if debating the path.

"Me?" Ewan asked and then shook his head. "Nae."

Kerr MacGorrick answered for him. "He's thinking this wench will be a handful, my laird."

"I can handle the lass."

"It does na' sound like it, my laird," Kerr replied.

"Aside of which, she's *my* wench. I rescued her and I'll decide what to do with her."

They all waited. The wench didn't say a word of argument about it.

"True. We give you that. You rescued her. Near lost your own skin doing so, but you've gained another wench. As to the why you'd wish another one? We doona' ken, do we, Ewan?"

Now, both of his clansmen were laughing. Aidan fought the heat down and swallowed the ire away. His voice sounded it. "I had to bring her! You saw it. They slaughtered everyone."

"You should've left her. 'Tis clear she wanted it."

"How so?"

"We've been listening."

"But you doona' hear! There's naught left to return to. Naught."

"There's the woodcutter." The wench spoke up in a soft feminine tone she'd been keeping hidden. "They wouldn't have reached there."

"You think not?" Aidan snapped.

She looked up at him with an innocence she had to have practiced, and he hadn't sufficiently readied to withstand the sight of her vivid blue-green eyes. Aidan had to look away before the flush gave him away. He felt discomfited and his thoughts jumbled together. He didn't like the feeling at all.

"They got the woodcutter, too, lass."

MacGorrick was speaking in a gentle tone. Aidan glanced at him before looking to the wench again. She'd put her hand to a tree trunk and appeared to be stabilizing herself against it with her head bowed. He watched and waited, and braced himself for the screaming and wailing she'd been threatening him.

"No," she replied finally, speaking to the foliage beneath her. "Aye. All of them."

Aidan met Kerr's unspoken question before lifting his shoulders in confusion. It was clear the woodcutter meant something to her, but it was all he knew as well.

"Very well." She'd straightened and was looking at him with a blank stare. She totally ignored the other two.

"You readied?" he asked, licking his dry lips.

"You won't . . . let me go?"

Aidan narrowed his eyes. He'd been hooked by her gaze the moment he'd first looked into it, and now, with a wash of moisture coating the surface, the sensation was worse. Aidan gave a shake before he answered.

"Why not?" she asked.

"There's Sassenach all about. Razing the countryside," he reminded her. "'Tis na' safe."

"You'd leave the dead without proper prayers and burial?"

Aidan sighed, long and loud.

Blaine spoke up. "Let her leave."

"Nae."

"We doona' need her! We canna' even gain a ransom."

"I said nae," Aidan replied.

"Why not?"

If it wasn't all three of them asking it, he'd not have been so stubborn. Such argument was unbelievable and against type. Aidan MacKetryck had a certain reputation. He'd earned it. He wasn't biddable or accommodating. He couldn't remember when he'd faced this type of dissention. It made the pounding in his head more painful. He glared at each one in turn, but saved her for last. He had his hands in fists at his hips, too. She looked away first. And that felt like a victory for some reason.

"We tarry and camp is na' getting any closer," he finally replied.

"You'll na' let her go? Truly?" Ewan asked it. Kerr had his eyebrows raised.

"She's staying with me. Safe."

"The laird has spoken. Come along, Kerr." Blaine took the lead this time. Aidan lowered his chin and waited. He'd haul her over his shoulder if he had to. He hoped the look conveyed it. It wasn't like him, but everything about this lass unsettled him and he didn't know why.

He made a walking movement with his fingers and got a look of hatred in response. At least, he thought that was what the scrunching of her features looked to be. He waited. Her jaw was so set he could see the delineation of a vein along one side. She gave a closed jaw exclamation of some kind before swiveling in place and following his men.

Aidan watched a leafy branch swish back and forth from the shove she'd given it. He'd won for now, and he could probably add to the victory. Not only was she moving toward the copse where they'd hobbled the horses but he'd managed to shut off her arguments, too. He lowered his head, shoved the branch aside, and followed. He still didn't know what was wrong with him and why she unsettled him so. Keeping her was yet another rash move, made without reason and continued without sense.

At least that facet of his character he could count on.

Chapter 3

This MacKetryck was a very rich laird, if the amount and quality of horseflesh was any indication. The saddled mounts were also testifying to how many clansmen he'd lost. Juliana counted twice before she was certain. There were seventeen horses milling about a small clearing and two young men were watching them.

Both lads leaped to their feet and shouted for Aidan the moment the small party broke through the trees. Then they were racing past her to reach her captor.

"Alpin. Arran."

Juliana turned and watched as MacKetryck had an arm about both young men. They looked like miniature versions from the same mold. That said a bit about their close relationship. Juliana was good at guessing and fair with accuracy, as well. Not that she cared at all who the new clansmen were, or what relationship they shared with her captor, but guessing was habit from a lonely childhood and helped pass the time.

The wide, welcoming grin on Aidan MacKetryck's face gave her pause. Despite his rudeness and arrogance, his handsomeness hadn't altered. If anything, the shafts of cloud-dim light penetrating the rooftop of trees showed her exactly how jaw-dropping and striking a man he actually was.

She swallowed the self-disgust at what had been an
instinctive jaw drop and forced her lips closed. It mattered
little that her captor was a beautiful man with a brawny
masculine size. Nor did it matter that he appeared to have
younger siblings that he cared deeply for. All she was concerned with was finding his weaknesses long enough to
escape him. She already knew one of them was his temper;
yet as she watched him with his brothers, he didn't look like
the same man who'd shoved her twice during the last bit of
trees without bothering to note when she'd tripped and spilt
some of her millet.

"Good lads." Aidan had finished his greeting and pushed
the young men toward the group of stallions. "Now, off with
you. Fetch the horses."

"And be quick on it!"

The one named Kerr ordered it. Juliana watched both
Kerr and Ewan join the boys weaving among the horses,
grabbing at ropes and reins. The MacKetryck didn't look like
he was handy at doing anything other than observing.

She stole a glance his way and instantly regretted it. He
wasn't just observing the men gathering horses. He had his
chin lowered and was watching her as well. She blew a sigh
and watched a shadow of a smile touch his lips before jerk-
ing her gaze away. She'd known better.

"Where is everyone?" one of the lads asked.

Kerr spoke again. "Dead."

"Dead?" The boy sounded horrified. The other lad was
perched on a stump with his eyes and mouth wide, looking
horrified enough for both of them. "*All* of them?"

"Aye."

"Wh-Wh-Wh . . . happened?" The younger one had a
stammer. He was also shy, if the blush overtaking him was
any indication as he caught Juliana's eye for a moment.

"Sassenach." Ewan Blaine answered them from somewhere

among the horseflesh while Juliana pretended not to note that Aidan had moved closer to her.

"But . . . y-y-you was reaving on Liddlesdaleby Village, a-a-and Biggstown-by-the-Dale. Both held by MacDonal clan. As is Castle Fyfen."

"True," Kerr MacGorrick answered. "At least . . . that's what we were told. We were told wrong, though. Dead wrong. Now we're just dead."

"But—I thought MacDonal took the castle back from that English sheriff . . . that Sir d'Ancen-fish. Or whatever."

"D'Aubenville," Kerr corrected. "Giles D'Aubenville."

"That's the one." The older one was the one talking. "D'Aubenville. Baron D'Aubenville. He was the overlord . . . or something near that. But MacDonal clan won Castle Fyfen from him over a season past. Before the winter. In battle. Bloody battle. I hear they beheaded him, too."

Harness was jingling amid their talking while the Ewan fellow was whistling and attempting to corner a stallion. Juliana kept her attention on him and not what they were saying. She already knew what had happened anyway.

"Strong clan, MacDonal," Kerr remarked. "That's why we planned this. Reaving from MacDonal is a good thing. Adds a bit of boast to a man's name, it does."

"We d-d-d-dinna' get one Mac-Mac-MacDonal?" the younger one asked.

"All we got was that lass yonder."

Juliana kept her features still and halted any reaction as they looked over at her. It wasn't easy.

"Who is she?" the older one asked.

"Doona' ken that yet, Alpin. All I know is Aidan rescued her. And then took her away from all the murder and burning and raping . . . and she put no end of argument to it since."

"Why?"

"He wants another lass. Doona' ken why on that either. He already has too many doing his bidding."

"I should have brought some with me, since you've done naught save stand about jawing when you've mounts to gather," Aidan said.

"I mean, why would the lass argue her rescue?" Alpin asked.

The older one was named Alpin. That meant the young shy one was Arran. Juliana automatically deduced it, and then did her best to ignore it. She didn't want to know their names, or anything else about them.

"Perhaps she fancies a MacDonal clansman . . . or anyone aside from a man crazed enough to attack a Sassenach horde."

"You a-a-attacked the Sassenach?" The younger one asked it.

"If I did, it was poorly done," Aidan commented from beside her.

"They were better armed," Kerr informed him. "There were also more of them. Near two hundred more of them. And they'd horses. And archers."

"They . . . a-a-ambushed you?"

· "Nae. They dinna' even see us. They were too busy doing the devil's work, murdering and burning," Ewan added.

"Then . . . how did everyone die?" The older one was talking. He didn't have the stammer, nor was he shy. Juliana wondered if it was something they outgrew.

"That there's the rub, Alpin lad. We were hid well. Waiting. They dinna' even see us. Nae one did. So . . . we up and decided to announce our presence. To a murdering horde of armed Sassenach. We mounted a rescue. Of the villagers."

Kerr MacGorrick put every bit of sarcasm to his words. Juliana felt the reaction in the frame beside her as Aidan stiffened. He didn't say anything.

"With twelve men?"

"Thirteen. You need some more learning on how to count, lad."

"But . . . everyone—is . . . *gone*?"

"Aye. We doona' rescue properly, although the liege did send a few of them to hell afore getting noticed. And that just turned the attack from the villagers onto us. It dinna' help much either. They still killed the villagers."

"Cease speaking of it and get the horses," Aidan ordered them. "And fetch me Rory's mount. He's docile enough."

"You need a docile horse now?" MacGorrick asked.

"I need less jawing and more action," Aidan answered. "We all do. We've a bit of a ride. 'Twill be harder as we'll all be leading horses. Can you ride?"

Juliana didn't realize he'd addressed her until she noticed the silence that came from awaiting an answer.

The young man named Alpin was leading a large horse over to where she stood. It might be docile, but it didn't look it.

"No," Juliana answered him.

"How well do you learn, then?"

Hard hands gripped her waist and tossed her atop the horse like she was a sack. Juliana's breath clogged her throat, but one hand automatically grabbed for the horse's mane as her feet left the ground. That gave her the pivoting point to spin right down into the saddle, facing forward and clinging with both hands wrapped about the horse's neck. She'd also split her legs. That position lifted her skirts to her knee, putting her lower legs against horse hair and her thighs on the cool texture of leather. She watched Aidan flick a glance to her well-tooled boots before going up her legs and torso, before finally reaching her face. There wasn't any millet left in the basket shape of her skirt either.

The older lad was chuckling, but he was the lone one she could hear. All about her horses were gathering, hemming her closer to where Aidan stood, hands on hips and not one expression on his face. Then he nodded.

"You're barbaric, MacKetryck," she informed him, lifting her chin with the announcement.

"I have been so described afore. Come. I owe you a meal."

He had her reins in his hand as he went to another horse. Juliana's mount walked alongside him without demur. She watched Aidan jump upward onto his horse's back before swinging a leg over, pulling her closer with the pressure of the reins in his left hand. That was when she knew for certain escape wouldn't be easy.

Rain started before they'd cleared the trees, peppering everything with large drops that just got harder and thicker and wetter until it was difficult to breathe. Juliana pulled her cloak over her head and hunched forward into her mount's neck. That made a sluice for the water to drain from, once the black wool got saturated. The wet wool smelled musty, while rivulets of water ran down her neck and into the neckline of her shift. It was uncomfortable, but it was warm. In fact, it was so warm that the slit she'd made to see through was venting steam.

The MacKetryck laird appeared to be in the same posture from what she could tell, looking like a sodden beast atop his horse. He'd decided to lead four horses, including hers. He'd lined them up, with hers closest to him. She assumed it was in the event she didn't learn how to ride fast enough.

Juliana made a face at him. He probably knew it didn't take much talent to stay atop a horse at a walking pace, especially when someone else had the reins.

She also assumed the other clansmen were following. A quick check back proved little. The rain blurred everything from two horses back while steam rose from every mount's head to hover with the rain mist, making it even more opaque and indistinct. She didn't know how MacKetryck could see to lead.

He never showed any hesitation.

Juliana knew when they started to climb by the pressure of her buttocks into the back of the saddle. She responded by leaning forward, hunching even closer to her mount's neck. That posture turned into a full body cling as the horse slid more than once on ground that looked mud-slick and treacherous, when there was ground. Some parts of the path didn't appear to have anything below the horse at all, except mist-filled air. On each slide, Juliana caught her breath and kept the screams from sounding, until the horse regained its footing. She refused to fall. Not only would it be undignified, but it might prove fatal as well, for not once did MacKetryck check on her.

There wasn't any warning when they reached his camp. The ground had leveled once they reached the top of the hill, and then they'd descended into a glen that was followed by another hill. Juliana counted one more glen before he led them into a lone copse and stopped, seemingly without reason. She parted her cloak opening, putting a critical eye to what was so grand about this particular bit of forest, and then she noted sharp angles that were tent tops meeting the leaves above her. It was well hidden.

MacKetryck's camp appeared to be two large tents settled among the trees, while a third was just an outline behind them. All were tautly set up, with pegged ropes, giving the rain an easy run-off. They all appeared to be constructed of a densely woven gray, brown, and green material, making them a perfect match of the forest, as well as hiding any light coming from within.

Her eyebrows rose in consideration. She'd assumed this Aidan MacKetryck a Highlander of low manners, combining a mass of brawn with a dearth of wits, but she was rethinking her evaluation. He appeared to be cunning and disciplined, and planned well. He also expected to be followed without question and without checking. All marks of leadership. That made his continual avoidance of his men's taunts strange, and started her pondering what use such insubordination might be to her, and when it was best put into play.

Food and rest came first, however. No escape back the way he'd just brought her was going to be successful without the same qualities she'd assigned him: cunning, planning, and discipline. And a horse.

"Heck! Gregor!" Aidan called the names once he'd dismounted and just prior to turning to her.

Juliana watched as two clansmen left the closest tent, took in the grouping, and broke into a run. Then, she ignored them. Aidan was approaching and that was the bigger problem.

"Where is everyone?" She heard one of the men asking it through the rain-soak.

"Dead," someone answered, and after that an explanation was getting spoken.

The MacKetryck laird was standing at her side, his head level with her cloaked throat, and his eyes not much farther than that. He'd tossed his plaid from his head. That gave her a very good view of what he must look like surfacing from a swim in the loch, dark hair plastered to his head, spiked eyelashes, and clothing that didn't mute a bit of his power.

"What's your name?" he asked.

"Juliana," she answered, and then sucked in the curse. Poor crofters didn't have fancy names. It was the first thing she'd altered. He nodded to her throat, although he looked to have skimmed her frame before returning there.

"I'm taking you into my tent, Juliana."

"Why?"

"I'd na' wish a fight over it."

"Again . . . why?" she responded.

He touched her eyes for a moment, taking her breath with the contact, before he shied away. If she wasn't mistaken, he'd flushed about the lower jaw and it was moving into his cheeks. Juliana narrowed her eyes. He looked to be blushing, but the rain could have affected her vision as it was everything else.

He took a deep breath. "I'm going to carry you now."

Juliana looked down to where mud and wet foliage appeared to be devouring his booted feet. "Very well," she replied.

"You'll come without issue?"

"I've no fondness for the elements," she replied.

"You're to keep your woman wiles to yourself," he informed her.

"My—"

Her voice stopped, clogging her throat as he plucked her from the saddle. The cloak slid from her head onto her shoulders at the move, because she couldn't hold on to it and his shoulders at the same time. It didn't truly matter. Rain added to the damp of her hair, turning it into a riot of red spirals that stuck everywhere they reached.

He held her close enough she could hear his heart beating. That was offset by the experience of his soaked form against hers, and then he added the rush of his released breath to the mix. All of which was terrible. And odd. And troublesome.

"Wiles," he answered her through closed lips, and then he started walking.

He called them *her* wiles when he held her so tightly it might as well be an embrace. The mist of drops that made it through the canopy of trees didn't mute the sensation of heat radiating through him and making everything on her even hotter . . . wetter, more alert and tense, until it became a condition near feverish. Juliana hadn't any experience with such a thing. Being held and carried while he negotiated safe footing brought a delicate throbbing sensation to her most sensitive areas, making her thighs shiver, and there was no hiding the tight pinpricks of her nipples, without pulling at the clinging material. The moment she did so, she watched his glance flicker to where she was holding the cloak away from her breast, then he looked at her, and then he moved his gaze beyond her head while his lips tightened.

"You're to cease that as well," he muttered.

"Put me down."

"'Tis muddy and slick." He punctuated that statement with a slip, gripping her even tighter while he regained his footing.

"I'm not afraid of mud . . . or slick," she informed him, and pushed at him with the hand he'd trapped between them against a chest that she already knew wasn't malleable.

"Na' until we reach my tent. And safety."

"I'll be safe there?" Juliana asked.

"Aye."

Her luck wasn't changing for the good. His tent was the smaller one behind the other two. She realized it as they passed between the larger structures.

"From you?" she added.

"Of course. I've na' ravished you."

Juliana narrowed her eyes and considered him. He had a flush of color coming through his throat and into his cheeks again. She nearly smiled.

"I mean . . . na' entirely," he finished, sounding slightly apologetic. If he hadn't chosen that moment to lock glances with her, she'd have been able to answer him instead of look at him wide-eyed and witless. She forgot how to breathe as well.

And then her back slapped high up against one of the anchor ropes, showing they would have been in the door flap if he hadn't been watching her with an unblinking look from unfathomable eyes, while his feet were still moving. A shower of wet dripped all about them, chilling and yet burning at the same time. Juliana licked at a stray drop on her upper lip.

"I warn you, lass."

He'd lowered his voice, making a trickle of shivers flow along her back.

"Jul—" she whispered back, making a pout from her mouth and not realizing what that signified until he moved his glance there and back. Twice.

He pulled his head back a bit and regarded her. Juliana gave him the same level look, although the sparkle of continuing rainfall on his features turned him into a fantasy creature she'd have dreamed of . . . if she'd have known he existed. She very nearly sighed.

"Women."

He muttered it at the same time he gripped her more securely than before, this time with just one arm. She didn't know it was to have an arm available for opening his door flap until he did it. She didn't care. She was trying to assimilate and ignore how being shoved against the hard mounds of his chest had ignited the flesh of her own bosom. She didn't know how to hide it. She guessed he'd noticed it, since he flicked a look to her cleavage and swallowed. Heavily.

"You doona' follow the slightest instruction, do you?" he asked.

"What?"

His words came with breath that gave her shivers. Or the closeness of rain-soaked male was responsible. Either way, it was difficult to listen and force the trembling away at the same time. It proved impossible the longer she tried it.

"Your wiles. And their use on me."

"I'm not using wiles on you."

He put her down with an arm that trembled slightly. She stumbled momentarily on the suddenness of the move, but he'd stepped back the width of his tent and didn't seem to notice. He was also breathing heavily, lifting his frame with each one, and scoring her flesh with the rush of air. He folded his arms and regarded her with a stone-cast expression. All of it was visual, and exciting, and forbidden, and totally alien. Juliana wrapped both arms about her torso and worked at getting her body to cease plaguing her. She didn't know anything about what was wrong, and she didn't want to know . . . especially if it involved a Highlander.

"It's a reaction to the escape," he informed her, although she wouldn't have asked, and without one bit of warning.

"Wh-What . . . reaction?" She wasn't feigning the confusion that was probably noticeable in more than her voice. She watched as nothing about him changed.

"To me." He nodded, like he'd said something sage, and then he smiled, revealing wide white teeth. Then he elevated it by a wink.

Juliana gasped and swiveled sideways before more of her wits failed her. The man already knew he was handsome, and was probably noted for such a beauteous smile, and yet he did it with such abandon! Without one bit of care to how it probably affected women, and not just her.

"Being so near death has a way of changing things."

His voice lowered again, and that caused such a tremor to go through her, she lurched. Fully and openly, and inescapably. She knew he saw it even before he chuckled. Juliana narrowed her eyes on the tent wall, silently cursed the body she couldn't control, and sneered with a dismay he wouldn't see.

"Makes one feel . . . more alive," he continued, slowing the delivery of words until he might as well be growling them.

"I'm hungry," she informed the wall.

He chuckled again, louder this time. Juliana stood straighter and added a bit of stiffness to her posture for good measure.

"Still," she added.

"I'll see a platter fetched. Doona' move."

Juliana frowned. She was hoping he'd fetch it himself and

give her some time and space. "I'm not allowed to get warm?" she asked, turning her head back to him. "And . . . dry?"

"I meant you're to stay here," he said finally.

"You'll see dry clothing fetched as well?"

He nodded.

"And something to wash it down? I'd take water. Ale?"

"When you've ceased ordering me about . . . perhaps."

Juliana shrugged. "You're near a stream. I can fetch it myself."

"It's na' safe."

"There isn't an Englishman anywhere near your camp, MacKetryck. I'm certain you're aware of it."

"I've nine clansmen alive still."

"Seven," she amended, before instantly regretting it. A simpleton was easily overlooked. That was how she'd managed for six months already—by using her wits . . . and hiding the extent of them.

Juliana swallowed, wondered if he'd caught it, and then knew he had. It was clear from the lifted eyebrow and sucked-in look to his cheeks as he evaluated and considered her. She nearly cursed and watched him note that as well.

"You have na' met Tavish and Stefan yet. They're guarding. No one enters. On my orders."

"Oh." It was all she could think to reply.

"Tavish noted and allowed our passage earlier. He's a good archer. Rarely misses."

"I suppose he'd shoot anyone . . . leaving your camp as well?" she asked.

He nodded. "If you're lucky. As bonny as you are, he'd probably keep you screaming first."

Juliana's face fell. And then it hardened. She felt and welcomed every bit of it.

"Are you going to see me fed or not, MacKetryck?" she

asked finally, but the words were croaked-sounding and indistinct. It was the best she could manage.

His reply wasn't voiced, but it didn't need to be. He regarded her for some moments, while each breath she made got louder and harsher in her ears and he seemed to grow in stature as he stood there, blocking his door.

And then he nodded and left.

Chapter 4

He didn't know what was worse: the lass's argumentative nature and her skill at it; the dead clansmen he'd sent Kerr and Stefan back to gather under cover of nightfall; the disastrous turn of events that had started with reaving against the MacDonal clan; the question of how he'd bear word of the dead to the clan at Castle Ketryck; the cursed weather; the unpalatable, overcooked venison that required seemingly endless chewing in order to swallow; the knack this Juliana had for causing an itch in his loins that frustrated and annoyed him; or the fact that he was outside in an evening rain watching a fire that was sizzling and hissing with stray raindrops despite the woven thatch of hemp strands they'd erected as a roof above it, pondering over it all.

He didn't know why the lass argued her rescue so! He'd saved her. It wasn't open to question. He'd saved her, going against type, and she gave him nothing but grief ever since. What was wrong with the lass?

Aidan wasn't a chivalrous type by nature, at least he'd never been before, but he just couldn't have left her standing there oblivious to what was coming. Everyone knew what a Sassenach horde would do to Scot women—the same thing they'd done during the Welsh wars, back when he'd been a boy and told the tales while at his uncle's side. If a woman lived through the murder of her family, the ravage of her property, and then the brutality of her raping, she still had to face her future as an Englishman's property.

As winsome as that Juliana was, it wasn't difficult to guess what fate would be hers . . . *if* she lived through the first of it.

Aidan grunted slightly and moved into a crouch. There was a shadow passing through the light coming from the bottom of his tent door flap. He didn't think she'd truly try to escape back to the villages, but he wasn't taking the chance. Perhaps no one had told her of the horrors of life as an English whore. Aidan sighed. He'd already exchanged too many words with the lass. Somebody else could tell her.

He swallowed meat that was the consistency of an old saddle before tearing off another bite. The entire time he didn't take his eyes from the tent.

He hadn't wanted to rescue her, take her with him, and then continually work at keeping her safe. He had enough things to do already. Why . . . he'd have labeled her mad, if he hadn't been at the receiving end of her tongue enough all day that he knew how sharp it was. The lass had wits and wasn't afraid to use them. That was trouble. She also had the most winsome face he'd seen in many a season. And that made her double the trouble.

Aidan stopped chewing for a moment and cocked his head. Actually, she might be the most beauteous woman he'd yet seen. He had a very good notion of how womanly her frame was as well, and when he factored in the wealth of curls she'd hidden beneath her cloak, all in the reddish shade of a rowan tree berry, he was certain. This Juliana was definitely the most beautiful wench he'd ever seen. He scratched at his groin absently. He hadn't wanted to rescue her and bring her back with him. *Jesu'!* What fool would?

Beautiful women were always trouble. It seemed to follow

them. Had his mum lived beyond Arran's birth, she'd have counseled her eldest son of it. Had his da, Grant Niall Mac-Ketryck, lived to see Aidan into manhood, he'd have probably made certain his son knew the pitfalls of bonny women. Instead, Aidan had his uncle, Dugald MacKetryck, to thank for everything . . . including this latest foray onto land held by MacDonal clan.

Dugald MacKetryck was known as the "Black" Mac-Ketryck because of his temperament and the darkness of his deeds. He'd taken over as regent upon his brother, Grant's death and shoved Aidan into adulthood, first by sending him against challenger after challenger in the lists for bouts of fighting; next by forcing his nephew to attend every session of his clan court and making him listen to every complaint and every issue; then adding lectures and book learning to the mix; and finally forcing a barely grown Aidan to a full battle that determined who was laird . . . and who was not.

But never once had Uncle Dugald brought up the subject of women. He'd let Aidan figure that out on his own.

Aidan swallowed another nonchewable bite of venison, pulled in a long draught of whiskey from his sporran to make certain he didn't choke, and when his head came back down, the shadow was moving beneath his tent flap again. He wondered if she was pacing.

As small as his tent was, that didn't give her but four steps each way. What a waste of time that would be. Aidan smiled slightly. He'd mistaken it. Sitting out in a rainfall, eating an unpleasant meal while he pondered the whys of everything, now *that* was a waste of time. He'd probably be better off pacing with the lass.

Aidan wasn't one for thinking over the whys and where-fores of fate, and not just due to his curse. Growing up under Dugald MacKetryck's tutelage had taught him one thing: things were what they were, not what they might be if given time and thought. Pondering was for old men like his uncle. The doing was for men like Aidan.

He spat at the fire, heard the instantaneous sizzle, and tore off another bite of meat to start chewing.

Action. That was what he liked and that was what he did. Reflex action was usually the best, too. He could almost sense where a claymore was going to be coming from next, the moment he'd knocked it aside with his own. Most of the time, being oriented on action worked to his betterment. Aidan was unbeatable at the castle list with any weapon chosen, and with bare hands as well. He acted, reacted, and moved, without taking time for thinking it through. It had saved his skin more than once.

As it had today.

The shadow crossed in front of the door flap again, and then it stopped before going to a large form that might mean she was on her knees. Perhaps the shock she must have suffered was finally coming to the fore. Perhaps she was grieving.

For a husband. And children.

She was probably wed—any lass her age should have been a wife for some years, and have nearly the same amount of bairns to her croft. But if she was wed, her husband must be the basest idiot born for letting her roam about the woods this morn, in predawn, with only an apron for a weapon.

Aidan sharpened his eyes on the shadow as it went dark and distinct for a moment, as if she was right at the door . . . maybe getting ready to shove the opening aside and creep away in what would be a failed escape attempt.

Foolish woman!

Aidan shifted, rising farther so he could forestall any such move. He wasn't allowing an escape! She was the only thing he'd done right today, and by thunder, he was not letting her go to her doom. He didn't care how much she argued. He was saving her, and he was going to keep her safe. That was just the way it was.

Aidan was more convinced about it now than he was before, but he'd decided to let the returning party with the dead clansmen speak for him. The only things waiting for her at that village were death and suffering. And pain.

He hoped she didn't have a spouse and children.

The shadow at his tent door shifted again, going back to an indistinct form before it moved away. Aidan did the same retreat, going back to the balls of his feet before turning his attention back to the fire and his meal.

The form of Tavish Findlay crossed in front of him before the man went to his buttocks beside Aidan. The man resembled a sapling in comparison to Aidan, lean to the point of looking frail. It was a lie. He could outwrestle half of them, outrun most of them, and easily outeat all of them. He had a thatch of brown-red hair that never looked groomed, even fresh from the loch, and sparse clumps of like-color beard he kept trying to grow. Aidan had the same issue. That was why he kept the whiskers scraped off with a skean. Tavish was also the best archer in the clan. Perhaps farther. Accurate and deadly. He was also fair with a slingshot, nearly as accurate and easily as deadly.

There was a companionable silence broken only by the sounds of a large quantity of wood burning in a bonfire amid a muted forest rain. It didn't last.

"Kerr tells us you hid well enough, the English should never have spotted you," Tavish commented to the fire.

Aidan swallowed. "Kerr has an aversion to truth. 'Tis why he's gathering the dead with my brother, Stefan, and Heck."

"You dinna' start it?"

Aidan shook his head. "'Twas Iain. With a whoop and a yell, and a charge, and then they took his head off. Foolish whelp. And damn me for being too far away to change any of it."

"What help would that have done?"

Aidan huffed. "None . . . but I'd have repaid the man in kind, instead of sending a half-dozen others to their maker just for being in the way."

"Kerr says you felled more than that. Near twice."

"And as I said . . . he has trouble with truth."

"Why don't you stay his tongue, then? You've taken men down for less. Many a time."

"Because that's what he wants. Ewan, too."

"They want you to hit them?"

"Nae. They want a full-out beating. I refuse."

"Have you been at your whiskey long?" Tavish teased.

Aidan pulled in a large breath, sighed long and hard, and shook his head. It didn't help. It was still chill, wet, and dreary. And Tavish was still waiting. "They hid when they should've fought. 'Tis why they lived. It was also cowardly. They know it. And they want to be punished for it. To mute some of the guilt."

"I'll hit them for you," Tavish answered.

Aidan shook his head. "They want severe punishment. Fit to the deed. From me."

"Why don't you give it to them, then?"

"I'd tell you it's due to pure joy that they lived, combined with my newly discovered meekness and compassion. But that would be a lie. Truth is . . . I'm guilty of the same transgress. I canna' punish them for hiding and then running. I did the same myself."

"You had to save them, though! And the lass."

"Doona' color it any other than it is, Tavish. Base cowardice. And we're all guilty."

"You should have sent Ewan as well, then," Tavish finally replied.

Aidan grunted. "Nae need. Ewan knows when to keep silent. He has na' taunted me."

Tavish grunted a nonanswer and then started speaking

again. "It'll take most of the night for them to gather our dead and return."

"Longer than that. I also want word on the woodcarver. I expect them back tomorrow . . . near nightfall. We'll wait." Aidan looked toward the tent and watched it until he saw the shadow pass again. It wouldn't do if the lass escaped while he was turned careless by the man supposedly guarding.

"I put Arran to guarding for a short span," Tavish said, as if reading his mind. "He needed it. He's off-put by your denial."

"He's more annoyed Alpin got to go. Speak true."

Tavish chuckled and then sobered. "It might be dangerous. Sassenach may still be about, killing any that survived."

Aidan pulled a dirk from his belt and started twirling it, looking it over for nicks, as if that was all he had to do for the evening. It was easier to talk to a blade. It was also easier to watch his door flap without looking like he was.

"Well?"

"They've still the castle to take. They'll put every man on that."

"You think MacDonal still has Fyfen?"

Aidan turned to look at his man. "That clan plays with the devil for sport. You ever hear of a MacDonal giving anything up?"

"That's nae proof."

Aidan sniffed and looked back to his tent. "I also heard his pipers. As we slunk away . . . leaving them to their fate. Mac-Donal clan was still defending the castle. They may still possess it. Kerr and Heck will have to be stealthy. Or deal with me."

"What of your brother?"

"They've orders to keep him safe."

"Nae wonder Arran's down in the pipes. You made it safe, and let his brother go . . . but na' him?"

"He already had a long day. And if he's true to type, he spent most of last eve awake. Doona' forget, the lad's young."

"He's fifteen."

Aidan's twirling of his knife paused. *Fifteen?* When had the lad grown up? "So . . . he is," he replied finally.

"You were wed at fifteen."

Aidan smirked. "True."

The man shoved a large bite into his mouth and started chewing. Aidan almost stopped to warn him before deciding the man's silence would be appreciated for a spell. He watched the shadow pass the door again. She was still there, still awake.

Prowling . . .

He wondered what she'd look like in the clothing he'd sent her. He hadn't any intention of dealing with her again until she'd dressed in clothing that wasn't stuck to her with moisture, skimming curves he was having trouble ignoring, and not unless she had the near-unbelievable color and volume of her hair covered again, and definitely not until he had the whorl of lust banished and controlled.

There wasn't any reason for such an issue either. She wasn't that special. She was beautiful, true. She was solid in the right parts and soft in other perfect places. That was also true. But the lass had also suffered today, and that made any action toward her wrong. Only the basest craven soul would slake his lust on a woman who'd lost everything and was in too much shock to even realize it. Aidan understood that, but his body wasn't listening. Even now, he felt the heavy pull in his groin and tightening of his lower belly.

It was hard to fight it out here in the rain with an unpalatable meal and a fire that wasn't giving much warmth. It would be near impossible if he got near her again. He'd already admitted it and then he'd tried to deal with it.

And why her?

Aidan wanted that woman. Physically. Hard. Pounding

hard. It was instinctive, and irrepressible, and instantaneous. And massive. And still there, dogging his every breath.

He nearly groaned aloud, alerting the man at his side. The woman was still working her wiles and he wasn't even near her. Such a thing was unhealthy and unbelievable. He already knew it happened when he was near her. He'd proved it during the rescue . . . but now? Hours away from her and a good distance of ground apart?

The urge that had started once he dove atop her wasn't changing, or muting, or doing anything except increasing. Intensifying. Escalating. Despite his every effort at putting a rein to it. It didn't make any sense.

Why her?

The fire didn't hold many answers, and he moved his vision back to include the tent door. And *her*. Juliana. She had a fancy name. Old. Roman. From other lands and other times . . . before Druids walked the land, erecting stones and speaking magic. He knew all that from when his parents had been picking girl names for Arran, since Mum had threatened his father with what would happen if she had another son. They'd been certain that time it would be a lass. Aidan had been ten. And the new child was another son. But Lady MacKetryck hadn't lived long enough to find that out.

Aidan grimaced. No wonder he detested thinking.

He hadn't much choice tonight. There was only one thing his entire frame wanted action on, and that was being denied. Aidan watched the tent flap unblinkingly until his eyes watered. There hadn't been any shadowed movement in there for some time. Odd. He decided to wait. A minute. Then, check.

"Why did you take the lass?"

Aidan barely controlled the jump as Tavish asked it. The man was gnawing at his joint of meat again, getting ready to risk another choking. Aidan sucked on both cheeks before answering.

"I dinna' *take* her." But he sure as hell wanted to. And damn Tavish for putting it in words! Aidan gulped. "I rescued her. From certain death. Or worse."

"That is na' what Kerr says."

"Kerr. And his stories." Aidan started rocking slightly, going to his toes and then back flat-footed. To his toes. Back. Toes . . . It had been half a minute at least. There still wasn't any sign from his tent. Had she finally given up her pacing, then?

"What are you going to do with her?"

"I doona' ken yet," he admitted.

"You already have enough women."

"I know."

"They serve your every need."

"Do you have a point to these words?" Aidan asked. He rocked back onto his feet. To his toes. Back . . .

"Some of them are na' going to much like . . . that." Tavish pointed toward the tent that Aidan was studying.

"I know that as well."

"You can always set her free. Kerr tells me that's what she wishes."

Aidan moved his glance over to his man for a moment and then returned to his tent. The lass's time was near up. If she didn't move soon . . .

"Well?" Tavish asked.

"Nae. She stays."

"Kerr says—"

"Kerr can say all and it will na' change things. The lass stays with me!"

Tavish was studying him. Closely. Aidan fought the urge to return the look. He didn't know why he'd just responded so vehemently either, but it might have something to do with the fact that time was passing and she still hadn't moved or given him one sign that she was still in the tent.

"I've na' heard of you having women troubles afore, Aidan."

"I doona' have them now. I rescued the lass and I'll keep her safe. Nae matter how much wind is jawed into place by arguments . . . and from whom. Simple."

Tavish finally pulled another large portion of meat loose and started chewing, smacking his lips like it was a tasty morsel, silencing the man and giving Aidan more time for pure thinking. The shadow was gone. Still. Had she finally given up her pacing? And if so, had she bedded down on the pallet he'd instructed Alpin to take for her use? Or perhaps she'd decided to use Aidan's bed, since his bed roll was already strung up, suspended from poles stuck in the ground and piled with blankets. If she'd done that, he'd use the other pallet that wasn't long enough, nor would it be thick enough to keep his weight from the ground. He might even forgo it and sleep on the ground. Gladly. Because sleeping with chill and damp might help mute everything he suffered.

Her time was up.

Aidan rocked forward and rose to his feet in one smooth motion, slipping his skean back into his belt as he did so. He'd taken two steps toward the tent when the commotion started.

Chapter 5

Juliana groaned, rolled over, and hit her nose into something hard, sturdy, and cold. She cracked an eye open, discovered it was the little chest he'd had at the base of his bed, and not a male Highlander. A further glance showed the bed in exactly the same condition as when she'd last seen it . . . covered with her cloak. She groaned again and stretched, pretending the emotion was due to soreness at sleeping on the ground and not sheer stupidity.

She'd known not to close her eyes!

The delicious aroma of roasting pork floated beneath the tent flap and she sniffed appreciatively. Then she listened. No drip could be heard, and she'd gone to sleep with the sound of running water. That meant no rain. Or if it was raining, it was of mist consistency. That would make it easier to run when she had the chance, but easier to track and catch her as well. Juliana concentrated. She couldn't hear much except the far-off chirp of a bird or two. And then she smelled the roasting meat again. That got her other eye open, and a bit of salivating to her mouth as well.

The younger brother, Arran, had brought her a dry, overcooked hunk of meat last eve. It had been served on a trencher platter that at one point might have been a flat fried oat cake. They'd let it get rain-soggy, though, and it sagged between his fingers. He'd ignored her blank look when he'd set it down on this trunk and left. He'd returned moments later with a tankard filled with what turned out to be watered-down ale. Unless she was mistaken at the first sip, they'd splashed some whiskey into it, too. It had smelled unappetizing, looked worse, and if she hadn't been so hungry, she'd have pitched the whole lot out the door at where their laird sat, watching the fire and looking like he hadn't a care in the world.

He hadn't even the sense to stay out of the elements.

Juliana had shivered in her double layers of dry plaid, purloined earlier from the dead clansman Rory's bundle, and still felt the chill. It had to be wet, uncomfortable, and cold sitting out there in the rain, even if it had softened to a continual shower from the pelting earlier. Anyone else would've had the sense to sit inside where it was dry. Or under a tent drape. Not MacKetryck. He'd chosen to sit out there by the fire, surveying the clearing like he owned it . . . and that gave him a perfect angle to watch her door.

She'd noted that the only time she'd peeked, and then stifled the frustration. He wanted to sit in the rain and guard her door? Well and good. She'd been up against more stubborn men. She'd wait him out. He couldn't watch forever, and Juliana had had all night. All she had to do was get to a horse, get hidden, and wait. She wasn't going to have any trouble with a horse either. She knew how to ride well enough. It had just been years.

But that meant she had to be ready to escape the moment he gave her an opportunity. Juliana had sighed heavily, pulled her finger back from the door slit, and smoothed the flap back into place with hands that trembled only slightly. Patience was one of her strong suits. As was stubbornness, headstrong behavior, quick wit, and a wicked tongue. If he knew who she was, he'd probably have heard all that.

Juliana had turned from the door then, put her hands on her hips, and surveyed her situation. Her shift and underdress were hanging from a hook. Her boots were upside down, near the wall. Her cloak was tossed across his bed, but she'd moved the blankets first. She'd wrung the garment out as best she could, but it was still going to be damp and cold when she donned it. It would warm up quickly though. Highland wool had that reputation. She had her hair combed and plaited again, and felt the satisfactory slap of the braid end on the back of her thigh. It wouldn't take long to put everything back on. She was only waiting until it was dry enough that it didn't make her conditions worse. Escape was the plan. Getting ill was not part of it.

Juliana sighed again. She was going to escape and get back somehow. She didn't dare do anything else. MacKetryck wasn't going to stop her.

And that was that.

Getting warm, dry, and well fed was an excellent start to her escape plan. And here she was getting gifted with all three every time Arran visited. The grand laird Aidan Mac-Ketryck must not know much about women he was keeping against their will if he was going to supply her with everything she needed to escape him. Stupid man.

Juliana had moved to sit as elegantly as possible on the rolled-up pallet brought for her and say grace. Then, she'd started munching delicately on her sup. It hadn't lasted. In her prior life, no one would have recognized the Juliana who'd devoured the meal, chewing venison into a swallowing state with bits of the wet bread, before washing each bite down with ale.

Juliana moved now to sit on her pallet in the dawn-lit tent and licked her lips in remembrance while she listened to her belly growl. It had actually been the best meal she could remember in a long time. But it had also made her drowsy. That was why she'd started pacing.

The fresh smell of roasting pork drifted to her again, more pungent this time, and it was accompanied by the faint aroma of frying bread. Or something they were frying . . . Juliana sniffed, smiled, and sniffed again.

These Highlanders certainly knew the way to satisfy a woman's hunger . . . if nothing else.

Juliana stood, untied the outer covering of plaid, and dropped it at her feet. She'd just untied and peeled open the inner red and black plaid layer as a cheerful voice preceded Aidan MacKetryck's head into the tent flap opening.

"You ken your way about a sickbed?"

He smiled and ran his gaze to her toes and back after he'd asked it, and then he stepped in. As if he'd been invited. His manners hadn't improved, but that smile of his sent a lurch through her frame and the heat of a blush right to her cheeks. All of which was unwelcome and horrid. Juliana forced herself to continue meeting his gaze, despite how it started an odd sensation through her breasts, and a weak sagging feeling to her knees. It didn't seem possible, but he looked even handsomer than she recalled. A night spent in the open must agree with him. He looked freshly shaved, which was ridiculous. Scot men didn't shave. He also looked like he'd made a further effort at grooming by finger-combing his dark brown hair before tying it back into a queue. He hadn't taken the same care with his wardrobe, and what he was wearing didn't cover enough of him. The *faile breacan* he'd draped about his frame was tied lazily at the hip and drooped from a shoulder. It didn't help that he'd forgone a shirt either.

Juliana held the plaid material together in front of her and considered him, and did her best to pretend the emotion was from being caught in such dishabille and not any reaction to him.

"Well?"

"You don't look sick," she replied finally.

He grinned wider, her heart thumped oddly, and then he nodded. "'Tis na' me. For the lad, Arran."

Juliana lifted her eyebrows. "Your brother?" she asked.

He sobered slightly and winked. "Aye. That would be the Arran I refer to."

If he teased with her, she was in trouble. Juliana hadn't any experience with devastatingly handsome men who flirted with her. Nor had she developed any weapon for such an event. It hadn't been an issue before. None of the males in her past experience had come close to the masculine force that was Aidan MacKetryck.

"Wh-What . . . happened to him?" She stammered through some of the sentence and then actually colored worse.

He pursed his lips into a kissable shape, creating a sensation almost worse than when he smiled. The shiver went shooting down to her toes and back before centering right at her nipples, making them rigid and sensitive against the wool. Juliana had no choice. She pulled the ends of her plaid covering up as she crossed both arms about her. He shifted his gaze momentarily to her move, as if evaluating it, and then he was right back to gazing at her.

"Well?" she asked.

He took a step farther into the tent, which she already knew was six paces deep and five paces across, and that only if she took small steps. His move made it look even smaller as his head grazed the roof. Juliana didn't back from him, not because she didn't want to, but because he'd managed to affect her knees now to the extent her legs were jittering, too. He was also heating up the enclosure, or something else was happening, since the flush covering her entire body was sweat-starting. The sensation of warmth radiating from him had an intriguing aroma, too. She couldn't avoid it since every indrawn breath was coming in rapid succession.

"Well," he replied finally, and pulled in a big enough gulp of air that his chest lifted with it.

Juliana's lips parted, she reached her tongue tip to the upper one, and then her eyes widened as his body seemed to react, pulsing in place. And then he released his pent-up breath, narrowing his eyes and lowering his chin at the same time. The look he gave her made the earlier sensations a rehearsal for the torrent of heat that spiked all the way through her. She had no choice. Juliana tightened her arms, backed up a shaky step, and tripped, dropping with a graceless plop onto his cot. Worse was when she released the material wrapped about her in order to hold to the sides of his bed as it rocked, crazily tipping her before righting again.

None of which went unnoticed by him.

His glance flickered to throat and cleavage flesh she couldn't cover fast enough. And then he lifted that one eyebrow and smiled. This one didn't have any mirth to it at all and instead looked predatory and sinful. Wicked. Elicit. Male. Primed . . . His plaid was warping into a haphazard pattern where the material hugged his loins, too, catching her eye on the enlarging mass of material, and making everything on her body warp with it. Juliana had never felt as she did now, and it was an all-over emotion—agitated, excited, anxious, tense. Edgy. Frightened.

"Aidan!"

His head cocked sideways with the shout, releasing her from his attention, and Juliana sagged before she caught the motion. She used the next few moments to grip her covering closed clear to her jaw, and steadfastly waited through his evaluation when he saw it. The man had that devilish ability to raise just one brow, and he was still wielding it, pinning her in place and making it difficult even to think of breathing.

"What does she say?"

The speaker was close, if sound was any indication. Juliana watched Aidan take a couple of deep breaths, and when he'd finished, he lifted his head from the visceral stance he'd been in. It felt like further release as he looked down at the ground and stepped back to his original spot. This time when he looked back at her, there wasn't one expression on his face. Then he turned his head and yelled an answer.

"Give me time to ask . . . Tavish!"

MacKetryck's yelling voice was loud in the amount of space he'd had to give it. If she hadn't been holding on to the material wrapped about her, she'd have her hands to her ears. She settled for scrunching up her shoulders. He'd turned back to her and saw that, too. Then he cleared his throat.

"Well?" he asked finally, in his usual tone.

"You've said that . . . already," she replied. As a flippant remark, it failed. It was too breathless and had a gap in it. She didn't need his instant eyebrow lift to know of it.

"Aye."

"And?" she asked, pulling the word out so he'd explain.

"'Tis my brother."

"Arran?"

"Aye. Arran."

"He's . . . ill?" Juliana questioned since all he did was answer in small sentences that told her nothing.

"Hurt."

"How?" That word put her lips in a pout. She watched him glance there and stop midbreath, before looking over her shoulder. She had to wait for him to finish his exhalation before he spoke again.

"He took a wild boar down. Last eve."

"Oh." That explained the delicious aroma. And if she was in time to prevent the overcooking, it would probably taste as good as it smelled.

"His first," Aidan continued.

"How bad?"

"He did well. But he was na' prepared."

"How bad . . . is he hurt?" Juliana clarified.

He touched his glance to her and then moved it to the material of the tent behind her head again. Then he shrugged. "Na' bad. I've seen worse. Had worse. By far."

"Then why do you need me?"

A half-smile played about his lips, but the moment he looked at her, the flash of amusement died, fading to a blank look. "Arran thinks it bad. Verra bad."

Juliana nodded. "So . . . what do you need of me?"

This time his grin was wide enough to show teeth, and she wasn't ready for it. Juliana's eyes went huge, the hand holding the material at her throat trembled, and she watched as he took in all of it. And then reacted. His grin died as he lowered his chin and narrowed his cheeks, before turning his head sideways to her. Juliana watched as a dark rose shade suffused him, and it looked to be originating from the middle of his chest.

"Aidan! Are you going to take all day? The lad's groaning away still." The tent flap moved and a strange man stuck his head in, nodding at her before turning his attention to his laird. "Powerful groans," he finished.

"Where is he hurt?" Juliana stood, holding her covering with one hand while pulling the cloak out from beneath her with the other one. No one offered to help her toss it over her shoulders, but she wouldn't have accepted if they had.

"The lad's a bit . . . bruised," Aidan supplied.

"There is na' much you can do for bruising. Have you tried cold water?"

"Aye," the man at the door replied.

"Does it need to be wrapped then?" Juliana asked.

Both men chuckled, sobered, and then guffawed again. Stopped. And then looked embarrassed. Totally embarrassed. Juliana folded her arms and regarded them.

"Nae. We've . . . na' tried wrapping it," Aidan finally replied.

"Then what do you expect of me?" she asked.

The man at the door answered her. "Well . . . you see . . . ahem. It's na' so much that he needs the bruising attended to, as he needs the fact he's injured attended to."

"Where is he injured?" Juliana asked.

Both men cleared their throats. Neither one replied. She noticed that neither of them would meet her eye either. Both seemed to be blushing now. Juliana raised her eyebrows.

"Oh," she finally said.

The man at the door grunted. "Name's Tavish," he supplied. "And we were thinking if Arran had a bit of sympathetic . . . female about . . ."

"He'd stifle the groans?" she finished.

"I think he'll appreciate the company." The man at the door was openly grinning. Juliana nearly returned it.

"Well then, cease delaying me. Take me to him."

The thin man pulled his head out of the door and opened it. MacKetryck preceded her out of the tent, but he was waiting when she exited. He wasn't the only one. There were another three men standing about, looking like they'd just come to their feet. Juliana watched as they doffed tams and straightened kilt bands, and nodded at her. She turned away quickly.

"Come. We'll do introductions later. I'll see you to Arran."

He didn't wait to see if anyone agreed, but she already knew he expected complete obedience from his clan. And her. She wouldn't argue it anyway. She didn't want introductions either.

She heard Arran before she saw him. He was in the large tent closest to the horses. He lay on a cot facing the side of the tent and he was rocking in place while voicing soft heart-rending groans. Either they'd lied about the extent of his injury, it was more severe than they'd known, or Arran was the weak sort. Juliana didn't know anything about wounds to a man's groin, but her heart immediately pulsed at the agonized sound as Aidan lifted the door flap.

"Arran, lad! Look!"

The young man rolled his head toward them. His face was lined with pain, but there wasn't a tear in sight. She'd guessed him as a young lad yesterday. Now, she knew the truth. He wasn't much younger than her seventeen years. He was as handsome as his older brother, too.

"I've brought you a visitor."

"I-I-I doona' wish—" His voice stopped when he saw her.

"This is Juliana."

"Na' her. Aidan! Why-why-why did you-you-you have to bring a-a *girl*?" He put such contempt on the last word that Juliana stopped, went to her full height, crossed her arms, and raised her brows.

"Now, Arran. This is na' just any lass. This is the one I rescued."

"I-I-I already ken . . . who she is." She watched Arran ease onto his back and lift into a semisit when he got there, scowling as he punched a roll of blanket into a back support to lean on, and catching his breath as he did it. He sounded slightly less pained, though.

"She wished to thank you firsthand for the fresh meat. How could I tell her nay? She's my responsibility now. I doona' take those lightly."

"Thank you-you-you . . . for visiting," Arran remarked and turned his head dismissively. He hadn't put much groan to the words. It was clear he wanted time with his self-pity. And he didn't want her. Juliana knew she wasn't wanted. Aidan must be immune.

"I'll have a joint of meat carved and brought in for you two. Gregor is handling the cooking. 'Twas a nice-sized boar you got, Arran. Nice-sized. Fit for bragging. Especially with the way you took it."

"I'm ru-ru-ruined, and you wish t-t-to-to brag?" the lad asked.

"What? I'll be crowing over how you took such an animal

with only a skean and little warning. That's what I'm for bragging."

The lad smiled a bit with the praise.

"As to the other . . . the ruined part? I believe we'll just pass on that. Fair?"

The lad nodded after a moment. Juliana silently agreed. She didn't want to discuss anything of his injury. She didn't even know what to say over it.

"Then why-why-why did you bring her?"

"Juliana wanted a bit of companionship."

"What's wrong with yours?" his brother asked.

"Plenty."

Juliana and Aidan said it in unison, and that surprise was added with the wide-eyed locked gaze that followed it. His left eyebrow was lifted again, and the man was too handsome for such an expression. She felt burned. Scorched. Sweat beads broke out near her hairline with the force of it. Then Arran coughed and Juliana looked away. There wasn't anything she could say. Looking at Arran was far safer, and her presence might be doing some good after all. The young man had moved into a full sit, propped against the bed roll, and had only the slightest grimace on his face as he finished.

"She does-does na' seem to-to-to fancy you much, Aidan," he remarked.

"True."

"Why?" He was asking Juliana.

"I'm auld," Aidan answered.

Arran looked skeptical. It was probably the match to Juliana's expression. "You've ten years on me. That's na' auld."

"To a young lass, it is. Trust me. I'll leave you two now and see what's taking Gregor so long."

"What am I to-to do with her?" the lad asked.

Aidan was hiding a grin. Juliana didn't find anything amusing.

"Talk. Visit. Eat."

Watch. Guard. Detain.

Her mind gave her the words as she stood mutely considering the entirety of Aidan MacKetryck's trick. She couldn't believe she'd been so witless and walked right into it. Juliana put every bit of ire she felt to the look she gave him. He smiled broader. And then he winked.

"You'll call out for anything, Arran?" he asked.

"But Aidan! Wh-Wh-What does a lass . . . t-t-talk of?"

Juliana spied a trunk, the match in size to the one she'd bumped her nose into earlier, and walked over to it. She had it pulled into position next to Arran's cot and was preparing to perch atop it before she spoke again. She ignored Aidan . . . completely and totally.

"I'm certain you'll find something. Lasses like flattery. You could try that."

"A-A-Aidan." The young man was embarrassed. It was in his voice and on his flushed face. Juliana glanced at him and then away. The emotion did nothing to hamper his comeliness. It probably increased it, if she was a young woman with nothing more on her mind than keeping an injured, handsome lad company for the day.

She settled onto the trunk, although it was too short and her knees were near her chest. "Oh. We're going to have a very nice talk, Arran. For most of the day, while I wait for my clothing to finish drying . . . and you to tire," Juliana informed him.

"And our dead to arrive. So we can bury them," Aidan added.

Juliana gasped. His voice held more than just words. It held raw emotion. She did her best to pretend she hadn't heard it, although the trill of gooseflesh down her spine was impossible to ignore.

"I'll be-be-be up by then, A-A-Aidan. Swear," Arran told him.

"I ken as much. In the meantime, enjoy your rest. And your company."

"So . . . wh-wh-what do you w-w-want to talk of?" Arran's stutter was even more pronounced when he looked at her through the talking. It took a while to get the sentence out. Juliana calmly waited, with her head cocked and her hands folded atop her knees, giving him her full attention.

"Oh . . . we're going to talk of your eldest brother," she replied. "What else?"

Arran was looking over her shoulder at his brother. She didn't have to check. She knew.

Chapter 6

Juliana attended the burial and consecration, despite every effort at avoiding it. She hadn't much choice, since her captor seemed to know everywhere she was, and when. Even now he hovered at her side, making certain of her attendance. She wasn't singled out, since she'd heard him order them all there, but it felt like it.

Usually in the aftermath of battle, the dead were buried where they fell. Or the bodies were burned. Or left to rot. Or displayed as a warning.

Juliana sighed. Nothing was usual about this. Thanks to her talk with Arran, she knew the difference. And she knew why.

Arran MacKetryck had been a font of information without asking for any of it. Once he got some food and three tankards of ale into him anyway. He'd spent the morn and into the afternoon regaling her with stories, and he'd lost most of his stuttering as well.

Juliana now knew MacKetryck land was north of Inverness, well away from any wars and conflicts over the Scot throne. They didn't worry over who claimed kingship since the Norman line died away. Could be John Balliol for all they cared, although the rebellion had faltered, leaving Dunbar

Castle, Edinburgh Castle, Stirling Castle, and Perth Castles in English hands; could be Robert Bruce, although he'd lost the great cause five years earlier in the vote for Balliol. The fact that it was now King Edward taking, and killing in the taking, was just further reason to avoid the Sassenach.

Arran rarely heard of such doings. In the Highlands, land and property were a fluid affair and always fought over. One man claiming total rule meant little. Proving the rule was what mattered. Aside from which, the best challenge and win was over another Highland clan. Always. Anything else was of little value. This included English-held properties, with the effeminate, overpowdered, and frilled lords and sheriffs that owned them. English landowners were detested. As were any Lowlanders that welcomed them.

So it was with Clan MacKetryck.

They hailed from the farthest reaches north, from a bastion called Castle Ketryck. It was named after some forebearer, who'd killed a Viking king in order to possess it. Arran didn't remember the Viking king's name and Juliana had stopped him from yelling for Aidan to get the information. It didn't matter. All that mattered to her was time passing.

According to Arran, the name "Ketryck" had been changed sometime in the past to the surname "MacKetryck," since the "Mac" stood for "son of." Juliana hadn't known that. She didn't know much about Highlanders at all. With her upbringing, it wasn't possible to come into contact with one of them long enough to learn any of this.

As the only daughter of Baron D'Aubenville, and heiress to all his holdings, Juliana had been well above any contact with them. Previously.

So Juliana nodded and frowned and listened or pretended to listen, and all the while she felt the time passing. A weight of time. A solid thickness of time. A whole span of time that no one could gain back. Her father would be awake in his grave if he knew where his daughter was and with whom.

If they'd put him in a grave after displaying him atop Fyfen Castle gatehouse.

Juliana swallowed to kill the bitterness of her thoughts and went back to listening and nodding . . . and waiting.

According to Arran, Castle Ketryck had been started by Norsemen, using gray stone that matched the rock it perched atop. The MacKetrycks had enlarged and fortified it in the centuries since then. Their castle was now the finest ever built, strong. It was impregnable. Insurmountable. Inescapable.

Or Arran was one for faery tales.

Juliana didn't discount it, since his description made her own holdings small and insignificant . . . or what would again be her holdings if the English had won . . . and if she could get back there before much more time passed. And if her betrothal to Sir Percy Dane still stood. And if the D'Aubenville steward posing as a woodcutter had escaped the carnage. And if a thousand other things could be handled . . . once she escaped Aidan MacKetryck's captivity and could attend to them.

Despite the tension from practicing patience until she was ready to scream, Juliana had found the information Arran gave her interesting. Unbelievable, but interesting. And it did help pass the time.

Throughout the large meal of roast hog, fried gruel, and fresh berries that was served with full, foamy tankards of ale, Arran had regaled her with stories about their home. He'd told her how Castle Ketryck had a solid stone curtain wall that took more than seven hundred steps to walk along on each side. Juliana had looked unconvinced. That would make an almost endless barbican. It would rival Stirling and Edinburgh Castles, if not exceed them. It might even be larger than Caerlaverock Castle, and that one still held out against Edward's forces. Arran told her Ketryck Castle's barbican was more than three arm spans wide, too, and he didn't mean his arm span. He meant Aidan's, and his voice had warmed considerably while telling her that.

Hero worship of his brother? She had to contend with that, too?

Juliana had worked at controlling any argument or answer to anything Arran told her. She wanted him sleepy, not awake with anger. Besides, she didn't care if he claimed a castle larger than those King Edward had just constructed in Wales. Nor did she care what size Aidan MacKetryck's arms were, or how long. Or how strong. Or anything else about the man proclaiming himself her rescuer. Aidan's image had been planted at Arran's words, however. That was bothersome and made her feel odd. It heightened her senses, making every-thing more alert, and she was slightly breathless as well. De-spite everything, she'd nearly sighed.

Arran hadn't noticed. He'd been too involved with tales of the walkway all along the top of this curtain wall, connecting all eight towers, each five stories in height . . . and possess-ing its own stairway. Juliana almost argued that before she bit her own tongue.

Tales. That was all they were.

Arran's voice had slowed occasionally and he'd yawned more than once by then, so Juliana just let him keep talking, while she kept waiting.

He'd described an improbable gatehouse next. It suppos-edly arched over an entry that was six stories high. On sunny mornings, the shadow cast by this gatehouse stretched across the drawbridge and a good walking distance into the heather as well. Arran must have noted Juliana's incredulous look at all this, because he'd simply folded his arms, said she'd soon see, and she could then tell for herself.

Castle Ketryck sat on a bit of headland overlooking a lake they called Buchyn Loch. This loch emptied into the North Sea and had water so deep and so blue and so cold, and so full of fish, it was no wonder the first lairds of Ketryck had fought wars to gain and keep it. They hadn't stopped there. The MacKetryck clan was rich in lands and holdings, but they had a thirst for more that seemed inbred. Arran boasted to her that they'd already gained so much land and reputation they'd had to go south for more. That was why they'd been at Castle Fyfen. They'd heard it had been taken by the Clan MacDonal, putting the land under Scot control.

And that was why Aidan had sent his men back for their dead.

Juliana had perked up a bit at that information and she'd sat forward slightly on her trunk.

It seemed that Arran's big brother was a superstitious sort. Aidan believed that a Highlander buried in Scot-held soil had a just death and rested with his maker, while a Highlander left in any other dirt was cursed to roam the darkest mists of the glens, dales, and forests, searching out and haunting those who'd allowed such a deed . . . to exact their vengeance. Aidan MacKetryck wasn't taking any chances.

That wasn't the lone thing he believed. He had amulets in his possession to ward off more curses than the one he'd received at birth. Aidan truly believed that despite everything he did, this particular curse followed him, and wouldn't release him until he reached the grave. Juliana had laughed aloud at that, making it a hearty sound on purpose. She'd guessed Aidan hovered outside the tent, listening. So she made certain he thought her completely captivated and entertained by his brother.

Perhaps then he'd relax his vigil, it would accompany Arran's rest, and all this passage of time would serve a purpose, and Juliana could escape. Aside from which, she didn't want to know any more about this clan. And she didn't want to get fond of them! When she returned home, she wanted to

forget everyone and everything that had happened since that
horrid night that started it all.

Everything.

Aidan MacKetryck hadn't been about when Arran had
finally slept, breathing thickly and rhythmically, even as
she'd passed her hand over his face twice to make certain of
it. It had been fairly simple to sneak to her assigned tent,
dress back in her own clothing, and then slip back to Arran
without getting spotted. It had also been easy to leave again,
although the second time she'd been in a slight crouch and
moving toward the horses.

And then that whip-thin Tavish fellow had loomed right
in front of her, frightening her into a squeal before shaking
his head and blocking her. She hadn't needed an escort back
to the tent where Arran was still sleeping either, but she'd
gotten one. And the next time as well. Only that time it had
been Aidan stopping her. Just as he did the time after that.

Juliana gritted her teeth now and pulled in a breath. He
might as well have her tied to him, as closely as he watched
her! And there was simply no reason for it. He'd saved her.
What of it? She was no man's responsibility after that. His
claim to keep her safe was too much! And for how long? And
what reason? The man had more than enough wenches at
his beck and call already, according to Arran. He didn't
need another one.

Juliana glanced over at where Aidan MacKetryck was
standing. Solemn. Head bent against the onslaught of new
rain, while body after body was lowered into the hole they'd
dug. The cloud cover hadn't dissipated throughout the day, so
the rain wasn't a surprise. Juliana huddled in her own shift,
underdress, and boots, covered over by her cloak, learning
the wet warmth of it again, and watched as they started shov-
eling mud atop the mass grave, covering over their dead . . .
as well as the body of the woodcutter.

And that was when the first physical stab of despair came.

* * *

The lass had some explaining to do.

Aidan tapped his sporran bag, which held a signet ring they'd cut from around the woodcutter's throat when they'd found him. It was MacKetryck property now, until he decided to give it to her. That wasn't happening until he found out what it meant and whose it was. He didn't recognize the crest of entwined serpent tails, but simple woodcutters didn't usually wear gold objects, nor did they have hands raw from woodworking. A woodcutter had calluses, not blisters. So if the corpse they'd brought was a woodcutter, it was a newly learned trade. He looked more like a scribe. Or a taxman. Or a clergyman who'd lost faith and forsaken his vows . . . perhaps on the promise of a bonny lass's hand.

Aidan hoped she wouldn't try talking her way out of giving an explanation. He added to that. He hoped she'd finally realize the futility of trying to escape him. There was nothing to go back to. Not anymore. The English had not only burned and destroyed both the village Liddlesday, and Biggstown-by-the-Dale, leaving nothing more than a church foundation to mark where the last had been, but they were fully in control of Fyfen Castle as well. The battlements were reportedly strung with MacDonal clansmen, since these Sassenach hadn't left one soul living.

Not even the piper.

Aidan sighed heavily, made the sign of the cross, and did his best to ignore where Juliana was standing beside him, her bent head reaching his shoulder. It was a position of abject grief. It matched the cry she'd given when they lay the woodcutter's body out beside the MacKetryck clansmen. It also matched her fervent hugging and grasping and checking of the body and the pale drawn face she'd turned to him when she'd finished.

He couldn't see her face now and was glad of it, although

that annoyed him. She had her hands clasped before her, holding her cloak closed at the waist. Demure. Grief-stricken. Quiet.

She bothered him. Endlessly. He swore he could tell where she was and what she was up to simply by a feeling he got. As if he sensed her in some fashion. That was worrisome, and he was spent with wasting any more time pondering. He'd given the orders. They had tonight to fill their bellies and rest up before they started for Castle Ketryck. At first light.

Aidan waited once the deed was done and ground shoveled into place, getting wetter in the downpour while the grave mound she stared at got the same.

"Lass?"

He spoke in a tone his men would be teasing him over if they heard. He frowned slightly as she ignored it. Or failed to hear it. Aidan cleared his throat, looked down at the mass grave, and that was when his eyes widened and he started silently cursing his own foul stupidity.

Facing death altered things for him. It always had. Aidan was a demon in battle, where there was too much action and force and split-moment maneuvering during the killing to experience much of anything, especially death. That happened later. Afterward, when the silence came, that was when he'd feel and experience chest-crushing suffocation, a heart that skipped and altered to the point it frightened him, and a numbness that more than once he'd feared he'd succumb to it. It was another curse he suffered, but this one he kept to himself.

Aidan fingered his sporran for the right charm, starting a silent chant in his head before he found it, while he worked at overcoming the heavy feel spreading beneath his breastbone. He sucked in, got a chest full of damp-filled air, but the tight feeling persisted. And then his heart missed a beat.

"La . . . ass?"

He tried again, only this time the word was in two syllables and had gone into a higher pitch, sounding choked and raw. He couldn't help it. He couldn't gain enough air to speak properly. She was flirting with fate the longer she stood in the evening rain making him wait with her. Because there was one sure thing that canceled out all the death feeling and made Aidan feel alive again. The joy. Power. The frustration, anguish, anger, thrill.

All involving a woman.

Oh . . . Christ.

Aidan lifted his head to the sky and watched raindrops fall all over him before he closed his eyes. His birth curse was shoving itself right in front of him . . . taunting him. He'd been rash. Impulsive. Reckless. Unthinking. He knew this happened every time he faced death and he also knew how much his body craved this Juliana . . . yet he'd done nothing to alter it?

The amulet wasn't working. Cursing silently wasn't helping. Sending hollow promises to the heavens did little good either. He should've left the dead where they'd fallen or had them buried before reaching camp. And if he had to be that foolish, he should have planned for this. Left her in another man's care. Sent her to the tent. Escaped to a different one. Put her back with Arran. Run away. Hid . . .

Aidan reached for her, locked on to her upper arm, and then swung her to face him. He might have used too much force, since he had to catch her with his other hand to prevent her from colliding with him. That was just as stupid, since that put Juliana in his hands, beneath his nose, and within his grasp. Aidan was further provoked when his own arms began shaking. His heart dropped another beat, startling him.

"Lass?" he tried again, but this time the word cracked, sounding brittle and dry. He swallowed, but choked on it since his throat felt like it was already closing off as it numbed.

She lifted her eyes to his, taking his breath with the

contact while his heart jumped instantly into a quick-paced hammering. She looked brittle, fragile, and everything her posture had been demonstrating to him throughout the burial. She was suffering. Grief-stricken. Pale. Bereft. Hollow-eyed. Completely passive. Only the lowest wretch would even think of taking her at such a time . . .

Lowest wretch . . .

Despite the slur he'd put on himself, Aidan pulled her close, lifting her at the same time, until he had her frame and face matched to his. Her lips parted and he swore the soft sigh of breath from them touched his lips. Even through the steady film of rain draped between them.

"Take . . . me . . ." she said.

Aidan stiffened, while the roar of reaction at the content of her words made his hold shakier, his chest fuller, and the numb feeling started dissipating. He couldn't prevent everything on him from ratcheting to a primordial level of want and need. Instantly. Voraciously. Noticeably. He gulped.

"It's na' . . . the best . . . place," Aidan replied before he lost his wits. The rain might be wet and carry a chill, but nothing about it damped the heat rising from contact with her. His voice was shaking now as well. He was incapable of moving his eyes from hers.

"Please?" she answered.

"Jesu'!"

His curse word carried a plea with it. Something about it bothered her, for a small line crinkled through her forehead as she frowned. Blushed. And then she smiled slightly.

"I meant . . . take me home," she whispered.

Aidan didn't have a strong enough curse word available. There was a whooshing sound filling his ears and it just got louder and louder, amplifying the volume of his own heartbeats as she put her mouth in a kissable pout right in front of him. Daring him. Begging him . . .

Fool! She was asking to go home; for him to take her

there. As if she still had one. Aidan sucked in a huge gulp of air that moved her with it and then he held it. Hard. Long. Steady. Counting the heartbeats that accompanied it. Before God, he wasn't taking a grieving woman! No matter what the provocation.

She blinked, instantly silencing the whoosh of sound in his ears, but then it hit his nose as he released the breath. She dropped her gaze to the area of his chin or throat, and then she shivered . . . and added a soft moan.

Aidan had her into a berth within his arms the next moment, well away from the torment that was her woman spot rubbing right against his lower belly. Then, he was stalking through the wet, soft ground. He was determined to carry her to his tent, deposit on the cot, and leave her there.

Women! They were the curse and bane of the earth. That was what they were. And women who looked like this Juliana were the worst. They were put here to torment a man, make him do and say and think things that weren't. Punish him for chivalrous behavior. Punish him worse for need. Keep him in a frustration of want fueled by his own honor and denial. Make certain he'd regret not only the saving of a bonny wench, but also the self-induced restraint that kept a man from taking and enjoying and savoring said wench until hell sounded better.

Aidan was shoving words through his head with every step, adding more transgression to beautiful women who denied a man at his lowest, before he reached the door flap of his tent. He didn't even slow down, pushing it instead with his momentum and making the piece of material cling to his head before he moved three large steps to the cot, set her down atop it, and then went to his haunches on the ground beside it.

He'd failed. He knew it. He only hoped she didn't.

The door flap settled into place behind him, sealing them into a personal bit of space that had only rain-lit dusk to light it. Juliana had her legs curved over the edge of the cot, her hands wrapped about her torso, and a wide-eyed look that gave him a full unsettling dose of her eyes. They'd stunned him when he first saw them, and it hadn't changed. Or muted. Or done anything other than intensify the dazed state of everything. Aidan shook his head to clear it. Then, he did it again.

Why her?

"Please?" she asked.

Aidan thought that was what she'd said, but the whooshing sound was back again, fuller than before. Nothing about her whisper penetrated it. All of which was an excuse for shaking his head again like he didn't understand.

"Why not?"

"You nae longer have . . . a home."

He answered brutally and watched her eyes moisten with tears she could blink into existence. But she didn't. Instead she watched him with dewy eyes and a frame that was shaking as she caught her breath in little gasps. And then she raised her little chin, narrowed her eyes, and argued with him.

"I do."

"Na'.back there," he replied.

"You don't know that."

He nodded. "I do."

"Let me go. Please?" She had a pretty plea tone as well. If he wasn't in a whorl of frustrated longing, he might even listen before he denied her.

"Nae." He made certain she understood by shaking his head.

"Why not?" She sounded cross. Strict. Stern. She didn't look it. Aidan roamed his vision over lush, lovely, and right-sized woman curves.

"Because I rescued you," he told her when he'd finished looking her over.

Her plea look changed to a completely blank one. If it

wasn't so shadowed in the tent, he might be able to find an expression, but he doubted it.

"So?" she asked.

"And I claim you."

"You can't claim me," she informed him.

Aidan raised an eyebrow, watched her glance at it, and saw her swallow quickly. She was acting a bit unsure and flustered. So, he raised the other brow as well and then moved them both several times. "Why na'?" he asked finally.

"Because I say so."

She'd replied quickly, but she sounded shaky, too. Aidan spent a moment on that. If she was feeling unsettled by his presence and what it meant right here and right now, then that was fair and just and right. He grunted.

"Well, I say different, and I'm the laird. My word is law."

She called him a name he hadn't heard before and Aidan raised his brows again, higher this time. He didn't say anything. He didn't know what to say.

"For how long, then?" she asked finally.

"Ever," he replied.

"Oh no. Never. And never you." She had a slight sneer to her mouth as she said it. She also shook her head as if she had a choice in the matter.

"Why na'?"

Aidan went up on his knees, crossed his arms about his chest, tightened the sinew to make it impossible to overlook the strength and power he possessed, and then he tightened every muscle in his chest to fullness, in the event she failed to notice. He was a prime male, in perfect health, and he knew it. He was also hard, enlarged, and ready to take her. Fully. Right here and right now. And without much more delay. Aidan didn't need to flex. She could see for herself. He watched her look to his groin before returning to his face. Her eyes were huge and filled with a fearful look he'd seen from the battlefield. But it couldn't have been, for the next moment she'd pulled her lower lip into her mouth and started sucking on it. That little move could easily release the severe hold he'd placed on himself. Aidan shifted his glance away before that happened.

"Well?" he prompted when he returned his attention to her and all she did was suck on her lip.

"Y-You . . . already have . . . women."

She was stammering, sounding a bit like Arran. She was also avoiding looking anywhere near him.

"I'll send them away," he replied.

"No."

"Why?"

"Please?"

She was using her plea voice again and jumbling everything in his head. Aidan was finished with games of words and emotions. And women who toyed with both. He'd been cursed and he wasn't forgetting it.

Rash. Reckless. Thoughtless.

"Come here," he ordered her in a raspy voice that didn't sound like him.

"No! Please?"

Her beautiful face feigned shock and confusion as she whispered it, or if she suffered either, he didn't know why. Everything on him was giving her a sign of just how ready he was and what he wanted. Aidan leaned forward, put his right hand on the rope ends that held the cot suspended, and yanked them backward, tumbling her forward, right where he wanted her.

Before she landed, he had her with his left arm about her belly, swiveled so she was sideways with her buttocks pressed into his groin, his right hand had moved to push the mass of cloak out of his way, and then he had his lips on hers.

Fire exploded all through him at the contact, sending a flame so bright, clear, and raging that he almost saw it. Heat flooded him, consuming . . . burning . . . and the contact of her mouth against his intensified the sensation. Aidan sucked on her lips, mingling his breath with hers, amid groans and whimpered words of ache, desire, and massive need. He pushed her cloak open farther, until he had her head pinioned in his right hand, his fingers separated strands of her hair, clenching and unclenching about the strands with a rhythm that coordinated perfectly with the shoves he was making against her buttocks.

The desire sensation was heady. Raw. Powerful. Potent. Aidan eased his lips from hers to trail his tongue along her jaw, flicking it slightly and totally enjoying the lurching of her frame as she reacted to his caress. He reached the delicate skin at the back of her throat and then tongued his way about her ear, licking at the goose bumps put into play by his attention.

Perfect.

He used his mouth motion to maneuver her head backward, giving him full access to her throat and soft cleavage that led to what he suspected was a bosom of flawless perfection. Aidan put his lips into a kiss and slid it along her skin . . . to the bottom of her throat . . . lower, bumping the valley between her breasts as he went, and lifting her with his left arm at the same time. He slit his eyes open to the sight of nipples that were small and erect where they pressed against her shift, and that tightened his arms and hands even more.

A crazed fever suffused him, charging through his veins with unadulterated need, want, and craving, until it became vast and erotic and all-powerful . . . and nearly too massive to contain. Aidan sucked on her skin and shook in place as he fought for control. This was too precious. Divine. He wouldn't take her swiftly and savagely and with little regard for anything save release. He wanted the full ecstasy of when he'd have her fully exposed, spread beneath him . . .

welcoming him. It was going to be incredible when he took her, and he knew it instinctively.

He still didn't know why her, and he no longer cared. Aidan released the suction of his lips with a smacking sound, glanced at the bruise he'd just made, and lifted his head. And then he stilled. Stiffened. Stared.

Juliana's eyes were scrunched shut, her hands were wrapped about the top of her head, and the shudders running through her didn't look like passion at all. She didn't look wanton or willing or welcoming. She looked frightened, and anguished, and small . . . as if she was about to be ravished.

Against her will.

Aidan swore. Sucked in a breath and swore again. And again. And again. And as many times as it took to pull back the primal tempest he'd nearly succumbed to. Then he started ordering his body. Silently, relentlessly, and with a determination that made his entire frame shudder.

His fingers obeyed finally, releasing her enough so that she sagged from the position he'd held her in. He rose onto his knees next and shoved her back onto the cot with a force that made it sway crazily. Then, he stood. Groaned. Made fists of each hand with enough force it burned to his elbows. And then he backed a step, his breath quick and angered and loud. His heart pumped through his entire frame with the same angered and loud effects. By the time he reached and pushed on the door flap, he was in an all-over ache. Everything on him felt angered and tensed and primed and frustrated, while his lower belly and groin pained and jumped unceasingly. It stung, burned, throbbed . . .

Aidan spun, took four large steps before he was at an all-out run for the swift-running burn they'd camped near. He scrambled into it before he changed his mind and regained his sanity. And then he was gritting his teeth to keep the howl at a level his men wouldn't hear.

Rash. Reckless. Thoughtless. As usual.

But he did feel alive.

Chapter 7

Aidan MacKetryck was annoyed with her. He wasn't making a secret of it, and more than one of his clansmen had glanced at her since he'd first brought her out of the tent, walked her over to a stump, and put her atop it. The extent of his ire at her was clear from the blank expression on his face, the tight, clenched look on his mouth, and the fact that he never said one word to her. Not one.

If it hadn't been for Arran bringing her a hank of boar meat earlier with the instructions to prepare and do so rapidly, she'd have probably been marched out without her boots on or her hair plaited and smoothed beneath her cloak. She watched as they went about systematically dismantling their camp, rolling and tying and flattening tents into packs with an efficiency broken with tongue clicks and whistles, and varied slapping noises that seemed to have a meaning she didn't know. The pot they'd used for cooking got tied to one horse, with the roof thing and poles balancing out the opposite side. Tent packs got tossed atop bare saddles. The little trunks she'd noted went behind saddles, making a backrest if needed. Juliana tipped her head in consideration at that.

No one spoke as if by order. Or they were following Aidan's lead. His annoyance was being demonstrated by every tight-lipped blank expression he gave as well as dark looks from narrow-lashed eyes, as if voicing anything would be a waste of time. He hadn't taken the time to tie his hair back, leaving long, dark locks falling about his face and shoulders that required flipping out of his way constantly. He looked more than annoyed. He also looked dangerous.

Juliana got to her feet when he came for her. She didn't dare do any different. She fully expected to get a fist wrapped about her upper arm while he marched her to her mount. She got neither. He simply looked at her for a moment, and then jerked his head in the direction he wanted her to go.

Ooh.

If she ever got out from under his control, she was not going quietly. She was going to make sure he knew every single reason why no gentle-bred woman welcomed contact with a barbaric Highlander like him. She stomped each foot as she walked in front of him over to where she suspected her horse was. That wasn't good enough. Before she got there and without one bit of warning, hard hands had gripped her waist and flung her atop one, in a move even more careless than the first time.

Juliana nearly went headfirst over the other side. Nobody helped. She had chunks of the stallion's mane gripped in her hands and she had to claw her way back upright. When she got in the saddle, it was to see that Aidan had taken her reins and was almost to the lead horse. But this time when he mounted, he'd started a jog step that became a run, and just before he reached his horse, he leapt atop a rock and that vaulted him into his saddle. It was perfectly timed and executed and rarely done, if the reaction of whistling and clapping from his men was an indication. Juliana's mouth had parted slightly at the move. Despite how he annoyed and bothered every bit of her, she'd have clapped in awe, too, except he'd punctuated his mounting with a slap of his knees to his horse, and a jerk of the reins. If she hadn't been holding on to the mane, she'd have probably fallen. He hadn't looked back to check on her then.

And he still didn't. Nor did he bother to check the riderless horse that took the space between them, mutely testifying to the extent of his annoyance with her.

It was all fine and good with her. She didn't want any contact with him anyway. She hadn't wanted it last eve, and she didn't want it now. Juliana sniffed slightly and raised her chin. She didn't know what was wrong with him anyway. It was clear he could have any woman . . . and probably had. Well! Some woman should have taken his arrogance down a fraction or two before leaving it to Juliana to handle.

She watched his stiff back from a distance of the horse between them, sucked in on her cheeks, and tipped her head sideways as she surveyed him. It wasn't him . . . exactly. He was manly. Immense. Brawny. Beautiful. He was a fine specimen. She'd give him that. Even sitting his horse, you could see his power. It was evident in the thickness of his chest, the width of his shoulders . . . the massive size of his arms. But she already knew all that. She'd had a very good look the prior evening, when he'd stolen every thought and breath and sensation and held her so rapt, she'd lost the ability to form words.

He thought displaying himself like a game cock was all it took to gain a woman's attention? Or perhaps he thought giving her a demonstration would have more effect. Juliana's nipples tightened again, sending a tremor through her that annoyed and disgusted her. It wasn't that she'd enjoyed his caresses. Never. She'd endured them, gripping her arms about her and breathing in short gasps of shock-filled existence while she suffered through each and every lap of his tongue . . .

Juliana tightened her thighs on the horse and felt the same quivering sensation, the same tightening in her womb that started a wellspring of damp to her core . . . with the same results as last night. All night. It still tingled, itched, and frustrated her with a craving for . . . *something*. She settled herself into the saddle, enduring the rocking of the horse against tissues that were so sensitive, she might as well be unclothed. That disgusted her even more.

She hadn't wrapped her hands about her head to keep from reaching for him! Oh no. Not Juliana D'Aubenville. She wasn't driven by lusts and passions and sinful, moisture-imbued desires. Those things weren't the catalyst behind the quivers running all over and through her, making the past night an agony of sleeplessness, filled with restless tossing, and heavy, heated, sweat-inducing rivulets of sensation. That was not what it had been at all. Not Juliana. She wasn't like other women.

. . . although he had said he'd send his other women away. *What other women?*

Juliana's eyes widened on what that might mean. She'd thought his women worked about his castle, just as those at Fyfen had. Now she wasn't sure. She knew providing women for a man's comfort was done although no one spoke of it directly. As the chatelaine of her father's estate, she knew how to provide for a distinguished visitor's comforts . . . if requested and agreed. And what a servant wench did with her evening hours was her own business. Usually. If she warmed anyone's bed, Juliana had turned a blind eye. Such doings were beneath a lady's consideration. No gentle-bred woman would consider such a thing as gracing a man's bed without a proper wedding ceremony.

Her thoughts stalled as well as her breath. *How dare he?* Even if she were the daughter of a village woodcutter, that was no reason to believe her a lass of easy virtue! And even if she allowed this captivity of his and this claim of her . . . she would *never* even consider such a thing!

Now that was going too far. As was making her ride through a day that lengthened into afternoon and then evening with nothing to do save remember . . . and experience the same breathless state of tremors. And then remember again. Experience . . .

Riding without stopping didn't seem abnormal to them. The horses kept up the steady pace past meadows and across rock, beneath canopies of trees, through heather, and at one point around a loch that had seemed as vast and endless as her continual thoughts and irritations. Her back got tired, sending her into a slumped position against the horse's neck, since she didn't have a small trunk behind her saddle. It didn't seem to affect Aidan. Every time she looked, he was stiff-backed and silent. Large. Powerful. Implacable.

At least it wasn't raining, although the heavy gray shade of cloud cover lingering at treetop level was threatening it, and she was just wondering if he planned on riding through the evening when he stopped, lifting his hand at the same time. Each horse did the same after a few steps, shortening the line as they did. Juliana watched as Aidan dismounted, and he caught her looking when he turned to them. He'd tucked his hair behind his ears, but his expression was still just as blank, and just as dark. Juliana returned it in kind, despite the unsettled feeling in her belly, as if a stone were developing there and had just dropped.

He bowed his upper lip over the lower, gave a whistle, and that brought Arran jogging from behind her somewhere. Juliana watched as the smaller man took the reins, releasing Aidan to walk to the bushes. She looked behind her and saw all the men doing the same thing.

"You doona' have . . . much t-t-time!" Arran called out for her benefit.

There was no appropriate moniker for an uncouth, bad-mannered, rude and ill-bred cur that would force a woman to dismount a horse, get into the bushes for nature's call, and somehow manage to get back without the courtesy of an assist. But she found a few, and was mumbling them beneath her breath as she moved a stiff and slow left leg to join the right. Then, she jumped forward, landing ungracefully on her knees, and when that wasn't enough disgrace, she found when she tried to stand that both legs trembled and failed to work properly. This put her in an awkward position with both hands and feet on the ground. The only good thing looked to be that the ground beneath her hands was slightly higher than her feet.

"You've g-g-got to wait a-a-a bit. For . . . feeling."

It was Arran again. He'd moved to the front of the middle horse, which put him near hers while he spoke to her.

"Try a-a-and stand. Th-Th-That's it."

He was young. And slender. He was only a little taller than her. He stuttered. His voice had a squeak occasionally when he talked. He was still absolutely wonderful. Juliana already knew what was wrong. She hadn't ridden for such a lengthy time, she'd gone soft. Juliana had to blink tears away before she turned her head to him.

"U-U-Use your arms!"

That made sense. Juliana walked herself upright, using her hands to close in on her feet, then she had her ankles, up her legs, and then she was trying to stand erect, arching oddly at the effort. She felt a fool and probably looked worse.

"N-N-Now go! Quick!"

It was a stumble, but Juliana made it to the shrubs beside her horse, and then she went in farther, shoving forward on hands and feet when the greenery dragged at her. Leagues of greenery. Shrubs and bushes and thorn-bedecked stems had to be pushed through until she reached a stand of trees where the air even went dim and quiet, as if she deserved a sentence of solitude from a forest as well. Tears started up before she could stop them, making everything even worse. Juliana shoved a hand into her mouth to stop the sobs and used the other sleeve to wipe at the wetness.

"Hurry, Ju-Ju-Juliana!"

She hadn't gone far, if Arran's voice was any indication. And she still had her privy to attend to. Juliana wiped at the tears brutally, but they just kept falling. She'd rarely felt as weak. She'd had to contend with worse than silence from an arrogant male and sore muscles, much worse. If he thought this punishment, he needed a lesson. He hadn't been forced in the middle of the night to run for safety. He hadn't seen his father's dead body hanging from a castle wall and been forced to pretend it was nothing. He hadn't been forced to do menial labor, while hiding and hoping and starving and freezing for months while a horde of barbarians pulled apart his home. And he hadn't had to watch the only soul who knew the truth shoved into a quickly dug common grave.

Aidan MacKetryck hadn't any idea of the backbone his captive possessed. No one did. And by the saints, she wasn't going to allow that man to break her.

Juliana had her impulse to sob sealed away and most of the signs covered over before she walked back, wondering if her delay had served to get the freedom she craved and they'd ridden on without her. She'd have tried tears earlier if they worked.

She knew the truth the moment she came out of the trees, looked across what had seemed like a huge span of greenery when she'd crawled through it, and saw the MacKetryck laird nod as he spotted her. He had his arms folded atop his chest, his feet apart, and the same expressionless look to him.

She could try being a horrid captive next, but doubted it would work. He wasn't going to let her go and she didn't know why. She wondered if he did.

Juliana had her face turned away when she broke through the last of the brambles, pulling her cloak free of them as she went. Her luck was cursed bad. Still. Aidan was waiting for her at her horse. Nothing about him had changed. He looked implacable, hard, and vengeful. Juliana glanced at the area of his chin, noted it was darker with a beard growth he hadn't scraped away, and looked away.

She knew he was going to throw her atop the horse again. It would be a gesture of punishment and ownership. They might as well just get it over with. She turned to face her horse, looking across the saddle and seeing little.

"You need a rest?" he asked.

The surprise of hearing it stopped everything. She watched the ground and gray sky mesh into a wash of color as her stupid eyes watered up again. She shook her head.

"You look to need one."

Juliana stiffened and put her shoulders back. If she didn't blink, the tears might stay where they were. And if she didn't speak, perhaps he'd get her reply without having to voice it. She shook her head again.

"Turn about and face me."

If his voice was any indication, he didn't like the way she answered. She wondered what the punishment for that would be. She shook her head again.

"I said, turn about and—"

He put both hands on her shoulders and physically swiveled her as he spoke. And then his voice halted. Since he'd taken away her choice again, Juliana did the only thing she could. She tipped her head back and faced him and hoped he'd read her reply in her face. She didn't need a rest. She didn't need his concern. She didn't need anything. Nor would she accept it.

She couldn't tell what expression might be on his face, since he was a blur. She could alter it by blinking, but that would send tears down her cheeks. And then she'd have to admit to them. She refused. Juliana D'Aubenville wouldn't cry over any man. Or what he might do. Ever. She swallowed constantly and shook in place and silently ordered everything on her body to harden.

He sucked in a breath and then he huffed it back out, sending air all over her. She didn't have to see it. She felt it.

"You make this powerful hard, lass." His voice had lowered to a near whisper and he'd stepped closer as well.

Dear God! She was in trouble, and if he didn't cease, she was going to turn into a blubbering fool. Her knees were already trembling, and each breath was a ragged effort. Why did the saints have to punish her with a storm of weeping now? She'd stood dry-eyed and hard when faced with her father's murdered corpse. She hadn't cried when forced to huddle in near freezing conditions in that ancient croft, listening as winds howled through every crack. She hadn't even reacted when they'd buried her steward. She hadn't even cried when she'd been unable to find the ring. No. She had to cry now. In front of Aidan Niall MacKetryck.

She only hoped he wouldn't think it due to him.

"You leave me little choice. You ken?"

He had little choice? That was almost laughable. If she dared let the hold on her emotions crack enough to let them out. Juliana shrugged very slowly and carefully, and felt the difference in him. Good. She'd rather deal with his anger.

"Verra well. We ride on . . . and I tie you to the horse."

Juliana's eyes widened, the tears slid out, and he was watching all of it. That made his image perfectly clear, but there was something wrong. The concern in his eyes didn't match the words he'd just said. And that confused everything. Juliana watched him smile slightly and that was so horrid her heart lurched, alarming her with the power of it and suffusing her with an all-over tingling at the same time. She had to look away. And quickly. She did it too quickly, since the world spun for a moment before righting, and there wasn't anything to hold on to when she stumbled.

Except him.

"My other choice is putting you on my horse. With me."

He ignored where she clutched at his folded arm as he informed her of his intention.

Juliana watched the ground steady, and then she eased her hand from him. As if it hadn't happened. The trouble she suffered was severe, and constant, and increasing. It had Aidan MacKetryck at the core of it. Something was wrong with her to react so to him. It didn't take a seer to see that. As for riding on a horse with him? In his arms? She'd rather die.

"Where is the rope?" Juliana asked.

Aidan tossed back his head and laughed. Heartily. Juliana wiped quickly at her cheeks with the heels of both hands and had them wiped on her skirt before he'd finished. She almost thanked him. His amusement had done what she'd been unable to. She no longer felt any desire to cry.

He must have sensed the difference in her when he'd finished his amusement. She hoped he planned on tying her quickly, and that it wouldn't be too humiliating. She could sense the volume of horses and men behind her, and if they were true to form, they had to be getting restless, watching Aidan delay their departure.

As if she spoke aloud, Aidan stepped to one side of her and shoved up a hand. Juliana turned to watch some of the men dismount and start pulling things from their packs, and then settling on the ground beside their horses. Five of them stood poised to one side, waiting. The reason was apparent as she watched. An unrecognizable clansman at the far end of the line of horses started tossing bundles to a closer man, who opened the bundle, took something out, and then tossed it farther. The same thing happened with the next one and the next. When they reached Arran, who'd been the closest clansman behind her, she watched as he loaded contents from the bundles into a small basket. It wasn't until he brought it to Aidan, who motioned with his head at her, that she saw what it was.

Food. They'd opened and served strips of fire-dried veni-

son, flat oat cakes, and clumps of blackberries. Arran waited
while she selected a meat stick and one of the cakes. Then,
he gave the basket to his brother. He was at a jog only to
return with a tankard of ale to wash it down. It was also given
to her. Aidan didn't partake. A glance showed he drank from
his whiskey flagon instead. Juliana looked about at the men
sitting and eating. She could hear the slight sounds of movement as they ate, but nothing else. Aidan hadn't had to say a
word. Such discipline was impressive. And frightening.

"I ordered a rest," Aidan informed her.

Juliana was gnawing on a meat stick by then. She nodded.
"Instead."

She frowned at that one word, but he didn't elaborate. He
was shoving one of the oat cakes into his mouth and washing
it down with a large gulp from his flagon. Then she knew
what he meant. He'd ordered a rest . . . instead of either
option he'd given her. That was considerate of him. If he
showed much more chivalrous behavior, she just might be
forgiving him for a bit of his behavior last night and today.
But not all of it.

Juliana put her ale atop the saddle, keeping it from tipping
with one hand while she finished the meat and started on her
cake. It was dry and had hard bits baked into it that tasted
bitter. It needed the ale. She gulped half of her tankard down
and resettled it, looking through the golden color at the omi-
nous gray cloud cover. And frowning. She was revamping
her opinion of Highlanders a bit. They were warmongers . . .
barbaric and crude. Coarse. Vulgar. Uncouth. Capable of
taking a castle, murdering the lord inside while his family
fled, and then displaying his dead body . . .

Juliana took another long draught of her ale, nearly draining the tankard. Replaced it atop the saddle. Looked at the
sky through it. Sighed.

She'd repeated that litany through her head too many
times and for too long. She was tired of it. And she'd been

only half-right. Highlanders *were* rough, arrogant, uncouth, lusty, and crude. But they were also strong, efficient, well disciplined, and they knew exactly what to feed a female they'd decided to rescue. This was the third wonderful meal she'd had.

She should revamp her anger over Aidan's rescue as well. She had that decided once she'd drained the tankard, washing down the last of her cake. Then she checked for the berries. She didn't have to look far, since Aidan was still standing beside her and held the basket out.

And if he hadn't decided to look at her with one eyebrow raised while she plucked a small stem of them, she'd have thanked him before turning away. He really shouldn't do that. It stilled a woman's tongue. And other ridiculous things.

She should probably thank him for rescuing her, rather than berate him in her head over it. The English soldiers who'd retaken her castle hadn't been asking names when they'd been chasing and slaughtering. Why . . . if Aidan hadn't grabbed her as he had, she probably would have died. Or wished she had. She popped a berry into her mouth.

"You ever sit a horse all night?" Aidan asked at her shoulder. Juliana jumped and then choked. Then she was sucking for air and coughing. He could have done more than laugh at her, too.

"Why?" she asked, after the wheezing had stopped and she could breathe again.

"I have nae wish to tie you."

Juliana picked up her empty tankard, turned to face him, and put the uneaten berries back into the basket. She would have put the tankard in there as well, except Arran materialized at her side and took it. She waited until he'd gone back to his own horse before speaking.

"Set your camp up here."

He pulled back slightly, raising his shoulders as he lowered his chin to regard her from a span of an arm away, looking too raw and male to avoid. He probably assumed such a stance when looking for a fight. At least, that was what it looked like. Juliana shivered. Bit at her tongue. She probably shouldn't have gulped the entire tankard of undiluted ale but that was hindsight.

"Is that a nae?" he asked.

"Aye," she replied.

"You've sat a horse all night?" He didn't have to pretend the incredulity. It was in his voice and on his face.

"Nay," she replied.

"Well, which is it?"

Juliana giggled and that brought his chin up slightly, taking him out of the threatening pose. She found that even more amusing and covered her lips before she sounded inebriated and silly. And then the first hiccough hit, shaking her with it and widening her eyes.

"You've na' drank ale much either, have you?"

"Aye," she replied from behind her hand. And hiccoughed again. If there was a purgatory before death, feeling this dizzy and happy when facing Aidan MacKetryck had to be it.

"You have?"

"Nay," she told him.

"Well . . . which is it?"

Juliana giggled again as he repeated the exact same question. Then, she hiccoughed a third time. He swore and she didn't even recognize some of the words.

He did that too often, and without any reason. She hoped he didn't do it around proper company . . . and in a proper setting, like his castle.

"Do what?" he asked.

Juliana put her other hand atop the first one on her mouth, slapping herself with the move. She couldn't believe she'd said it aloud. And if she was capable of doing that, there was no telling what she might let slip. And what he might find out. And what he'd do about it.

"You ride with me," he informed her when all she did was look at him between hiccoughs. "And doona' dare touch me."

Now . . . how was she supposed to do that? His horse wasn't that large. Juliana looked at where Aidan's stallion was standing, placidly munching on foliage at its hooves.

"All women ken how. It's inbred."

That time she hadn't said a word. Not a peep. Maybe another hiccough, but not a word. Juliana's eyes went to his, and the wretch winked. She had to look away before her legs dropped her, but that was a misused wish. She realized it as the gray sky and green grass spun and there was nothing she could do about it.

He had her up and over his shoulder and was walking with her before she reached the ground. Hoots and calls reached her ears over it, proving Highlanders weren't perfectly silent and disciplined after all, given enough provocation. She just wished it hadn't been her.

Chapter 8

The woman felt good in his arms. Solid. Lush. Her lips were parted slightly, sending little purrs of sound with each of her breaths. She was a comfortable weight where her shoulder rested beneath his arm, her head below his chin, and even where she'd brought her knees up to prop them against his other arm. She had her right hand open and held against his upper belly as if caressing the flesh. Some of her hair had escaped the braid, letting spirals of red peek from beneath her cloak. He wouldn't change a thing. She was comfortable and warm, and making his heart experience strange antics within his chest while his breathing wasn't far behind.

He'd been a fool.

Only a dim fellow tried the love act with a woman who'd just buried her husband. Or brother. Or whatever the woodcutter was to her. Aidan decided it didn't much matter what the woodcutter had been. He was dead and she was Aidan's now. And that was that.

Keeping Juliana safe when he thought she detested him had been a severe test of will. Aidan didn't know how he'd managed it. And it had been for nothing! She'd been crying, making his heart hurt when he saw it. He wanted her safe from hurt . . . and then he caused it? He'd felt like a bull elk. In rut. Without sense or sensibilities. All of it due to a false-hood his mind had conceived. *Jesu'!* He hated thinking. He should have just asked, or approached her earlier. He wouldn't make that mistake again.

She hadn't rejected him last night. She'd rejected his timing.

He got further proof as the lass accepted this arrangement. She'd gasped when he'd jumped atop his horse with her still on his shoulder, but she hadn't demurred or argued when he'd brought her from over his shoulder, sliding her into the front of his saddle. She hadn't fought him when he'd wrapped an arm about her and pulled her back into his chest. She'd gone readily and fully, and even wriggled herself into this curled-up position with a little sigh of contentment that had him openly grinning.

Aidan yawned now, lifted his head, and gave three sharp whistles. Juliana moved, rubbing her cheek against him with her disturbed sleep. Aidan held his breath until she'd fin-ished, and settled back into him.

He slowed and moved left, making it easier for Heck to pass him, taking over the lead. As the eldest of Aidan's honor guard, he had first right. After that would be Kerr, followed by Stefan, and then Tavish, if needed. Until Aidan had enough sleep and led again. They'd done it often.

It showed.

Aidan knew the change was made and accepted by the in-creased gait of his horse. Once that happened, he moved his chin forward, settling it atop her head. He thought about bringing his sett farther atop his head, but dismissed it in the event the movement or fresh chill jostled her. The night was filled with moisture, but she still wore her cloak, and how she'd bundled into his arms was very secure and very warm. Aside from which, the rain wasn't doing more than filling the air with moisture, making a fine mist to coat everything until there was enough of it to turn into a drop and drizzle away. It would most likely end come daylight, if the sun came out and burned the clouds off. He'd slept through worse.

And the girl felt so right in his arms!

Perfect. The word filtered through his head again. She was perfect, and she felt perfect, and what he felt right here and right now as he held her was perfect.

Aidan made the decision to change horses come morn in order to ride straight through to Castle Ketryck. Four days' worth of riding could be shortened to two and a half if they didn't stop or set up camp. They had enough food. They had normal late spring weather. They had a change of horses now. And he had a warm, dry, luxurious, private chamber . . . with a large bed . . .

Aidan tightened his arms subconsciously on the sleeping goddess, took a long whiff of her smell, and decided he'd delay stopping and changing anything for as long as possible. And that was the last thing he remembered.

Oh no!

Definitely no. And again no. And another no.

Juliana blinked again and got an eyeful of near-naked chest, since the shirt was stuck to him with moisture, making it transparent and useless as a covering. That was exacerbated by the absence of the hank of plaid that was supposed to be across him but was instead gripped in her hand when she must have used it to balance herself. And all of that was added to by heavy breath hitting her nose from above her.

She had not slept this way. Not in his arms. Oh no.

Juliana jerked upright, the horse shied, and Aidan reacted as if he'd been fully awake the entire time, tightening his hold and pulling her tight against him while the horse beneath them rocked and swayed, and worse. She had no choice but to feel every bit of where he was hard and thick and pushing against her buttocks with his man-rod. Again. The man was an animal.

"Jesu', lass! Do you always wake so . . . rough?" His voice was a growl of sound, and he immediately added to it by lifting his head and whistling.

"Put me down," Juliana replied and started wriggling in the event he didn't understand.

"Give me a—*Christ!*"

The last was due to her elbow contact where he should have been protecting, rather than using his arms to imprison her. Aidan went concave, trying to scrunch into a bowl shape, gripping her to him in the meantime, and that was just stupid. There wasn't space on his horse for it. Juliana hadn't even time to cry out before they tumbled from the horse in a jumble of entwined limbs.

He was probably lucky it was soft, wet, and marshy where they landed, since he was on the bottom, and that just got her more cursing and groaning. But when she tried to rise from him, he just tightened his limbs more.

"Let . . . me . . . up!" Juliana spaced out the words with her struggles, gaining just enough gap for an arm or a leg, before he had her wrapped up again. Her cloak was against her, too, since it had slipped from her head and gotten hooked beneath him, and that pulled and held her shoulders. As well as releasing lengthy curls that had escaped her braid.

"Na' . . . until you . . . explain." He had gaps in the words, showing that it wasn't as easy holding her as he made it look.

"Explain what?" Juliana stopped moving, turned her head to where she thought his face was, and gaped. Closed her mouth to swallow, and gaped again. Her breath caught, restarted, caught again; her heart fell to the pit of her belly, where it pounded with a crescendo of deafening thumps; then an ocean wave went roaring through her ears, blotting that out. She was going to faint. Rage. Scream. Explode. Dissolve.

She'd known she was in trouble, but not the extent of it.

Aidan looked wild. He was in a semi sit-up with her astride him. He hadn't bound his hair back and it was in severe need of a grooming. Strands went everywhere, across his face, all over his shoulders. Some strands even went straight up. His eyes were slit, his nostrils flared for breath, his mouth was a thin line, sharpening his jawline and narrowing his cheeks, and everything on him was bunched up and tight, making ropes and bumps of muscle her hands were gripping and her upper thighs were sitting atop. And since he was breathing hard, she was rising and falling with it.

Then something changed. She could only hope it wasn't something in her face.

Aidan opened his eyes from the slits they'd been in, showing their amber color through the mesh of lash. Then he cocked that one eyebrow, drawing her gaze to it before she looked quickly at the horse legs behind his head.

"What?" he asked in a soft voice that didn't match anything else on him.

Juliana forced her slack lips back together and gulped. Glanced over at him before shying away and gulping again, although it was dry and scratchy-feeling the second time. She wasn't going to cry. She wasn't! And she'd never admit why! Even to herself. If this was a feeling, it wasn't a good one. It was harsh, real, raw. Huge. So vast, she started shaking with it. That slackened parts of him, starting with the legs at her back and moving through his belly, and dropping her slightly as he did so.

"Lass?"

He had a confused tone to the word. She didn't dare see what might be on his face.

She did not love him. Oh no. Not him. Never.

"You called a rest?" A voice spoke from behind her, sending a shadow onto the top of Aidan's head from a weak morning sun.

"God's—"

Aidan cut off his curse and moved his attention to the speaker behind her. His move made the mass of muscle beneath her apex contract, and shift . . . and connect. Juliana reacted instantly to lift away, but was gripped at her waist by hands that weren't gentle. Or slack.

"Alpin?"

Aidan asked it of the man behind her, and looked to be giving him full attention. As if the way she was pinned to his belly experiencing a worse sensation than when the horse had rolled beneath her wasn't affecting anything.

"At your service . . . and hers."

Alpin was probably bowing. Juliana didn't turn her head to check. She was concentrating on ignoring everything about the man holding her, what he was making her experience physically, as well as the tumultuous beating of her heart.

"Where's Arran?" Aidan asked.

"In the bushes. He . . . uh . . . overimbibed last eve."

He wasn't the only one, Juliana added silently.

"Ill?"

"You should ha' stopped the serving of Killoran's stock. That ale has a bite to it. A large one. Serpent large."

"Kerr," Aidan answered.

Juliana closed her eyes to it but that made it all worse. And harder to ignore. She knew she was turning pink, and then passing that to red. The sweat at her scalp told her of it. She opened her eyes again and looked over Aidan's shoulder at his horse's legs. It was safer.

"Aye."

"Why is everyone standing about, taking in the morn?"

"Well . . . you did call a rest."

That was Kerr again. Sarcastic. Amused. She recalled that from when they'd first met. Juliana silently cursed the fates.

God. Aidan MacKetryck. She still didn't want to know them or recognize them. Now, more than ever.

"Go rest then," Aidan replied in a growl of voice.

"And eat?" Alpin asked.

"The lad's an empty hole. Needs filling," someone explained.

"Verra well. Go. Eat. And do it far from me."

"We came to check . . . on your safety." That voice she didn't recognize.

"Verra well, you checked. I'm safe," Aidan replied.

"How about the lass?" Kerr asked. Then he snorted what was probably withheld laughter. They all sounded fairly amused.

Aidan swore again.

"I believe that's Aidan's way of saying the lass is also . . . perfectly safe." One of the men answered in a teasing tone she also recognized. It had to be Ewan.

"We have time for oat mash?" That was Alpin.

"My laird?" one of the men asked.

Aidan sighed, lifting her with it, before lowering her on the exhalation. "We near a burn?" he asked finally.

"Beyond the thicket. Stefan has a great nose for that."

"Then aye. We've time." Aidan wasn't paying much attention to the men behind Juliana. She didn't have to see his steady regard. She knew it. She could feel it. Sense it. Nearly touch it.

"Fetch the kettle, Gregor. Tavish, the kindling. And Alpin! See how you are at starting a cook fire. We'll cook up a pot of gruel that'll fill even you."

"Can we have more Killoran ale?"

They were starting to leave if the voices were any indication.

"You can mix it in if you like."

"But . . . what about the laird . . . and her?"

Someone had to ask it. Juliana shut her eyes for a moment

before opening them and finding Aidan's. He still had his eyelids lowered partway and one eyebrow cocked, and the moment she locked gazes with him, she gave the most appalling, wild, uncontrollable full-body pulse. And before it ceased, it got repeated by him.

Her eyes went wide. He lost his half-lidded look as well. He looked stunned and shocked and bewildered. Juliana only hoped it was mirrored, but already knew it wasn't. The blush stealing over her features told her of it.

"You heard the laird." His men hadn't waited. They were definitely walking away. "He's safe. The lass is safe. Everyone's safe."

"Except your bairn brother, Arran. That one is na' safe."

"Poor lad."

"Give him more of that keg. That'll cure him."

Laughter followed that announcement, there was some more banter that got indistinct with distance, and then more hooting and calling and laughter. Then there was silence, broken only by the sound of her own breathing.

"You ready?" Aidan asked.

To get up, seek the bushes herself, and then get fed? Juliana was more than ready. She nodded.

"Good."

Nothing like that happened. He stayed in the half-sit position, taut muscles against her nether region and his attention fully on her.

"Start speaking."

"A-A-A-bout what?" She wasn't feigning the confusion. The slight lift of his lips on one side wasn't helping either. She had to look away if she wanted her tongue to work at making words.

"This."

He added to the word by moving every bit of him against her, in a continuum of sensation, making a shiver that rippled over and through her before finding a center at each nipple, making them darts of awareness and sinful itch.

"Do you need to . . . visit . . . the bushes?" she asked, gapping the sentence with gasps of air.

"I did prior to the hurting you gave me," he replied. "Now? I believe it can wait."

Juliana wrinkled her brow. *Hurting?*

"And you'll wait with me until you explain."

"Ex . . . plain?" she stammered.

He sighed again. She moved up and down with it. She truly wished he'd cease that.

"You slept in my arms," he informed her.

Oh . . . Lord! She swore the words for him. Silently.

"Slept. All night. And you went there willing. Of your own accord."

"No . . . I . . . It was . . ."

"Look to me," he commanded.

Look to him? Now? She shook her head.

"Why na'? So you can keep lying?"

"I am not lying!"

Juliana turned back to him before she could think it through. It wouldn't have changed it, because he was right. Avoidance didn't do any good. It wasn't anything she wanted to deal with, but she might as well face it and get past it. She only had one thing left—her betrothal to Sir Percy Dane. She had a large worth to the man, once the king restored her property, and if she could get back to it.

And if she remained untouched.

Betrothal to Sir Percy Dane had been a large coup for her father. Sir Percy was a knight of great renown and distinction. He claimed powerful blood links to the crowns of Normandy, Saxony, Sicily, and England. If he hadn't been away, crusading for the noblest of causes, none of this would have happened. Castle Fyfen would never have been taken and she'd have been wed already. She wouldn't have even met a Highlander, especially not Aidan MacKetryck. And she would never have been astride the man with nothing covering her woman place while he looked at her with such an honest expression on his handsome face that the fates decided to shame her again with another nonrhythmic lurch of her frame against his.

There was nothing to hide behind, so she didn't even try. She met his look without flinching, enduring the shivers it gave her and then the flutter within her rib cage as her heart decided to join in.

"I'm going to kiss you, lass," he whispered.

"No—"

He stopped her with his move, made so swiftly his lips were filming hers before the sound left them, and her denial ended up sliding against his skin instead of being voiced with disapproval and strength. He'd moved to a sit and moved his hands, too, releasing her waist so he could slide both arms about and across her back, latching her right against his chest and making her experience the short huffs of breath he made, the increasing thud of his heart, and the damp heat his skin was exuding.

Every thought just disappeared, granting Juliana the freedom just to feel, experience . . . enjoy. Light filled her, gaining in strength and volume and luminosity. It was accompanied with song, light and joy-filled and melodic. And that was covered over by vast vistas of clear sky, large fields . . . wide oceans. And that changed to the wonder of water. Clear, fresh, open running falls of water, filling her consciousness as it rushed through her, engulfing her with the magnitude and intensity of it. An entire realm so filled with ecstasy opened for her that she nearly wept at the beauty and scope and grandeur of it.

And then it slowed . . . faded. Disappeared. Shut off. Ended.

The groan that released his lips paralleled her moan in length and timbre and meaning. Exactly. Aidan pulled his head up, releasing her, before looking down at her with such a tender expression her heart stopped. Restarted. Went into a ragged beat.

He licked his lips. "Deny that," he whispered, and then he smiled in that cocky motion that only lifted one side of his mouth.

"No . . . I—"

"You serious?" His smile dropped.

"It's not . . . I'm not—"

"You truly . . . deny . . . what you feel?"

He didn't have to put a description to it. She'd rarely experienced something so precious. And wrong. Her throat was closing off and her eyes were filling with useless stupid weak tears before she nodded. She was always going to deny it. And she couldn't tell him why.

"Doona' cry again." He had a pleading tone to the words. He'd also opened his arms and set her atop one of his legs, at the prone bent knee. Or thereabouts. She couldn't feel for certain and didn't look to check. She couldn't. Her eyes were hooked, watching him yank up on his shirt, pulling it from beneath his belt in order to offer the end to her.

Juliana smiled slightly, and then it widened. He was so sweet . . . and so rough-hewn. Coarse. Uncouth. Only a Highlander would offer up cloth that had been right next to his skin for days. But only this Highlander put naked flesh right where she had no choice but to see it and be bothered immensely by it. Juliana dropped her eyes to his lower chest and belly and then looked aside as she colored. She could appreciate why he'd do such a move now.

"I am a beast," he said, and from a side glance, she watched his hand drop.

She shook her head.

"It . . . is still too soon. I ken."

Too soon? Oh no. It was not ever. That was what it was.

"Your husband has been but fresh buried—"

"Husband?" she asked.

"The woodcutter," he answered.

Juliana stiffened and then she giggled. And then she was snorting through her nose to keep the laughter at bay. The release was akin to being filled with ale foam, and about as frothy and unsubstantial.

"What?" he asked.

He thought her wed to the D'Aubenville steward, with his airs and pontificating and complaining and pinched-nose features?

"The woodcutter . . . was na' your spouse?"

She shook her head.

"Then who is?"

"No one."

"Face me when you lie," he answered.

"I am not lying." She was grinding her teeth, however. And regretting every single moment of the morning. Almost.

"You're na' lying? Truly?"

"I am not lying and I am not wed."

"Widowed?" he asked.

"I am not a widow and I am not a wife. I have never been wed. Listen closer."

"At your age? What is wrong with them?"

Juliana was sucking in air at the insult and then losing it at the confusion. "With whom?" she asked frostily.

"The men . . . in that village. Doona' they have eyes?"

His men weren't the only ones with a teasing tone. They'd obviously picked it up from him, she decided.

"I'm getting up. I've nature to see to."

"Tell me why you're unwed," he replied, snatching her upper arm with a move that was invisibly quick.

"Now, MacKetryck," she ordered and pushed on him with her free arm. It was foolish and did nothing other than prove how warm he was and how stout and heavy.

"Was it your . . . argumentative tongue?"

He was going to get a good dose of her argumentative

tongue if he said one more word. He was also going to get the cook pot against the side of his head the moment his younger brother had emptied it. And the moment he wasn't looking.

"Or perhaps it's . . . your prickly . . . wit?"

"Have you finished?" she asked.

He sobered suddenly, oddly, and completely. "Please doona' tell me you're a maid."

Juliana debated every option in a matter of two heartbeats. If she claimed a lover or two, he'd probably want to join them. But if she claimed the pox, he might not. If she told him the truth, he might be even more curious about her. And probably more amorous. Trouble. It just kept getting deeper and wider.

"Jesu'!"

Aidan swore and stared at her, ending her quandary. She didn't have to say anything after all. He'd read it in her face.

Chapter 9

The lass was a virgin.

A maiden.

Untouched.

Every step of the horse beneath him echoed the words through his head and his nether region, making the sway of the animal erotic and stimulating. Strands of unkempt hair he should have tied back were slapped across his mouth wetly. That was erotic and stimulating. The scratch of woolen plaid against his skin was rough and itchy, and even more erotic and stimulating. *Hellfire. And damnation.* Even the wind-blown spurts of rain wetting his chest, right shoulder, and arm were erotic and stimulating.

A virgin . . .

Aidan cursed the fates again and lifted his face to the gray low hang of cloud. He opened his mouth, pulling in fresh, cool, wet air, and licking at the hair strands as well as drops on his upper lip. Even that started feeling erotic and stimulating. And forbidden. He lowered his head and went back to looking ahead.

This problem was without reason and against all logic.

Juliana had been unsettling and bothersome since he'd rescued her. He could feel and sense her about . . . and that was just wrong. There wasn't a charm to ward off unsettling women with bottomless eyes, lush lips, beautiful features, hair that demanded a touch . . . and nice-sized woman curves. He was already alert and aware of her enough, without the added fact that she'd never been touched by a man.

Except him.

Aidan wasn't an untried whelp, whose every waking thought was filled with women. He smirked slightly at the untruth. Near all his dreams had been spent in the same fashion. Arran was a prime example of that age. The lad reddened, danced with nervousness, and stammered worse if any lass looked his way. And if one approached, he'd probably faint. Aidan wished his brother well of it.

Nor was Aidan a young prospect like his brother Alpin, whose every move seemed accompanied by giggling lasses from the moment he arrived anywhere. They'd yet to pick a suitable wife for the lad. Aidan was waiting for him to do it. He huffed the amusement out. Alpin usually looked to be on the run from his admirers, looking for contests of skill, challenges of strength, or game to hunt. The lad had discovered the best ways of dealing with urges and hungers and lusts, all of them manly and accepted and useful. Aidan wished his brother well of that, too.

All of that was proof. Aidan was too old for any such awkward yearnings and desires. Where the love act was concerned, his body was fully his. If he needed or wanted a woman, it wasn't a difficult thing to gain. But it was under his control. His. He no longer suffered wild cravings and aches and hard hunger from just a glance at a girl. Or the thought of one.

She's a virgin.

An immediate blast of heat filled him, sliding through his belly to encase and torment his loins. The rush of sensation fisted his hand about the reins, pulling his horse's head up and halting the line. Belatedly, he put a hand in the

air, signaling the rest. He sensed the line behind him coming
to a halt, and he also sensed their interest. It was the third halt
he'd called, and it was not yet eve. Aidan whistled and waited
for Arran to come for his horse. He used the time to send unspoken commands, and then curses, and then pleas, to cease
the hardening and engorging and preparing . . . for her.

Jesu'! He was cursed. Beset. Spelled.

Aidan sat his horse to give Arran instruction, ignoring the
curiosity on the lad's face. Then he waited for the others, all
the while sending unspoken demands and orders. Useless.
All of it. His body had a mind of its own and it wasn't interested in obeying. This angst was for lads the ages of his
brothers. Not him.

A virgin . . .

Aidan sucked in a breath. Held it. This lass he'd rescued
upended everything. Again. Everything.

Aidan let the breath back out. She was changing his plans
now. They weren't riding through to Castle Ketryck. He
didn't dare. She couldn't sit a horse while asleep and he
wasn't tying her, although if this got much worse, he was
fully considering it. But that would require getting near her . . .
touching her . . .

God blast and damn . . . everything!

Aidan lurched against the saddle with an instantaneous
uncontrollable flash of pure hunger. Craving. Need. He
pulled in another breath and looked heavenward again. Then
he shifted his shoulders and rolled them as if to stretch away
soreness. His men were gathering on his orders as given
through Arran, standing about, awaiting further instruction.
None of them would believe this. He didn't even believe it.

Aidan . . . she's a virgin . . .

Aidan looked up again at the answerless sky before he
lowered his head back. Nothing worked. Nothing stopped the
litany of thought that struck him without warning, and nothing muted it. It wasn't fair and it wasn't just and it wasn't

right. It just *was*. He cleared his throat in the event his voice came out high-pitched or shaky. Then he sent Stefan and Gregor ahead with the tent horses to set up camp and get a fire started. If they had sense, they'd use the one left a fortnight ago, at the beginning of this accursed foray. Then he sent Alpin and Tavish for what they did best: hunt game.

Aidan licked his lips and grimaced at how shaky that minor act was. His hands were shaking, too. This was not happening. He tightened every muscle he still controlled before the tremor reached them. Before God and His Mother Mary, Aidan was not going to let this happen . . . he couldn't. And his youngest brother was watching! He concentrated and felt the response in his chest. Arms. Lower legs. Back. Neck. Belly. He dared try lower. His upper thighs . . . buttocks. He forced the image of a large fire with a roast slowly turning atop it on a spit, sending heavenly smells into the air.

She's a virgin.

"Oh . . . blast!"

"Wh-Wh-What did I do?" Arran burst out.

Aidan scrunched his eyes shut, took another deep breath that did little except make the tight knot of muscle in his belly pound, and then opened them to regard his brother. The lad appeared to have jumped back at his outburst.

"Why are you na' in the bushes?" he asked.

"I've no n-n-need."

"Nae?"

"W-W-We but st-st-s-stopped an hour a-a-a-ago."

"Oh."

"D-D-Do you ail?" Arran asked, lifting a hand to protect his eyes as he looked up. Aidan hadn't noticed it before but his brother had the same one-eyebrow lift. It was cocked up to meet his hair as he asked it.

Aidan tipped his head in consideration. It might be better to look weak due to illness. "Perhaps," he replied.

"Oh. I-I-I'll ask Juliana—"

"Nae!" Aidan interrupted his brother with a shout that made the younger man stumble backward and nearly fall. He felt like a bear. Nothing was going as it should. Nothing. "Can you just go back? Get on your horse. And cease delaying us?"

Arran nodded and then spun. And took off at his usual run.

Aidan was twisted slightly without thinking. He watched Arran, and that just put the center of his torment right in eyesight. Juliana sat one horse behind him. She had a quizzical expression on her lovely face, and calmness everywhere else. And that just wasn't right. Aidan swiveled back around, lifted one half of his lip and cheek in a grimace at the hard contact of his saddle, and started up again.

Things had better improve, and quickly.

It was a forlorn order. He smelled camp before he saw it, proving not only their expertise at erecting tents that protected and hid a fire even in another day of rain, but that Alpin and Tavish were successful at the hunt as well. The aroma of roast venison pricked his nose and would probably have started his mouth to salivating and the pit of his belly to growling, if there was any sensation that broke through the other.

The need. Want. Absolute lust.

Aidan avoided everything to do with her once they filed through the trees. He lifted his arm and stopped the line without looking at her. He sat for a few moments, practicing at ignoring her and trying for control over his frame. And then he planted both hands, palms down, against the horse's neck. That gave him a fulcrum to push up and out of the saddle using upper body strength. Then, he rotated using his shoulders, moving his body the exact amount he needed so he could drop in an arched fashion onto the ground beside the horse. It was the best he could manage and he didn't care what anyone thought. A glance in her direction showed Arran jogging toward him, but he'd stopped at her side, his mouth dropped with the awe. The object of all this torment, Juliana, just sat atop her horse and looked at him. Without one expression on her beauteous face.

"See to her!"

Aidan pointed in their direction before he turned away. They were near MacKetryck land. They'd camped near Loch Erind. He knew it was fed by melted snows and emptied into Buchyn Loch before draining into the North Sea. It was bottomless, white-capped with the weather, and heavy with fish. And cold. He was at a full run before he got to the shoreline and dove.

"Beast."

Juliana said it beneath her breath after Arran had given her a hand to assist her down. Once he had some substance to him, he could lift both hands up and accept a lady's hands against his. That way he could bear a woman's weight as she stiffened her arms and he assisted the drop from a horse. Done correctly, that was the only portion of a lady's form he'd need to touch. Or if they had proper acquaintance and the lady allowed it, he could put both hands about her waist and lift her down safely to the ground beside him. It certainly wasn't done by reaching one hand for hers, and using it to pull her down against him where he stumbled, making them both nearly fall.

The lad needed some training but he had a great sense of where to start. At least he knew to try and treat her differently and a bit gently. She could work with it.

"F-F-Forgive m-m-me," he stammered, releasing her almost instantly.

"I meant your brother. He's the beast."

Arran's face cleared. "Oh. Him."

"Aye. Him."

"Doona' b-b-blame him. He's ill."

"Ill?"

Arran nodded.

"How ill?"

"Uh . . ."

Juliana watched him look about furtively, as if telling was a great crime. Then she realized it might be construed as such. He was their laird, and Aidan told her that his word was law. In an English household, that meant charges and trials and punishments. She didn't need to ask about a Highlander. She'd already been the victim of it. Juliana forced the thoughts away. She already had her justice. MacDonal no longer held her castle. He was dead. Perhaps his body was hanging from the rampart right now . . . without a trial.

Men. It was all the fault of men and their lusts for power and property and victory, and then more of the same.

"Will I get the little tent again?" she asked, releasing Arran from the worry of answering.

He nodded. He did it often. Probably to avoid the chore of speaking through the stutter, she decided. She hoped he'd outgrow it. Then again, with his resemblance to Aidan Mac-Ketryck, the lad didn't need to do much talking anyway. His brother didn't.

"Oh. Well and good," she continued, walking in the direction of the smaller tent. Arran was trailing behind her as if seeing to her meant allowing her to do whatever she liked. Juliana stopped. Aidan had put her in Arran's care? The least decisive and youngest member of his band? And she'd balked?

"Once there . . . you'll fetch my sup?"

He nodded.

"I'm hungry. Could you bring me . . . a large sup?" *For packing.*

"If-If Alpin has na' eaten it all," he teased.

Juliana smiled slightly to herself as he lost more of his stuttering. That happened the last time he was with her. She'd wondered if it could be repeated until he lost it entirely. She almost wished she'd be around to try and test it.

"And perhaps water?"

"I'll bring ale," he replied without a hint of stutter.

"Not to drink. I need a pail. To wash with. I've not bathed in . . ."

Juliana stopped. Had it been four days since the attack? She wrinkled her forehead. Five? Being near that Aidan MacKetryck was affecting her wits. Her heart stumbled slightly before a heavy, painful beat restarted it. She tamped it down, ignoring it. However long, she'd guess at twice that time to get back. She wouldn't be riding through the night, she wasn't sure of the direction, and she'd have to be careful. She'd be an easy target.

She looked about as if unsure which way to go, although they were at the tents and their cook fire. The small tent was behind and to the right of the large one, with the overhang and fire in front of it. A small deer carcass was impaled on a pole, and she recognized Gregor as the man watching over it by turning it every so often. He'd stood at their approach, and then pulled the bonnet from his head and nodded. Juliana's heart pinged slightly within her breast, but she had it covered over before returning the nod.

They were putting the horses on the downwind side of the large tent. On the left. Just past the first bit of tree line. They'd probably post a guard. They always did. She'd face that if she got that far. She'd get a palm-sized rock before attempting it, since that was how she'd learned. Hitting a man didn't do much unless he was surprised and the fist she hit him with contained a rock. Or she aimed for the groin. Juliana swallowed. She hoped it wouldn't be Tavish.

Aidan was ill. That was all she needed.

* * *

His wife hadn't been a maid.

Aidan lay on his back, his muscles and lungs spent and aching with the effort of continuing the fight against the loch. So he'd ended up floating and watching the rain above him as it pummeled the waves rocking him about. She'd played at virginity and thought to fool a younger lad that she was being forced to wed. Afraid if he suspected, Aidan would beat her, as would her father afterward. So he'd allowed it, acting untried and new to the act, and listened to her complaints of how he pained when he'd taken her. She'd been slender—he remembered that—but well aware of her charms. And how to use them. He'd acted like an innocent fool.

Because otherwise he'd have had to beat her.

He instinctively knew she wouldn't survive the beating he'd felt like giving. She'd been too frail. Too slight. Too full of her own beauty and what it did to the men about her to care that she crushed her new husband's dream.

It hadn't even been his child she'd died birthing.

A wave crested over him, bringing a choking volume of water, and Aidan flipped to renew the swim. It had gone dark while he swum, mercilessly pumping his limbs through the water until his arms and legs ceased responding. Then he'd stopped, near the center, rotated onto his back, and just floated. And existed. And remembered.

Fighting the elements had a certain power. The quest for survival made a man forget old hurts and new frustrations. Aidan rolled over and started back. The water had grown colder while he'd tarried. The force of each wave carried the same effect of parrying an attacker's claymore. The challenger always going for the head so a good upward thrust could take off a man's lower jaw. Or they'd swing up for his groin, for any hit there put a man on his knees. Or a slice across the inside thigh, making a wound so deadly a man could watch his lifeblood race out with each heartbeat. Or they'd take off an arm, so a man could bleed to death unless he knew to tie it off and stayed conscious enough to do it. The waves had the power of an attacking horde and the force of a hundred claymores, pounding into him and pummeling him into the depths, making him fight for the surface over and over again.

He was flagging. Tiring.

Each breath burned with the quantity of water he was also inhaling. Each stroke of his arms had the weight of a fifteen-stone boulder attached. Each pump of his legs was hampered by an opposing force of bog-thick mass. He didn't stop, though. He fought it . . . but it wasn't enough. He was going to sink beneath the waves, tossed about by an ocean of fury, and not a soul would guess what had happened.

Not even the girl who'd caused it: Juliana.

If she hadn't been a maid, she'd have no question of what he'd been fighting, but she'd never know why. And never for certain. He went beneath another wave and fought for the surface while his heart pounded loud in his ears and his chest thudded with withheld air, until he broke the surface again, floundering weakly and ineffectually against wave after wave of assault.

He'd put her in Arran's care.

Juliana? His mind was playing tricks. The lass that so unsettled and disrupted him that he'd chosen to play with death rather than take her maidenhood and make her his . . . he'd put her in his brother's care? The youngest MacKetryck? The unsure, untried, untested Arran?

Aidan spit out water and coughed on it until it burned. He'd been a fool! Arran was no match for Uncle Dugald if he took a fancy to Juliana . . .

Just as he had Aidan's wife.

Anger shoved through Aidan then, pushing for air and making him take it. And that was followed by rage, a rage so severe his fists went to hammers of fury that slammed into the water, launching him up from the waves to his knees. And that made it possible to give his most gruesome battle cry. He hadn't finished the yell before he attacked the waves.

Aidan's shoulders went to a perfect rhythm, sending his arms in stroke after stroke of power and intent, making a motion that churned its own waves. And his feet kicked, feeling renewed strength and vigor against the bog-like consistency of the water, until it foamed and frothed behind him in surrender.

Heat pumped through him, sent from every beat of his heart and intensified by every breath he managed to gasp from beneath his arm with every other stroke. Over and over, and again and again, pushing and shoving and churning and gaining, his motions fed by a pain and ache and anger so intense, everything about him looked red.

He touched sand. Earth. Rocks. Shrubs. Aidan kept moving and stroking and pumping and then turned it to crawling, pulling plants out by the roots as he used them for his climb, until the ground leveled out, the world about him started changing from heavy red-dipped hate to a softer rose shade . . . and then altering altogether . . .

And then it turned to Juliana's concerned face.

"Aidan?"

He reached up with arms that were still shuddering with the effort, gripped both her arms that were wrapped tightly in her cloak, and pulled her down to him, smashed his face against her in a kiss that had no rebuttal, and kissed her until she returned it. And then he flung the vision aside, ignoring it completely, and started laughing.

The Red MacKetryck had won this time.

Chapter 10

Juliana sat cross-legged on the pallet and watched Aidan sleeping. It was easier to see him in the predawn light, but that hadn't stopped her from watching through most of what should have been a night spent in escaping them, but instead had been this—restless, sleepless, thought-filled, thrilling, exciting . . . frightening. She'd been unable to sleep whether she covered herself with the blanket they'd given her or not. It hadn't mattered. Sleep had eluded her regardless of how many times or in what position she tried on the pallet. It hadn't mattered how often she berated or counseled herself, or sprawled on her back looking at the darkness that was tent weave above her, doing her best to obliterate every thought of it. The reason behind her failure wasn't going away. It wasn't faltering. It wasn't muting. It wasn't fading.

It wasn't doing anything except breathing in heavy slumber on his cot.

Aidan was the handsomest male Juliana had ever seen. He had a wealth of dark hair that was usually pulled back, putting a sculptor's touch to his features. Since he'd been in the water last night, it had been plastered to him at first. Now it was just fanning out all over his cot, wild and untamed . . . like the man. He'd been blessed with dark eyelashes the

match to his hair, and if he allowed the shadow of beard that
was darkening his cheeks time to grow, it looked to be just as
dark. He'd probably been blessed with that healthy, brawny,
muscle-filled frame, but then he'd added to it, working it into
jaw-dropping ability and mass.

Most of that she'd accepted from the first time she'd seen
him. She didn't have a choice. It was too blatant to ignore.

But then she had to factor in the man himself. The inde-
finable portion he wielded with such ease: the pumping,
heated, thrilling, rousing, inspiring . . . *sensual* essence . . .
that came with the promise of so much more. He changed the
elements, stirring awareness of him with every look he gave,
every gesture . . . every word. The man had an incalculable
effect on everyone. Not just women. Not just her.

Juliana went to her knees and scooted closer to the cot
where Aidan rested, rhythmically pushing air in and out of
his frame as if he hadn't a care in the world. As if he hadn't
come crawling from the lake like a creature hatched from the
mists hovering on the water's surface. Grabbing her to a full-
body hug against chilled naked flesh, altering her plan,
changing her purpose, and stirring every emotion she'd been
fighting right into her consciousness. That was before he'd
collapsed into a laughing buffoon on the shore beside her, the
noise bringing all his men, and putting her in such a shocked
state, she hadn't even used that small bit of confused time for
the perfect escape opportunity it presented.

Now it was lost. Gone. Whisked away and changed. Completely.

In the torchlight they'd brought, it hadn't been possible
to hide a naked and exhausted and wet Aidan lying on the
ground, nor why she was outside the tent, swathed completely in a tartan atop her cloak, a stone still gripped in her
hand, and near the horses, while the bundle of dry venison
strips and oat cakes she'd dropped told the same tale.

It took four of them to haul Aidan to this tent since he'd

gone to his knees both times he'd tried to stand. Four. They each grabbed a limb and hefted while his brother Arran held the torchlight high and gave her continual troubled looks she'd refused to meet or return. They hadn't acted like hauling Aidan was easy, with cursing and low grunting and an occasional huff of slipped breath as the four of them worked in tandem.

It took only one man to make sure she accompanied them. She thought it might have been Stefan, since she didn't recognize him. He didn't speak to offer his name or anything else. He didn't have to. The grip he'd used to make her drop the stone, and the further manhandling she'd endured to get her down to her underdress with no sign of a weapon left to her, had been clear. He hadn't needed to point after the others.

They filled the tent with the volume of them before dumping Aidan onto his back on the cot, bowing it to the ground with his weight. Juliana wasn't ordered into the tent until they'd taken everything from the enclosure except the pallet on the ground and two blankets crafted of their own sett. One they'd pulled in a haphazard fashion atop Aidan, not even covering his lower legs or feet. The other was meant for her. She didn't ask and no one explained. They'd filed out then, giving grunts and signals as they went that probably meant her recapture and doom if she tried to escape again, as well as specifying who the perpetrator would be. Then her escort, if it was Stefan, gestured her into the tent with a jerk of his head and added to the severity of the order by his crossed arm stance and lowered jaw. She wasn't given the chance to mistake it, since Arran was right at his shoulder holding the torch, projecting another confused and worried look toward her that he didn't need to explain. She could guess. With his hero worship, he'd probably been classifying her as a deranged fool for trying to escape Aidan MacKetryck . . . and doubly a fool for being an unprotected woman doing so.

Then she'd heard the sounds of leather or something akin
to it sliding through material. All about her. With the torchlight behind them, Juliana had watched them weave the door
shut with strips of rawhide, going in and out of prearranged
holes that looked like large unsymmetrical sewing. She
could guess that it was happening at the corners as well.
Smart. It would be difficult to escape this mesh of tent without a blade . . . and that was what they wanted. She wasn't
going anywhere until Aidan was recovered and went back to
specifying his wants about it. Always his. Never anyone
else's. They probably blamed her for his illness, too.

Or whatever he suffered.

She could have told them then they didn't need to bother.
They could have left the door wide and a horse at her dis-
posal, and even given her a trunk filled with foodstuffs.
Something had happened to her. Something so large and vast
and inescapable, that all the chains in the world wouldn't
alter it.

Juliana had looked then for the first time over at the bulk
that was Aidan MacKetryck, his image dimming as they'd
moved away, taking the torchlight with them. Her heart had
pulsed sharply and distinctly in her breast, reminding her.
Again.

She wasn't going anywhere. She couldn't.

The way they'd prepared the enclosure kept it quiet and
private, and yet so totally abuzz with the sensation of Aidan
MacKetryck stretched out on his cot . . . naked . . . that no
matter what position she tried atop her pallet, she couldn't
alter it. Or change it. Or ignore it.

I love him.

It was so totally wrong. And yet the more Juliana tried to
block it, the more the certainty grew. She thrilled to it, vibrating all over with it while shivers coursed throughout her, and
then got covered by more of the same. It was akin to the

warning before a storm of weeping combined with the happiness from seeing a new batch of kittens being attended by their mother. And yet more severe at the same time. Unbelievably. Intimately.

And now Juliana was on her knees at his cot, lifted to a position above him, and filling her eyes and every other sense with what she'd never allow if he were awake and conscious to it. If she had to fall into this horrid emotional state over a man, at least this one was deserving of it. She'd never met a more powerful male. The lords and men of court her father had entertained wouldn't show well against him. Even her betrothed, the lauded knight, Sir Percy Dane, was a shadow beside Aidan Niall MacKetryck.

Of course, MacKetryck knew it. All of it. Every waking moment, the man projected self-confidence and arrogance and awareness of just who he was and what that meant. That was galling, but as Juliana perched next to him on her knees, she realized she wouldn't have him behave any other way.

She reached with a hand and slipped a stray bit of hair from where it was clinging to the eyebrow he was able to lift and move with such subconscious ability and appeal. Juliana thanked the dimness for covering the tremble of her fingers from herself. She held the lock of hair between two fingers and her thumb and rubbed slightly, separating the strands and feeling the silkiness. He'd never know. None of them would.

Nothing altered about the body before her. Aidan continued breathing deeply and rhythmically as he had all night, sleeping heavily. A condition that had annoyed and frustrated her as she'd sought it, and now was a balm and catalyst to what she was doing.

She opened her fingers, releasing the hair strands to sift onto the cot beside his face, and smiled slightly in appreciation of boundless, awe-inspiring male beauty . . . right in front of her . . . available . . . without one soul knowing. A tremor ran through her at the thought, flowing clear to her bare toes before it found a centering site, at the tips of every finger.

Juliana tucked her lower lip beneath her teeth and sucked on it as she moved both hands to the edge of the blanket covering him. He hadn't moved from where they'd placed him. They should have taken care to pull the plaid piece fully over him and tuck it, rather than leave it mostly dangling off the other side. If they'd done that, the flap covering him wouldn't be so easily lifted and peeled back, folding onto itself atop his wealth of muscle, revealing his chest and shadowing his belly. Juliana didn't dare reveal more. Not yet. The chill of morning air might alter his sleep . . . as well as make other things happen, such as worsening the tingling in her fingers.

Aidan had a wealth of chest, tanned to a golden color from running about without clothing. The skin was also mostly free of hair. Juliana smiled slightly and glanced again to his chin and cheeks. The hair growth on his cheeks told her the truth. He didn't grow a full beard because he couldn't, and for the first time, he didn't look like a full-grown, proud, boastful, mature male. He looked young . . . new . . . fresh . . . and more like Arran than ever. For some reason, that endeared Aidan Niall to her even more.

Juliana's smile grew at the idea of a youthful Aidan. He might have even stuttered.

She moved her fingers to his mouth, hovering atop his lip flesh with a tremor that was easily seen, even in the predawn dimness. Breath touched her fingers in a modulated span, matching the rise and fall of the chest in front of her. It was daring and breathlessly so. Juliana lowered her hand slightly, touching just minutely on his lower lip with one digit before heaving with the resultant spark that scored all the way through her.

There wasn't anything dim about that flash of light. Juliana was gasping small breaths as a result of it, blinking rapidly, and wondering how such a small tent could contain and hold something so vast. Her fingers had gone past trembling. They were shaking, and it was getting worse from the effort of holding them so close and yet still keeping from touching him.

This love emotion was a powerful thing. No wonder she'd avoided it.

Juliana waited long moments of time . . . locked in place. Sending ceaseless quick breaths into existence and just hovering. Watching. Waiting. Nothing about Aidan appeared to have changed. If anything, he looked to have settled even farther into his cot, although the binding ropes stretched above his head hadn't moved. Nor could she sense any difference in the closeness of his cot to the ground in front of her knees. Nothing had altered. His features were calm and beautiful in repose, and his breath was still the same slow rhythm, making the chest rise and fall in front of her with the same tempo. Strong. Constant.

Juliana gulped around the odd ball at the base of her throat and skimmed both hands above the revealed skin of his chest and upper belly, not touching. She didn't dare yet! Just . . . skimming. And feeling a sensation so close to touching, it was as if his skin rose to reach everywhere she hovered. Juliana's eyelids got heavy, closing to a slit of view, and her breathing deepened, sending her belly to the edge of his cot with the depth of each one. Sensation wove about the edge of her consciousness, heightening awareness, making such heat fill her, her skin moistened with the release of it, and imbuing her with such glow, the dimness of the tent was incapable of stifling it

"Ah . . . lass . . ."

The whisper alerted her. As did the roll of him toward her, connecting her palms against skin with a crashing effect of lightning to ground. Hard hands followed, gripping her about the waist and hauling her easily from her knees and onto the span of flesh she'd revealed. And even more of it, since it appeared the blanket hadn't waited to fall off the other side of him.

"This had best be a dream."

He whispered the warning against her lips, before taking them, and sending any answer into the confines of breathless sucking, licking, and toying. Pleasuring. Adoring. Juliana matched him with every stroke, learning the caverns of his mouth as he was hers and elevating the length of his groans with her own.

She felt hands about her buttocks, the backs of her upper thighs . . . her knees, and then the slide of material as her underdress moved, bunching in front of his assault. And then a touch hit her core, striking raw and brilliant lightning all through her and sending her into an arch with the instant shock and thrill.

Hands brought her right back, taking her cry of pleasure into his mouth with the force of his kiss, while the hot, heavy, hard power of his groin slid against where he'd left her vulnerable, open and taut, and still quivering with reaction and want. And need. And craving.

And urgency.

The cot collapsed sideways with his roll, sending her to her back on the pallet beside it, with her legs spread to accommodate the bulk that was atop her, his mouth capturing any denials she might make, his tongue licking away any doubts she might harbor, and his lips sucking at her essence, turning everything into trembling, sobbing, needy female.

"Ah . . . *lass* . . ."

The second word trembled against her mouth, matching the quake of his back where her hands had spread and explored, enjoying and thrilling and calling on the exquisite sensation that her fingertips had suffered earlier, only it encompassed her entire arms, her torso . . . her core.

"Lass . . . lass . . . lass . . ."

The whisper slid into her mouth, slithered over her back, and filled her loins, as he matched it to the motions he was making against her. And then he was lifting from her, and she lost the contact with his chest and belly from her as he went to a bowed position. Then he slid his hands from her waist to her hips, where he gripped her and moved her into a position that elevated her loins . . . so he could rub, slide, and moisten the entire length of his shaft over and over against her, while driving her mad the entire time.

"Aidan . . . please? Aidan . . ."

Juliana moved her hands over him, running them along every ridge of his back . . . his buttocks . . . everywhere. Up to where his wild mane of hair tickled and itched with each movement, back down the curve of his spine. Her body sinuously moving beneath him . . . aching . . . yearning . . . begging.

Aidan slammed his mouth onto hers, sucking with magical ability, while his hands went hard and strong and inescapable, and then he was shoving and pushing and making her endure such agony, her back arched on the pallet with the onslaught. Again. Farther. Deeper. Using small strokes of movement against the quivering, moist, raw flesh being forced to accept him. Aidan pushed at her, entering slightly . . . moving away. Entering again. Farther. Pushing into her in a continuum of motion, pulling her hips upward each time, opening and spreading her, and forcing her to swell and enlarge and take him. And using his mouth to capture the sounds she was making.

And still he pushed. Lifted her more. Pushed. Tightened his shoulder muscles and arms to elevate farther for a better angle. Pushing . . . farther. Going deeper. Making her accept the burn as it approached scorch level. The action sent shivers all over her that started where the agony he wouldn't cease was, went up her spine, and climbed over her head, where it hit her open, shocked eyes, making them water uselessly and completely.

A sob escaped her, separating their lips. He raised his head away, filling her eyes with the taut cords of his neck, the red color infusing his skin, the grimace lining all of his face . . . Yet still he continued maneuvering into her, adding burn atop burn, tearing and hurting and enlarging and forcing until he finally stopped, ceasing time and space and everything except solid, unforgiving sore and hurt and anguish. He'd even ceased breathing, although the pounding of his heart was full and heavy and massive, matching hers. If he waited for her body to accept this, it was wasted. Where they were joined was a solid wall of burning throb, and it just sat at a near unbearable level, until it became one solid experience of pain and tears and blood.

Juliana blinked the tears into existence, and more filled their place. No one had told her of the pain. The fire. The suffering. The continuity of it. And then a sob escaped her as she realized the obvious. He wasn't finished.

Aidan dipped his head slightly and met her eyes for a fraction of time that stopped and restarted her heart with a force akin to a blow. Juliana's eyes went wide with the flash of ecstasy that suffused her from just that one look, releasing the blur of tears. The power of it hit the lump in her throat with such fury, she gulped. Blinked at the experience. Gulped again. Then, he narrowed his lashes and tipped his head lower, blowing exhaled breath all over her and sending goose bumps from the contact . . . altering the experience just slightly . . . and it was all to hide what he planned.

Juliana's back arched in further shock and fear as his fingers tightened even more, as did the sinews of his shoulders where they were pressing against her with breath-stealing weight. Then she realized why as he pulled himself slowly out of her, pushing her away at the same time, and mitigating the pain from excruciating to nearly bearable. Giving her a moment or two to relax and just begin to comprehend the relief before rolling and holding her hips farther upward, making it easier for him to move right back against her and into her. Again. With painful depth and size. With unbelievable scope. Heaviness. Heat. Range. Fully. Until his groin met hers . . . encasing him. Completely.

Juliana gasped in a breath, and then lost the exhalation in his mouth as he moved his head toward her again. She didn't know it was to kiss her until he did it, lapping at her tissues and swirling his tongue, and sliding his lips against hers time and again, making shooting stars fill the tent. And it was all to disguise and make her accept the next time he moved to pull away from her, sliding slowly from her sheath, amid the same sigh of relief that was immediately followed by the return of pressure and bulk.

Again and again, and countless times more.

He lifted his lips from her, moving across a cheek to her throat and murmuring the same thing over and over as he went. "Lass . . . lass . . ."

"'Tis . . . pain, Aidan." Juliana whimpered the words.

"It'll ease."

He'd reached her ear and the words were soft. They were the only thing about this that was. Everything else on him was hard and strong and taut and rigid. And not changing. The opposite was happening. His body seemed to get even harder. Everywhere. Every breath was getting sucked in and pushed back out with a vicious motion that just kept intensifying. His heartbeat wasn't far behind as it pumped louder and stronger, putting a thump into every place she touched. Heat infused everything, dispersing any chill and putting a moist film atop every portion of him she touched, making every slide of her fingers skim along skin that warmed markedly, until the finger pads of each hand burned with it.

Where they were joined was changing as well, going to a moving sensation of remembered ache amid flashes of beckoning pleasures that flashed through without warning or rhythm or constancy, halting her breathing with the spasm her body involuntarily made. And that sparked a resultant grip he'd immediately put on all of him, before resuming filling and emptying her body with a pace that had the indefatigability of a wave-tossed sea and the constancy of a summer rain.

"Lass?"

"Aye?"

He'd lifted his head away and waited. Juliana thought she was prepared for the eye connection. She was wrong. It was as obvious as the nonmelodic lurch she gave against him, mashing their loins together with a mightier movement than he'd put into place. And that resulted in a sucked-in breath from him that came out with a curse that sounded more like a prayer.

"Christ."

"Aidan . . . I don't—"

"Wrap your legs about me, love. Now."

He didn't wait for her to comply before releasing her hips from the grip he'd had on them, in order to shove his hands palms-down into the meshed top of her pallet, squashing the feathers flat, and then sending everything on his body into full-out muscular perfection as he lifted his upper body away from her, and just stayed there, with arms that had the consistency of tree trunks and loins that continued rocking in place.

"Now . . . lass. Now!"

The urgency in his whisper matched the increasing spread of flush happening all through him, the breaths he was pulling in, holding, and then heaving out, as well as the increased motions he was pulling and pushing into her. Juliana tried. Her back fought her and her legs weren't far behind, while the continual movement at where he'd joined into her was warning her of barely forgotten pain and fire. For a moment, she didn't know if she could do it.

"Hurry, lass. Jesu'!"

Juliana barely got her ankles hooked behind his back before everything in his buttocks and loins lowered, putting weight and rigidity and bulk with such emphasis against her it shoved her up to where the restriction of his propped hands had to stop her slide. And then he groaned, gritting his teeth, and tightening everything to the point his belly was a vista of ropelike tendons while those deep in his chest mounds made indentations in the flesh as they held him in place. Poised. Holding. Shaking.

And then he moved, changing the movements, gaining volume to them, and strength and timing, putting them one after another in a tempo that just kept increasing. And increasing. Harder. Faster. Pummeling her body with a primordial rhythm only he heard. And then he went onto one arm, moving his right hand beneath her buttocks, grabbing and lifting in order to manipulate and move her exactly as he wished. Over and over and faster and faster until Juliana feared she'd melt. Sparks of sensation and fire started flitting everywhere, sparking from their loins and shooting throughout her body, outside of it, to the tent . . . and then beyond that.

Flares of feeling careened clear up to the heavens above, and she followed. Juliana's body went into a jolt of amazement, arching into a bow of such perfection and strength it moved him with it. She was exploding. Rising. Soaring. Even the heavens couldn't contain such rapture. Her eyes scrunched shut on worlds of wonder, vistas of sky . . . endless blue sky. Her arms and legs locked about the mass of man creating it, causing it, propelling her into it.

She was still flowing with the rapture when he changed everything. Stopping in a lurch of movement and holding it, while his frame went rigid with a rush of pulses that she could feel. Juliana opened her eyes slightly and watched as Aidan held himself rigid for an infinitesimal amazing moment as his eyes locked with hers. She was still watching as he shoved his head back, pulling his throat taut, while the deepest growl started in his throat, before surrounding her with a visceral throb of tone. Juliana kept her arms and legs locked to him as he became a thing of wild, primitive, raw, basic, sensitive, heavy lunges that propelled her shoulders into the arms he was using for a base, over and over again, looking like he was struggling and fighting a foe, while every bit of his nakedness was darkening with a flush.

The ferocity of his movements slowed, turning into jerks of motion against her. The growl changed to a sob of sound through his gritted teeth, keeping rhythm with the quick little pulses that were emanating from deep within her. Every other part of him became a trembling, tautly pulled, sweating mass of man, before he lowered his head, met her eyes with a look so dark, Juliana's eyes filled again. And then he heaved to one side, so the upper portion of him collapsed onto the mat beside her with enough force, air puffed out of the material weave. And then he just lay there, heaving great breaths while facing the other side, away from her.

"Oh . . . Jesu', lass. Oh . . . Lord. Oh . . . Damn."

He said more, whispering of wenches with spellbinding ways, and charms to keep a man safe, while the place they were joined jumped and twitched and started feeling moist and sore . . . and wicked.

"Aidan?" she whispered.

"Doona'—"

He didn't specify what he didn't want her to do, but the raised hand at his far side did. He didn't have to request it. She didn't know what she was going to say anyway. Juliana pulled her lower lip into her mouth and started sucking on it, while she waited and breathed in soft little gasps that were all he left her with his weight atop her belly. And between her legs . . . where the flesh was cooling, getting sticky . . . feeling vulgar, unclean. Wrong.

"I dinna' . . . expect—"

Juliana stopped breathing while her heart began a hammering that reminded her of its presence. And its power. And then it started hurting.

"This."

He still wasn't looking her way. Juliana winged the silent prayer to the heavens over it. She didn't want him looking . . . until she had everything hidden. In one morning the man had shown her what heaven existed on earth for a man and woman . . . and now he was locking her out. She didn't know what had changed, but everything about him projected it. She'd thought he wanted her. Exactly like this. And Juliana D'Aubenville would've shamed her ancestors and herself by accepting it. The moment he offered. Without thought.

Exactly as she'd done.

A flood of tears hit then, and she looked up at the tent roof to fight them. Wave after wave of them filled and flowed out the sides of her eyes and then refilled. She'd done something wrong. It hadn't been what he wanted. Or expected. Or demanded. Something about the act with her was wrong. He shouldn't have to say it in words. She wondered how to go about letting him know . . . and getting through the next few moments of her existence. Starting with how to get him to leave.

"My . . . legs," she started, the words sounding like a complete sob to her ears. She could only hope it wasn't audible to him.

The massive muscles in his back were undulating as he moved his arms to rise and then roll to face her. Juliana kept her vision on the bare weave above her and waited as he looked at her. At emotion she couldn't hide just yet. Maybe later . . . after he'd gone, but not now.

This time his curse was vicious, and punctuated with a move to his knees, sliding from the embrace of her body, before going to his feet. Juliana knew he was looking down at her and she avoided everything about it, watching the weave above her blur and clear and blur again with tears her body wouldn't quit sending.

He gave a heavy sigh, but didn't say anything. Juliana was grateful. She didn't want to hear any more. Not yet. Maybe never. She felt Aidan pulling at the blanket they'd given her what felt like years ago, rolling her slightly as he pulled it from beneath her. She heard the shift of fabric and knew if she looked he was tying and looping it about himself, covering over any signs of what they'd done.

Then he moved to the bottom of the pallet, grabbed both sides of his sewn-together door flap, and ripped the tent fabric at one side open, proving it wasn't an obstacle even without a blade.

For him.

Chapter 11

Rash. Reckless. Thoughtless.

Aidan walked into the mist-covered waves and added one more: cruel.

And then she had to cry her woman-tears.

He didn't know what to do when he'd seen them. She cried? He'd done his best to be gentle. Stifled every massive urge for momentum and speed plaguing him and replaced them with self-discipline and endurance. Contained the building pressure of ecstasy as long as possible in order to bring her with him . . . and it hadn't worked. He hadn't pleasured her. He'd hurt her. It didn't seem possible, but there it was. He'd been a thoughtless lover with her. Rash and reckless as well.

And now he was cruel.

Aidan rotated his shoulders and slowly moved with his legs, barely churning water. It was the best he could do with the way she'd depleted him. Drained him. Satisfied him. Fulfilled him. Everything about the love act with that woman had elevated him to another place, taking him so high his very soul received wings. He didn't know how. He didn't know why. The bliss had been unbelievably sweet and lush and wide, with a breadth Aidan couldn't comprehend or contain. It had never been that way. He didn't know how to explain it. And his attempt at words hadn't done more than make her cry more of her woman-tears.

He shouldn't have just left her, though. He could have pulled her into his arms and told her such a thing was bound to happen. There was too much want and need and lust between them. He'd been conscious of it since they'd met, and had it barely constricted and caged before she'd had to go and stoke it with the caresses she'd done on his body. To him. Making this her fault.

When the hum of sensation moving from her palm to his flesh had filtered through his wakeful stage, Aidan hadn't possessed anything to fight such raging instantaneous desire. Nothing. He'd been primed and ready and hungering for days now, the need in every thought and the want coloring every action. Until he'd worried that all she'd have had to do was look at him, and he'd have leapt.

That made it his fault, too . . . but she shared the blame. She'd ignited the barely controlled flame and turned everything into sensation atop pleasure atop glory. It had been such huge glory that he still radiated it, feeling strength and power and joy flood every limb until it couldn't be contained and had to be worked through. He'd suspected it would be good with her, but not this good. Not . . . incredibly good. Blissfully good. Rapturously good. In the span of one bit of loving, that woman had taken every prior experience and dimmed it, altered it . . . obliterated it.

He'd never felt so good.

Aidan stroked until his arms were too heavy for continuing, and then he flipped, floating on his back and looking up at cloud-strewn breaking day and grinning. And then he was laughing. His men would think he'd gone mad. The swimming wouldn't spare a thought, but the slow languor of it this morning . . . that they might question. The waves had calmed to a lapping motion with the storm's movement, and Aidan had always been a strong swimmer. He'd found it helped with working through the red times . . . the aggressions. It also increased agility and stamina and everything he needed on a battlefield.

And in a woman's bed . . . *Juliana* . . .

He shouldn't have just left her, but he didn't know what else to do with a woman shedding tears over what had been the most amazing experience of his life. He hadn't meant to cause pain, but he must have. Juliana hadn't just been crying. She'd been sobbing. If he'd been blessed with a glib tongue at birth, he'd have been able to say something to the lass . . . perhaps ward off some of her tears.

But his tongue hadn't worked. He hadn't said what needed saying, and now he was out here avoiding doing so.

Aidan's laughter died off and he lifted his head to look toward shore. It wasn't far, although the mist hampered and altered distance. Loch Erind was but a third the size of Loch Buchyn, and Aidan had been crossing that one since his youth. He saw the four men standing at the shore, watching him. They probably waited to fish him out again, if needed.

Aidan passed the thought by. They had more to do than worry over their laird's wits. They should be taking apart his camp; preparing the ride to home; anything other than watching and worrying over him. Wondering why he'd take a swim without doffing his attire first. And he wasn't telling. Nobody else needed to know how the freshwater swim was washing the leavings of what he'd done from the material weave.

Aidan blew the sigh of thanks over that small blessing. Other than the underdress he'd pushed and crumpled to her breasts, and small specks of blood dappling what were creamy, perfectly curved, and molded woman thighs, there hadn't been a sign of his perfidy anywhere on Juliana. Or the pallet, since they'd been atop this particular plaid the entire time.

Aidan shut his eyes, felt a shiver that had nothing to do

with the water's chill, and reopened them on pink-and-purple-kissed clouds as the new day's sun peeked through. If he had to take the lass's maidenhood, it was better they didn't know it. Or guess at it. Aside of which, they should know he didn't swim naked all the time. He hadn't taken anything off the prior eve before taking on storm-tossed waves and nearly perishing.

Aidan's eyes went wide and he lifted his head. He'd had his sporran with him as well.

His charms!

He'd lost his sporran . . . and it was a powerful long shoreline they now had to search. He flipped and started the swim back.

Juliana rocked in place on her perch atop a flat stone, smiled occasionally at Arran, who was her guard as well as company, and watched the MacKetryck clansmen about their search. Aidan and his band of clansmen had walked every speck of shore on this lake more than three times throughout the day, calling whistles and making other noises that meant nothing to her.

She had Arran to thank for everything. Almost. From his first visit once the sun had come up and they'd all stirred. If he wondered where Aidan was and why the tent had been ripped open, he hadn't said. He'd looked at her sitting on the pallet with the other blanket about her and asked with only a slight stutter if she wanted a pail of water to wash.

And that one request endeared him to her completely.

That was followed by a repast of a porridge they'd fashioned with the boar meat and oats, and he'd given her some of the ale with the huge bite to it to wash everything down. That tankard made a delicious breakfast even better as it dulled the edge of what had every indicator of being a day she didn't know how she'd live through.

Arran had then asked if she needed to release herself. And he hadn't said one word at how stiff and oddly she'd walked. Not one. He'd waited for her, though, his head above the shrubs, alerting her of his duty as guard. It hadn't been onerous then, and it still wasn't. He wasn't thorough or vigilant. On several occasions, he'd even asked if she'd allow him a moment and promise not to move while he was gone. Of course she wasn't moving. She was having difficulty doing anything with motion . . . because of his big brother, Aidan.

That was the only thing she didn't thank Arran for. He had nothing to do with her weakness . . . including the silly tremor of her knees, the continual and endless throb of soreness radiating from her core to crawl through her belly and down each thigh, nor each instance of gooseflesh that would run across her skin, making her catch her breath and making her relive it again. Soar with the memory. Lurch oddly with the reverie. And each time came without one hint of warning. If she closed her eyes, it was worse!

· That kept her awake and looking like she devoured every tidbit of information Arran gave her, despite the way her back started aching with prolonged sitting on the boulder and the drowsy effects of the ale. She wouldn't change it. She'd been worried they'd be leaving on horseback. She hadn't been certain she could manage it . . . and leery of telling their laird if it was too painful.

She had Arran to thank for being out in the wind-filled day, too. It was another gift to her. He'd given her the choice. Since they were staying until Aidan's sporran was located, she could go back into the tent or stay out as long as the weather accommodated.

Go back to the tent?

Even if the day turned wretchedly cold, and the wind filled up with rain as it kept warning, she'd have chosen this . . . sitting atop a flat boulder, listening to Arran, sipping on another tankard of ale, and watching the MacKetryck clansmen about their errands. Anything involving that pallet and that tent, and that particular memory, would be more than she wanted to try and absorb and live through.

All things considered, Arran was a wonderful jailor. If she didn't already know what the heart-burnings of love felt like, she might have believed herself in that emotion with the young Arran, rather than the real object . . . Aidan Niall MacKetryck.

Aidan was hard to spot, but she knew which dot he was as if by rote. He'd decided to go the farthest and stay out the longest each time, going to a small speck of man on the opposite shore at times. But he still loomed large in her emotions, stopping her breath, and making her quiver until she had to move her glance before Arran noticed.

He brought her yet another tankard of that same ale with a hard biscuit thing as the day wore on, the wind started carrying droplets of moisture with it, and the MacKetryck clansmen didn't look to be accomplishing much. Each time they returned to the camp for sustenance, they looked more downhearted, and needed more words of encouragement. Looking for the laird's charm-filled sporran obviously wasn't going well.

Toward dusk, when the wind was near word-stealing strength, and the clansmen were coming in, weather-dogged and weary, Juliana began to wonder what was next. The laird had lost his sporran, and with it all his luck and amulets and potions. That was when she asked Arran what would happen and was told of replacement. More would be crafted specifically for Aidan . . . by a seer, using smoke-induced visions, and special oils and objects. They'd most likely be set to the chore the moment the party returned to Castle Ketryck. In two days. That made the entire day even stranger.

Aidan Niall had obviously never had his life upended and had to replace things . . . all his things. Juliana wondered at luxury and security that could provide such an upbringing, and then dismissed it. If he'd never had to start afresh, it was an excellent time to start that lesson. She took another sip of her tankard, giggled, and went back to listening.

According to Arran, his big bad brother was bereft. The fates were against him. Aidan had been in a struggle against them forever . . . or at least ever since Arran could remember. Juliana would have laughed aloud if Arran hadn't been so serious when he said it, or if the rain hadn't decided to fall in earnest then, bringing side-falling moisture, or if the men weren't returning, and with them . . . the large, exasperated, frustrated male that was Aidan.

The man was suffering. Or something. Wind was whipping his hair all about his head, making it look alive, and flapping his *feile breacan* all about him, showing strength and sinew and rain-lashed limbs. Juliana flashed more than one glance at him before she was caught and just stared. He really shouldn't wear his clothing so loose and improperly fastened. Or if he did, he shouldn't have worked his entire frame into an eye-catching work of masculine beauty. Or if he had to do that, he should have the sense to stay out of her sight. Then he wouldn't have to lower his chin and glare at her through dark strands of hair fingering about his face, while portraying anger at her open-jawed regard . . . because it was entirely his fault.

He pointed at her and shoved it in the direction of his tent. Juliana didn't need translation. She was scooting to the edge of her boulder and holding out the half-empty tankard before the youngest MacKetryck turned to request it of her. Then she was running, all soreness forgotten or ignored, to reach the tent before he did. And she didn't even know why.

Aidan wasn't there. Juliana shoved past the ripped opening, surprised at how breathless that small run had made her. Her eyes flew about the small enclosure, flicked on her pallet stretched about the ground before shying away at the instant stab of giddiness . . . to his suspended bed, which made her entire body pulse, to the wall behind it. She'd been so right! The entire tent felt imbued with sensations and cursed with desires and passions, and everywhere she looked she had the same issue.

But that would never do. If he arrived and found her just inside, with her hand to her throat and her eyes wide, and everything else feeling elevated and primed . . . it just didn't bear thinking on! Not with the way he'd left her this morn, after showing without words how inadequate he found her.

The trunk seemed the safest. Juliana pulled it from its position against the wall so she could use it for a stool. Then she sat, the position putting her knees above her waist. The plaid she'd been wearing atop her underdress was scratchy. And wet. And suffocating. Juliana slid it from her shoulders and laid it across the end of his cot. The boots on her feet were restricting, and chaffing against her ankles since she'd forgone socks, and even if she knew where she'd put them last, they needed rinsing and drying. As did the underdress she still wore, looking crumpled and ill worn and imprinted from where his hands had shoved it.

Juliana fingered the fraying hem, lost for a moment on that thought. And then she cursed beneath her breath. It was exactly as she'd feared and avoided all day! And he was due any moment.

She moved to arranging the dress to cover her legs, tucking it beneath her toes, and then pulling it out again as that outlined and framed her legs too easily. So she twisted and turned, rearranging again, until she had everything on her lower body covered by the drape of fabric, covering any hint of shaky legs, quivering thighs, and tensed buttocks atop the rigid frame of his trunk. And even that felt sensuous!

Juliana gritted her teeth and moved on. She wished the shift had sleeves. That might hide some of the goose-flesh roaming over her arms, and the resultant tightening of her nipples. That sensation was added to by the power of her increasing breaths, making everything pointed and longing . . . yearning and begging and annoying her until she groaned the disgust through her locked jaw.

Juliana looked over at where she'd tossed the plaid, studied it sightlessly for a moment; debated which was worse; decided. It was warm in the tent enclosure, even with the ripped opening flapping about in the wind, and getting hotter with every passing moment. A sheen of moisture was already making her skin gleam. She didn't dare make it worse by adding the wool. All that aside, the blanket was damp and scratchy, and if she awaited him with it draped about her, it might alert him to her trouble the moment he saw it. And trouble it was. Her nipples were putting darts in the fabric with how tight and hard they were, as well as demonstrating how quickly she took each breath.

Perhaps if she hunched her shoulders, it wouldn't be so noticeable.

Juliana tried that, pulling the material out at the same time, and then smoothing the pinched portions where her fingers had just been. She gave another repressed groan. Everything she did kept adding to her discomfort and distress . . . and giving all of it away. Juliana straightened back up, making the little chest groan with the movement. There was nothing for it. She'd just have to keep his eyes off her bosom. Or something.

That was when she started fiddling with where to put her hands. The first effort of folding her arms across her felt awkward due to how low the trunk was. It probably looked exactly like what it was, too: defense. She pushed a bit of curl behind her ear, where it had escaped her braid. The action trailed a finger across her cheek. Juliana caught a breath as a wellspring of want and warmth and moisture almost instantly erupted right at her core, jolting her atop the trunk, and plaguing her with more accursed wantonness she'd have to somehow stifle and ignore. Or hide.

Then her eyes went wide. Juliana brought both hands in front of her face and watched them shake. She tightened her arms, sent the command, but nothing changed. She was shaking. Visibly.

How was she to hide *that* from him?

Then Aidan was there, standing at the tent opening, blocking the elements with his bulk and looking at her. Juliana slowly lowered her hands to her knees, and pressed her fingers into them, willing any response away.

She watched as he parted the rip, and bent his head to get through it, although she had to crane her neck to do it. Dark eyes held hers, making the breathless sensation even worse, and then he cocked that one eyebrow and earned a lurch of her entire body that had nothing melodic or graceful or hidden about it.

His lips shifted slightly into a pout at the same time he lowered his chin, favoring her with an unending look that was causing ripples all over her, tormenting and teasing and frightening with their intensity.

He started moving, pulling skeans from his belt until he had a handful of thin blades. She saw it at the edge of her vision. He didn't see it at all, since he wasn't releasing her gaze. And then he spoke.

"You have one chance to refuse me. One."

Juliana's eyes went huge. Her throat stopped up. Her heart moved to join it with a hurtful thud. And everything else on her body went totally alert and aware and watchful. She couldn't have pushed words through her throat if she'd wanted to.

The pursed look to his mouth changed to a smile, showing a shine of teeth, looking predatory, before he blinked slowly, and then he nodded. Juliana nearly fell off the trunk with the surge her lower legs did. All of her preparations were useless, unwarranted, and stupid besides. Nothing would have protected and hidden what she felt and what she wanted.

Aidan turned back toward the tent opening. Juliana leaned to one side to watch, and had to accept the appreciation of just how sharp these Highlanders were. She watched as Aidan took each skean, one after the other, and wove them into the material, first slicing across, and then putting another blade vertically atop the other, locking and sealing fabric with the two conjoined knives.

He'd run out of skeans before he reached the bottom and pulled more from the back of his belt as he went to one knee, securing and sealing clear to the earthen floor. She'd already noted how loose he wore his plaid, and that made it easier for the strip of it about his shoulder to slip down to an elbow, and that just made it impossible not to watch his back ripple and shift with every movement.

And be caught looking when he'd finished, took a deep breath that expanded all that back muscle, before swiveling in place on one knee, putting him at her eye level. Juliana sat atop the trunk absorbing the impact of his gaze and reacting with little pulses of movement that took all her breaths away, while a high ringing hit both ears. Juliana shifted her glance away, endured the shivers that coursed all over her, and focused instead on the middle of the cross-piece of knives he'd designed.

"I'll na' allow . . . tears," he informed her, putting a gap of silence before the last word.

Tears? They were the farthest thing from her. All of her felt primed and readied and it kept ratcheting higher and coiling further, until the fingers on her knees clenched tightly with it. She opened her mouth to tell him, but nothing came out.

"You had your chance, lass."

His voice had dropped to a whisper, but that didn't lessen the forceful, intimidating, and threatening tone behind it.

Nothing did. Especially his stance. Aidan had gone to both knees, raised to the full height he could, and punctuated it with both hands draped on his hips. The tartan wrapped about him had slid lower, wrapped haphazardly about his lower belly and groin. He was pushing that portion toward her, too, making certain she couldn't mistake him. Juliana gasped when she saw, and he knew all of it. The certainty was in the roped tendons of his belly, the heaving mass of his chest muscles, and the lowered jaw. He waited until she moved her gaze all the way up to his eyes.

"I'm na' one for words," he told her.

She snorted, giggling slightly. That sent a release to all the tensions running rampant through her, before they just started up again, wrapping and coiling tighter and tighter.

"And I'm na' a small size."

Juliana heaved, grabbed her knees for stability, and endured the rush of quiver that ran her back.

"Due to your maiden-wall, it pained. Afore."

Her eyes went wider, her throat closed off with the lump harboring there, and she still tried to gulp around it.

"You're to speak if pain happens. Not cry. Speak. You ken?"

He'd tilted his head slightly and was giving her such an aggressive, arrogant, and antagonistic look that everything responded. Instantly. Juliana felt the rush of heat through her lower belly, the thrill of weakness that hit the back of her legs, and total hardening of both breasts, shoving her nipples into the underdress weave with a rawness that felt erotic and delightfully sinful. She nodded. Her throat was useless.

"I'll na' hurt a woman when I take her. You. When I take you."

His voice had lowered along with his chin, while his eyes remained affixed to hers. That look put the lower curve of his amber-shaded eyes in silhouette against the whites. Juliana had never seen anything as primitive, hungry, and enticing.

Eliciting a response so dark and earthy and unbelievable, her lips opened to pant for each breath.

"You ken that, too?"

He'd raised the one eyebrow, and if he didn't do something, in a moment Juliana was going to be screaming with the overpowering rawness emanating all about him, permeating the tent, her tissues, the very air. She was near to tearing the restriction of her underdress from her skin. She nodded again. Rapidly.

"Then . . . get off that trunk and come here."

Chapter 12

She'd done what he asked. Without question or hesitation. And without one show of woman-tears. Aidan hid the massive rush of satisfaction deep, shoving it into his depths to keep company with the ache and want and lust and desire he was dedicated to controlling this time. She was upright on her knees, facing him from the length of an arm away, and breathing her sweet smell all over him.

"Aidan?" The soft words kissed his chest.

"Aye?" He licked his lips. Pulsed in place. Licked them again.

"You—you're . . . going to . . . take me?" The slight hesitation on the words was heightened by the rise of color through her cheeks and the way she ducked her chin, unable to meet his eye.

"Oh. Aye," he returned.

His eyebrow went up as he watched her twist her fingers together, looking altogether nervous and flustered. He staunched the desire to smile before she saw it.

"I may even manage it more than once," he informed her.

She pulled in a gasp. He heard it and saw it, as her breasts rose under that dress. And that was too much impact. Aidan transferred his view to the tent weave behind her for a moment, put both hands to fists at his sides as he pulled in on muscles throughout his frame, and breathed slowly and rhythmically. And had the surge of lust tamped down. For the moment.

He moved his gaze back to her. And waited. Counted heartbeats. Worked at it. He was determined this time. He didn't care how much his body fought it. He was giving pleasure. Not pain.

"What . . . should I do?" she asked in such a light voice he had to cock his head to hear it.

"Na' much more," he admitted.

That had her moving her head too rapidly to avoid catching the blue-green, endless, bottomless gaze of hers. Aidan wasn't prepared and had to narrow his eyes slightly and tighten his belly even more. That made the lust noticeable as his hips pushed inward and forward, without any permission from him . . . as if daring a look from her. So he could react to it. Doing exactly what he wanted to avoid.

Aidan licked his lips again, cursed the fates that had taken all his amulets and charms and everything else he relied on and replaced them with such massive need, he was trembling with it. He rolled his fists inward where they rested on his hips, stretching the sinew on his arms until it burned . . . put a thought to the ache . . . and then rolled them farther. It helped, but not much. Working at controlling this was harder than he'd suspected. His heart was giving him trouble, too, as the beat deepened and got larger and fuller and started deafening him to everything except his breathing. Those were loud. And coming faster.

"Why?"

He thought that was the word she asked, but sound wasn't penetrating the solid thump in his ears. She'd also shimmied closer or the pallet had shortened. But that was wrong. He'd been locked to her eyes the entire time. She couldn't have moved. Aidan shook his head slightly.

"What?"

She had a little smile hovering about her mouth and her eyes had softened . . . as if she recognized his distress, and knew why. She was going to find herself in his arms, and shoved beneath him, while his mouth plied her lips to give her those answers. That dress of hers was going to get the worst of it again, too. He glanced at it and immediately wished he hadn't. Her sweet, tight tips were pushing against the fabric, beckoning a touch, a tongue . . . a taste.

Ah . . . Jesu'!

Aidan cursed silently, closed his eyes, and shook with reining in the complete and total longing his body was suffering. The lass was new to this. Innocent. She didn't realize her power. She couldn't, or she'd not wield it so completely and carelessly.

"Can—can I touch you?"

The breath from her stammered words hit him first; followed by the hearing of them . . . and then came the realization of their content. Aidan's eyes went wide, his breath slammed from him, and the heartbeat in his ears went to a solid hum of sound.

He nodded. And forced down any desire to watch. He kept his eyes on her nose and cheeks, where the feather of her brown lashes flicked with every blink, while waiting with everything tight and the inhaled breath as she reached a hand for him. She was shaking. Her fingers had the same affliction. They were also cold. Aidan sucked in farther at the contact on his belly, thanked his luck she was above his belt level since any touch there and he'd be leaping right onto her and into her . . . and cursed it as well. He flinched and flexed against the plaid atop him in a never-ending torment of tension and ache and repressed need. He was also heating up, putting a glisten to the flesh she was running her fingers across, her motion sending tingling sparks coming off her fingertips and shooting right to his groin.

Despite the hold he had on everything, Aidan nearly groaned, but kept it in check by swallowing it down, pushing it to where the thump of his heart was rapid and harsh and stuttering between beats.

She moved closer, sliding her knees on the pallet until she was just below his chin, putting the bare hint of her breath all over his chest and belly. As if her touch wasn't sufficient torture. Her fingers warmed further as she moved them, roving about his belly, first to his right and then back across, and then she had both hands on him, spreading them about his lower belly and leaning in a sinuous full-body move as she did so. She was also rolling her head, leaning it against his throat to make it worse . . . putting her scent right beneath his nose.

Aidan groaned then . . . instinctively. He moved . . . despite the rein he was exerting, lurching with his hips fully and totally right against her palm. Then he had to stay affixed in one stiff position in order to endure the rash of reaction since everything male in him had made certain his tip touched.

"Oh . . . Aidan."

The whisper filtered through his ears, although he'd already felt her make it by the breath against his skin.

"Lass . . . you are verra close to being seized. And ravished."

The guttural tone didn't sound like him. He still made it. Her head jerked up from him but not her hands. She had those stilled in place, one at his belt line and the other atop his chest, right at his heart, where she couldn't fail to miss the hard thumping. He tipped his head and watched her move her gaze slowly up his chest, where everything bunched and moved as if desiring a caress, and then she was looking up at him through a lush fringe of lash, and sucking her lower lip into her mouth in that gesture of hers.

And then she let it out, glistening with moisture and smiled. Slyly.

"I am?" she asked, raising her brows, as if it were questionable.

Aidan moved against his own volition, grabbing for her arms, hauling her against his chest, and finding those lips were just as luscious and sweet and tantalizing as he'd guessed. Her moans weren't making much sound, since he captured each and every one of them, and added a groan punctuated with a push of his groin against her cloth-covered legs. Over and again, until he was crazed with it.

He tilted his head, holding her with his chin in order to wrap one arm around her back, supporting her collapse, while the other slid with perfect precision to her waist . . . around to her hips . . . and then he was going back onto his haunches and pulling her onto his lap at the same time.

It wasn't enough. And everything on him knew it. Her lips were driving him mad, and making it impossible to curb the absolute rage of need and want he suffered. Continually. End-lessly. The same one she'd stoked to an unrestrained level.

Aidan shoved a hand to the garment edge, pulling and yanking on it, and then he was bunching it in front of his hand all the way up her leg. He lost his objective the moment his fingers felt the curve and plump range of her hip . . . and buttocks, and that was where he moved next. He filled his hand with her flesh, the motion lifting and holding her, so he could shove against her . . . squeezing, massaging, manipu-lating . . . in order to push over and again. And again.

Aidan groaned heavily into the caverns of her mouth, where the wizardry of her tongue was flashing onto a thou-sand places, sending hammers through his skull. Her breath was mingling with his, matching every hard surge of air he made, and then she had her hands against his chest and was pushing.

She was pushing . . . at him. Away.

If he sobbed, that was the sound Aidan made at the mani-festation of denial. He yanked his mouth away from hers, lifted his head, and watched the tent weave flex and bow and then turn red with a pressure behind his eyes that pained with each ping of his pulse. He gulped, gritted his teeth, and sent the agony of need through every hiss of breath he made.

"Jesu', lass! Na' now! Christ!"

He was frightened. Of massive lust. Red-hued and vicious. And uncontrollable. Totally. Everything on him shook with the attempt at holding it back. It was a choking presence and then it went shoving all through his chest and belly and loins, propelling his hardness right between her thighs and against the sweet buttocks he was still holding to.

"I . . . need to remove my dress."

She was tapping at his cheek with a hand, sending a sensation of sharp cuts through the skin with each touch.

"Aidan?"

She had both hands on his chin and was forcing him to look down . . . at her. He blinked the red haze in a pink wash. He'd lost. He couldn't stop. She didn't know. Aidan's eyes pled with her silently as he released her buttocks, moving the hand quickly to his groin, shoving plaid aside and fishing for the opening, and then ignoring it completely, to bunch the material out of the way.

"But . . . my dress!"

She spoke again. Breathlessly. With more words . . . and none of them made sense.

"Forgive—"

The word accompanied his move. Aidan yanked his plaid up and apart, grabbed for her hips, and pulled her atop him, burying himself to the hilt in her moist depths and feeling the trill replicating all over from being sheathed. His groan that accompanied the complete bliss wasn't deep. It sounded exactly like the sob it was.

And it got worse as the rush of emotion ran through him, raising gooseflesh and making everything shudder as he fought it, suppressed it, groveled against the onslaught of it.

He wasn't taking her rapidly. He wasn't! He'd promised her pleasure.

Pleasure.

Aidan kept her affixed to him, with such a tight lock on every muscle, he forgot to breathe. Or blink. Or exist. He was afraid to do anything. The pink haze colored everything, going redder with every heartbeat before dimming back to pink. Red. Pink. Red.

"Aidan?"

The goddess in his arms was whispering his name, lifting the bit of hair plastered to his earlobe with the whiff of breath. Bringing him back to what he'd done. Forcing him to accept it. And finish it.

Aidan closed his eyes. Reopened them with a slit just enough he could see and still disguise the self-loathing. He pulled in a huge lung of air that came with an instinctive and unwelcome urge to rock backward from her, and then back in, the entire motion accompanied by the tightness of her embrace.

"Ai . . . dan?"

This time she split his name with a worried tone to it. He rocked again, slower this time, modulating the impulse with the need and recognizing a flash of victory at the control he might be winning back. But there was no help for it. She kept calling him. And he couldn't change it. He was in her woman-place and he was finishing this and he was taking every bit of the experience before he left to castigate himself. Even if she was unwilling. And no matter what she said. He tipped his head down toward her, steeled himself for the look she'd have on her face, and forced the eye contact.

The pink still colored everything, including the slight pout on her lips as she asked him something.

"I—can I remove . . . my dress?" she asked.

"What?" he asked, blinking around the pink as it hit him. She hadn't fought him. She wasn't denying him. She wasn't unwilling, or if she was, it wasn't in her voice. She didn't act unwilling either, with a hand about his neck. And nothing about her rose-tipped cheeks looked it either.

"My . . . dress?"

"Wh-Wh-What dress?" he asked, swallowing around the stutter on the first word. *Christ*. He truly did sound like Arran.

She giggled, and that sent the tumble of motion through her nether regions, rippling down him, and then she sent another one. And another. And a further one.

Aidan gave another huge groan that trembled in time with the shudders running him. He barely caught the instantaneous lurch he was primed, ready, and compelled to do, finding and using a power no man should have to. It was impossible to tighten everything further, but he tried, going into a bow shape that put his head right next to hers.

"Jesu'! Doona' do that again," he begged.

Her eyes were wide on his but she must have been obeying, since other than a tighter hold on him, nothing else happened. And then she ducked her head a little and went a further rose shade.

"But . . . my . . . dress?"

He looked down at the offending garment she kept mentioning. It was balled to her waist, in a crumpled mass . . . hiding what were probably luscious breasts and tempting nipples. But it wasn't in his way.

"I'll get you more."

She pinched something about him, massaging and caressing, and Aidan had only a moment before responding. Immediately. Instantaneously. Completely. Her mouth wasn't far and he slammed his lips to hers, sucking and slurping and taking all her arguments to perdition, while he gripped her to him with a hand cupping a wealth of buttock flesh and holding her exactly where he needed.

Pressure.

Exquisite pressure seized his loins and began building. Aidan leaned forward, dropping them onto the mat, keeping from stifling her with his weight by one stiffened arm to support him. The other hand wasn't moving from where he had it cupping buttock flesh, making certain she stayed sealed to him. And then she made it so much more by wrapping her legs about his lower back, locking her ankles in position, and making everything on him react and start pumping.

Aidan lifted her to him to make each movement give more, and be more. His hand squeezed without mercy while his loins pummeled. And created the ecstatic pressure. Over and over, sending hard knots of building sensation right to his lower belly, between his legs . . . into his lower back. Creating sensation atop commotion atop tumult, until he was powerless to modulate or control any of it.

Juliana writhed beneath him, alternately matching him in a sinuous dance of her own creation, and arching away to experience her own special pleasure. And then she'd return, sending her joy over it in little gasps of breath that went all over and through his frame. Again. Countless times. Still he thrust. Pulled out. Thrust back. Over and over and with such intensity and strength and force that it was propelling her along the pallet with each lunge into her sweet cavern.

Again. And over. Aidan felt the pressure ratchet higher, locking his lower back and buttocks in its grip, and gripping him in a primordial rhythm that had nothing controlled or ordered or influenced about it. Her hands pulled at the hair beside his ears, her lips slid to his ear, and Aidan's movements got wilder. Slamming into her. Pulling back out. Slamming again. With primitive motions, hard thrusts, and massive pushes. The sensation increased . . . becoming an elevated range of motion and power and strength that pumped through him with every pulse beat.

Harsh sounds of breathing blended with the heavy beat of his heart, and that was tempered by her soft sighs and cries of pleasure. Aidan pummeled her hips with his, lifting her higher, positioning her so he could fill her completely, taking every bit of the intensifying and building pressure and sending it back at her, over and over. Again. And just when he thought he'd reached breaking point and was going to explode, it happened.

The mass of pressure burst, releasing bliss and contentment and rapture throughout his frame, pumped there by the solid heavy beats of his heart. Aidan flung his head back to voice the sobbed breath that filled his chest cavity, keening with a throat that felt raw when he'd finished. Aidan was ramrod stiff the entire time, holding the pulse of ecstatic release to him as long as possible, twitching and rocking and pulsing deep in her womb . . . making her take him. Own him. Contain him.

Aidan moved his head down and met her gaze, memorizing and encapsulating the one brief moment in time when he had absolute and total heaven, and then it dispersed. The power ebbed with every continued beat of his heart, pushed out on the heels of the pleasure, and getting replaced with lassitude and complete satisfaction . . . combined with a weariness dogging every limb.

He dropped, doing his best to land at the side of her, rather than atop her, and turned his head toward her, breathing heavily and deeply as he waited for his heart to calm back to a range that wasn't frightening in bulk and depth and speed. The pinkish haze had vanished, bringing her into perfect focus. Aidan was still huffing for each breath and pulsing into her but they were jerked in smaller, longer-spaced intervals. He searched her face for tears. Fear. Worry. Disappointment. Anger. And saw nothing but wonder. Wide-eyed wonder.

He smiled slightly. She went a rose shade and tipped her eyes away, putting the brown feather of her lashes onto her cheeks again.

"Oh . . . my," she whispered into the air.

Absolute emotion hit him. From those two words. Aidan put the thumb and fingers of his free hand against his eye sockets and held them there while pings of sensation stabbed at him. He'd never had to deal with this before. Ever. And from those two words.

It wasn't like him, and by the saints, it was ceasing. And before much longer.

Aidan held his fingers where they were and modulated his breathing. And begged the fates for a little time . . . time to get control over this odd condition that couldn't possibly be weeping. He should've known it was useless. As was every prayer he'd winged this day. He'd lost his charms.

"Aidan?"

He cleared his throat and lowered his voice, trying for a masculine range. "Aye?" he asked.

"That was . . . oh *my*."

Satisfaction and contentment warred through every limb, and then it hit his torso and throat. Aidan moved his fingers away and blinked her into perfect focus. He didn't know how to answer her, or even if he could.

"Is it that way . . ."

She was having trouble pulling in breath for the words. She was blushing, too, if the pink tone of her cheeks was any indication. Aidan's lips twisted.

"What way?" he finally asked.

"Uh . . ."

She flashed a glance up at him, pulled her lower lip into her mouth to suck on it, and then looked away again.

"Nae," he told her and squinted slightly as she looked back toward him. "'Tis na' . . . that way. At least na' . . . Ever. That was the most—you are the most—Jesu'." And that came out exactly as lame and stupid as it sounded.

Her smile was brilliant. Heart-stopping. He had to look away for a moment. Blink. Return to her.

"But . . . I don't understand."

She was speaking to his chest. Aidan waited for her to glance back at him, and he waited what seemed a long time before she did it. And then she shied away the instant she touched his gaze. From there she appeared to be looking at his chin.

"What?" he asked.

"I'm . . . not supposed to . . . enjoy . . . *it*."

The complete pleasure of hearing that choked off his throat for a moment. Aidan had it disguised by a huff of breath all over her frame. He watched what looked like shivers ripple over the exposed flesh of her throat and the hint of perfect breasts he had yet to see. Due to his rash, reckless, and thoughtless curse. He swallowed and tried for a low masculine tone again. "Who would tell you such a thing?"

She ducked her head again. Aidan had a finger beneath her chin and raised her again to face him, although she kept her eyes lowered, giving him a view of brown sweep of eyelashes against perfect skin.

"Well, whoever they were . . . they either dinna' do it proper. Or . . . they dinna' wish you to know. That way they could save your maidenhood. For a spouse." He lowered his lips to her nose, pressed a kiss there, and felt her gasp.

"I appear to be a tad . . . impatient." He moved to the neckline of her shift and ran his fingertip along it. And watched her blush deepen.

"You didn't grant me time . . . to take it off."

"True," he replied finally. "And that is my loss. Again."

"What?"

She had deep blue-green eyes. Deep, fathomless blue-green eyes. They'd stunned and enraptured him from the moment he'd first seen them. Taking his wits and tossing them aside. And they did it to him again. He swallowed. "It won't happen again, lass. You have my promise."

Her eyes widened. Aidan winked. And then he rolled onto

his back, separating them with the move. Then, he wet his lips and pursed them, and gave a weak attempt at a whistle.

"What . . . are you doing?" Her voice rose slightly.

"Calling Arran. Poorly." He wet his lips and tried again, with the same result: a weak, barely audible whistle.

She gasped loudly. "Now?"

Aidan sucked in on his cheeks. "You have an issue with now?"

"You—you're not wearing anything."

She sounded embarrassed. Aidan tipped his head to look. She looked embarrassed. "'Tis only Arran," he told her.

"Aidan!"

She gave him a moment of time before she moved, pushing at him, although it didn't do much except slide her along the mat. He watched as she went to her knees, shimmying with her body and working her shift back into place. It wasn't just wrinkled at his impatience. It was darker in spots as well.

"What?"

She didn't answer him. He watched as she pulled her legs beneath her in a cross-legged sit. And just sat there watching him. With those blue-green eyes, and that reddish cloud of hair all about her. Aidan pulled in a huge breath and tried to whistle for Arran again.

"Aidan . . . please?"

She sounded shocked. And then she sucked her bottom lip between her teeth again. He smiled slightly.

"Aye?" he asked.

"C-C-Could you move . . . to your cot? And perhaps . . . dress?"

His eyebrows rose. "Why?"

"So Arran won't see."

Aidan grunted. "Lass, I am na' moving anywhere. I'm na' interested in moving anywhere, and I'm na' caring to move anywhere. Aside of which, I'm na' certain I can move anywhere."

"But . . . why?"

"Because I'm . . . drained. Weak." He pulled in another breath, pursed his lips again, and whistled. It was stronger. Louder, too.

She gave him a look he couldn't decipher. Then she lifted both brows, putting disbelief into that look. He didn't have any trouble reading it.

"Weak?" she asked.

"Aye. Weak. Were you na' new to this, you'd already ken it."

"How weak?" she asked.

"Uh . . ." Aidan didn't finish. He didn't know how much weapon to give her. He decided to show her. He pulled in a breath and sat up. Curved forward over his legs and stretched.

"You don't look weak," she said.

Aidan sighed out the breath and sat fully, put his hands on his thighs, and looked across at her. He watched as she glanced at his nakedness before moving back to his face. The blush was easy to spot, even in the storm-washed twilight outside their tent. He decided to go against his instincts and tell her. "Should an enemy accost my door, I'd find strength and fight him," he told her. "But 'twould be against nature. Tupping a woman drains a man. Especially . . ." He cut off the words. He didn't know how to explain it.

"Especially what?" she asked.

"E-E-Especially . . . you." He finished. With a cursed stammer. It came out even lamer and stupider than his earlier words. She had an odd expression on her face. But it was soft and luminous. A slight smile touched her mouth first, and when it reached her eyes, he had to glance away.

"I don't understand."

Oh Christ! And damnation! He wasn't explaining. He couldn't. He didn't know why it was she who did these things to him. And he didn't know how. Aidan looked at the crossed knives at the tent door and cursed the impulse that had him deciding to talk and explain anyway. It was the loss of all his luck amulets and charms. He wasn't doing anything normal and by rote. Nothing.

So he gave her silence. She filled it in. Just like a woman.

"I mean . . . you said—more than once. You'd take me . . . more."

Aidan scrunched his eyes shut. Reopened them on the improvised fastening he'd put in place at the door flap. "Oh. That. After sufficient rest . . . aye. I'll perform again. You'll have nae complaint." He tried not to sound defensive, but didn't manage it. He kept his eyes on the locked knives and fought the rising flush.

"I have no complaint now . . . Aidan."

She sounded completely content and close to a purr. Aidan licked his lips, put his head back, and whistled again. This time it was loud enough to penetrate the wind-whipped rain outside.

And then it penetrated his skull that he was looking at locked knives Arran couldn't get through. There was nothing for it. Aidan went onto hands and knees and crawled to the door and started pulling knives. He put a curse on innocent lasses with winsome faces and bonny frames, who wouldn't allow a man respite from questions and emotions. And he added to that. And all the time, he could sense her behind him.

Chapter 13

There was something to say about these Highlanders . . . something large. They truly knew how wonderful it would feel to be ensconced in a sturdy tent, with a lit wick in an oil bowl for light, fed a large bowl of stew created from a combination of their game meats, given a foam-topped tankard of ale that was refilled, washed off with a rag dipped in clear, cold water, and been directed to open the little trunk and fetch one of Aidan's clean shirts while the underdress she'd rinsed dried where it was laid out.

They'd crafted a very sturdy tent with what looked to be thin hemp strips, interwoven with wool. She couldn't be sure, since the ale made everything nice and blurred and unclear, but that was what it had appeared to be when she'd first been imprisoned in this small tent. The impression didn't fade or change as she ran her fingers along the side she leaned against. Such material woven as tightly as it was made a structure that was impervious to the elements, although it did look darker along the top edges where water must have been getting absorbed. She already knew light didn't penetrate easily, so rain must have had the same issue. Very sturdy and very well made. About the only thing the material couldn't withstand was their laird, Aidan, when he wanted out. But maybe cutting the holes in the fabric in order to lace the opening closed had weakened it.

She shrugged on her supposition and took another sip of ale, rubbing at the foam that tipped her nose.

Such a tent would be of great use in any season and in any clime. She wondered if the English had anything as finely worked and useful. She didn't remember the D'Aubenville family possessing any. Then again, she hadn't been involved with any of her father's weapons, including his siege tents. Nor would he have allowed her to. Machines of war meant men, and Juliana hadn't been allowed near them. As a lady of quality, she wasn't in any man's company without a chaperone.

She could see the wisdom in that.

Juliana looked over at the sleeping lump that was Aidan Niall MacKetryck and snorted. She took another sip of her second tankard, swallowed, and considered it. She wouldn't have met him if the castle hadn't been overtaken. And that meant she wouldn't know this love emotion or the sheer rapture he gave her. Sir Percy Dane certainly wouldn't have raised it in her, if the one time they'd met was any indication. Even if she accounted for her age at the betrothal ceremony, the man was tall, thin, and hawk-nosed, with beady blue eyes and a weak chin. Nothing about him had set her twelve-year-old heart to racing . . . but he did look good in his chain mail.

Juliana sighed. That future was gone. Any wedding with Sir Percy Dane was gone. She was ruined. She had been the moment she admitted she loved the laird of the Mac-Ketryck clan. And then it was solidified when he'd taken her maidenhead. She might as well admit it and carve out another future . . . with him.

Juliana pulled another sip from her tankard. She didn't know much about it, but she was willing to be his woman . . . sharing his chamber and his bed. The old Juliana would have hung her head in shame, covered herself in sackcloth and ashes, and fought the idea with every fiber of her being. The Juliana that admitted loving Aidan MacKetryck was different. She'd take what he offered.

She moved the mug, watching the ale swirl with the oil wick behind it. She'd be his mistress . . . Her eyes narrowed. But she'd be the only one. Some mistresses had more power than wives. It was ever true. She stopped the mug's movement and watched the light waver and glow through the amber color. He'd better follow through on his promise to dismiss his other women, regardless of what position they claimed in his life. Juliana D'Aubenville wasn't sharing. Ever.

She looked over at Aidan atop his cot, since that was where he'd gone once he'd finished affixing the knife fastening, after giving Arran to the count of three to hie his arse back to his own tent before being sent there with a skean in his buttocks to make it memorable. That was her fault. She'd asked for more of this wonderful ale, and Arran had informed her, amid a smattering of stutters when he brought it, that this particular tankard was the last of it, and if they wanted more, they'd need stop by Killoran's croft. The others were already thinking to make it by eve. If they found the sporran easily. Or if Aidan forewent finding it. And that was what got the lad threatened.

Aidan hadn't looked interested in partaking of the stew. He hadn't wanted a drink. He hadn't even stayed awake to peek while Juliana bathed, and she'd looked for it.

It must be as he'd said, then. He needed rest after . . . tupping. Juliana closed her eyes and suffered the shivers and heated blush at the repeated memory. She rocked back against the tent side while the fabric bowed slightly, but held. It seemed Highlanders not only knew how to make a tent, but knew how to anchor it. Juliana forced that thought into her consciousness, since reacting to Aidan's touch wasn't getting her much of anything except discomfort. She went back to her ponderings. And sipping at the ale they'd brought for her.

They'd anchored this tent well, but it was ever so. The sides were taut with tension from their mooring ropes, easily supporting any number of things . . . including her weight. Juliana turned slightly and flipped a finger into the material. It bounced back, answering that question. It was extremely well anchored.

The roof was pointed at the center, lifted with more rope, creating a slope for runoff. They'd have to position this tent near a taller structure like a tree . . . or one of the larger tents. This time, they'd placed Aidan's tent between the two larger ones, solving that problem and making it even more sheltered. If the storm that had ended their search was still raging outside, it was nearly impossible to tell. Except for the occasional whiff of air sent through where he'd locked the blades together again.

She looked that way for a moment, watched the bottom of his door flap slide along the ground, and when she looked back, Aidan was on the pallet in front of her . . . fully stretched out on his side. Naked. And she hadn't even heard him. Juliana gasped, the tankard in her hand trembled, and she ordered her eyes to stay focused entirely on his face. It wasn't easy. The oil bowl was on the little trunk behind him, putting a flickering gold glow to his outline and a mass of shadowed male everywhere else.

"Good eve," Aidan said, putting a finger out to slide it in a circle on the mat. He didn't look to see it. He didn't move his eyes from hers.

"Uh . . ."

Her mind wasn't working. Her tongue was right with it. Juliana held the gaze for as long as she could without blinking. Then he started widening the circle circumference, moving muscle on his chest and dragging her attention, despite her effort. Juliana's glance dropped there, imprinting the amount of naked male behind his hypnotic movement, before blinking and returning to his gaze. It was nearly impossible to hold it, though, since he'd raised the one eyebrow and had what appeared to be a slight smile on his lips as well.

"You found my shirts," he remarked.

Juliana's eyes dropped to the shirt that she'd tucked beneath her knees. It hadn't been onerous. The hem reached past her knees. The shirt was sewn from finely spun linen, making a flow of material that didn't crease much, especially as it had been rolled into a small bundle and then shoved into a trunk. He had four more of them, and a beautifully woven plaid in that trunk. As well as silver armbands and a brooch of the same metal. He had enough wardrobe with him he shouldn't have to go shirtless and half-naked all the time . . . most of the time, she corrected.

"Pity," he said, bringing her glance back to his face.

"What?"

"I'll just have to remove it."

Her gasp matched the twinge of her entire frame and the widening of her eyes. The slosh of ale in her tankard gave most of it away, too, as it was the only sound for a bit. He was definitely amused. The slight lines at the sides of his eyes matched the upward tilt to his pursed lips.

"Naked . . . ness . . ."

He put the word into existence, splitting it with a long pause, making little sense and yet too much of it at the same time. And that finger of his was at the edge of the pallet and nearly to her toes. Juliana fought the urge to look.

"Me."

He didn't have to specify it! A rush of emotion flew through her, chasing the gooseflesh down each arm, tightening each nipple, and forcing a wellspring of warmth and want into existence at her core, and making her knees quake against the fine linen of his shirt.

"Awake. Readied. And naked."

Breathing was going to be an issue. She couldn't gain

enough air with the short pants her body cursed her with. She had to open her mouth to pull in and push out each one. Aidan hadn't moved, but it looked like he had, getting larger, and fuller, and creating a heat and awareness that had not only a warmth to it, but a sensual aroma afflicting her, too.

"Just . . . as you requested."

He rolled onto his back, spreading both arms wide, while his head had swiveled to keep his gaze locked on her. The tankard dropped from nerveless fingers, spilling ale onto the dirt beside her. Both hands were atop her mouth, covering over the jaw drop as well as holding in the cry. Aidan was in a full grin now, while the one cocked eyebrow was daring her to ignore or argue, or do anything other than gape.

Juliana had never seen what she was looking at now. God had been extremely heavy-handed in regards to Aidan MacKetryck. He was a beautiful male. He was in prime condition and in perfect physical stature. And well endowed. And he knew it. There was no stopping the urge to look and keep looking.

Then, he was moving the hand closest to her and pulling in the fingers, over and over in a rapid fashion, beckoning her. Juliana's mind told her not to allow such an arrogant gesture, but her body was already moving, shoving forward onto her hands, which put her so close to him, she didn't have to move another step.

And then he reached for her, wrapped both arms about her, and pulled her right atop him, locking her arms down at her sides, while her legs split to accommodate the bulk of his belly and hips, just as she would a horse. And then he took her lips, canceling every thought with emotion and sensation. Lips plied hers, breath touched her nose, raw and intensifying, and then his tongue reached the caverns of her mouth, sparking everywhere it touched.

Juliana writhed atop him, matching the movements of her moans, while his arms unlocked to accommodate it. Her hands slid along his sides, over massive pulse-pounding bulk to his shoulders . . . alternately wrapping about his neck and gripping into his hair so she could use the same kissing motion on him, slurping and sucking and licking. She felt his hands . . . moving along her back, her buttocks, to her knees, and then he pulled up the shirt hem, sliding it over her thighs, her hips . . . to her waist.

He had the shirt bunched at her back before letting it go, losing his objective to return to cupping and squeezing and maneuvering her buttocks, in order to push her down and pull her back up, sliding her against his rod. Over and over, liquefying her in place and sending shots of feeling down her legs and up through her belly, making an exquisite torment sensation of her nipples against him, with material still restricting.

Without warning, he pulled his lips from her, and shifted, locking her against him with an arm about her waist while she wasn't loosening her grip on his hair. He flipped, the move putting them on their sides. And with the next one, full out on her back. She wasn't given any time to assimilate it before he had his hands on both sides of her torso, right beneath her arms, and used that as a base for a shove up from her and onto his knees. The swiftness of the move unlatched her fingers from him as well as took all the warmth and heat and moisture away, and leaving a cold shiver in its place.

"Aidan?" Juliana whispered.

"Lift your arms." He didn't give her time to comply since he was shoving the shirt to her neck and then reaching above her to pull it off. Leaving her complete open, defenseless . . . and naked. And covering her bosom with both crossed arms.

"Oh . . . nae. Na' now."

The whiff of air accompanying the words riffled across her flesh, and Aidan had his fingers about each arm, coaxing her to remove them. Then he was adding to it with his kiss, draining her fears and canceling out her shyness. The exquisite

sensation followed his mouth when he trailed along her chin
to an ear, breathing shivers of reckless desire and shameless
need into existence the entire way. She was covered in them,
being tormented by them, enduring them. And Aidan was the
conductor, lapping more of them into existence at her throat.
Juliana started lifting her hips and that was the beginning of
the undulation that heaved her from the pallet and against
him, time and time again.

And his chuckle made the entire tension of sensation worse!

Juliana barely felt his warm, hard fingers sliding along her
body, roving her flesh, before locking on to her waist in order
to hold her in place while he propelled his entire body down
her . . . taking his heavy bulk and fitting it between her knees.
Where he was touching was igniting a thousand fires and
even more shivers. And the sensation just kept building as
Aidan slid his tongue from her throat . . . down the center of
her . . . stalling time and her breathing and her heartbeat as
he went.

And then he reached a nipple and started the same hypnotic rotation around it, and Juliana went absolutely wild,
bucking her body from the pallet, mashing her frame against
every part of him she could reach, her knees squeezing over
and over on his hardness. And then he put his entire mouth
atop her and suckled. The keening cry tore her throat, even
as she tried to quiet and end it. Juliana threw her head back
and arched in a complete and total crisis of energy and
wonder and ecstasy.

She forgot to breathe. She couldn't do anything except
feel. And exist. And experience the thrills coursing over and
through her, again and again . . . accompanied by his chuckling,
which just made everything more alert and tormented and
grasping. And then Aidan moved to her other breast, and did
the same things.

"Oh! Aidan . . . Oh!" His name was a sigh of sound meshed
between exclamations of delight and enjoyment.

"You complaining . . . over my rest . . . wench?"

He asked it with a hoarse voice, looming over her. Then he was lowering his mouth to hers and moving her head with each lap of his tongue on her lips. That gained him a rain of fists on his chest, bucking motions with her hips against where he was poised, and moans of frustration with the way he tormented and teased her.

"More . . . complaining?"

He split the words with a grunt and pierced her with a look that went straight to her heart. Juliana already had her legs apart, allowing him entry, and with the one look she went to a bow shape in order to embrace him closer, locking her ankles at his lower back. Nothing. Aidan held himself from her with his arms, jerked toward her opening with nonrhythmic lurches, readied, hard. Engorged. Yet still he denied her.

"Please, Aidan? Please?"

"Now?" The word was hissed at her through his teeth. It came with a heavy pulse of his hips, pushing him through her entrance and punishing her with more slowness.

"Aye, Aidan! Aye. Now! Please?"

Juliana grabbed both sides of his head, filling her fingers with lanky strands of hair, locked her gaze to his, and willed a consummation. She watched the immense satisfaction hit his features. It was in the slant of his swollen lips, narrowed cheeks, and the half-slits his eyes went to. And then he slammed his lips to hers, and rammed home in the same instant. Juliana went crazed with it, flinging her entire body into the whorl of anger and intensity and rapture he took her to the brink of, and then shoved her over with each increasingly wild thrust he made into her.

Waves of ecstasy lapped over her, ebbing and growing and then rioting through her entire frame . . . ebbing again. Through it all she clung to Aidan, gripping his heated, moisture-imbued flesh, feeling the caress of every heavy breath he made against her nakedness, and the symphony of his grunts with each repeated move. Again. And so many times, she lost feeling with the pallet at her back, there was nothing but blue sky, endless vistas of wonder . . . and Aidan.

Grunting. Sweating. Pushing.

And then he increased his motions, going to massive rapid lunges against her, and forcing her to accept them. Deep. All-encompassing. Heart-touching.

"Lass . . . Ah . . . lass. There. Right . . . there!"

Each whispered word came with a corresponding move of his body within hers, but with the last, he stopped, taking her from the pallet with her cling as he arched upward for a perfect few moments. His heartbeat thudded against hers, his groin pulsed into hers, while every muscle and striation of his frame was bulging and taut and going purplish with a flush, and he was making her nose vibrate against his throat with the low groan that went on and on, and lingered in the air even after it was silenced.

Then, it was over.

Aidan lowered his head, opened his eyes, blinked rapidly for several heart-stopping moments, and then he dropped. Juliana dealt with the bulk of him, breathing in tandem with him, the action sending cool air over them until the volume and cadence of it slowed. That was when he rolled from her and onto his side. Juliana was watching, enthralled, as he opened his eyes again and turned his head. The instant it happened, her heart gave a near-painful thump, shooting a reminder of how she felt all over her. She didn't know if she gave a sign, but a slight smile touched his mouth before he rolled farther, putting him half on the pallet and half off. It also separated them. Juliana watched as he lifted his head. Dropped it with a slight groan. Lifted it again. Dropped it. And then he pulled in a huge breath and huffed it out.

"Aidan?" she whispered.

He put a hand up in his gesture for silence. Juliana surprised herself by obeying. She watched his dark eyelashes dust his face with his blinking, before they closed. She counted for more than fifty heartbeats, listening to his breathing calm, until it sounded like he was going to sleep. Again. And in that uncomfortable position.

Juliana rolled onto her side and supported her head on a bent arm. "Aidan?" she tried again.

"Aye?"

It was a grunt of sound, but it was an answer. He wasn't asleep. She watched him lick his lower lip into his mouth before releasing it. The man had perfectly formed lips. And they looked swollen . . . mauled. Juliana's body pulsed in a long disjoined motion from her side of the mat. The man was so beautiful! It was just unfair.

"I'm na' calling for Arran," he informed the air above him.

"What?" she asked.

"I am na' calling for Arran."

"Why?"

His mouth tipped into a smile. "I'm worse off than afore . . . although it does na' seem possible."

"Nay?" she teased.

"You . . . uh . . ."

"Yes?" she prompted.

He lifted his hand as if to ask for silence again. She watched it tremble for a moment before he dropped it again.

"You're drained again?" she asked.

He nodded. Juliana giggled.

"And . . . this is not the usual?"

He sucked in on his cheeks and twisted his lips as if considering either the answer or if he should give it to her. He finally shook his head. Juliana was glowing. It was probably visual. If he looked. He didn't.

"Aidan." Her tone warmed . . . lowered.

"Aye?" he whispered.

"You've feelings for me."

"Lass—"

"Admit it."

He gave her a huge intake of breath before his long, drawn-out sigh, probably trying to sound harried and put-upon. It didn't work. He was too visual. Stirring. And with the flicker of the oiled wick, it was impossible not to note the shadows and dales that delineated him with every breath he took. Especially the large ones. She roved her eyes about him. Such power. Such presence. Such a man.

Drained?

"Aidan." She tried again using the same exact tone.

"What now?" he asked.

"You've feelings. For me. Admit it."

"You will na' let a man rest. Will you?"

"Aidan."

"He works into a massive tired pleasing you, and you just jaw him to death as a reward. This is what you do."

"Aidan," she tried again. "Your feelings?"

"All right, lass. You win. I do. I've feelings. Most of them tired and blurred and getting stepped on."

"You . . . have feelings for me?" She couldn't help it. She hadn't truly expected him to admit it. The surprise colored the words.

"Of course I do."

Her eyes went wide, and her mouth nearly split with the absolute joy of what he'd just admitted.

"What man wouldn't? You're a bonny wench. With a bounteous frame."

Her face was frozen in place. Then it started settling into a blankness she had to work at. Her breath was another problem, burning at the way she held it.

"Aidan." She said his name in exactly the same tone and inflection as before.

"And a penchant for jawing a man's ear at the worst times," he continued.

Now it was her turn to sigh. She watched how much that pleasured him. It was in every bit of his smile.

"You need to seek rest, lass. We leave on the morrow. First light."

"That is not what you told Arran."

"First light is na' much time."

"You're impossible, Aidan Niall MacKetryck!"

She slapped at the mass of muscled belly he was exhibiting. Her hand bounced. His smile widened. Not much else happened.

"You are na' the first lass to say so," he informed her.

Juliana didn't answer. It hurt too much. There wasn't any way to disguise it.

"Does your silence mean you'll leave a man to rest?"

"Aye," she croaked, and then swallowed. He smirked. It was still endearing. Juliana watched as he shimmied himself into a more comfortable position, although it appeared to be by flattening the mat to match the ground level. He folded his arms atop his chest, making everything even larger and more muscular-looking. He didn't open his eyes. He didn't turn back to her.

He went to sleep.

Chapter 14

They came upon the Killoran crofts toward dusk. Juliana didn't have to be told. There wasn't a hint of rain in the heavy cloud hanging about the deepest darkest section of this glen. Her nose was alerted well before they'd got beneath the overhang of cloud carrying the faintly sour smell of dredge mixed with a bare whiff of rising bread odor, and that was blending with wood smoke from their kilns. It was easily recognizable and unmistakable for the ale brewing industry it was.

As were the fields they'd traversed through since midmorn.

As chatelaine of Fyfen Castle, she'd overseen the brewing of ales, including the perfect dredge to mix with water. And perfect dredge required barley wheat . . . fields and fields of it. The size and scope of this particular glen was jaw-dropping. If Juliana hadn't been watching Aidan's back and feeling the most unsettling knot of worry start an ache at the base of her belly, she'd have probably had the jaw-dropping affliction as they passed from field after field of ripening wheat interspersed with fallow fields.

All of it belonging to the laird of MacKetryck.

Arran was a font of information during their midday stop, settling amid one of the tilled fields that wouldn't be harvested until late in the season. Juliana hadn't asked, but it hadn't stopped his mouth.

Killoran ale was the finest in Scotland, and the barley grown the best, as well as the oats that were added to make wort. As vassal and clansmen to Laird MacKetryck, the Killoran owed Aidan a portion of every hogshead brewed and sold. As well as supplying any number of oaken kegs the castle needed. And a household the size of Clan MacKetryck required a lot of ale. But she'd soon see for herself. They'd be at the castle about midmorn. They could continue over the next two drums, and arrive during the night, but Aidan had already given the orders. He wanted the time to regroup, bathe properly, and dress for the ceremony of arrival at his castle. And he also had to import the sad tale of their only son, Beathan Killoran's demise at the hands of the English dogs.

That was going to be difficult. Killoran had more than eight daughters to his credit, but Beathan had been the lone son. Arran didn't know how the old man would take the news. He didn't envy Aidan the telling of it, but as liege, it was his responsibility and his bane.

All this information affected her more than she wanted to admit. A man owning all the land and lakes and forests they'd been in since she and Aidan had fallen from the horse was a very rich man. Powerful, too. Frighteningly so.

Arran's tales added to the knot of worry until it pressed against her backbone as well. No wonder Aidan acted so arrogantly and assertively. As if he owned the world. The sound of a lone pipe filtered through the low-hanging fingers of fog, giving an eerie feel to everything. It was difficult to tell where the notes were coming from. Once that piper was joined by more of them, it was impossible. They were probably sending word of MacKetryck's arrival. Or something.

It appeared Killoran had several lovely, lush daughters who weren't afraid to show it. He also had more than a score of other lasses working for him. Juliana sat atop Rory's horse and watched the mass of clansmen and women surrounding Aidan's group once they arrived in the cleared area comprising Killoran's compound. Since it was at the bottom of the valley, it felt darker than it actually was. The reason was apparent as soon as she saw the mill. A heavy fringe of trees loomed throughout the opacity, outlining the far bank of what looked to be a good sized, fast-running, and deep river. All of which made it feel darker and more mysterious. Perhaps if the sun were shining, it would temper the impression.

She already knew Killoran claimed eight daughters and they were easy to spot. It was apparent by their clothing, since their dresses were crafted of finer materials, with embroidered necklines, while at least two of them had made an effort to conceal their hair beneath veils, although the veils were atop their shoulders with the effusiveness of their greeting. All were very lovely girls, with very obvious charms, and not immune to showing them off. Nor were the other women, if the amount of wagging hips beneath low-necked bodices was any sign.

Juliana watched and listened as more than one of Aidan's men called out greetings from behind her, recognizing Alpin's voice. She didn't note who the others were. She was watching Aidan to see if any of these women were the women he'd claimed he'd dismiss. She wondered if she'd have to assert herself already, and not only how to go about it, but if she had the daring. The knot loosened just slightly as he didn't appear to do more than tip his head and smile before ignoring all of the women about him.

It wasn't returned. Juliana intercepted more than one sly glance toward her after failing to catch his eye. She sat atop her borrowed horse and waited. And then she started surmising again since Aidan dismounted and left them to greet a large, robust, white-bearded fellow who was shoving through the crowd to him.

The Killoran family compound appeared to have five crofts of varying sizes. Two had lean-tos extending out the sides, for protecting their horses. Those buildings were probably housing for all his workers and kin. She turned a bit in the saddle. There was an odd-looking structure built right into the side of the hill. Grass covered the roof and one side. From the amount of people coming and going from either door at the end of it, she'd assign it their living abode. The design probably made it easy to cool and heat as well.

"Nae! Please, my laird! Tell me 'tis a lie!"

Juliana's heart pumped painfully with the amount of anguish in the voice that canceled out all the other sounds in the clearing. And then she heard the rumble of crowd noise as the news was disseminated, over and over again, catching phrases now and again that she preferred to ignore. Juliana wasn't going to be affected by their grief. Not at all. It was their fault. If a Highland clan hadn't taken Fyfen Castle in the first place, they wouldn't have dead to mourn over. Nor would she.

Juliana turned her attention to the kiln building, easily tagged due to the amount of smoke coming up from the roof to mingle with the mist, creating the thick overhang of fog. They'd also use that building for cooking. To save time and wood . . . or whatever they used for fuel.

Then she heard the unmistakable sounds of weeping. Wailing. Lamenting. From all about her. Displaying the emotions she hadn't been allowed to.

Juliana blinked at the blur in her eyes and moved to consider the building just decipherable through the mist beyond the kiln. This one looked easily as large, but had a sloped thatched roof. That sort of roof would have the perfect conditions for starting the malt process. Grains had to be moistened and spread in a cool dry place that vented . . . exactly like a loft beneath that roof would allow. Such a building would also be easy to keep warm, since that stage of the process generated heat. If she didn't miss her guess, the interior would be filled with oaken kegs being stored, aged, or readied for transport.

"You show me the Sassenach! I'll carve out his heart! I'll cook it for me sup!"

The old man was brandishing a wicked-looking sword, using both hands. Juliana had seen one before. It was called a claymore. It was an ugly weapon, unwieldy, much heavier than an English-made sword, and usually crafted from inferior steel. It was still capable of hacking a man's head from his body. As long as the man brandishing it had enough strength and stamina for the task. And enough hate.

"Then show me any Englishman! I want blood! My son will na' rest without blood!"

There were more words to the threat, said in a loud, sob-filled voice that cracked occasionally with the depth of the man's emotion. Juliana started humming to herself, and then rocked in place atop her saddle. It was still their fault. They'd started it. As far as she was concerned, they'd gotten what they deserved.

She had to blink quicker, however, and focused on the indistinct shape of the large waterwheel of their mill. She'd been right about the size of their river. It had to be deep and fast-running to spin a wheel of that size.

"My lady?"

"Yes?"

Juliana's chest went concave with indrawn air, bowing forward with the shock. She held it from a gasp by sheer will. Her eyes went wide with the horror, allowing a lone tear to escape, while her hands shook where she had them holding on to her saddle.

"The laird . . . has told us of your plight."

"He . . . has?" Juliana watched the fingers of fog for a moment longer and then swiveled to the other side to face the woman standing at the side of the horse. She wasn't one of the daughters. And she wasn't alone. There were four of them.

"Aye. It be a sad day when the MacDonal clan gets such a thorough drubbing. Near wiped out, I hear. And at the hands of the Sassenach. 'Tis just terrible. Terrible."

"Aye," she replied. The woman was right. It was terrible. All of it. Juliana wiped at the tear on her face, and smiled shakily. She was being tagged as MacDonal clan. It was almost amusing.

"We've got a spot for you to freshen yourself and get a bite to eat."

"What . . . of Aidan?" And curse her tongue for asking it! Juliana felt the warmth of a blush from the other's regard, as well as the raised eyebrows.

"Laird MacKetryck?" one of them asked. And then she giggled, which started them all to it.

"Aye. That Aidan," Juliana replied in a tight voice.

"The laird is with Killoran. At the burn. 'Tis where the men go. To drink and bathe. And prepare themselves. As usual. Women would na' be allowed."

"Prepare for what?" she asked, shrugging slowly and carefully, while she blanketed every emotion and expression she might have. She hadn't forgotten how, she'd just ignored it. Love had changed her.

"Sup. But will be a subdued affair. Due to Beathan's passing."

Juliana moved her far leg across the saddle preparatory to sliding off by herself. *Highlanders!* If any of them had possessed manners, they'd have seen she had an assist, or at the very least, a stepping-off point. Juliana rolled her eyes, putting her distrust and bias about them back to the fore of everything, and jumped to her feet.

* * *

If sup was subdued, there was a distinct speech difference here.

Juliana sipped at a tureen of broth one of the women had fetched for her and licked at the drop leaking through a bottom hole before it reached her borrowed shift. They didn't worry over bowls that leaked since good porridge had the consistency of bog, and no one else needed the stock broth heating on the fire for tomorrow's stew. Or whatever they planned on cooking. It hadn't been given to her in a gracious fashion, but Juliana hadn't cared. If she didn't get something other than what they were eating, then she was going hungry. And that was that.

Only a pig could stomach the table load of steaming entrails they'd heaped atop huge flat chunks of bread that served for a platter. The food was covered in a shine of grease that reflected the torchlight scattered about, and it was still entwined exactly as it had been when they'd taken them from the animal belly. Juliana had watched from her long stool against one wall as the fare was applauded and then attacked from both sides of the common table. If a diner didn't have a knife, they bit off a portion, or pulled at it until it split, scattering the rough-hewn table with more grease, and gaining laughter that had a drunken tone to it.

Everything in the large croft built into the hill had a drunken tone to it. From the loud slapping and clapping and voices, to the belching and cursing, and laughter. Everything. It was clear they had well-brewed ale, and weren't immune to partaking of it. Juliana had glanced once from the safety of her stool and requested water. And it better not be a goblet from the pail set atop each table to water down the ale. The same pails that weren't getting more than a hand or fist dunked into it, although one at a neighboring table had been dumped atop one unfortunate fellow, amid guffaws and general hilarity. He'd taken it well, after getting another tankard of ale and a wench at either side. Juliana told the woman serving her that she wanted her water fresh drawn from the well, and if the woman serving her wouldn't fetch it, then Juliana was prepared to do it herself. That was a threat that worked. Not much else did.

The bathwater had been slimed with use. The shift smelled stale and well used, and self-pitying tears were hovering so near the surface she had to consistently swallow and blink to send them back, and that was accompanied by unpleasant shivers that raced down her arms and then her legs joined in. She was surrounded by humanity, and had never felt so alone. She missed her chamber at Fyfen. She missed her father. She missed the woodcutter's croft. She missed Arran.

And she especially missed Aidan.

Something jostled her elbow, sloshing soup onto her fingers, and she quickly licked at them before her dress received any further stain. This experience was everything she'd heard and believed and had described for her in her worst memories. And more. She couldn't believe she'd been ready to toss all her upbringing and sense of decency aside in order to fit in with such a race. She finished licking at a finger, swallowed, and then Aidan walked in, ducking beneath the doorframe, while a piper filled the room with sound.

Juliana forgot to breathe. Think. Exist. There was the most horrid, low-pitched buzz in both ears, overriding all the other sounds in the room, including the piper. She held the bowl at her chin level and stared as everyone seemed to be doing. The only difference was that Aidan wasn't looking at anyone else but her. As if he knew exactly where she'd be sitting and what she'd be doing.

Moments passed, feeling like sennights of time, while several heads started turning her way. It didn't change anything. She loved him. Totally and completely and with a breadth and scope that altered everything. Then he turned his head, releasing her. She watched him shout and clap some clansman on the shoulder before moving farther into the crowd, greeting so many clansmen if it hadn't been for his height, she'd have lost him.

She caught a glimpse of red and black plaid and then the bench beside her shifted slightly. "Aidan asked me to check upon you."

"Good eve, Arran," Juliana said.

"Alpin. Jesu'. Arran stutters. And is a failure around women. And has little resemblance to me."

Juliana couldn't prevent the smile at how put-upon he sounded. She had it stifled before turning to him. They truly didn't know how much they favored each other?

"I would guess he looks just as you did at that age. And exactly as Aidan," she replied.

His face fell and he looked toward the ceiling before returning his gaze to her. She'd been wrong. He wasn't going to be as full in the chest unless he started soon, and the size of his waist probably rivaled hers. The legs sticking out from his plaid also needed a good bit of muscle added to them. He didn't have the same mouth as Aidan, nor the same length of eyelashes. And as he sat, looking bored and harassed, she noted that he didn't have the same amber shade to his brown eyes either. Alpin MacKetryck hadn't been slighted, though. He was a very handsome man . . . as long as one hadn't seen his elder brother first.

"So? Are you?"

"Am I . . . what?" she asked.

"Satisfied? Well cared for? Fed. Jesu'."

"What if I weren't?" she asked.

He put both hands on where his knees were and leaned back against the wall. Then he puffed out his cheeks before blowing the sigh. It was filled with his disgust. He didn't have to voice a word.

"I'm to make certain of it, then."

Juliana giggled. Had him turn his head against the wall to give her a look akin to Aidan's threatening ones, and that was even more endearing. She tried to prevent her eyes from softening, but knew he'd seen it as his face fell again.

"You're not fond of the duty, are you?"

"What was your first inclination?"

His voice had a snide undertone that matched the aggressive words. Juliana shook her head. She was close to rolling her own eyes. She hid the urge by lifting her tureen to her lips. "Why didn't he send Arran?" she asked the broth.

"Because Arran is na' a man."

Juliana snorted the soup she'd mistakenly tried to sip, getting a nose full of liquid and suffering the tears that came from choking, while he just sat there and regarded her with a sneer on his upper lip.

"It eats better if you swallow it rather than breathe it in," he informed her.

"Oh, do tell . . . dear youth," she replied in the iciest tone possible and watched his eyes narrow.

"I'm nae youth," he replied, attempting a deadly tone akin to Aidan's when he was out of patience.

"I'd rather have Arran. Go. Alert Aidan of it."

"Well, you canna' have Arran. Na' tonight."

"Why?" she asked.

"Because Arran is on a short leash right now."

Juliana gasped. "He tied him?"

"Of course na'. Jesu'! We're nae barbarians."

Juliana had to look back out at the crowd before he saw her amusement again. It was too easy to toy with him, and a simple matter to raise his ire. He'd need to learn how to temper it before too much time in her presence.

"So explain. How is he tied?"

"Tavish was assigned a guard on him."

"Is he in danger?"

"Only from Killoran ale."

"Oh," she said, nodding sagely and keeping the effervescent sensation of laughter right at her throat.

"So? Are you?"

"Satisfied with my eve? Settled? Well fed? And enjoying your company?" she asked.

"Aye. All that."

"Totally, dearest Alpin. Totally."

"So . . . I can go?" He was already rising, showing the complete lack of manners the lad possessed. But it could be corrected if Aidan kept up the pretense of her status in the MacDonal clan. The introduction as a lady had given her respectability. And position. She might even have a chance at teaching Alpin MacKetryck manners once they reached Castle Ketryck . . . if she had enough patience.

"Can I ask something first?"

His sigh was full of disgust and dismay. He sat back, rocking the stool, which had been his intent. He was much too easy. Obvious. Not at all like Aidan. Alpin was determined to make further contact with him as annoying and frustrating as possible. That way, he'd be released to freedom sooner.

"Are you betrothed?" she asked with as much innocence as she could muster.

A complete look of horror crossed his face. It was enough to send her into more giggles. She settled with tipping her head to the side while she waited for his answer.

"You're too auld!"

He said it finally with such conviction and aggression that Juliana couldn't help it. She dissolved into helpless laughter at his side.

Chapter 15

"Juliana?"

At the whisper her head shot up, connecting sharply with what felt like Aidan's chin. His indrawn breath and hissed curse verified it.

"Aidan?"

"Hush!"

He had a hand atop her mouth, and with his next move she was on her feet, with dizzying speed. If he hadn't had her clasped fully to him, she'd have probably fallen. She'd have been in even worse straits, if she'd been in a deep sleep rather than lying awake on her specific mat.

"Come."

He gave the command, but since he had an arm about her waist and lifted her occasionally before she'd have stumbled over a sleeping form, it was a moot order. The air outside in the dark was fresh, chill, and clear, showing a quarter-moon and star-strewn sky, answering another of her ponderings over if Killoran ran his kiln day and night. Remnants of the smoke cloud were still apparent in fingers of haze, lit with moonlight. If one looked close enough for them.

"What . . . are you doing?"

Juliana asked it after he shoved her through the barely

open door and then brought it closed behind him as he joined her. Their doors didn't latch, which was another moot issue. They were fit to the frame and bolted if needed. Aidan was in luck that this one hadn't been.

Or maybe he'd planned it.

"Kidnapping you," he answered.

"You can't kidnap me!"

"Hush!"

She'd added a bit of tone to her whisper. Aidan grabbed her and moved to one side of the croft, standing in the roof overhang shadow with her pressed behind him. Long moments passed with nothing more than the sound of heavy heartbeats in her ear. She couldn't tell if they were hers or resonating from the back she was pressed to. Through the obstruction that was Aidan she heard a sharp whistle followed by two more, then nothing. Aidan relaxed slightly, moving back muscle against where her nose and cheek were pressed.

"You've posted your men?"

"Killoran, too."

"He posted men, too?"

"Aye."

"Then . . . why are you here?"

He swiveled his neck and tipped his head to one side, meeting her eyes with a shadowed one, making all the flesh at her nose and cheek undulate, as well as the thick waist of it she had her hands about. The man was easily two of his brother Alpin. And he'd been wearing full attire at sup. She didn't know why he had to run about shirtless now. Not that she'd complain. She wouldn't change the contact of her palms to his flesh for much of anything.

"I already said."

"But—you can't kidnap me."

"I'm laird. I can do what I want. Now ready yourself."

Juliana's eyebrows rose. "For what?"

"Running."

"Aidan." Her whisper was as deadpan as she could make it.

"Now what?" he asked.

"I do not have shoes."

He cocked the one eyebrow of his, making a larger impression since it was on the moonlit side of his face. "Fair enough," he answered. "Prepare to be carried then."

Her eyes went wide. He didn't give her any time to assimilate it or do more than gasp as his left arm looped about her waist and yanked her around to his front, sliding her shift into a tight wrap about her with the motion. Then she was up in his arms with her arms about his neck and gripped there for one heartbeat. Two. On the third, Aidan ducked his head and started running. Juliana closed her eyes, tucked her nose against his throat, and breathed deeply with him, experiencing a hum of what was probably happiness all over her. Nothing had felt as wonderful.

He'd reached the kiln building, where they dried their sprouted barley prior to grinding it. Aidan hadn't slowed, but turned so it was his back slamming against the structure as he waited, breathing hard and sending air all over her. And then he caught his breath as a slight coo of sound came.

"Were we spotted?" Juliana asked.

"Aye," he answered.

Juliana stiffened.

"Doona' fash, love. 'Tis nae Killoran, but Heck. Or Gregor."

Love. He called me love. Not lass. Love.

Oh, dear heaven. The storm of reaction flooded her, sending tears to her eyes and making her nose run, and making everything start shivering.

"Sounds closer to Heck," he added. "Ready?"

Juliana pressed her nose closer to his throat and nodded. Swallowed. Chastised herself silently for even thinking of crying at such a time, and waited. She knew when he was preparing to run by the harder grip on her thighs and back and how he ducked his head. She clung to him through the turns and twists he made, dodging things, and this time when he turned them about to shove against a wall, she could see they'd made the large thatched roof building. She could smell the slight sour odor of moistened barley grain that was laid out to sprout.

Aidan stayed against the wall in the thatched roof shadow, the same as before, and waited, breathing deeply. This time the sound wasn't recognizable as a signal. It sounded like the rustle of tree branches. Twice.

"Aidan?" she whispered.

"Aye?"

"If your men know where you are . . . why are we hiding?"

He shoved out his lower lip and blew a sigh that ruffled the loose hair at his forehead. "I already told you. I'm kidnapping you."

"From who?"

"Oh. Me."

The last word was accompanied by a tighter grip on her thighs and back. Juliana didn't have any time to question anything before he'd ducked his head slightly and was running across a span of dirt and shrub that had little for cover. Juliana clung to him, trying to make it easier, and just when she thought he'd run straight into the river, he turned about and slammed up against the wall of the mill.

This time his breathing was so hard, it raised and lowered her with each one. It was also making it difficult to hear any of their signals, especially if it was another subtle one. Juliana pressed against him and tried to listen for any sound.

Nothing. She couldn't hear anything. Aidan held his breath and Juliana tried to match it, but gave out long before he did. And still there was nothing.

"They don't give a signal this time?" Juliana whispered.

He grunted.

"Lack of a signal . . . is a signal?"

He nodded.

"Oh my. That's—"

"Hush!"

Aidan slid along the wall, probably gaining slivers in his flesh since he'd deigned to wear a shirt, as usual, moving toward a darker bit of shadow cast from their ladder. At the same time, the slight rattle of weaponry or other bits of a man's attire alerted them to the Killoran man's approach. Juliana's eyes were wide as she watched him come around the side of the mill where they'd just been. The arm behind her back released, causing Juliana to grip tighter at the loss of support. She could feel Aidan moving about as his shoulder rubbed against her side. She hoped he wasn't fishing for a skean, but had to swallow the dismay and shock when he brought one from around her.

Oh . . . Aidan.

She didn't say it aloud, but something must have alerted the man. He looked right at them, opened his mouth, and that was when Aidan's blade hit him. She hadn't even felt Aidan move. Juliana watched the Killoran man waver for a moment before sagging into a lump of plaid next to the building.

"You killed him!" It should have been screeched, but was instead a breathless, frightened, horrified whisper.

"Nae." Aidan looked down at her and grinned. "I'm na' that dense."

"You didn't . . . kill him?"

"Hilt hit."

"Hilt," she repeated.

"Handle. Leaves a large bump. When he wakes."

"Oh . . . dearest God." She was in luck he'd put his arm back about her as she sagged against him with the relief.

Aidan raised his head and made three odd grunting sounds akin to an animal. If she hadn't heard it, she wouldn't have believed it.

"You're calling . . . Heck?"

"Aye."

"Why . . . now?"

He gripped her tighter, preparatory to running again.

"Aidan," she hissed.

"To hide the man and get my blade back. Now, hold the questions."

"I don't understand, Aidan. None of this. You're the laird."

"Spare my ear until we reach my tent. I'll answer anything then. Now, hush."

"You're staying in the tent?"

He turned to stare down at her and give his threatening look. Juliana's lips twitched before she put her nose back against his throat, hiding the smile. He was taking her to his tent. She knew only one reason why. Everything on her body knew it as well.

The last bit of her abduction had some sloshing to it as the bridge they'd built to span their river wasn't above the spring thaw line. Juliana heard it with a portion of her hearing. The rest was impacted by her elevated heartbeat and quicker breaths. Aidan didn't run across the bridge, although he walked it with a rapid pace. She made guesses as to why. It wasn't stealth. The sound of rushing water covered over any echo his boots were making on the wooden structure, and the moon sent the tree line shadow onto the water, and that included the bridge. He might be walking because it was too slick to race across it holding her, or perhaps there wasn't another Killoran man posted beyond the mill.

And then they were amid the trees, passing one of the large tents before reaching his. Aidan didn't even slow his steps. He ducked his head and used it as leverage for the door slit, and then he was on his knees on the pallet, leaning forward to lay her atop it and then covering her mouth with his own.

Juliana's arms unlatched from behind his head and

started massaging, molding, and caressing his upper back . . . shoulders . . . arms.

"Ah . . . lass. Lass . . ."

Aidan's murmur accompanied his lips along her jaw to her ear, and that was matched by his hands along her legs, pushing the shift up her thighs. His fingers trailed her skin with the motion . . . to her buttocks.

"I canna' wait another moment, lass. I canna'!"

"Oh . . . Aidan."

Juliana tried to convey her own frustration and need, with the hands she ran all over his chest and belly, before delving beneath his kilt, delineating the massive muscle of his thighs with her fingernails as she trailed them over and over up and down each limb. She was lifted, a hand beneath her buttocks while the other shoved and bunched and pushed the shift out of his way, and all of him began rocking and pulsing and pushing in the primordial rhythm she craved.

"Aidan . . . yea. Oh, Aidan . . . please?"

Juliana tried to wrap a hand about him, before adding the other one, filling her palms with solid, hard, pulsating thickness. Aidan went totally stiff at the first touch. It was her moving, bringing him closer, and shoving her hips down to meet him.

Hard hands grabbed her hips and he rammed in, stopping her cry of ecstasy with his mouth. His kiss deepened, accompanying his movements to pummel into her, denting the mat and her conscience with the glory, expanse, and totality of it. She writhed beneath him, accepting every lunge, every push, every movement, as they got harder and faster and more raw and brutal, grabbing every surge of ecstasy and holding it as long as possible.

Then Aidan was stiffening, pushing into her in little surges that matched the sob vibration running his throat. Juliana pressed a kiss there and experienced his groan with her lips as well as her ears, while he angled up into a full arch of his chest above her, pulsing over and over into her with lunges that raised her hips from the mat. And then it was over.

His collapse this time was onto the pallet beside her, planting his face into it and just lying there twitching and trembling and breathing more heavily than when he'd run with her. The oil bowl he'd left burning showed all of it. In perfect silhouette.

"Aidan?"

He rolled his head toward her, opened his eyes, and met hers. The resultant flash of sensation went all the way through her before rippling to him. The width of her eyes matched his when he'd finished the odd lurch.

He blinked several more times. Licked his lips. Pulled in a huge breath and released it . . . all over her.

"Aye?" he replied finally.

"How can you kidnap me . . . from you?"

His lips went to a slight smile and he rolled his eyes upward, reminiscent of Alpin's posturing. Juliana waited. She was still waiting for her answer when he looked back at her.

"Lass. I—"

"Promised me answers," she interrupted.

He puffed his cheeks out with the next breath. "Aye. That I did."

"Then why? And how?"

"I could na' sleep," he admitted. "This entire night. I've been beset—bothered—nae. Worse. I was plagued. 'Tis torment . . . and never-ending. That's what it is. I need . . . your body. What you give. I had to have it. 'Twas a fierce want."

Each word sent another flash of sensation through her, matching the spurt of her heartbeat.

"So I was rash. Again."

He rolled from her completely, using his head as a fulcrum, and pulling them apart with the move. He ended up on his side, facing her with his head supported atop an upward flung arm. His kilt went to a puddle about his hips and upper thighs, hiding most of him. Juliana wasn't as lucky. Her shift was still in a mass of material bunched up past her waist, forcing her into a curve about the wad of it, while her lower limbs and hips were open to the air and his gaze.

She watched him look to her nakedness and then he looked back at her. "And always," he added.

"Always . . . what?"

"Rash. I am ever rash. And reckless. 'Tis a curse. Look at you."

Juliana looked down at her nakedness, wantonly displayed for him. Then she returned her gaze to his. She didn't change a thing.

"I canna' even wait to unwrap you."

"Actually . . ." She rolled onto her side, facing him and nearly touching. "I think this was my fault."

His one eyebrow rose. Juliana moved a finger to trace it, and then moved her vision back to his. "True?" she asked.

His grin was heart stopping, even if it was followed by a yawn. She already knew it, but the sensation caused a stutter feeling within her that made the finger touching him shake. Juliana slowly moved her touch to his temple and pushed a lock of hair back behind his ear before he'd finished his yawn.

"You're a blessed sight, woman," he informed her and nuzzled his head about her outstretched arm.

"So . . . you've answered the why. But not the how," she informed him.

He blew out a heavy breath, hard enough it caressed her naked loins, and he closed his eyes. "'Tis a powerful potion you wield, lass."

"What?"

"With this frame of yours. Powerful. Draining . . . perfect . . ."

And with that one statement, he canceled her argument. Juliana closed her mouth and forgot the words. It wouldn't

have been easy to get an answer from him anyway, as quickly
and deeply as he went to sleep. She still had a hand touching his ear, and used it to finger and then smooth the hair
strands that had escaped from his queue back against the
mass of it. Then, she was sliding the back of her finger along
his cheek, giggling a bit at the twitch of reaction he gave,
although it didn't wake him.

It wasn't a potion. It wasn't a spell. It was an emotion. She
wondered when he'd discover and realize it.

"So . . . Ewan, what will we do with the woman?"

"'Tis painfully simple, Kerr MacGorrick. The laird will
turn to a *poucah* and wizard her back to the women croft."

"Or . . . leave her wandering about, lost in her grief over
her clan's near demise."

That's an idea. Aidan twisted his lips and considered it.
Aidan could get her to the clearing by the kiln and set her
onto one of the benches he'd had to dodge earlier. She could
have walked in her sleep. Grief sometimes did odd things to
a person. It would be light soon enough, but he hadn't wanted
to move her from the curled-up sleeping goddess position
she'd assumed. Not yet.

"Aye. That's a great plan . . . but does it na' answer the
problem."

"What problem is that, Kerr?"

"You going to make them cease that?" Tavish asked from
Aidan's side.

Aidan looked across their fire at where Kerr and Ewan
were squatting, trading teasing words, before looking back to
the man at his side. "Nae," he replied.

"Why na'?"

"Listen," he replied in a near inaudible tone.

There wasn't much heard for a few moments. Not much

was seen either . . . unless one looked into the fire, trying to decipher its secrets. Or watched the thread of smoke wending its way upward to the hang of mist that was brought into existence by the night air atop water. Aidan smirked slightly.

"The problem is the woman. You should listen without so much dirt a-tween your ears. You'd hear more." Kerr added to it with a shove on Ewan's shoulder.

"Oh. Aye. The woman. 'Tis always a problem, is na' it? Especially for the laird."

"'Tis na' his lone fault."

"Nae?"

"They swarm about him like bees. To a honey pot."

"Aye. A honey pot. Our laird. That's a good one."

Both men guffawed loudly and smacked their knees. Aidan turned his head and sucked in on his cheeks to hide the smile.

"What are we listening for?" Tavish asked.

"My conscience," Aidan replied. He watched Tavish puzzle it for a bit, but had his attention caught again.

"Our laird should na' have taken it into his head to give her a title."

"You think not?" Ewan asked.

"Makes it powerful difficult to bed her."

"I'll be calling you out," Ewan replied quickly. "You even hint at an issue with that. The laird has nae issue with that. Never."

Aidan got his glance toward them intercepted.

"You see there, Kerr? The laird heard that. I will na' have to give your sorry arse a whipping. He won't leave enough for me."

"And if you'd listen instead of jawing, you'd hear it right. I would never cast aspersions on that. The MacKetryck laird is known far and wide for his manhood."

Aidan cleared his throat. Loudly.

"Then explain. 'Tis clear we all want to ken what you're saying. Don't we, lads?" Ewan gestured widely to the encampment.

Aidan ignored them. Tavish didn't.

"Doona' look to me," he said. "I have better things to do than decide the whys and whens of my laird's wishes."

"You weren't behind the slab of wood?" Kerr asked.

"What slab?" Tavish asked.

"The one placed beside that Killoran clansman. To make him think a log fell on him and knocked a bump into his head that had him dreaming of large-bosomed lasses . . . instead of one of my laird's skeans."

"That was a good shot, wasn't it, Ewan?"

Both men took turns shoving each other's shoulder on their side of the fire.

"Aye. That it was. 'Tis a pure pleasure serving Aidan Niall. Pure pleasure."

"Which does bring me back to the woman, Ewan," Kerr said.

"You and that subject. I vow, Kerr—"

"The woman is a problem, Ewan. Now, more than ever. Just look at this eve."

"What of this eve?"

"He granted her the title of lady."

"What of it? The lass acts and behaves just like one. You've already noted it. Doona' take it back now."

Kerr sighed heavily. "It's na' that. She is a *lady.*"

Ewan shrugged. "So?" he asked.

"You're dense, Ewan lad. One weds a lady a-fore bedding her. Unless they wish problems with her clan. Hmm. That could be the plan. If there are any MacDonals about the face of the earth still to insult. God rest their souls."

"I am not dense," Ewan replied to all of that.

"Then use your head for something aside of hanging your hair on! Think, man!"

"Why do you ken he kidnapped her? Practice? Jesu'! You need to do something with all that hot breath you fill the world with, Kerr."

"'Twas rather well done, too . . . wasn't it?" Kerr added.

"Aye . . . that it was."

Both men nodded and grinned. Aidan watched them at it.

"You ken the problem yet?"

Ewan had lines across his forehead now. They probably matched Aidan's. Kerr made a sound of frustration.

"Castle Ketryck is na' filled with Killoran's slack men. 'Tis teeming with menfolk. Women, too. Every nook. Every hall."

"So?" Ewan replied.

"We're going to need eyes in the backs of our heads, extra ears, and the luck of the saints. Think, man! Ponder it out."

"Why?"

"Because . . . someone should have pondered it afore the doing of it. That's what I'm saying."

"Pondered what?" Ewan asked

"Tagging the woman a lady! Would you think, man? If she was another of his women, none would care! But . . . taking a lady? That'd be an insult."

Aidan stiffened noticeably.

"Oh," Ewan replied.

Oh? Aidan could think of a lot more words, curses most of them.

"Tagging the woman a lady was reckless. A man doing that dinna' think afore he acted. He should've. Then there'd be nae problem at all."

There was a general moment that could have been Ewan sucking in breath at Kerr's daring. It would match Tavish's reaction at Aidan's side. Aidan didn't react. He listened to his blood pounding through his ears, modulated his breathing, and then cocked his head to one side. Kerr was right. And Aidan had done it to himself.

"You should spend time pondering the whys of your wenches, Kerr MacGorrick. And the lack of them."

"I had offers," Kerr replied in a mock defensive tone. Ewan hooted.

"You had womenfolk running from you last eve. That's what you had."

"You'll pay for that, whelp!"

A bit of good-natured slugging happened across the fire.

"I ken what you meant," Tavish said from Aidan's side. "About the conscience."

"How's Arran?" Aidan asked instead.

"Sleeping. With his arms about a smallish keg."

"Smallish?"

"Aye. Mostly water as well." Tavish smiled widely.

Aidan returned the gesture, and ignored the two men, who were now wrestling, from the other side of the fire. "How did he take it?" he asked.

"He drank me under the table, he did."

"Under the table?"

"More akin to . . . under a pallet. Which is where he's sleeping. And aye. I matched him tankard for tankard . . . even as they became nothing more than water. I let him win."

"You did, eh?"

"Aye. Why . . . right now, I'm prostrate and stewed to my gills. I may na' be able to sit my horse on the morrow. This is how stewed I am."

Aidan grinned.

"I may never live this down. You ken? Your bairn brother has a large mouth."

Aidan snorted the amusement. And then had his attention gripped by the duo on the other side of the fire. Talking loudly. Both men looked a bit disheveled, but with their arms about each other's shoulders and a tankard in the free hands.

"We should do more than ponder the doings of the laird, Kerr."

"True," the other man agreed.

"He's laird. He can do what he wishes."

"Can he get out of the Campbell betrothal?" Kerr asked.

"Campbell . . . betrothal?"

"You dinna' hear? Our laird sent off a missive more than three sennights past. Requesting the Campbell heiress's hand in wedlock. Without pondering that one much either."

Kerr was wrong on that account. It had been at the back of Aidan's mind since Dugald MacKetryck had proposed it over a season ago. Aidan just hadn't acted until right before leaving to reave against the MacDonal clan's new holdings.

"Go on with you, Kerr MacGorrick! The lass is but a child."

"She will na' always be so. And once she reaches her woman-time and can be wed, our laird wants her hand. And the land and treasury that comes with it, of course."

"Maybe the Campbells will na' accept," Ewan replied hopefully.

"It's the laird of MacKetryck clan, Ewan," Kerr replied.

"Oh. Aye."

The sinking feeling in Aidan's belly was overridden by the tight band circling his heart in his chest. He didn't know he had the capacity for feeling each heartbeat with a painful thud.

"Which does bring me all the way back round to the problem of this particular woman, Ewan Blaine. Does na' it?" Kerr asked, each word distinct and clear.

Aidan looked across at both of them, ignored the spurt still happening in his chest, and smiled slightly. "I still have na' located my sporran, lads. I'm thinking a team of two might have a much better chance at finding it."

"Right."

Ewan was the first on his feet. Kerr put his tankard down first.

"We've a *faile breacan* to prepare, doona' we, Ewan?" Kerr asked.

"Oh. Aye. For the laird. He canna' arrive in less than the best."

"You ken that, do you? Perhaps you should ken other things a lot quicker as well. Then I would na' have to keep jawing until we reach trouble."

"Trouble follows you everywhere, Kerr MacGorrick."

They were still trading insults when they faded from the light.

"Aidan?"

Aidan raised his hand for Tavish's silence. Then he stood and very carefully smoothed his kilt band across his chest, checked for his skeans, and stomped a bit to bring feeling back to his feet.

"I could see the woman back for you," Tavish offered.

"She's mine," Aidan replied.

"Oh. Aye," Tavish replied. "I'll go back to being drunk and prostrate, then."

Chapter 16

Arran hadn't been telling faery tales.

Juliana had gotten glimpses of gray rock between the low-hanging mists throughout the morn. The match of sky to castle was so close, it didn't look entirely real. Perhaps if the day had been filled with sun and blue sky, or anything other than overcast and wet, she'd have experienced the awe sooner. But by midday, there was no stopping the jaw-dropping effect every time a cloud parted enough to frame what her eyes wanted to deny but couldn't. Castle Ketryck kept growing and spreading until it looked to span the horizon, leaving little delineation between rock and castle and water and sky.

The entourage about them had grown apace with the castle's size, beginning with a lad from a nearly hidden croft. After that, the crowd just kept growing, as clansman after clansman walked from fields or trees and around buildings until the width and depth and noise about her threatened to overwhelm any individual thought. A lone piper joined them at the beginning of a field of heather that stretched from either side as far as the eye could see. He was soon joined by more of them. Juliana hadn't much experience of it, but she decided MacKetryck pipers were probably known for their melodic tone and volume as the sound swelled to join all the others about her.

Juliana heard calls and greetings being flung about the men behind her, as well as questions and some heartrending cries of names that had only been shadows before. She recognized a few: Iain. Filib. Rory. Her thigh muscles twitched from atop the dead Rory's horse as that name got called out with a question and answered with silence.

Aidan didn't turn his head, or move from the grim stance he'd assumed that morn when she'd first seen him. He was nothing like the wild, intense man who'd kidnapped her, and sent her into the heaven of pleasure just last night. Juliana ducked her head for a moment, to gather that thought before it showed on her face, then turned again to watch Aidan's stiff back, one horse in front of hers.

He was fully arrayed in what Arran told her was the MacKetryck black and red chieftain plaid. Aidan had his hair neatly combed and tied back, making a queue that reached midback, where it grazed the plaid band atop his sleeveless shirt. That garment had come from his trunk. She already knew how well the woven flax skimmed the skin. It had been large on her, hiding the fact that they'd been sewn exactly to his proportions, or maybe when he'd been a tad bit smaller, since the seams looked near to splitting every time he moved. He'd put on carved silver armbands, one on each upper arm. He had a long claymore with an elaborate jeweled hilt strapped to his right side, where it hung perpendicular to the horse's side.

He looked like a laird capable of controlling and commanding a clan the size of the MacKetryck one. He projected power. Leadership. Authority. The kind of man one looked up to. She could understand Arran's hero worship.

Easily. If this presentation was the reason they'd stopped at the Killoran compound, it was effective.

The clouds decided to part just then, putting a ray of sunshine directly atop Aidan, lighting him, making him sparkle, and sending evil-looking glints from the claymore's unsheathed blade with every move of his stallion. The sight stopped every bit of the crowd noise with the awe. Juliana had to admit it was breathtaking, because it took hers away. And then, the light spread farther, putting not only light but warmth atop her head as well as those farther down the line.

All about her she heard the reaction, with words of omens and signs, said with a dialect and thick speech that made it difficult to understand. Juliana kept her head dipped slightly and her smile hidden. The entire lot of them sounded superstitious. And foolish. It wasn't a sign of anything more than the rain might be breaking.

The clouds lightened more the closer they got to Castle Ketryck, making it impossible to avoid the structure and what it stood for. Power. Might. Strength. Rule. Arran hadn't told her enough . . . or he needed better words. The castle was stout, massive, impregnable, and invincible. Juliana felt a knot of apprehension settle at the base of her spine, worrying her with every roll of her horse.

Before they reached the river-sized moat at the base of the wall, and the large swath of ledge meant to support a drawbridge, she turned her head surreptitiously from the right to the left and back again, eyeing and evaluating that mass of rock barbican, and trying to find a way to ignore the lump of worry at the same time. The curtain wall looked longer than seven hundred steps, and it appeared that Arran had misrepresented the thickness of it as well. It easily looked more than three times Aidan's height. The wall was crenellated all about the walkway at the top of the five stories of wall, and each merlon opening had a clansman at it. Some of them appeared to have more than one. The gatehouse surpassed all of it. Juliana had to guess at a width of rock that would accommodate a group as large as the one standing at the center of the gatehouse wall, looking eight to ten heads deep.

There were also drummers somewhere inside that structure, for a thrumming of noise was accompanying pipers from inside to join the sound outside, making a swell of sound that was impossible to ignore, in the event anyone missed the laird of Clan MacKetryck's arrival.

It was better to watch Aidan.

Juliana dropped her eyes from the massive fortress facing her to the man claiming lordship over all of it. And felt humble and small and insignificant and dowdy . . . especially in the used, cast-off shift and with her hair in an unkempt braid she wouldn't have washed in that tub last night even if they'd begged her to. It was just as well that the braid was tucked beneath the plaid they'd given her to wear, while she sat on the end of it. Juliana had never felt so alone. Isolated. Desolate. Despondent.

What was the love of a lone woman to the man who commanded this? Especially a woman he'd tagged a lady from the MacDonal clan? He'd given her respectability with such a title . . . but the cost was more than she could absorb. She had no choice but to shove it away. Ignore it. Until later . . . much later when she was ensconced in a room in this keep. All by herself. Alone. Bereft. Cut off from any of them. She guessed a lady of the MacDonal clan wouldn't be allowed near unaccompanied males. She might never get near him again once inside this monstrosity.

The knot of emotion spread, going to a stone in her belly and pounding a reminder with every beat of her heart. She had to look aside and away from Aidan and swallow ceaselessly while her hands went to fists on the horse's mane. She was afraid . . . so afraid, especially of the sensation reaching her heart.

And she'd been wrong. It was better to look at his castle.

Juliana moved her vision from their laird and tipped her head back to fully see Castle Ketryck as an Englishman might . . . who'd just come to besiege it. She smirked, but it was a shaky expression. King Edward hadn't come this far north, or he'd have brought more men.

The gatehouse looked closer to seven stories in height. Juliana would never believe Arran's descriptions again. Since it was early afternoon and the sun was partial with its light, there wasn't a sign of shadow being thrown by the gatehouse. There was a huge sound of grinding and creaking and whining and a trembling sound coming from the mass of rock, which must have heralded a drawbridge getting lowered . . . a large drawbridge, capable of spanning a moat this size. Juliana eyed it again. The moat was a large span of water, glistening with a blue-green color when the sun speckled it, showing the depth of it as well. It must have been fed from the loch behind Castle Ketryck.

Her father, Giles D'Aubenville, had been a wealthy English baron, but he'd never seen anything like this. Castle Ketryck looked to match or exceed anything the king had built in Wales, too, but Juliana had only rumor and drawings for those. Here she was faced with solid stone.

They lowered the drawbridge in chunks of space at Aidan's approach. He was in place, patiently waiting on the rock ledge of this side when the bridge slammed the final span of space to the ground. Juliana covered her mouth and nose at the air that puffed up from the ground at the impact. Aidan's horse reared back, but he had it controlled instantly and completely, and perfectly. Then he was leading them onto a span of wood that echoed and thumped with each hoof being marched across it, Juliana's mount included.

She'd been right. The width of stone was more than three of Aidan. It was a solid matching of blocks that fitted without leaving enough space between the stones for a sword blade. Her shoulders drooped slightly and she moved one hand to put it atop the sensation at the pit of her belly before they'd cleared the dark tunnel beneath the gatehouse and appeared on the other side.

Aidan didn't stop. He proceeded across a span of grass that looked to house an entire village of structures as well as the populace of one, and then he neared another curtain wall, this one without a gatehouse. Arran hadn't said a word about baileys, nor how many Castle Ketryck had. Not a word. Juliana nearly twisted around to give him a glare that would leave no misunderstanding over how much his lack had affected her, but settled with frowning at the hand she had wrapped about horse hair.

This wall had another archway they passed beneath. It didn't look to be three of Aidan either, although it was a closer match to that description. It was crafted from the same gray rock. It was as if the builders had leveled a mountain and then used the rock to construct another mountain of castle in its place. But that was impossible. Unbelievable. It would have taken an army of men and centuries of time. But what did she know of it anyway? Juliana knew life only as the protected and pampered daughter of an English baron. What Juliana experienced now was fit for a king.

They reached the inner bailey. This one had another courtyard of sod, peopled with more clan. Aidan's progress was slowing as they neared a stone building that appeared to interconnect with more of them before joining another wall. It might have been the outer curtain wall, overlooking the loch . . . or it might have led to yet another bailey. Juliana couldn't tell, and she wasn't asking.

If this was a keep, it was impressive as well. It looked four stories in height, although the two structures abutting it were taller. There were towers at the far ends, with the same battlement running all about the top, although it dropped at the keep rooftop before slanting back up for either taller building. Crenellations were only allowed for a king or with the permission of a king. Juliana was beginning to think Highland lairds might be in the same category as kings . . . or fancied themselves as such.

Having crenellation on a building this far inside its walls seemed overstated and boastful and of little use. It was useful only in the event a rival clan managed the impossible and broke through both walls. Juliana narrowed her eyes in thought. She decided these three buildings must have been part of the original structure, constructed centuries earlier by the Vikings. That could explain the defensive fixtures.

Aidan stopped and raised his hand, halting the line. The sounds of drums and pipes ceased as well as the crowd noise. A shiver went along Juliana's arms and across her back at how eerie and odd it seemed. None of the sun percolated into the area they'd stopped in. It would need to be late morning for that to happen, she surmised.

Aidan dismounted and everyone watched as he patted his horse and gave the rein to a squire. Then he turned about and walked the one horse length back to her and stopped. Just . . . stopped.

"Come, Juliana."

He held both hands out for her, as if he knew the correct way to assist a lady in dismounting. Swallowing every bit of unease, Juliana complied. It was a mistake. The moment they touched, her palms sparked, and she jerked them back.

Juliana's eyes flew to his before dropping. The lump shifted and she tightened her belly on it, trembled in place, and there was nothing she could do. No one she could turn to. No way to run. No place to hide. No one she could trust.

She had too many secrets. Love for him was just one of them. And if she had to fail at hiding it, why did it have to be in front of God, and Aidan, and the amount of MacKetryck clan gathered all about her in a hushed silence that made everything so much worse?

"You will na' appreciate it if I pull you off the horse, Juliana."

He hadn't moved. Not a muscle. She had to do it. Or . . . try. Juliana commanded her own hands to reconnect to where he was standing and starting to look annoyed. The hands she held out shook visibly. She didn't know what expression might be on his face. She didn't dare look.

Aidan MacKetryck had been trained in the art of romance and chivalry after all. Not only did he know how to assist her, but he was well versed in supporting her weight as she slipped to the ground, and once there, on how to provide an escort. He released her to stand on legs that wobbled beneath her shift where no one else knew anything of it, but he didn't allow her to stay that way. He had his shoulder tipped down just slightly and his arm crooked and held out for her to hold on to. And he just stood there, with one eyebrow raised quizzically while a slight smile played about on his lips.

"Welcome to Castle Ketryck," he said, and gestured with his head to the mass of stone all about them.

She opened her mouth to say something amusing and biting at the same time, and had to close it again as nothing came out.

"What? You thought I'd ride through a broken door? With you across my shoulders? Screaming and kicking?"

Unbidden tears pricked at her eyes, blurring the ground beneath her since her gaze flew there. Juliana cursed the fates and a deaf God for making her face this, and having it happen now, when everyone and their mother could tell his captive hadn't had the sense to keep from falling in love with him. Just like any number of other women before her.

Aidan's men had also dismounted, although there wasn't much noise to accompany the act. She could sense their presence all about and behind her, settling in as though to create a shield about her and Aidan. Guarding. Protecting. It was a ridiculous notion.

"Juliana?" Aidan whispered from somewhere above her.

Juliana nodded slightly, not enough to upset the tears hovering at her lashes, but enough he'd know she heard.

"You need to place your hand atop my arm. For an escort. You ken?"

He was counseling her on etiquette. Juliana would've laughed, except it might break through everything and she'd end up sobbing. Or throwing her body against him, which would have been immeasurably worse. She settled on another nod.

She put her hand out without looking. She couldn't control how it shook visibly, or how cold it was. The next moment, he had her hand in his and guided it to his arm, forcing her to accept a contact that tingled more, heated worse, and reverberated with an emotion difficult to contain. It was too beautiful. Tears slipped onto her cheeks and she licked at them before they reached her chin.

"Doona' fret so, Juliana. I've claimed you. You're safe."

He thought her frightened? The instant reaction cleared her nose, making a sound that was loud, uncouth, and crude. The only good thing was that it didn't sound like a sob. Aidan turned from her, placing her at his right side for the escort, and acted like he hadn't heard it as he started walking. The movement pulled her with it, whether she wanted to go or not. Juliana walked slowly through a narrow corridor of bodies she could sense, since she wasn't chancing a glance at anything. Not until she had this weakness under control and covered over and hidden. Juliana could think of more august ways to enter the MacKetryck chieftain's lair than walking at his side, sniffing back tears, while swathed in a plaid that was still rain damp and beneath that a shift that needed washing, but she didn't have another choice.

Aidan moved suddenly, putting his free hand atop hers to pull her close and move slightly in front of her, bringing them to a halt in the same moment. Such a position made a barrier of his body, shielding her. It felt protective. It probably looked it. Juliana caught a breath and held it, ignored the skip of a heartbeat, as she waited for what further torment he could possibly devise. Then she saw them. Fancy, embroidered, pointed-toed slippers were in front of them, blocking the way, and if those slippers belonged to a woman, she had the biggest feet of any female Juliana had ever seen.

"My laird," a melodic masculine voice said.

"Lachlan," Aidan replied from beside her.

Juliana stole a glance at the slip of a fellow and then back to the ground. The man standing there didn't look like he could stop much, especially Aidan. He looked small and frail in comparison to Aidan, as if the slightest whisk of Aidan's hand would send the man flying. His attire didn't help with the impression. His cassock was of heavily embroidered satin in a dark blue shade. It made his skin sallow and gaunt. He'd had his head bowed, but it wasn't deferential to Juliana's practiced eye.

"Your presence is required." He hissed the words at Aidan.

"I'll see him at the return feast," Aidan replied.

"Return feast?"

"Aye."

"We'd nae warning."

"Now you do. Go, Lachlan. I've returned. I require a feast. Order it. And order the Lady Reina to report to my chambers."

"My laird!"

"What?"

"But . . . your chambers?"

"You hear well," Aidan replied. "As always."

"'Tis most . . . unwise, my laird."

Aidan grunted. "She's na' attending me, Lachlan, but Juliana."

Oh . . . dearest God!

He'd clarified her position in his household, sent lightning flashing through her body with the surge of her heart, and released the weight that was cursing her belly. And he'd done it with one sentence. Juliana was quivering at the mix of emotions. Elation. Horror. Giddiness. Fear. Shock.

"Juliana?"

Aidan swiveled without warning, pulling her in front of him and right beneath the gaunt fellow's nose. She did a perfect half bow for him, which would have been deeper and more respectful if he'd deserved it, and watched the cloak scrape the dirt beneath them. She should have been prepared for the man's insulting tone, if not his words.

"You wish Lady Reina to attend—"

"My orders are na' questioned, Lachlan. Recollect that. Apprise my uncle, too. Or he can wait until my banquet and hear of it."

Aidan shoved past the man and within moments they'd reached three lengthy stone ledges that served as entry steps. The Lachlan fellow had trailed behind Aidan, or he was on his other side. Juliana didn't check. She had enough to handle stifling and hiding the stunned feeling while still touching and experiencing Aidan. She hadn't known love was such a potent thing. And if this Lachlan fellow guessed at it, Juliana wasn't sure what he'd do about it, or with it.

Or why that frightened her.

They'd constructed the steps for giants. Or for standing atop while issuing edicts and commands. Or to keep visitors from riding into the hall without dismounting from their horses first. Juliana stopped at the base of the step ledges beside Aidan and considered immaterial things that spared her from pondering the real ones.

Clan MacKetryck may not seem barbaric, but these steps showed different. Juliana could see improvement would be needed here. No lady should be forced to make a climb in order to walk steps. It couldn't be accomplished with modesty and grace, especially if holding a gown at the same time. They'd also need an assist from a strong male such as Aidan MacKetryck at their side. Or use their hands on the steps.

Juliana negotiated the steps without too much difficulty, although Lachlan looked for it. She had Aidan to thank. He tightened the arm she pulled at to climb the first step, lifting her at the same time. And then he repeated it. All she had to do was hold on while he lifted. All about her, Aidan's men flanked her, ready to step in if needed. She knew Lachlan noted it as well. Her fingers were tingling when they arrived, and her back had an icy sensation crawling along it to center at the base of her neck.

She'd been raised in such an environment. She recognized intrigue and power struggles, as well as spies with vindictive tendencies. It appeared Aidan had enemies in his castle. Juliana didn't know who, or why, or how many, but she had no doubt she would.

They'd stopped and were standing in a great hall lit only by a banked fire at one end and a smattering of torches about the walls. It took a moment to accustom her eyes to the lack of light, making it possible to pick out long tables, benches, and screens, arranged about the massive space without much symmetry.

"Your uncle will be displeased. He has an answer from Campbell clan!" Lachlan hissed the words.

Aidan stiffened beside her, and a moment later had the reflex covered over. If she hadn't been attached to him, she wouldn't have felt it. "You have your orders, Lachlan," Aidan replied.

Juliana recognized the metal behind his voice. Lachlan must not have been as sure, for he argued it. Again.

"But your uncle—"

"Uncle Dugald can meet me now if he likes. On the list. Go. Speak of that to him. But until such time . . . I'm laird. By birthright and victory . . . and you have your orders."

Aidan was moving across the room before he'd finished speaking, pulling her toward where a change in available daylight showed a hallway to be. The scraping of boots and clanking of weaponry established that his men were accompanying them as well.

"As you wish, my . . . *laird*."

It was softly spoken and the last was a slur. They all heard it. Juliana could tell by how the body of men tensed as if holding a collective indrawn breath. Then, it dissipated and they went back to following Aidan. He hadn't reacted visibly. Apparently, he was used to pretending a complacency that the taut condition of his arm didn't match. Juliana's quick glance showed the fisted hand before he opened and twisted it, making the sinew beneath her hand roll and vibrate. That was too much sensation beneath her finger pads. Her knees wavered and her breath caught, which was too much to show when surrounded by so many. She had no choice but to terminate the contact. Immediately.

Aidan reached out and across his chest with his other arm and had her held in place before she'd finished the thought. He did it without looking and without breaking stride, sending a jittery weakness throughout her legs she had no choice but to endure. She only hoped her legs supported her for the climb. His pace slowed, making it a bit easier. The slight incline of the stone steps, worn a bit in the middle, was also helpful as they spiraled up the dimly lit tower they'd entered.

She was still reeling from what he'd done, and tempering the absolute rush of emotion with the realization of what had just happened to her. She had an unspoken status now . . . as the woman settled into his chamber. If they were in an English household, she would. She would be in a status just below that of wife. The Lady Juliana D'Aubenville was now a Highland laird's mistress.

Chapter 17

The chieftain chambers opened off a landing of the stairs, directly above the great hall. It appeared to be bisected by a floor-to-ceiling partition of wood. The area gave the same impression of dim, dark, and massive space as the great hall below. The effect was not as severe, however, owing to a light source from somewhere behind the wooden wall outlining width and height, and because of the dimness of their tower stairwell. The darkness wasn't a poor design. The stairwell had sconces positioned in the outer wall for torches, but none were lit at present, making the slits at the very top of the stairwell tower the primary light source, and forcing her to hold to Aidan tightly since he wasn't unsure of any step.

Juliana waited for her eyes to adjust before she could make out the arrangement and furnishings in the room, but he had control of their progress and was already near the center of the room and swiveling to face his men before that happened.

There were a lot more clansmen at their heels than the nine he'd had with him, Juliana noted, looking back to the floor.

"You heard?" Aidan asked.

"Aye." Someone spoke and more chorused it.

"Then go. Prepare. Arran and Alpin. Follow me."

Aidan swung about again, and took her with him to the wooden wall that contained a door and several empty niches. Juliana pondered that for a moment before he pulled the door handle down and shoved the structure open, and walked in, keeping her with him for every step.

"Lads, the shutters."

Both brothers were at the far end of the room, pulling open shutter after shutter along the far wall. After the first one, Juliana could see the inverted V shape had been carved and thinned, so the windows were linked closer than the original thirty-foot depth of wall granted them. The result was a series of narrow windows, spaced closely together, gaining a view encompassing Buchyn Loch, a bit of dark land that was the opposite shore, and past that nothing but open sea.

The sky had cleared more, for sun sent the shadow of Castle Ketryck's battlements out to skip along the low-hanging wisps of clouds. Juliana's eyes followed the jagged outline of castle projected onto mist that was stained with the most unearthly glow as it reflected the multihued shimmer from the water beneath.

"Oh . . . Aidan."

It was as if he'd planned for her to see this, and at the most perfect moment. Juliana's eyes were wide, and the same thing happened to her lips as her mouth dropped open. Her heart was hammering until it felt like a caged thing, shoving at her chest wall with every bit of how the experience touched her, spoke to her . . . entangled her even more with him.

Aidan cleared his throat beside her. "Arran? You're to fetch whatever the Lady Reina requires."

He released the hold atop Juliana's left hand as he spoke, but she barely felt it. She was rooted to the spot in awe. And then she felt him pulling her hand off his arm before he turned away, although he didn't move.

"Alpin? You're to make certain she stays here. Guard the outer chamber. Nobody leaves. Nobody but Lady Reina enters. You ken?"

He was somehow in the space right in front of her, although she hadn't seen him move. He'd also tipped his head down and toward her, putting him so close his breath meshed with hers. Juliana was gripped by his gaze. He sighed out a huge breath, sending air all over her nose and lips.

"And now . . . I must go."

She opened her mouth to say something, but didn't know what it would be. She should thank him. Something stopped her. Pride. Juliana stood to her full height, which was just below his chin, and faced him.

"You're safe now, Juliana. With me." He swiveled from her and gestured for his brother. "Alpin . . . now!"

The last was clipped and rapid and angered. He was at the door in four steps, Alpin at his heels. Juliana watched him pull it open and then shut it behind him with a slam.

"You've brought a lady with you."

Aidan lowered his chin and blinked, trying to bring into focus the elderly woman who was perched atop a stuffed stool engrossed in her sewing. Myriad tall vases of odd-smelling oils sat on shelves and tables in her tower. And then she'd lit the wicks within them, putting a haze of smoke into the room that was being caressed and then grafted by what daylight came through her window. He didn't know how she could see to sew.

"Have I?" he asked.

She smiled at her project. Murky sunlight washed her lined face, giving her a beatific and innocent aura and hiding the vituperative, malevolent, and evil woman.

"You knew it the moment you landed atop her."

Aidan shrugged. "Which time?" he asked.

Dame Lileth Fallaine-Dumphat chuckled, bringing the lines into even more definition. She bent back to her sewing, putting two more nearly invisible stitches into the cloth, with thread that had the same issue. She might as well have been sewing with air between her needle and the fabric, Aidan decided.

"Every time . . . sweet laird. All of them. You knew her innocence. And you still took it."

He grunted an answer.

"And now you come to me."

"Aye."

"It's . . . too late. Almost."

He rolled his head atop his shoulders, listening for the cracking of bone, and then looked back at her. "Well . . . 'tis your fault. All of it."

She laughed again at that. She lifted her bit of material and perused it while she spoke. "Your da had the same idea. He erred. I doona' control the fates. I only read them."

"Then . . . read them." He took a step farther into the room and looked about before trying to pierce the haze, which appeared to have thickened. This tower was granted to her by his grace, and taken away by the same. He watched as she assimilated the threat and then nodded.

"Rash. Reckless." She shook her head and made a clicking noise with her tongue. "But there is also courageous. Victorious. Exactly as I foretold. Your da was a fool to argue it."

Aidan pulled in a large breath and nodded. "So. Assist me."

She stood with the heft of old age dogging her bones, and wadded the material into a roll on her arm. Aidan tried to pierce the smoke at her movements. She pushed at her material, shoving it onto itself again and again, over her lower arm, and from there to her hand, while it packed tighter and tighter and got smaller and more compact, until when she'd finished, there was a tear-drop-shaped thing that fit in the palm of her hand. Aidan watched it and still didn't believe it.

"When did you decide to make her your woman?" she asked.

"I dinna'," he replied.

"She is in your chambers . . . as we speak."

"Oh. I dinna' decide that," he clarified. "'Twas an impulse."

"And when did this impulse happen?"

"The moment Lachlan stopped me."

She nodded. Lifted her piece and twirled it in front of her face, back and forth, while what sunlight there was picking out facets on the thing. Aidan shut his eyes and shook his head; reopened them. It looked jewel-like, and that wasn't possible, either.

"Lachlan . . . MacGorrick. That one is a mistake of nature."

"Aye. Kerr's father's cousin. That would be the Lachlan I speak of," Aidan replied.

"You did it to keep her . . . safe?"

"I canna' keep her from the Black MacKetryck's machinations if I doona' ken where she is."

"And . . . in your bed is the safest place?"

Aidan tilted his head to one side, sucked in on his cheeks, and still couldn't prevent the flush. He knew it was happening even without the slight reddish tint starting to color the smoke hovering in the room. She didn't see it since she'd decided to go to her fire, and poke a full blaze into existence from just a few embers, but he knew she was aware of his reaction. It was in the chuckling she kept doing.

"So . . . now the grand MacKetryck laird needs a charm from me?"

"More than one," he admitted, blinking the red haze into a pinkish washed one.

"Lady Reina would have sufficed for that. Yet . . . you seek me. Despite your fear."

"What fear?" he asked, lowering his voice and chin farther.

Dame Lileth Fallaine-Dumphat spun up from the fireplace and tossed something at him. Aidan twirled to one side, listening to the rain of blades hitting the floor from the skeans she'd tossed. And then popping with a distinctive sharp sound, making nothing more than black spots where he'd been standing.

"Rash. Reckless. And quick. I forgot to add that one," she informed him before nodding. He watched her go back to her fire.

"You should have been put to the stake and burned," Aidan said, watching her as close as possible through the red fog coloring his vision, getting deeper and then fading along with each beat of his heart. Red. Pink. Red.

"You'd be the third MacKetryck to try such. And all that happened is . . . the Lady Reina got disfigured. Scarred."

"And that because I halted it and saved you. Both of you. Me. Aidan MacKetryck."

She stood, pondered her fire for a moment, and then looked over her shoulder at him. Aidan tightened everything, preparatory to evading whatever she tossed again. Instead, she smiled.

"So . . . what do you ask of me, Aidan MacKetryck?"

"I need a charm. Of vast potency."

"Vast?"

"To turn back time."

She shook her head. "You think me a sorceress?"

"You doona' wish to ken what I think you," Aidan replied. "I would not ask it, if I were you."

She turned fully to him to stare from across the span of room. The fire leapt higher behind her, silhouetting her smoke-blurred, thin, frail form. With the red coloring everything, it was macabre and sinister. Aidan locked his teeth and returned her look exactly as given. She finally sighed.

"Sweet laird . . . it might be something if you . . . had the ring?"

"The ring?" He shouldn't be surprised. He still was.

"The one with entwined serpents. Tucked into your sporran. That ring."

Only three men knew of it. And none of them would betray him. Aidan put his hands on hips, attempting a relaxed, indifferent pose, but knew it was to stop the trembling. Dame Lileth Fallaine-Dumphat had always frightened him. Very few of his clansmen would be in the same room with her. And never alone.

"I doona' have it any longer," he informed her.

She shook her head. "Pity."

"What else would work?"

She ignored him for a moment and turned back to her fireplace and the small kettle that was now hanging from a hook in it. He narrowed his eyes on a smoke that was starting to itch and burn his eyes and watched her toss the strange prism she'd created from her material into the kettle. Then she put in one drop of liquid from another tall container. She stirred her kettle slightly to a clanking sound of metal on metal.

"'Tis a verra powerful thing . . . to turn back time, Aidan Niall MacKetryck. It also begs the question of why. What perchance would you change . . . had I the ability to do it for you?"

"What else would work?" he repeated.

"Would you wish to keep from meeting with her? Aidan Niall." She was clicking her tongue again, fussing over her fire, shaking her head and speaking more to the flames than to him. "Fate canna' be changed so easily. She'd have crossed your path again. With even worse happenings."

"Fate?" he asked, raising one brow.

"Or perhaps you need a potion to stop her potency to you?

Is this what you came to Dame Lileth Fallaine-Dumphat for, sweet laird?"

He opened his mouth. Shut it.

"There is nothing against a love such as you both have. You ken?"

You both. His ears heard it, but his heart was already hitting at him over it, putting a red wash to the haze in full, hued shades, coloring everything about the scene.

"So . . . what else can I do for you, Aidan Niall?"

He shook his head slightly, blinked, and cleared his throat. "Since you canna' do what I need, I ask a charm. A potent one."

"I will na' stop the bairn you've planted in her belly. If this is what you wish . . . I warn you. The male child she carries is the start of your legacy. I will na' destroy it. You ken?"

His legs wobbled. His ears started ringing, and everything else on him was twitching. Jumping. Giddy with it. Giving him such a huge rush of sensation, he was weak and dizzy with it. Red colored everything and everywhere he looked. Aidan locked every muscle he owned and broke into huge heavy gulps for breath as if he'd just come in from a battle on the list. He heard her cackling in the background as an oddly resonant sound. He broke into a full sweat before he had the urge to faint finally conquered and buried again. His limbs were sore with it. His heart was a huge heavy pounding force with it.

The bairn.

"'Tis a pure shame . . . you requested a betrothal with the Campbell heiress. You should have seen me afore sending the note."

"Can—" Aidan had to stop and clear his throat. It sounded like he'd stuffed a hunk of dried bread in his mouth and was choking on it. She found that even more amusing. He couldn't see her clearly, but he had no trouble hearing her laughter.

"Can I alter that? Is this what you ask?" she asked, once she'd ceased the hilarity and gone back to stirring and clanking the object in her pot.

He nodded.

"The Campbell clan is a verra large clan, Aidan Niall. Strong. Rich."

He nodded again.

"Even more bloodthirsty than MacKetryck clan. With more warriors. More weaponry."

His head was pounding in rhythm with the red, sending a bloodred hue through him and onto the fog that was billowing about the room . . . before fading back to a light wash. He blinked, but it just kept coming, filling his vision, heating his blood. Dark red. Light wash. Dark red. Light wash. Blood-hued . . .

"Is that a . . . nae?" he asked finally.

"Make certain the child is a MacKetryck, Aidan Niall. Legal and binding. Doona' let it be born a bastard."

He sucked in a huge breath, held it until it burned his chest, matching the dark red all about him. Then he exhaled. "I risk war with the Campbell clan then."

Her answer was slow and distinct and said with a hint of laughter. "But Aidan Niall MacKetryck . . . you listen, but you doona' hear. You have . . . two brothers."

And that was when red washed over everything.

Aidan pulled his sword with his right hand and backed against the wall as a huge swell of red flared right out of the fireplace, filling a fog that was near impenetrable, and then it approached him.

Dame Lileth Fallaine-Dumphat was laughing hard. The sound reeked of ill-will and triumph. Aidan blinked the moisture from his eyes and it just kept coming. Aidan Niall didn't cry. Tears were for the fainthearted, the weak, and for women. They weren't for him. He shoved his left arm across his eyes and the blur hampering his sight and swung his sword out with his right arm, creating havoc and hitting less.

The floor moved, rolling beneath him and sending him to his knees. Aidan rolled and was immediately back on his feet, hitting again at the thick shape in the fog she'd summoned. And moisture just kept blinding him, making it even harder to fight and conquer.

"And it's all your own doing, Aidan Niall . . . yours."

The moan of voice hampered him, weighing his arms with a sow's bulk and his legs with anchor chains. Still, his body cursed him with sobs. Aidan shoved his arm across his eyes again, reacting blindly to an image to his left, spearing a weightless banshee, before it disappeared, sending him to a full-out fall, which would have been on his front, except he twirled midfall and landed on his side . . . his sword side. Half-winded, he was again right back on his feet, after completing the roll. The move cost him breath and stamina for countless moments, while he pulled for air through vapor that resembled a wall of sodden plaid.

"May the great laird, Grant Niall MacKetryck . . . witness this!"

His father?

The blow caught him full on the back, taking him to his knees, where he bent forward, retching and sobbing, although he'd never admit to the latter. He staggered back to his feet before another one could land, and stumbled backward until he found a stone wall with punishing force.

Aidan did another shove across his eyes, lifting his sword at the same time. Then he was moving along the wall, lashing out at anything that had substance or moved. But there was too much. In the reddish tear-blurred vision the room was alive with *poucah*, peopled with demons, and filled with evil. Everywhere he turned, swinging, and stabbing and moving, there was another red, fog-dense shape. Aidan kept hacking and slicing, and carving a way to the hag, who wouldn't stop her tormenting words.

"Alpin will make a great husband for the lass."

Alpin? Aidan's heart pumped anger and rage through him hard and swift, drying his eyes as nothing else had. That gained him vision and clarity with every blink, turning the moisture into bloodred scrape and dust dry. Juliana would wed Alpin over Aidan's dead body.

"Aye . . . my laird. Alpin. His is a world of game and fish and wine. He may na' even mind that her maidenhead was stolen. Unlike your first wife." And then she laughed.

She knew about that, too? Aidan had never told anyone. He was taking it to his grave.

Heat reflected through the red haze, her fire glow glinting off his claymore, and Aidan swiveled toward it, in an arc of motion that had the kettle hooked and flung across the room, while a bit of red coal hung up on his blade.

But she'd moved. Aidan blinked through eyes that burned, swinging his head in an opposing motion to his blade. Waiting. Listening. For the hag to speak again. Just once.

"Or . . . you could choose . . . the Black MacKetryck as her husband. Dugald. He would like that."

The breath from her insidious whisper touched his right side and Aidan flipped his left hand over his shoulder before she'd finished, swiveling his body to follow, putting his sword out at the ready while gripping her old throat and squeezing. Listening to her choked sigh of breath. Squeezing more. Lifting her from the floor with the pressure of his fingers, and seeing nothing but red. Bloodred.

"Enough!" he hissed, bringing her close enough he could see the fright in her light gray eyes.

And then everything changed. Aidan blinked and watched it. Disbelieved it and still watched. The fog dissipated, turning back into sun-kissed smoke haze. The red faded and then disappeared as if it had never been. The fire was burning merrily in the hearth, and the only sound was a kettle glancing off a wall.

Dame Lileth Fallaine-Dumphat was right in front of him, looking small, frail, elderly, pathetic, and worried. Aidan stood, breathing hard while he looked down at the woman in front of him, wringing her hands and looking up at him with an innocent expression. Aidan stood to his full height, gave two heavy chest breaths, and then looked back down at her.

"You should na' burn so many . . . potions," he told her through clenched teeth.

She smiled, but this one didn't have much mirth to it.

"It clouds things."

"Na' enough, sweet laird." Her voice was raspy-sounding, as if she'd just been choked. Aidan sent a swift glance there, but there was no mark of fingers. Nothing. Just old, pale skin.

He grunted and lifted his sword above his head, while his left hand reached for the tip, to guide it back into the scabbard.

She moved her glance to it. "Your charm, Aidan Niall?"

His fingers didn't find a sword tip. They found a jewel. Aidan pulled the long, slender pendant off his tip and twirled it in the light while his sword lowered again. It was a purplish cast stone, near a thistle in color. And it was wrapped with two bands of etched gold, exactly like serpents, in a like configuration of the ring he'd lost.

"What does this mean?"

She shrugged.

"What does it do, then?"

"Makes everything . . . clear," she replied.

Aidan lifted a brow, twisted his lips, and looked back at her. Nodding, he flipped the gem into the air with his thumb and caught it easily. Then he was fingering his sporran bag open without looking to slip the little charm into it. He backed up three steps from her while he did so, bowed his head slightly, backed up four more steps. Aidan was at the door before he swiveled to leave. It was a defensive move, and they both knew it.

Heck, Kerr, and Tavish waited for him in the hall, lounging against the walls as if their laird hadn't been in danger. They all stood and stretched when he came around the corner from her door. They looked sheepish. Tavish was the first to speak.

"I see you escaped unscathed," he remarked.

Aidan shouldered through them and shook his head. "Nae thanks to my honor guard," he muttered, continuing down the hall.

"We'd have come had we heard screams," Heck informed him.

"So . . . what happened in there?" Tavish jogged around Aidan to ask it.

"Come with me next time. You'll see."

He watched the man's face fall and ignored it. "Come, lads! We've wasted enough time. To the loch! I fancy a swim."

All three groaned.

"Across," Aidan added.

"But—we've but newly returned. And we've preparations . . ."

"Or the list. I'll meet every man on the list instead. Your choice."

"And have bruises to sport for the fest?" Tavish asked.

"A swim it is. Right," Kerr piped in. "It's a challenge."

"A challenge? If we try to match the laird, we'll be worthless to the wenches this eve," Tavish replied.

"Aye," Kerr responded. "Weak as bairns."

They'd reached the spiral steps and Aidan had to consciously keep from tripping on the first one as his knees involuntarily flexed. Flinched. Betraying a weakness he'd never known.

"Just get to the loch. And any others you can rouse. That's an order."

Aidan was jogging down the steps as he said it, and then he took two at a time, then three, doing anything to block the thinking. Anything.

Chapter 18

The view was truly awe-inspiring. Juliana was on her knees, shoved into the narrowest portion of one window, staring at it and blinking and listening to a heartbeat that matched the gentle ripple of wave far below her. Just . . . existing.

"Now . . . wait! I never said—"

"Y-Y-You can-can-canna' go!"

Juliana pushed back from the window point, carved so narrow an archer would have difficulty fitting, before turning her head. Alpin was being shoved into the chamber surrounded by women. His ruffled hair, plaid that was askew, and red face gave mute witness to how amenable he'd been to their attention. Until now. Arran was flailing his arms and stuttering.

"N-N-N-Nae! You m-m-must go! A-A-All of you! Alpin . . . stop them!"

"They say he's installed her in his chamber, Arran . . . lad." That voice and the way she said his name had Arran standing open-mouthed and turning red. It was attached to a beautiful dark-haired woman.

"We just want a small look, Alpin." That voice had a

throaty charm, especially when she lowered it for Aidan's brother's name. Juliana couldn't spot the speaker.

"Aye. We doona' wish to disturb anyone."

"Just a wee look, Alpin? Please?" The throaty one again.

"But—I never said you could—nae! Aidan will kill me!"

Juliana stood to her full height, watched the general melee as it looked to be more than a dozen women pushing their way through the two young men. She spent a few moments looking at them and swallowing the reaction. She'd never seen such a varied assemblage of women, each vying with lush curves, lengthy hair, and pleasant features. She gulped, put her head back, and whistled. Just like she'd seen Aidan do. And surprisingly it worked. Loudly.

Everything stopped. Juliana put words in the space.

"Alpin? You may explain, please."

Juliana used her haughtiest voice. She watched as most of the women in front of her pulled back slightly, with raised brows and pulled-in breaths.

"My lady, uh . . . these women! I—"

"Had a bit of trouble holding the door. So I see," she finished for him. "And I well see your problem. All of it."

Juliana started walking among them, feeling insignificant and dowdy and unkempt, as well as small where she should be large and short where she should be taller. She didn't let any of it show on her face. She met each woman's look and waited until the other dropped her eyes. Except for three of them. She nodded at them before moving on. Those would be the tougher ones. She already knew it.

"So . . . is there a . . . favorite amongst you?" Juliana asked, coming full circle and arriving back at the windows, where the fresh late-day breeze at her back gave her an odd sense of courage. She asked the question to the space above them, wondering if that was correct etiquette, before discarding that stupidity. She'd never been in this situation before.

She didn't know where and from whom she was supposed to learn proper behavior.

"A . . . favorite?" One of the three she'd already tagged as trouble spoke up. It was a blond woman, possessing a very large bosom and hips, which were then complemented by a very small waist. She knew how to walk to make certain all noted these features first, and demonstrated it as she pushed through the throng.

Juliana sighed heavily and drew out each word. "A favorite. Of Aidan Niall MacKetryck. The laird."

"My lady! I truly think you should—"

"Oh hush, Alpin. You're the one who allowed them entrance."

"I never allowed—" he began.

"Are you saying they . . . forced their way in?"

"Na' truly . . . forced. More of . . ."

"Are these the women Aidan favors, Alpin?"

"Well, they . . . uh . . ."

"Exactly as I suspected. So I ask again. Is there a favorite among you?"

"The laird doesn't have a favorite. That way there's no trouble. We're all his favorite . . . my *lady*."

Juliana narrowed her eyes at the new speaker, easily tagged as the throaty-voiced one. It belonged to a striking woman with darker blond hair flowing freely all about her, and a more willowy form than the previous woman. Juliana waited several moments before moving her vision above them again in a dismissive fashion. "Very well. Is there a leader amongst you then?"

"Leader?" the first blond woman asked.

"Someone willing to speak on behalf of all. That type of leader."

There was a bit of whispering. And then the beautiful, dark-haired woman stepped through the crowd to the front.

"Aye. I'll speak," she said.

"And you are?"

"Sorcha. And this here is Una. And Siniag, Robena, Maisie, Lorna—"

"I prefer the others stay nameless, Sorcha. Otherwise, I have to specify punishment . . . by name."

There was a collective indrawn breath.

"Pun . . . ishment?" Sorcha had lost a bit of her aggressive behavior.

"For accosting me in the laird's chamber."

"Accosting you?"

"Aye. You . . . accosted me. The woman installed in his chamber. As his favorite. His only . . . favorite." Juliana spaced out the words, giving them a threatening quality she didn't know she could wield. She watched the others' eyes widen.

"But, my lady—"

The second blonde shoved the words out. She'd lost her sarcastic bent. Juliana looked over their heads again.

"You're dismissed," she announced.

"Dismissed?"

"From my presence. And if any among you have chores to return to . . . I would allow it. This once," Juliana continued. There was some shuffling of feet, and then she watched as they started leaving, from the back where she couldn't see. She could feel the tension relax just a bit, until Sorcha came close. Juliana hooded her eyes and tipped her chin up to meet the other's eye, while tightening her back as if to withstand a blow.

"He'll tire of you." The girl had lush eyelashes about very dark eyes that flashed with her emotion. It heightened her appearance, which was unnecessary. She was already beautiful.

"You truly seek punishment, don't you?" Juliana asked.

"He calls you 'lass' . . . does na' he? Always. He never uses a name. 'Tis for a reason . . . *lass*."

It was a blow Sorcha gave and she didn't even have a

weapon. There wasn't a stiff enough spine to take it. Juliana spun before the woman saw how deeply it had affected her.

"Alpin?" She cleared her throat to rid it of the weak sound. "See this woman from the chamber. And alert Aidan that she may need duties assigned to her . . . outside the keep."

Sorcha's reply was in language no woman should use. That made it worse for some reason. Juliana kept her eyes on the view, which wasn't as beautiful or serene or awe-inspiring anymore. It had been fouled. She slid a glance to the immense, three-sided bed sprouting from the far wall. It was also fouled.

She'd rather watch the sun-speckled loch. The view blurred, but she wasn't truly looking at it. She was reliving Sorcha's parting statement and experiencing the unpleasant gooseflesh running across her frame, over and over. And over. And then she was joined by Arran.

"Hasn't she . . . left yet?"

"Al-Al-Alpin just took her. Hear the door?"

Juliana glanced toward him, saw the worry on his face, and tried what was probably as sick a smile as it felt to give it. "Oh, Arran . . . did he have one for every day of the month?" she asked.

Arran wrinkled his forehead. "N-N-Nae," he finally replied, as if he'd actually been counting and she'd been serious.

"I tease, Arran."

"Oh," he replied. He shuffled his feet, and looked at her again, with one eye partially closed. "Wi-Wi-Will you . . . t-t-tell—"

"Your big bad brother, Aidan?" she interrupted his stutter. "What will I tell him, Arran? What? That he has such a large unruly batch of loose women that his brothers couldn't keep them away from me? Why would I do that, Arran? I'm one of them!"

He looked like she'd slapped him, and Juliana burst into tears.

"Oh nae. Nae. This will na' do. Arran. What have you done?"

Juliana had subsided into a ball in one of the window al-coves, feeling worn and used, and especially down-spirited and contrite at how she'd treated Arran. She heard yet another woman speaking the words and turned her face away to look at the gray stone, since the view outside had lost every bit of its luster.

"Arran MacKetryck, I spoke to you."

"I-I-I-It was na' me!"

"Then who?"

"The w-w-w-women."

"What women?"

"Don't answer that, Arran!" Juliana was on her feet and moving into the room. He wasn't capable of handling yet an-other of Aidan's women. "I can't keep quiet about it if you tell it."

"Oh," Arran replied.

"So . . . who am I dealing with now?"

"'Tis the Lady Reina."

Arran moved toward the slender, tall woman standing just inside the chamber door, waiting. Lady Reina didn't have the same look about her as the others. As she came farther into the chamber, getting touched by the light, it was obvious. She was dressed too richly, clearly indicating her status at the castle. Juliana wondered how Lady Reina felt about attend-ing one of Aidan's women.

She didn't ask. She didn't have to. She tipped her head up, and tried to look self-confident and poised and refined de-spite her surroundings and status, and unkempt appearance. It wasn't entirely her fault that she'd been given no correct

clothing, or decent bathing facilities, but it was her fault
that she'd been weeping, leaving telltale signs on her cheeks,
although the red and black plaid wrapped about her covered
over any dark spots. She ignored all of that to look over this
lady with the same reserve she was facing. It was especially
galling in contrast to the other.

Aidan's Lady Reina was dressed in a rich samite fabric of
pale rose, with elaborate stitching all about the hem and
bodice. The underdress looked to be of bleached woven flax,
and it was fashioned to cover her bosom and throat with
pleats that shadowed and covered. She was another blonde,
with golden hair braided in long strands that were then fastened in loops and attached to a headdress fashioned of real
gold filigree and set with a multitude of colored jewels. She
had a heavy cream-colored veil pulled to one side, shadowing half of a face possessing clear blue eyes, pale flawless
skin, and lips the same rose shade as her gown. Juliana
recognized the material, the expense, and the craftsmanship
that had gone into such an ensemble. At one time, she'd had
clothing just as rich and just as elaborate.

"Juliana?" the vision in rose asked.

Juliana nodded.

The woman clapped her hands as if entertained and de-
lighted at the information. "Hand me your plaid."

Juliana looked at Arran. He shrugged. She looked back at
the woman.

"Why?"

The blonde laughed slightly. "Because I am Lady Reina . . .
and my laird, Aidan, has put you in my care." The woman
turned to Aidan's brother. "Arran? Order a tub. And hot water
to fill it. Hurry! Assist them. We've little enough time."

Arran turned with a jog. Juliana didn't watch as he went
through the chamber door. The woman had moved and was
nearing her and then circling her.

"The plaid, Juliana." She motioned with her fingers. "And quickly!"

Juliana unfastened the brooch clip with trembling digits and then slid it from her shoulders. Before she dropped it to the floor, the blond woman gave a cry, startling her.

"'Tis exactly as they said! Exactly."

Lady Reina came nearer and Juliana backed up, but there wasn't anywhere to go once her shoulders reached rock. But she'd brought the blanket wrap with her and clasped it again with both hands.

"You needn't fear me, Juliana. I'll na' do more than . . . take a snip or two of this hair . . . just so."

A small blade had appeared in the woman's hand and she had snipped a coil of hair from Juliana's shoulder before Juliana could free a hand to slap at her.

"It is as foretold!"

The blonde gave a joy-filled cry again and danced her way back to the center of the room, the movement making her veil flutter. Juliana slid along the wall toward the door. And Arran. And safety. Softly sliding her boots against old rushes so the woman wouldn't know what she planned. She was near the door before the woman spoke again, stopping her in place.

"It does nae good to avoid your fate, Juliana." Lady Reina had sobered, and spun, and was pointing the small blade in the exact location Juliana had reached.

"My . . . fate?" she whispered.

The blonde smiled, revealing perfect white teeth. "Aye. Your fate. As written."

"You're mad," Juliana replied without thinking. Aidan had put her in the hands of a crazed woman.

"Gifted, lass. Gifted," the woman whispered with a volume louder than speech. And then she changed, making Juliana jump as she shouted the rest. "That lad best return quick! I've other errands for him. Green. I've a feel for . . . green!"

The woman spun in place with her arms high, stirring the smattering of rushes on the floor with the hem of her gown. Then, she stopped midspin and focused her one-eyed gaze on Juliana.

"Pale green . . . the lightest hue. In . . . satin. Much thinner than this . . . Nae! Your bliaut must be of pure linen! From early-pulled flax! Na' . . . yet . . . ripe. With darker strands woven through it for mystery. And beneath that? An underdress of . . . white satin! Aye! That is it! But it must be so white . . . 'tis blue in torchlight. You ken? This is what I see. Where is that Arran?"

Juliana sagged minutely against the wooden partition wall. Clothing. Lady Reina was talking clothing.

"We'll need oils . . . savory . . . lavender . . . And perhaps a bit of heather. Aye! Heather sprigs! Masses of them! And thistle! We need purple thistle. To weave through your hair. Or lavender! You do see it? Where is that Arran?"

The woman's excitement was growing with each description, making her voice loud even in the immensity of Aidan's bedchamber. It was also infectious, Juliana was finding as she came away from the wall without conscious volition.

"But we must have that plaid. Come, Juliana. Hurry!"

The blanket fell to the floor behind her, and then she found herself right beside Lady Reina and looking at her. Juliana didn't know how she got there either.

"He was right to put you in my care. This hair . . ." Lady Reina was unfastening and brushing Juliana's hair and it didn't feel as if she touched it. "There are sonnets devoted to hair such as you possess, Juliana lass. Sonnets! Written by love-struck swains with no outlet for their unrequited love. There you are, Arran! You have a tub? Well . . . have them bring it in! Now! And set it down . . . near the fire!"

There was a large fireplace on one wall. Juliana hadn't noted it because it had been dormant and dark. Now, as soon as Lady Reina mentioned it, Juliana noticed flames filling the hearth area with warmth and light and the smell of wood smoke.

"Verra good. Verra." Lady Reina clucked her tongue and clapped her hands as a large tub was set on the floor, and then pail after pail of water was brought in, filling it until they could see the water reflecting the flames. If she looked close enough, she could see the steam rising from it as well. Juliana sensed the added moisture all about her, like a veil of invisible threads. She could feel the increased heaviness in the air she breathed. "Now run, Arran. Run. Fetch me three chests from my chambers. They're already set out. Go, lad! And take your brother out with you!"

The last was directed at Alpin, who'd entered the chamber and was staring at Juliana with a thunderstruck look. She hadn't realized until then that he hadn't seen her uncloaked and with her hair unbound, in a riot of curls that happened whenever her hair was wet . . . especially around steam. Not many of them had. She blushed as she turned away.

"There's only one man for you, Juliana lass." Lady Reina's voice lowered to a hypnotic level as she walked around Juliana, circling her over and over and making her dizzy with watching until she gave up and looked instead at the tub and fire. "One man. And 'tis na' Alpin MacKetryck. Poor lad."

"Who is it then?" Juliana asked.

The lady responded with a fit of laughter and then she sobered again. "Ah, lass . . . you question that which you already ken, and ken naught what you must question."

"What?" She might as well have drunk too much ale, Juliana decided, wrinkling her forehead with confusion.

"Your fate. 'Tis already foretold . . . as I've been saying."

"Are you a . . . seer?" Juliana asked.

Lady Reina found that totally amusing, too, with laughter

stronger than before. It was so merry, Juliana found herself smiling.

"Nae, lass. Dame Lileth Fallaine-Dumphat is the clan seer. A wiser, more fey woman you'll na' meet. She was my teacher. My mentor. Me? I . . . am but a novice."

As superstitious as he was, why would Aidan put her in the hands of an understudy?

"Because he trusts me, lass," the woman replied, as if Juliana had spoken aloud. "Aside of which, I ply the fastest needle. You'd never be finished in time if anyone else attended you. Or if you were . . . faeries would have to assist. Now . . . cease this worry. 'Twill line your face afore you've aged. And hand over your shift."

"What . . . of Arran?" she asked, already reaching for the hem to pull it off.

"He'll na' see you, lass. I'd na' give him the chance. Nae man sees what belongs to my laird, Aidan."

Juliana's hands froze on the shift hem. She felt stewed, dizzy . . . light-headed. She nearly stumbled. *No.* Somewhere in Lady Reina's words there was a hint of sin and pain and blackness. Something about fouled pleasure. Juliana shook her head to clear it and to dispel her foolishness. She couldn't decipher the thought enough to ponder and worry over it.

A knock heralded Arran's reentry. He had three clansmen with him, each burdened with a trunk nearly the size of the porter. They scattered rushes with the passage of their boots and added grunting and heat to the room with their efforts. Juliana watched as they set each trunk down in perfect line with what looked to be immense caution. All of it happening under the watchful eye of Lady Reina. Juliana stood mutely observing, with her hands still clutching her shift, raised to her knee level.

"Now, unfasten them. And open . . ."

The most amazing aroma of lavender and heather and

field flowers filled the air, emanating from the trunks and adding to the room scents.

"Now go. And doona' bother us again. You, too, Arran. I'll be calling for you when I've a need. Come, Juliana."

Lady Reina didn't look to see if her orders had been followed. She probably didn't need to. Juliana heard the door closing behind her as she approached the open trunks.

"Fresh heather. Sprigs of lavender. Oil of rose . . . oil of rose?" The woman wrinkled her nose and shoved the wax plug back into it. "Nae. Rose is for old loves . . . na' for the enjoyment of fresh ones. Lavender . . . now that is what we need . . . and look here. You see? Green linen. Just as I foresaw."

She was holding up a rolled span of linen that looked the shade of old lace in Juliana's eyes, but as the woman unfolded and rolled it in the light, darker shinier threads caught the torchlight from all about them, rendering a hue that resembled night-lit fog. Juliana looked at it with awe, and then moved her eyes to Lady Reina's unveiled one, and then looked farther about, at torches lit in their sconces, and all about the room.

She hadn't seen them getting lit.

Juliana blinked several times, counting to more than twenty as she looked about the room. She was worse than stewed and drunker than when she'd partaken of Killoran ale. She had to be. She was seeing and experiencing and feeling things that couldn't be.

She was tired. Overcome.

Juliana blinked again and then shrugged. She'd missed the lighting of the torches and the men who'd done it because she'd been caught up in the pleasure of sensation wrapping all about her; the scent of lavender and savory; the heavy vapor of her warm bath; the crack and smell of burning wood; the feel of the linen Lady Reina was placing right in her hands where the material draped as if poured atop them.

"Oh . . . my," Juliana breathed.

Lady Reina laughed again, and clapped her hands. And then she was up and dancing and twirling and making everything rotate and getting Juliana dizzy. Juliana sat down, realized it was on his bed, and immediately stood back up. Then she grabbed for one of the end posts, connected at the top to a wooden canopy and two other sides, making an enclosure that looked erotic, sensuous . . . and wicked.

Lady Reina was back at her chests, pulling sprigs of what looked like freshly plucked heather from them . . . but that couldn't be. Juliana swayed in place, holding to the post for stability, and watched as white satin was pulled from another trunk. From her vantage she could see the blue-cast shimmer of the material, and that was just improbable, too. The woman had already planned what she'd say and what she'd design well before she'd walked through the door. There wasn't another explanation.

"You need to undress, lass, and you need to do it afore too long. We've lavender oil to soak you in, hair to oil and comb and arrange, and I can't see to everything. I've got a dress to craft."

The woman was planning on sewing a dress while Juliana bathed? The idea was absurd. Impossible. Unfathomable.

"Go on, lass. Undress. Sink below the water. It's heavenly. I've added oils and potions to the water to guarantee it."

When had she done that?

Juliana stumbled slightly when she released the bedpost and that was just a harbinger of the rest of her walk as she neared the tub, crossing one way and then the other as if the room were moving and she had to compensate. She'd never felt as odd. Otherworldly. Rapt.

She had the shift pulled over her head and tossed aside before she reached the tub, and then she dangled her hand in liquid warmth that promised heaven. She lifted a palm filled with the substance, and saw little flower petals stirring about with the motion. There was something wrong about that. Juliana lifted her hand to her nose and sniffed of windswept freshness, dew-filled morns, and oiled heat . . . and decided she didn't care. She peeled off her underdress, which felt crusted and stiff with wear.

There was a sigh of sound behind her. She didn't look to see what it was.

"Slip beneath the water now, Juliana. Step in. I'll be there in a bit for your hair. Go on, lass. Doona' fret. 'Tis na' harmful."

Not harmful? No. It was totally pleasant, and intoxicating, and luxurious, akin to being wrapped in the softest of fur and snuggled into the warmest of soft beds. And then it began exceeding that.

Juliana lay back, resting her head on the tub rim, and ran her hands over limbs that felt silken to the touch and warmed clear through. She couldn't remember when she'd ever felt such comfort. She had nothing to compare it to. Aidan's embrace perhaps . . .

Right then.

That was what this feeling was closest to.

She heard a noise behind her that sounded like choked laughter. She ignored it. The Lady Reina was too vast and strange to ponder. It would take more time than the span of a bath to try it.

Juliana lifted an arm, studied it before running her hand along it, touching the light spots of bruising that were Aidan's grip when he'd moved her to carry while kidnapping her. He probably hadn't even known it.

Behind her she heard Lady Reina chuckling, and then the woman was humming. That might make sewing go quicker. Juliana didn't know much of sewing and needlework. She hadn't the patience for it and hadn't attempted it. Her father hadn't objected. He had a vast estate to run and no son and that disappointment was so vast, he hadn't spared much emotion or care on what his only heir did with her time.

Juliana sighed and lifted the other arm and did the exact same maneuver down this one, running her fingernail along the flesh and loving the silken feel, the heated flesh, the sinful stir . . .

Hands appeared beside her, guiding her head into the water, and then fingers worked at her hair, soothing away the dirt of days, the neglect of sennights, and the worry of months. Until the only thing she felt was an underlying vibration that turned into her heartbeat if she thought long and hard enough about it.

Before she knew it, she was sitting on a cloud of MacKetryck plaid coverlet before the fire, wrapped in more of the material and watching the flames as Lady Reina worked her fingers through coiled locks that needed plaiting to make them behave. Juliana tipped her head to look at where the other woman sat.

"Are you a . . . witch?" she asked, lowering her tone to a whisper at the last word.

"Dugald MacKetryck thinks so," Lady Reina replied.

"I've na' . . . met the man," Juliana replied.

"'Twas a great day when Aidan MacKetryck won back his legacy. A great day."

"Won?"

"Dugald was guardian and regent during Aidan's minority. He grew fond of the position. He dinna' wish to pass it on. The Black MacKetryck was a bad choice. Dame Lileth Fallaine-Dumphat tried to warn the auld laird. To nae avail."

"Black?" Juliana asked.

"Aye. Black. It suits the man's soul. Aidan's suits him as well."

"What is Aidan?"

"Aidan is called the Red MacKetryck. For a reason."

"Red?"

"The color of rage. Fury. Anger. He wears it well."

Red . . .

Aye, Aidan did wear red well, Juliana decided. She watched as Lady Reina's one unveiled eye softened.

"He's a beast when challenged. Verra angry. Verra furious. 'Twas a great battle. Took half a day to fight, but he won. He wrested the castle and his birthright from Dugald."

"When?"

"Near . . . seven years past." Lady Reina frowned just slightly as if in pain.

"That would have made him younger than Alpin. How is that possible?"

Lady Reina smiled. "You ask the oddest things when you already have the answers."

Juliana wrinkled her forehead. "I do?"

"Oh . . . aye. You do. But just look here. It's time for your rest."

"Now?"

"You've time, and I'm na' quite finished with your attire. You doona' wish to shame me in front of Dugald Mac-Ketryck and the household, do you?"

Juliana shook her head. She was beginning to see why Aidan had placed her in Lady Reina's care. The woman always got her way.

Chapter 19

Nothing killed it. Nothing silenced it, tempered it, or even made it waver. Nothing.

Aidan crawled onto Buchyn Loch's shoreline expending every bit of what strength he had left, and then lay there panting and heaving for breath, while his heart still beat ache through every part of him. He'd thought the worst heart pain had been burying his parents three months apart. Now he knew better.

He was sitting on his buttocks, with his arms wrapped about his lifted knees, awaiting the return of his men from the water. Not one had kept up with him. And rather than making them finish the swim across, Aidan had started back and turned them all back around. They probably thought it punishment. He'd gathered that from their groans as he'd passed them.

It should have exhausted him beyond all reason, taking any want for pondering and thinking away. Physical challenge had always worked before. The sense of death and the thrill of cheating it always left him with a heart-pounding newness of spirit. Now all each heartbeat brought him was pain. Unmitigated. Massive. Increasing. The water blurred before him, and Aidan blinked rapidly to still it. He had to. He wasn't in the water anymore. He hadn't donned his plaid yet. There was no way to hide anymore.

He knew what he had to do. He knew he had to do it quickly, before anyone could dissent, or argue, or change it. And discover how much it cost. And before the hurt encompassed everything and made him sacrifice the very thing he'd nearly died for. He'd known when he gained the title of laird of Clan MacKetryck that it came with responsibility. Great responsibility. And it came with great honor . . . centuries of clan honor . . . that he'd sworn to uphold.

At all costs.

He blinked more. The view cleared. Blurred. Aidan kept blinking, shuddering through another breath that burned. Blinked again. Tavish was the first to join him, lying flat out on his belly, in a lean eel shape, and breathing hard enough to displace earth.

"Where's Heck?" Aidan asked.

Tavish pointed backward. Aidan grunted. Watched the loch surface glint with fading sun as it blurred again. He blinked again. Rapidly. Tightened his arms about his knees and breathed as shallowly as possible before bowing his forehead and shuddering until the dirt beneath him cleared enough that he could go back to looking out at the loch and waiting for his men without anyone being the wiser.

Nothing killed it. Nothing even muted it.

Heck was the next to crawl out of the water. Tavish had gained his breath back, although he was still stretched out, putting a lean frame on display that could use not only more meat to it, but more sun. Aidan nodded at Heck.

"Where's Stefan?"

Heck did the same motion Tavish had, pointing back out to the water. Aidan grunted and went back to watching. Blinking. Watching the lines delineating water from land from sky blur and mesh. Blinking faster. Breathing shallowly and evenly and with a modulated rhythm that was vicious with inflexibility.

Kerr pulled himself out next, although he just lay there, half in and half out of the water.

"Go fetch him," Aidan told Tavish.

The man rolled, did a somersault motion, gripped Kerr's arms, and without looking like he expended any strength, hauled the rest of him onto shore. Then he crawled back to sit beside Aidan and look out over the same view.

"You want to tell us what this is all about?" he asked.

"I'll be . . . useless to the lasses . . . thanks to this."

Kerr panted the words from just beyond Aidan's feet. He dropped a glance to him and then looked back to the waves.

Heck snorted. "You're always useless, lad," he replied.

"When I get some strength back, you'll regret those words, Heck Blaine."

"Ooh. I'm shaking here," Heck replied.

Kerr was straightening and attempting a push-up. He decided it was easier to flop back on shore, however, and did it, making a groan of sound at the effort. Aidan's lips lifted slightly at the man. Stefan was next from the waves, crawling amid churning water and huffing breath and cursing soundly at Ewan, who was right with him.

"There! I've won . . . whelp! And you'll . . . pay up. Soundly." The words might have sounded more threatening if they hadn't been panted amid gulps for breath. It would also have helped if Ewan wasn't churning earth with pumps of his arms before collapsing a half-length farther than Stefan.

"Tie! 'Twas . . . a . . . tie!"

"Now wait here. If anyone wins, 'tis me. I was first," Tavish announced, getting to his knees.

"The laird was first," Heck replied. "And he went clean across and back."

"Aidan's part fish. He does na' count," Tavish replied.

Aidan barely heard it through what he recognized as more ache. His heart just kept sending it. He blinked again and turned back to the waves. Cleared his throat to make certain the emotion stayed hidden. "Where's Gregor?" he asked.

They all pointed out at the water. Even the two who'd fresh come from the swim. Aidan squinted and could just make out the head of his last man, bobbing about without any sign of swimming. He looked more to be floating on his back. "Go fetch him, Tavish," he ordered.

"He'll have my skin if I mount a rescue."

"And I'll take it if you don't," Aidan replied.

Tavish grinned. "True," he replied, and walked back to the water before putting lean white buttocks into the air in a dive.

"You want to tell us what this is about yet?" Heck asked at his side.

Aidan looked sidelong at his senior honor guardsman and then looked back out to where Tavish had reached Gregor. From the looks of it, there was a challenge getting made and another race started. It was all well and good. Entertaining. Almost took his mind off what he had to do. But nothing stopped the reminders coming with each beat of his heart. Aidan blinked on the sight of churning water where the two competitors were. And then sighed heavily.

"Fetch Alpin," he replied. "Get him to his rooms. I'll meet with him there."

"He's na' in his rooms already? Perchance . . . with a wench or two?" Kerr asked.

Aidan kept the wince inside, but kept his attention on the swimmers nearing shore. "He's guarding my chambers," he replied.

"Oh," Kerr replied.

"Can I don my plaid first?" Heck asked.

Kerr spoke up. "As little as you possess a-tween your legs, it'd be a pure shame na' to."

"You'll be regretting every word, MacGorrick. Every single one." Heck was tossing his sett atop his shoulder and wrapping it as he spoke.

"Just name the place. And time, my man."

"In the hour," Aidan said. "At the list. With poles."

"The hour?" someone asked.

"Aidan! We've but caught our breath from this torture and you want more?" Kerr complained.

"Aye. I want more. So much, I will na' be able to stand! You ken?" Aidan snarled it and blinked more cursed moisture out of his eyes. Nobody said anything for long enough he could feel the burn of more than twelve heartbeats. Then Heck spoke up.

"Right. I go to fetch Alpin. The rest of you? Get your carcasses to Alpin's rooms with the laird."

They made a solemn group, following him with only their weapons and boots evidencing their passage through the halls. Aidan took in the bustle happening in the great hall before shoving his way through all the people there. He was midway before he stopped, looked about him, and glared.

"They're preparing, Aidan," Heck informed him. "For your fest. To celebrate. As you ordered."

Fest. To celebrate. He'd been rash. Reckless. Again. There was nothing worth celebrating. Aidan returned his gaze to the archway at the end, where torches replaced the faded daylight that normally lit the spiral stair to Alpin's chambers . . . the same chambers he'd claimed until winning the position of laird from the Black MacKetryck. Aidan set his features into a blank look, kept blinking away the emotion his body cursed him with, and preceded the group to the stairwell. He hadn't made it before his way was blocked by Lachlan MacGorrick, in another effeminate

robe of green samite this time, with silver embroidery en-
circling the hem and sleeves and even the neckline, where
it managed to peek through all the ruffling the man had on
his shirt.

"My laird?" Lachlan announced.

"Someone remove this buffoon from my path." Aidan
turned his head away in a dismissive gesture.

"Move, buffoon!" Kerr announced.

"Hush, cousin, I've come on an errand of Dugald Mac-
Ketryck."

"I ceased being your cousin when you swore off manly
attire, Lachlan MacGorrick," Kerr replied.

Aidan sighed heavily. He hadn't managed to evade his responsibility yet. He didn't know why he still tried. "What is
the message, Lachlan?"

"Your uncle regrets that you'll na' come to him. He would
rather this was done in private."

Aidan rolled his head on his shoulders, listening for the
cracking sound that released pressure through his neck.
He turned back to Lachlan, lowered his chin, and narrowed his eyes.

"The message, Lachlan," he said.

"Here."

The man pulled a piece of parchment from somewhere
in the folds of his robe. At one time, it had probably been
rolled and sealed with a family crest. Now, it was looking
creased and worn and folded several times. Aidan regarded
it with as much interest as he had everything since leaving
Dame Lileth Fallaine-Dumphat's chamber.

"What is that, Lachlan?" he asked.

"The Campbell clan's missive. You must answer it."

"I am na' reading that now." Aidan's voice didn't sound
like him. His men must have recognized it, for he could feel
them closing about him, although none made any sound.

"But you have to! They expect—"

"I am na' answering it now!" Aidan's voice cracked. He couldn't help it. That was when he knew the full power of this love thing as his sense of honor and duty wavered. He wasn't dealing with the message now, because if he did, it would all be real. He'd have to give her hand to Alpin in wedlock. He'd have to stand by and watch the woman who held his heart given to his brother. He'd have to live through the hours of their consummation. He'd have to survive the growing girth of his son within her . . . and then he'd have to survive the bairn's birth . . . with Alpin as the sire.

Aidan looked to the ceiling of his great room, and struggled for control over the onslaught of what could only be tears. If it killed him, he was gaining control of this cursed reaction, and he was doing it now. He reached for the purple amulet tucked in his sporran and had it in his grasp while the silent prayer winged upward. That was when a red wash of color started permeating the space between the arches above him. He sucked in a huge breath with the thanks, brought his head back down, and glared at Lachlan with an expression of hatred and revulsion and anger that had the man stepping back.

"Give me the message."

His voice matched his expression, and he watched Lachlan gulp as he heard it. The paper in the man's outstretched hand shook.

Aidan reached to his belt and pulled out a dirk. Lachlan's eyes went wide. He snatched his hand back at the same moment Aidan speared the paper with his blade. Then Aidan spun and flung the knife up and across the room and into one of the wooden arches supporting the floor above. They all heard the hard thud as it hit. And stayed.

"There. I answered it," he informed the man, who was opening and closing his mouth without making any sound.

"But, my laird—"

"Now, will someone move this buffoon?" Aidan interrupted, and lowered his head and chest, preparatory to shoving past him. Lachlan must have sensed it, for he retreated. Hastily.

Chapter 20

Juliana knew she looked astonishing. Breathtaking. Wholly maidenly. And completely ethereal. Draped in mist. As if spring itself had come alive for a visit. It was impossible to believe an ensemble of this magnitude could be created and crafted in the span of an hour's sleep, and yet it had. It was clear Lady Reina had an artist's touch and sense of drama that made Juliana impossible to overlook. She was almost afraid to leave the chamber.

The white satin underdress hadn't been fully complete. The sides were stitched in intervals, but that was because Lady Reina had put her expertise and quickness into the bodice and shoulders. Little puffed pleats of satin framed and supported Juliana's breasts before sliding beneath the shoulders of her gown. Those same pleats then reappeared at the top of each arm. There hadn't been time for sleeves. On a colder day in a different season, she'd need covering. In the steamed torch- and fire-lit warmth that would be the Castle Ketryck's great hall, it wasn't an issue.

The green-cast linen of her shift had darker tones running through it that refracted light whenever she moved, giving an appearance that she wasn't wearing fabric. Instead real meadow grass of the thinnest consistency and lightest shades looked to have been plucked and gathered and woven and then sewn to her frame. The Lady Reina hadn't compromised on that measure either. She'd fit the linen bliaut so close to Juliana's proportions that it skimmed and molded every curve. Where the fit wasn't close enough for Lady Reina's eye, she'd scrambled about in one of her trunks for a girdle of small hammered silver links that seemed alive with movement. That item rested on Juliana's hip, sparkling with light every time she moved.

Her attire was eye-catching; elegant, refined, and yet earthy . . . arousing the senses in a way difficult to define, but it was only an accompaniment to what Lady Reina had done with Juliana's hair.

Except for a few loose spirals about her face, her wild array of curls had been pulled back and held in place by a caplet at the crown. Lady Reina had brought out a caplet made of more silver links, although these weren't movable. Each link was joined by a drop of metal that a smithy had heated before pressing a flower emblem into it. Juliana's mass of ringlets had been smoothed and fingered and forced into a waterfall of red that nearly reached the backs of her knees. The length was a surprise. She'd never had it straightened and held that way before. The tresses behaved because they'd been wrapped and woven through a mesh of nearly invisible silver wire that had then been fastened to her caplet. The tresses would probably start recoiling and pulling and moving once Juliana reached the moist atmosphere of the great hall below. It couldn't be helped. There'd be too much steam from the foods and the ales and the breathing of so many bodies, and too much heat from torches and the massive fireplace that was all they had for light. It might also add to the effect Lady Reina had envisioned, making everything about Juliana look young, fresh, and alive . . . and ethereal.

And like a creature of the mist.

Lady Reina had stepped back and forth several times, flitting all about to add a sprig of lavender here, a bit of heather there, more of both, a thistle top, tiny, barely green leaves, and then the lady stood back, tipping her head back and forth before she'd clapped her hands and gave the laughter that was so infectious.

Then, she'd opened the door and called for Arran, but received both him and two of Aidan's honor guard. Juliana had to stand and blush at Arran's thunderstruck look since his mouth was open as well.

Juliana had Lady Reina to thank for her appearance. She'd had the lady's continual discourse throughout her dressing for the full description of what the great hall would look like and what would be happening as well. It wasn't enough preparation. She'd forgotten to add the laird, Aidan.

He'd never felt less like celebrating.

For this eve, he'd honed a skean to razor sharpness in order to scrape at the scattered beard growth, tied his hair back, donned a clean shirt, and another *feile breacan*, this one woven of dark-hued threads. He also wore the heavily jeweled MacKetryck clan brooch and armbands that Gregor had to fetch from the treasury, as well as the sword said to have defeated the Viking king Kenneth MacBruid so many years before.

Such a sword needed a sizable height to carry it. The tip of the scabbard occasionally scraped the floor even when strapped on Aidan. Such a weapon mutely spoke of the size of his ancestors, from whence Aidan gained his stature.

And then those in his great hall proceeded to eat and drink, taunt and laugh while Aidan watched it with a morose expression. His honor guard weren't far behind. They sat on his dais with like expressions to their laird.

His uncle had joined the festivities sometime after Aidan's third tankard of ale. He wasn't counting. And he wasn't trying for a celebratory drunk. He was trying to dull the ache that his heart wouldn't quit sending and the crowd noise about him that just made it all worse. But the moment Dugald MacKetryck entered, a strange hum started throughout the area, alerting Aidan and making him push his chair back to stand at his full height, hand on sword, in a stance no one would question.

The table reserved for the laird and his family stood on a raised platform between the chieftain tower stairs door and the fireplace. It was a long table, fashioned of heavy oak, capable of seating Aidan, his brothers, their companions . . . and anyone else he cared to invite. Aidan's place was at the center, in a high-backed chair specially crafted for the clan chieftain.

And only him.

There was another table of honor, set on a lower dais, farther along the wall, on the other side of the fireplace. That one was reserved for lesser members of the laird's family, and their guests. Aidan, Alpin, and Arran had been relegated to that position the moment their father had died, in a move against all clan stricture and laws. While Dugald Mac-Ketryck had usurped the position.

It was the same table Aidan relegated to Dugald with pleasure each time . . . except tonight.

Aidan didn't puzzle the why of it. He was afraid to. It was enough to realize the dull ache spreading through him had the power to alter things, changing events that used to have significance into nothing more than wasted time. There wasn't much that affected him. There wasn't much pleasure to be gained from anything. There wasn't anything except heart pain and endurance. And it looked to be a forevermore thing.

Aidan sighed, swallowed, and blinked to soothe the dry scratchy feeling in his eyes. Then he lowered his jaw and watched his uncle's approach from a distance well over the man's head.

The sconces all contained lit torches, sending flickering glow in the immediate area of each before fading. Candles burned in all four of the iron circles they'd winched back into place above their heads, and the fireplace was stocked and shedding a large volume of heat and light onto the floor in front of it. The area of the common floor was still dim, however, highlighted in pockets of glow from lit wicks in bowls of oil and stray candles. Even in the dimness it was still possible to see the richness of Uncle Dugald's attire, including a jeweled kilt band, and flashes of metal from the many dirks he'd seen fit to tuck into his belt and kilt band.

The crowd din lowered markedly before dying off completely while everyone waited. And watched. Dugald was flanked by his steward, the gaunt, overly dressed, and effeminate Lachlan MacGorrick on one side, while Dugald's current favorite, a young girl Aidan didn't recognize, was on the other. Dugald didn't have family with him, nor did he have a wife. The man had buried three of them in his search for an heir, and had no offspring to show for it.

Behind Dugald filed the eight members of his honor guard. Aidan felt his own men standing, shoving stool after stool back until they were in a solid row at both sides of him, with Alpin on Aidan's right. It wasn't necessary. He was willing and capable of fighting and winning over Dugald Mac-Ketryck. He'd proved it.

"So . . . you've returned."

Dugald's voice was deep and gravelly, akin to shale rolling down a hillside. Despite being a decade and four years older than Aidan, the time hadn't softened him or granted him wisdom. If anything, it had made him stouter, thicker with muscle, and more filled with jealousy and ambition than before.

Aidan nodded.

"Successful?"

Aidan's upper lip lifted on one side. Dugald already knew of their failure and the loss of life that accompanied it. He raised his hand and encompassed the room.

"Uncle Dugald! Take your place. Wait with me for my guest of honor . . . Juliana!"

"Juliana? I'd na' heard of her."

Aidan gave a half-smile. It wasn't amusement. Lachlan was his uncle's spy. It had taken years before Aidan knew for certain what that meant and whom to trust. His uncle not only knew of Juliana, he probably had a good description as well.

"Juliana is the lass I rescued, Uncle. And claim." Despite the control he'd put on his voice, Aidan heard the waver in the words. Cursed silently and waited. He didn't want his uncle knowing what Juliana meant to him. He rephrased that to himself. He didn't want *anyone* knowing.

"I . . . see," his uncle replied.

A collective gasp rippled through the crowd below him, turning the crowd's attention from him to the aperture on his left. Aidan turned his head for the reason, and a mailed fist of reaction hit him right in the chest.

Sweet Jesu'!

His knees wobbled. He sucked to regain breath the fist had slammed out of him, and fell backward with the shock. The MacKetryck battle sword catching against the high-backed chair saved him the ignominy of falling back into that chair and then toppling right off the back of his partition.

Someone shoved a cup into his hand. Aidan tossed it back, discovered whiskey. Inhaled. Choked. Burned. Coughed. Someone else smacked him across the back of the shoulders, sending him palm-first against the top of the table, rattling tankards and bowls and making the entire length of his table tremble and groan at the attack.

It was Juliana.

She was walking slowly and hesitantly into the crowd with Arran at her side, and if Aidan didn't do something and quickly, she was going to reach where his uncle's entourage had all turned about to wait. Aidan wasn't letting that happen. When she met the Black MacKetryck, it was going to be with Aidan at her side, making certain his uncle recognized not only Aidan's claim, but his willingness to assert it.

He acted. He didn't know how he did it or how his limbs handled the effort, but he vaulted up and over the trencher table without another thought. He landed lithely in the space beneath it, moved swiftly the eight steps toward her at a crouch, shoving through bystanders, and when he'd straightened, he was right in front of her, becoming the barrier he'd needed.

She gasped at his arrival, and moved her free hand onto her bosom, covering flesh that needed more material about it in Aidan's opinion. A lot more. Aidan's heart pumped unmercifully through him, heating everything, and probably turning him as red as the color coating everything. He glared at Arran. He glared at the rest of his honor guard accompanying her. He turned to glare at her. And then Aidan was in trouble, for he couldn't hold the look. He'd known she was beautiful . . . he just hadn't known *how* beautiful. He couldn't think. He couldn't do much except deal with the buzzing that had replaced his heartbeat in his ears. He just stood there, breathing hard and looking at her, caught and held in place by the clear blue-green of her bottomless, wide eyes.

"My . . . laird?"

Juliana's greeting was stammered and then she dropped her head and curtsied. Aidan had her hand and was pulling her to him. It was instinctive and it was massive. He didn't question it. The ache was muting, getting replaced by such an urgent rush of joy, he could barely contain it.

He had her nearly crushed to his chest and his lips atop hers, revealing every bit of what she meant to him, before something smacked into his belly with such force, he bent double with it. That sent his head into the space he'd just vacated and looked like he was returning her greeting. Aidan glanced at Tavish's grimace as the man rubbed at his fist. Of course it would be Tavish. He was the lone guardsman capable of making the same jump over the trencher table.

Aidan was paying that back. The moment he had the man on the list. With poles. In the meantime, he had an entire gathering to fool, and his uncle was first. Aidan pulled upright, pushing out a bit of air at the bruising he'd just sustained, and stood looking down at her, inhaling her particular scent. His fingers began a methodical drumming against hers and he felt her tremble. And that nearly buckled his knees with the slide of shivers. He was so grateful he hadn't looked at the Campbell missive yet, or spoken with Alpin, or moved her to another chamber, or changed anything about anything.

He loved her and it was a massive thing, with the power to change the very elements. He blinked and gazed around the great hall, which looked sunlit and bright.

"This your . . . foundling, Aidan?"

Dugald's words cut through the haze encompassing everything about this. Aidan gave a last warning glare to everyone in range, getting a quick grin from Tavish in response, then he sucked in a huge breath and turned around, bringing Juliana with him held close to his side. Dugald MacKetryck had gone to the front of his group in the interim, and stood to his full height. That put him below Aidan's cheek, but nearly a head above Juliana. With both fists atop his hips and legs slightly apart, he made an outstanding figure. Aidan looked him over as Juliana might and was surprised to feel self-doubt akin to how he'd felt as a young lad presenting his newly wedded wife.

Dugald MacKetryck favored his nephews in all save the color of his eyes and shade of hair. He was in perfect physical condition, with thick, brawny muscles. But those eyes of his were an emerald green that everyone noted first thing. He also sported a thick head of black hair with only a few white strays in it. He was eyeing Juliana before smiling slightly, and Aidan watched as he exerted a charm women supposedly found irresistible.

"Jul . . . iana?" the man asked softly, elongating her name into a caress and putting a hint of air on the last of it.

"My lord?" Juliana answered at Aidan's side, bending into a curtsy while she used his hand for support. She was showing far too much bosom, if his vantage was any indication.

Aidan lowered his chin slightly, enlarged every bit of his frame, and regarded the shorter man as Dugald looked Juliana over. It wasn't noted. Dugald was giving Juliana his full attention and liking what he saw. His uncle started nodding, licked his lips, and then tipped his head in response to her greeting.

"Dugald MacKetryck, my dear Juliana. I am patriarch of Clan MacKetryck, uncle to these lads, and a man completely humbled and silenced . . . at your beauty."

Aidan's hand clenched around hers, as both arms flexed instinctively. Completely. Involuntarily. She flashed him an upward glance before looking back at Dugald. Aidan clenched his jaw as he looked over her head, trying to ignore her. He hoped she understood. He couldn't possibly look toward her again. Everything in the room was starting to get a red wash coloring it. Controlling his anger had always been an issue. Calling it on wasn't.

Juliana's head bobbed with a nod, brushing his shoulder with her caplet, and then she answered with a bit of prose about meeting such a grand figure, and all of it was said eloquently in the Frankish language of the royal court. Aidan lifted an eyebrow at the words and how perfectly she spoke them. Then he had to suffer through how that little bit of fluidity coming from her mouth affected him and knew the tremble of his hand about hers gave it away.

She tipped her head, catching his glance as she looked straight up at him, and took all his senses apart. The most incredible, loud, rhythmic sound filled his head, obliterating every other sound. He didn't realize it was his own heartbeat until her mouth stopped moving and she stood poised, with a questioning look to her features. Aidan was lost. He couldn't possibly hear over the sound crashing through his head. He lifted his gaze, focused on the far wall, and swallowed. He was acting like a lovesick fool. And probably looked it.

Arran nudged his side, and when Aidan turned to the lad, he saw they'd cleared an aisle of space through to his dais. Juliana squeezed his hand, drawing his glance to her, and then she smiled. Aidan's eyes narrowed, his heart leapt into rapid-fire stance, and then his knees started quavering. She motioned with her head toward his table, alerting him to exactly what she'd asked and what his reply should have been. And what Arran had been trying to show him. Aidan nodded although it was a jerked motion, and then he managed to accompany her back to where, if he was lucky, he'd be able to fall into his chair and pretend none of this was happening.

Aidan looked at the tankard in front of him. He didn't know where it had come from. He also didn't know how he'd reached his chair, but he was forgoing any more ale.

"Aidan?"

It was Juliana. She was right next to him, seated on a padded stool, with her hands folded atop her lap. That was the farthest he was looking. Some fool had seated her next to him. In Alpin's place. Of course she'd be next to him. Making his world a whorl of longing and frustration and barely tempered ache. And making certain he knew of it. He couldn't answer her. Not yet. He could barely function.

Aidan quickly turned to the room before him. His uncle had just reached his own dais and was being seated and served, speaking with a wit that had others about him applauding and laughing and waving his arms wide like a magnanimous benefactor to all before him. Aidan caught the glance Dugald sent toward him. No . . . the glance sent toward Juliana. Dugald caught his nephew's glare and nodded. Then he turned aside, chattered some more, and got another burst of laughter.

It was probably at his eldest nephew's expense.

Aidan moved his gaze past Dugald . . . to the far wall, where three rows of shields hung, each displayed atop the sett captured with it. They were battle trophies. From valorous days, victorious forays . . . clan conquests . . .

"Ai . . . dan?"

Now she broke his name in half with a slight hint of tears wrapped about it. His luck was cursed horrid. He should've put her on the other side of Alpin . . . so he could watch them together. See if he could handle how his future would feel without trying to kill someone. That was what he should've done . . . if he were one for thinking first.

Aidan sighed, steeled himself, and turned his head to answer her. That was another mistake. He could tell it the moment his eyes connected with hers. The whoosh of sound started in his ears again and then built. The quiver in his lower limbs was back, running down both tensed thighs to his toes in the soft leather boots. And the discomfort of a full whiskey flask atop his groin did little to staunch the hardening, enlarging, and building evidence of vicious desire.

Ferocious want. Brutal need. Violent yearning. For a woman he shouldn't claim.

Christ.

She smiled slightly, moving his rapt gaze from her eyes to perfect rose-shaded lips . . . that were moving with her words. Words he hadn't a prayer of hearing.

"I'll fetch it!"

She'd asked for a sup trencher. From above her head Aidan watched Arran jump from his seat and gesture to two serfs, who began to fill a trencher platter with meats that had been roasting since their arrival, leeks and onions that had been stewed and mixed with blood pudding, and cheeses that bit a man's tongue with tartness. Aidan didn't move anything else. He was locked into position, filling his senses with the sight of Juliana attired in a gown that didn't look to cover enough, and smelling of such freshness, she might as well be clad in mist. And not much else.

Lady Reina had outdone what he'd asked. No man should have to put up with seeing Juliana with her hair all unbound and rippling to her knees or wearing a thin weave of barely colored flax that skimmed all over her, making it easy to see a waist his hands could span, breasts that would lose their shelter of satin when crushed against his chest, and a hint of thighs that led to absolute bliss.

Aidan licked his lips. Swallowed. His ears popped, clearing the constant whooshing sound of his heartbeat . . . before it started right back up again. He lowered his head slightly. Grit his teeth. Settled straighter against the back of his chair to give him more room beneath his sporran bag. Swore.

"What . . . is it?"

He didn't have to hear it. He knew her words from the movement of her mouth and the curiosity in her eyes when he dared move his gaze there again. And that was just stupid.

He was locked within her gaze while the breath got sucked out of him and refused entry back in.

"I . . ." The rumble of voice had to be his, as was the slight shaky sound to the one long-drawn word.

"I must thank you."

She had a blush blossoming through her cheeks. Right in front of him. Making everything about her look younger, sweeter, and more appealing. She looked down shyly, the move fluttering eyelashes against her skin. Aidan pulled in a gulp of air. Swallowed again. Leaned forward for more room. Cursed the hard wood of his chair bottom, as well as the lack of give beneath him, and then he cursed the immense desire he couldn't even temper. Aidan pushed down on the sporran with more strength.

"For . . . this dress. And Lady Reina's . . . help."

She was speaking the words to her conjoined hands. Aidan forced himself not to shift or move and prayed she wasn't looking anywhere near his lap right beside her.

Lady Reina's . . . help?

This wasn't help. This was longing and yearning and hunger, washed over with anguish and suffering and pure, unadulterated torment.

"I . . ." He spoke again. He had the same rumble to the word, although he should've cleared his throat before attempting it. That might've firmed the shake out of it.

Aidan blew the rest of his breath out and moved his head, looking out again at the crowd on the common floor. Then the view changed to include Arran and the serfs as they materialized in front of them, the table level with their shoulders. Aidan watched them lift trencher bread, heavy with the meat, puddings, vegetables, and cheeses. Both platters were also bowed with juices from the elk, deer, boar and duck, since it looked like they'd carved the most succulent pieces.

Juliana said the proper words of appreciation that had Arran stammering and stuttering and turning a definite shade of red, before he left intent on a mission for a goblet of water the lass beside Aidan requested . . . using a voice that was quiet and melodic and unbearably sweet. Adding to the intimate torture of listening.

Aidan watched her reach for a piece of duck, noting they'd even carved the meat into bite-sized pieces . . . moved the poultry to her mouth, parted her lips . . . ate . . . and then licked at the meat juice that touched on her lower lip. The lurch in his entire frame slid his buttocks against hard wood beneath the thin weave of kilt, despite how tight he immediately made his thighs against the chair bottom. He groaned.

Juliana reached next for a piece of venison. Aidan watched her make the same moves, although this time she didn't lick at her lip for no juice dribbled. This time, he had such a grip on the wood the reaction that flared through his frame didn't do more than make the chair creak. The same thing happened with the next bite she took and the next, although by the time Arran returned with a goblet of liquid, Aidan had the response to a tremor that didn't make sound and wasn't visual.

"Aidan?" Juliana asked it suddenly, turning to him with a piece of cheese in her fingers. Aidan locked on to the morsel and watched as she just kept it at her lips . . . hovering . . . tempting . . . promising . . .

He gritted his teeth harder, lowered his chin, and forced his gaze from her mouth to her eyes. And felt his heart sink clear to the pit of his belly, where the pounding was a worse problem than when it deafened him. He watched as something dawned within her as her eyes widened, pulling him in inexorably, and then holding him with a vicious grip no woman should wield so easily and fully.

"Aye?" The word was croaked. He was actually surprised to hear it.

"I-I-Is Lady Reina . . . your . . . ?" Her voice ended without finishing.

And then she released her grip on his gaze to drop her eyes to the region of his chest while full red crept through her face and through her bosom as well. Aidan glanced there, earned the heave of his loins against the sporran that he shoved right back, and cursed himself for being every brand of idiot.

"My what?" he asked.

She shook her head.

"She's Dugald's sister. Through marriage."

Juliana gasped, put a hand to cleavage that was already his bane and hell, and looked up at him with wide, surprised eyes.

"Dugald? She's related . . . to . . . *him*?"

Aidan nodded, felt the glimmer of satisfaction at the way she said the last word, and that nearly righted everything in the room again. Except she was still looking up at him and breathing a reaction, which might be her dismay and disgust, all over him. Hooking him within her gaze, and all the while making him accept the sweetness of her breath and the shivers it engendered.

"Then . . . he'll punish her."

"Nae," Aidan reassured her.

"He will, though. I know the type. For this . . . dress. This . . . presentation. He'll see her punished, Aidan. He will."

"He can't. I protect her." Aidan's voice still growled, but he felt the satisfaction like a cool wash all over him, soothing muscles he still held taut against the onslaught of Juliana's femininity. She hadn't been fooled by the old lecher's charm.

"You?"

"Aye. Me," he replied. "Just as I will you."

Her eyes went enormous. And then she dropped them. "I see," she whispered.

Chapter 21

The magic was gone.

Juliana blinked out at the humanity in the great hall as if for the first time. It was dim and shadowy and the glow of candles at her table made it look even more so. There were so many people and so much happening! MacKetryck had loaded his great hall with clansmen and women of all ages and abilities, great platters of steaming fare, huge barrels of ale, bowls of wick-lit oil, and scattered pockets of musicians. The din was constant and loud and discordant. Laughter was everywhere. The feasting and reveling looked to have been going on for some time. And she hadn't even heard it.

It was as if Lady Reina had encased her somehow in a bubble, not unlike those that frothed at the bottom of a waterfall. Juliana had been here through all of it . . . she just hadn't noted any of it. There'd been a low-pitched vibration running through her, creating warmth that coursed through her veins, a glow surrounding wherever she looked, and a primitive blend of scent that permeated every pore, making this evening the most immense, sensual, and visceral of her experience. Food had never tasted and smelled better, colors had never looked so vivid and appealing, and the hypnotic quality of being beside Aidan MacKetryck—catching his gaze, feeling her heart skip at his eye contact, and near swooning with his touch—had been so vast and overpowering, it felt like she'd been transported to another world.

And just like that, the bubble disappeared.

She'd not only forgotten she was in a heathen castle deep in heathen land, in the control of a heathen laird, and before the eve was finished, she'd be ensconced in that befouled bed with him, but she'd been enjoying the accoutrements that readied her for it. She'd been looking forward to it with desire, longing . . . and craving. She'd been in a fog of want and yearning and desire, and every breath she took accentuated and heightened it.

Juliana blinked and brought her focus back to Aidan's table. It wasn't difficult. Directly to her right stood a candle stand, holding five lit tapers that wavered and flickered and sent a tiny plume of smoke wafting upward. There was another candle stand two settings down and more beyond that. If she looked, there was probably another candle stand at Aidan's left with the same arrangement.

She didn't look.

That amount of light made it not only easier to see and converse and dine, but also impossible for anyone in the room not to see the richness of those on the dais conversing and dining.

Aidan had loaded his table with riches. Juliana blinked again on the quantity and quality of them. The goblet Arran had brought for her looked so encrusted with jewels the smithy had to have had difficulty attaching all of them. It should have been akin to hefting stone, yet when she'd lifted it to her mouth earlier, it had felt the weight of feathers. There were two-tined forks set out, giving an impression of elegance and refinement. A long blade rested alongside each fork. Both pieces had been smelted with jewels encrusting their handles. Juliana hadn't seen them because she hadn't looked. She'd eaten with her fingers because she'd been expecting that. She hadn't felt gauche or barbaric while she'd done so either. Until now.

The haze of perfection and wonder Lady Reina had some-how woven about Juliana had dissipated, taking the fantasy quality from everything and putting it back to reality. Juliana couldn't do anything other than accept it, and suffer through the reasons why.

She was appalled and disgusted. With herself. And getting more so the longer she sat there listening and watching and evaluating. By his own mouth, he'd said he'd protect her, but that wasn't odd. He'd been saying it often, in as many ways and as many times as the amount of days he'd known her. She was under his protection . . . just as the Lady Reina was?

Juliana's eyes flitted about the chamber, picking out the women with the most winsome faces and lush curves. The gathering had a surfeit of them. Everywhere she looked, they graced the tables with men all about them. Juliana checked the table beside her with a surreptitious glance. More than twelve clansmen ate with Aidan. They were accompanied by five women on her right and at least three that she could see on the other side of Aidan, most possessing features that were very pleasing to the eye, as well as fine forms.

Juliana's lip lifted. She clasped both hands together and tightened them. Self-disgust was covering the jealousy, and she wasn't admitting to that until she got all the other emo-tions under control.

She looked next at where that conceited ass Dugald was holding court, laughing and gesturing broadly to a rapt table of diners, as well as an audience he seemed to have gathered on the common floor in front of him. They were shouting back and forth and gesturing and lifting tankards for toasts, and laughing. Raucously.

She didn't know why. There was nothing amusing left in the world.

Not for Juliana.

Dugald had five winsome lasses at his table. There wasn't one that had any imperfection that Juliana could tell. They were all beautiful and all looked to be her age, if not younger. Juliana shivered slightly in a delayed reaction from meeting the man. The bubble had her fully encased back then. Now, she was not so lucky. She had to feel the revulsion full-scale.

One of the ladies at Dugald's table reached forward and spilled her goblet, sending a froth of liquid over the edge. Juliana gaped as bodies jostled and fought and struggled for the right to lie in the mess of rushes beneath the table and catch the drops of liquid as it fell. From where she sat, she couldn't tell which gent had been the victorious one in the pile of clansmen.

Barbarians. Heathens. Savages.

She'd known. She'd feared. She'd tried to escape. Now, she was here . . . and caught. And there was nobody to blame but her.

The spilled drink was gone and there was a general clapping and laughing and slapping of shoulders about the floor below Dugald's table. The girl who'd spilled it was laughing, too. It coarsened her, altering the beauty she'd had moments before. Juliana's lips thinned. The girl would have need of her beauty. It was obvious to a trained eye that Dugald's favor was a fickle one. Any lass catching his eye had a finite and short reign. He obviously replaced them the moment they had some age to them.

"Juliana?"

The voice at her left ear sent a whisper of air over her shoulder and onto flesh she should have covered. Juliana felt the ripple of reaction at her throat and then the shiver that followed it, racing along her skin to center right at her nipples, giving him every sign she wanted his attention . . . if he looked.

Juliana turned her head slightly and glanced up. He definitely looked. And then he moved the dark ale color of his eyes to hers. Juliana's heart sank. She lost her disgust, dismay . . . everything. She gained pure intensity and potency and awareness in their place. A buzz affected one ear and she tilted it slightly. His features softened into a smile and she returned it. Instantly and immediately. Why had no one warned her of the power this love emotion wielded?

"You doona' eat any more?" He gestured toward the trencher plates. Juliana followed his hand before returning to his gaze.

"I'm . . . not hungry."

He cleared his throat, grimaced slightly, and tilted his head back to look toward the ceiling before lowering it back to her. "Then, come. We've finished."

Come? With him? Now? With everyone watching?

"Wait!"

She stopped him midmovement. She could tell by the tension all along him from where he'd risen from the chair and the rapt attention he gave her.

"For what?"

"You . . . didn't eat."

Juliana waited with a baited breath before he relaxed and lowered back into a sit. Then he reached out, plucked up a piece of something, and popped it into his mouth, chewed maliciously, and swallowed. Then he turned back to her.

"Verra well." He nodded. "I ate."

He was on his feet and pulling her without giving her any time to assimilate anything else. He had her gripped against his right side next, with an arm looped around her torso, making it easy to lift her from the ground and start walking toward the end of his dais.

His men were rising to their feet, one by one, before Aidan reached them, assisting their ladies either to their feet, or shoving them closer to the table, making a pathway for Aidan to walk through.

It was perfectly orchestrated and carried out, as if planned.

Then Aidan was on the common floor, lifting her even more securely against his side, and Juliana buried her face into his shoulder. If he had to make it apparent to all what she was to him and where he took her, she didn't have to see it.

Crowd noise swelled about them, due more to her new awareness of it than interest in their exit. Shouts and cries and lyre music and swells of laughter were still occurring all around her when Aidan forwent any appearance of escorting her in a genteel fashion. Juliana gasped as he swung her up and into his arms without one hint of warning. That position put her level with the clansmen all about, since Aidan was so much taller. Juliana turned her face fully into his upper chest.

He'd reached an exit and shoved past anyone standing in his way, and then he was walking by any spiral stairs that would lead to his chambers. Juliana turned her head slightly and peeked. She didn't see much. They were still on the lower level where no window slits or other weaknesses had been constructed into the structure. There were torches lining the walkway, but they weren't sufficient to overcome the gloom.

He jogged up three steps into another corridor, and then turned right. Juliana moved her head farther. Men were following him, but there were more than three steps, if the way their heads bobbed was any indication. Aidan must have taken two at a time. Or more.

"Where . . . are you taking me?"

She moved her eyes up, caught Aidan's instant glance before he looked ahead again. He had his jaw locked if the taut look of it was any indication. He didn't answer but she knew he'd heard her. They entered a room, long and high, with a ceiling of wood supported by arches, and Juliana's eyes went wide as she looked up at them.

"Where . . . are we?" she asked.

He glanced sidelong at her before looking over her head again. "My household," he replied, before going to another jog of motion, crossing the room with footsteps that echoed.

"Not . . . your chamber?" she asked in a little voice.

He stopped, right beneath an archway at the far end. He pulled in a huge sigh of breath, making her rise with it. He had everything scrunched on his face and his arms so tight about her, Juliana was having trouble breathing. Then, he started shuddering, making her shake with it. He opened his eyes when he released his breath and met hers with a wary look that elevated her pulse to a nearly unbearable speed.

"Is . . . that what you want?" he asked.

Juliana's entire body lurched against him. *Yes. No. Yes! No . . .*

He smirked, sending a huff of breath about her forehead, then he did that slight head duck he made before moving again. They entered another tower, containing more spiraled stairs, with halls leading from them at intervals. Aidan didn't stop. He didn't hesitate. He went clear to the top floor and turned into that hall. There were scattered torches in the cavernous hall, making a darkness that engulfed them as he walked. The clansmen accompanying him were still climbing the stairs. They could be heard but not seen yet as Aidan approached a large, iron-studded door and kicked at it.

"Come in, my laird."

Juliana's eyes were wide not only at the ancient-sounding voice, but the surety behind it as to who would be calling.

"Dame Lileth."

Aidan said the greeting as he walked to the center of a large room lit mainly from the fire in her fireplace. There were myriad scattered candles all about shelves and niches, putting a cloyingly sweet haze into the air. Then Aidan was tilting to put Juliana's feet toward the floor. He waited for a few moments while she found her balance before opening his arms. He released her fully and started backing from her toward the door. Juliana turned to watch him.

"You brought the lass to me?" the old woman asked.

"'Tis the lone place she'll be safe."

The old woman laughed heartily, but it had a jarring sound not unlike that of broken pottery. "'Tis ever safe with you, Aidan Niall MacKetryck," she replied.

"Na' from me," he replied.

"Where is your Campbell clan missive?"

"Stuck to the ceiling of my great hall," Aidan replied.

"'Twill be hard to answer from there."

Her laughter got even louder. Aidan stepped back farther, leaving a vast chasm of chill between them. Juliana rubbed her arms together at the loss of his warmth.

"True," Aidan said finally.

"Go then. I'll keep your Sassenach lass . . . safe," Dame Lileth announced.

Juliana heard Aidan's grunt of surprise from the door. It covered over her own gasp, but nothing stopped the shocked look they exchanged.

"Sassenach?" Aidan finally asked.

"She has the look of one . . . and the bearing. She probably speaks the Frankish tongue. Doona' tell me you dinna' note it yourself, sweet laird."

"Juliana?" He didn't say it warmly. It was said with every bit of how he must have felt about being deceived and tricked. Juliana swiveled toward him.

"Y-Yes?" she asked with just a hint of warble to it.

"Is this true?"

"Yes," she replied, ignoring the unpleasant shivers running all over her arms.

Aidan looked to the ceiling while taking huge gulps of air. His men had caught up to him. They appeared to be shadowing the torch-lit area behind him with even more man-shaped darkness.

"MacDonal clan took the castle and the villages . . . but they left some of you alive? Perhaps those that had a use, or surrendered . . . or hid?"

"Yes," she replied.

"So . . . this last massacre . . . the English killed their own? Including the woodcutter?"

She nodded.

"This is why you fought your rescue."

She didn't answer. It wasn't really a question.

He grunted. He pulled himself to his full height and crossed his arms about his chest. In the spliced area of shadow and light he stood in, he looked massive, immovable, and frightening. Juliana's shoulders ducked slightly despite the hold she was exerting on her entire frame.

"I must ask you something, Juliana. Afore I decide what is best."

"That does na' sound rash and reckless." Dame Lileth spoke up from the fireplace.

Aidan put up his hand toward the woman. "Juliana, when I ask this, you must be truthful. Fully. You ken?"

"Yes," she said.

He sucked in another breath, making his chest enlarge and moving his locked arms up with it. "Could you cleave unto a Highlander, forsaking your own kind?"

"C-C-C-Could . . . I?" she asked. She was stammering worse than anything Arran managed. Her eyes went huge as an emotion so close to glee filled her, she felt surrounded by the brightness of it. Blinded by it. Juliana suspected she glowed with it. She clasped both hands together and shoved them to her breast in an effort to contain it. A lump was completely blocking her throat and pounding huge beats from there to fill her with what had to be absolute joy. There was no way to contain it.

"Could you cleave unto a Highlander of the MacKetryck clan? Putting nae other man afore him?"

"Oh . . . Aidan." The words didn't make much sense, since they were shoved past the obstruction in her throat and filled with the shake of tears. Juliana couldn't believe what he was asking. For him, she'd forsake heaven.

He looked stern. Unforgiving. As if he detested everything about this . . . and about her. As if he hated asking what he was asking. Juliana had to drop her eyes.

"Juliana. I ask again. And be clear. Could you cleave until a MacKetryck Highlander, putting nae . . . other man afore him?"

His voice was choked-sounding and raw. She couldn't tell what that meant, and she wasn't looking. She was too afraid.

"Yes," she whispered.

"You would forsake being English, and become Scot?"

"Yes," Juliana whispered again.

"You vow it?"

"Yes." How many times did she have to tell him yes? *Yes, Aidan, Yes. I love you! I'd give up heaven for you!*

Juliana looked up then and wished she hadn't. His eyes looked like black stones, with the sheen of moisture atop them. His mouth was set and hard into a look of hatred. Everything about him looked filled with hatred. And he'd aged in the light cast from the woman's fire and tapers as well. Then he moved his gaze to the old woman behind her, and spoke words to her. Words that sent ice right through Juliana.

"I'll get word to Alpin to prepare."

Alpin?

"Aidan . . . no!" Juliana's cry was barely audible, although she screeched it around and through the block in her throat. "No!"

He was turning away, shoving through the honor guard at his flank. He didn't see her sink to the floor. Only the woman behind her did.

Dame Lileth's floor was cold and hard. It had been swept recently. Juliana turned into a quivering shaking ball with her legs tucked up beneath her, and her arms wrapped as tightly as she could about her torso, while her forehead hovered just above the surface of the floor. There were deep cracks in the wood. Her tears disappeared the moment they touched.

"Doona' hold it against him so." The old woman dropped something atop her. Juliana recognized it as a blanket made of the MacKetryck plaid. She shoved it off.

"You disavow your own promise already?" The woman was cackling from over beside her fire.

"Wh-at promise?" Juliana whispered.

"To cleave to a Highlander. You vowed it."

Fresh tears filled her eyes and dripped onto the floor, sinking into it as if they'd never been.

"He has nae other choice. You ken?"

"Everyone . . . has choices." Juliana tried to sound disgusted. She didn't. Her nose sent moisture into the words, and no matter how she sniffed and struggled against it, more just kept coming.

"Name them."

"Marriage . . . to me," she replied.

"The man will na' answer his missive. And the Campbell clan awaits that verra thing. Clan honor. Ah, lass, there is nae honor above that of clan laird. He near died earning it. You believe he'd toss it all over for you?"

No. That truth hurt. Just about everything did, though, to one degree or another. Juliana shuddered and absorbed the pain, and watched as more tears fell onto the wood and disappeared.

"Aidan Niall would rather slit his own throat than disavow his honor."

"Then . . . he can have me as his . . . mistress."

"A born lady like you?"

Juliana's eyes went wide on the floor. She stiffened. "You don't know—"

"Lady Juliana D'Aubenville would never stoop to being a man's plaything," Dame Lileth said.

"Yes . . . she would," Juliana whispered finally.

"Well, the bairn took that choice away, too."

Juliana caught a sobbed breath and looked at the floor in front of her nose as a tear dropped off it. The old woman was crazed. It had been mere days since she'd given herself to Aidan. Days!

"You ken the truth, lass. Just as he knows it."

"You told Aidan this . . . lie?" Juliana wiped at her eyes.

The woman huffed out an amused sound. "He has to protect his bairn. That's why he'll wed you to Alpin. You ken? To give his bairn a name. And legitimacy."

"I won't do it. I won't say the words."

"As a member of Clan MacKetryck, you canna' go against the laird. You ken?"

"I'm not a member of Clan MacKetryck."

"You will be. You just vowed to it."

"I vowed to cleave to a Highlander named MacKetryck. I can pick any I want."

"Lass . . . Aidan will say the words for you. You need to believe it. He is the law. He'll wed you to his brother."

"Give me something to stop it, then! You can do that. All seers have that ability. Perhaps some tansy? In the smallest portion?"

"Nae."

"Why not?"

"'Tis the perfect vengeance, lass. Perfect. Fulfilling. Special."

"Against . . . Aidan?"

"All of them! His father. His uncle. The men who dinna' trust me! You ken what a year in Ketryck Castle dungeon does to a body, lass?"

Juliana shook her head.

"How about fire? You wonder what being tied and set afire does?"

Juliana shook her head again. She reached for the blanket

and pulled it over her shoulders. She was cold. Tired. Her belly and back hurt, and where her heart had been was a solid block of pain.

"If it hadn't been for Dugald's defeat, I'd have perished. Lady Reina at my side."

"So . . . Aidan saved you?"

"In a way. He gained his position back and halted the punishment the Black MacKetryck devised and ordered."

"He . . . saved you. And this is your repayment?"

"Nae. This is."

Dame Lileth went to her chamber door, opened it, and started whispering. As if someone was there. Juliana lifted her head from the floor, looked through the swirls of smoke the door had put into motion. She squinted her eyes, but still couldn't see who the slender, shadowed figure was. Then she heard the name . . . Lachlan. And then Alpin's name. And then hers. Fear invaded her entire frame, as insidious as any viper, chilling her as it pumped with every beat of her heart.

She was on her feet with the plaid wrapped fully about her, and still couldn't stop the shivering as Dame Lileth shut the door and came back through the haze of smoke toward her.

"What have you done?" Juliana asked, trying for an aggressive tone.

"Paid him back." The old woman went past her toward the fire.

"I'll wed . . . Alpin," Juliana said.

"Now . . . why would you do that?" The woman was clattering and clinking with items over by her fire.

"Call Lachlan back," Juliana insisted. "I'll do it. I'll wed Alpin."

"And I ask again, my lady. Why would you do that?"

"Don't hurt Aidan. Please?" Juliana's eyes were swimming with more tears.

"You love him that much?"

The woman had turned from her fire, and the glow behind

her outlined her easily. Juliana nodded. Dame Lileth grunted an answer and went back to fussing with racks and things.

"Stupid man."

"Please?" Juliana whispered.

"I canna' hurt the man more than he does himself. He really does need to learn the value of reflection. Truly. He does."

"Please?" Juliana tried again.

Dame Lileth pretended not to hear. "I'm just setting about making a nice hot drink. I'll make enough for you, my dear. Doona' fret. 'Tis safe. I'd na' do anything to harm the bairn."

Juliana watched through the swirls of smoke as the old woman put deed to word over by her fire. And she was humming to herself.

Humming.

Chapter 22

As the sun pierced through the cloud cover atop Buchyn Loch, Aidan watched with eyes that scratched and burned and attempted to tear up occasionally in defense. The light spread fully before him until it reached his panoramic windows. Then it glinted off his scabbard, lying atop the table at his elbow, as well as the pile of dirks he'd assembled next to it, making that hurtful to look at as well. Aidan tilted his sporran flask and dribbled the last of the whiskey into his mouth, but missed. He swiped at his cheek and chin with a desultory move, and then flipped the flask away. There was a dull thud of sound as it landed and then the sound of it rolling until it was stopped by one of his bedposts. Watching it forced him to look at the chieftain bed, still perfectly made with heavily embroidered linens and blankets of finely woven MacKetryck sett. Readied. For him. To sleep within. Or play with the perfect lass.

Aidan smirked and went back to tormenting his eyes not only with the view, but with sunlight his eyes had to squint at in order to make it bearable. He didn't know why he'd bothered drinking. There wasn't enough whiskey to dull the pain, temper the reality, put him to sleep . . . or keep him from this horrid state called pondering. Aidan put a hand to his eyes, his thumb at one, fingers to the other, and pressed, seeking relief. They were sore, probably red, and drier than anything Tavish had ever attempted to cook. The one thing they weren't was weeping.

Aidan huffed out a shaky breath.

Alpin had taken the news well. Having at least two lasses giggling from the bowels of his chamber behind him probably helped with that. The command to marry Juliana was burning a hole through Aidan's belly, and his little brother had simply asked, "Is that all?" with a massive amount of impatience and moving about in the hall. Before receiving a nod and bolting back into the arms of his waiting women. That was when Aidan had decided to get a full sporran of the best MacKetryck whiskey he could find, making certain there was plenty of it and nobody to see.

Is that all?

Aidan uncovered his eyes, put his elbows on the table, and supported his head in his hands.

"Aidan!"

The sound reverberated through his chamber and then it was accompanied by some fool pounding on his door. Disturbing him. Bothering him. Making him face it. Despite his warning to the two honor guardsmen he'd put in control of preventing that very thing. And the bolt he'd dropped in place. Both were clear signals not to do exactly what they were doing. Aidan lifted his head and looked in that direction, ignoring the ache in his neck at the movement. The pounding got worse as more of his guardsmen joined in. *By God! The castle better be under attack!*

He didn't have to imagine the red. His sore eyes were cursing him with it. Aidan shoved the chair back, knocking it to the floor, grabbed for the scabbard, and strapped it on with vicious movements. Then he was checking the skeans in his belt and adding those from the table's surface. And then he was striding to the door, shoving up the bolt and opening it with such a reddish cast on the fury, the seven men standing there all backed at least a step from him.

"Aidan—"

Aidan had Tavish on his skinny buttocks with a hooked ankle, a skean to Heck's chest, and another one at Kerr's throat before anyone else said anything.

"It's Alpin!" That was Stefan, who had the sense to be out of Aidan's arms' reach.

Aidan pulled back, sucked in on the ache behind every eye blink to glare at them. "What of Alpin?" he asked slowly and distinctly.

"He's heading to the list!"

Aidan pulled in a huge breath, and watched the reddish color about everything wash out into a pinkish tone. "Being on the list is a good thing after a night spent wenching. Jesu'!" He put one foot behind the other and used the move to pivot back toward his room.

"Against Dugald!"

Aidan continued his spin, ending back facing them. He lowered his head, endured the immediate throb of his heart adding to his discomfort by thudding within his chest with increasing beats, and glared. "What?" he asked.

"Dugald challenged Alpin!"

"Aye. Afore the sun even rose!"

"To the death!"

"What the devil for? Alpin does na' have anything Dugald . . ." Aidan's voice dribbled off as it dawned on him exactly what Alpin did possess.

"For the Lady Juliana's hand."

"Who betrayed me?" Aidan blinked around soreness a good sleep would cure and pierced each of them until Heck spoke.

"The lone mention was in Alpin's hall. With you. When you gave him the word."

"So?"

"Was Lachlan MacGorrick anywhere about?" Heck asked.

"Jesu', Kerr!" That was Tavish.

"Me?" Kerr cried.

"He's your cousin."

"One does na' choose their cousins," Kerr complained.

Aidan shoved through the three closest men. The others had already made a path for him. "Move," he commanded.

He led them down the steps, taking two at a time, before reaching the hall, and then came to a stop as he watched the scene unfolding to the dim light cast from the open door at one end, his staircase at the other, and a still burning fire. Kerr's cousin, Lachlan, was atop one of the trencher tables. He was waving his arms and chattering and instructing. He'd ordered two serfs atop the structure, and then he'd made one serf get atop the other's shoulders. And the higher one was waving a stick up into the air at wherever Lachlan pointed.

"Lachlan MacGorrick!"

All three jumped. The movement had the serf on the other's shoulders landing ungracefully on his knees, before he moved to his feet beside the other two. All three stood looking down at Aidan and his men, and looking like fools. Aidan watched them and tempered the immediate wash of anger with a deep breath and a large gulping motion.

"My . . . laird?" Lachlan asked finally.

"My tables are for dining upon. Not standing atop." Aidan enunciated through his teeth.

"I was trying . . . to get the missive . . . down."

The man had ever been effeminate. His squeaky tone added to it and made everything worse somehow. Aidan's heart decided to add further ache to his issues this morning, sending pinging thumps throughout his head with every beat.

"What for?" he asked.

"Some . . . body needs to answer it."

Aidan pulled a skean from his belt, looked up, and flung it toward the first one. There was a collective gasp as they hit, and then both knives fell to the chamber floor, while the paper floated about in the dimness.

"There. It's down. Now get off my tables."

He turned away from the scene and started toward the door. He was at a jog before he reached the step plateaus, deep worry behind the pace. Lachlan wasn't at the list watching the outcome of the contest. That was another sign of what Aidan feared. If Alpin MacKetryck fought against his uncle Dugald, the winner was a foregone conclusion.

The sound of a large crowd beckoned him toward the outer bailey, and Aidan was at a full run before reaching the archway between them. His heart was hammering loudly in his ears, reminding him of its presence and capacity for pain. It felt like a fist of immense strength and dimensions was gripped about it, squeezing along with each beat until they were at a painful level and scope.

Dawn was just passing over the wall, putting a gold tint onto the tops of heads and from there reaching the churned-up mud comprising Castle Ketryck's battle list. His ancestors had planned and constructed well. The list was long enough for a run with horses and wide enough to accommodate whatever moves a struggling mass of men might make. It had been designed to highlight the spectacle within. While both far ends were the same level of the courtyard, making for a head start atop a horse, the ground had gradually been removed and sloped down until the center was a full body jump down from the rock walls that had been built up on each side.

The sound of metal striking metal could be heard over the crowd, and Aidan felt the first slight easing of the fist wrapped about his heart. He jogged the last steps, and then came to a halt. He stepped aside so his men could make a way through to the wall. A loud roar went through the people all about him, and Aidan couldn't wait. He plucked people out of his way and shoved, and when he reached the wall, he was right in time to watch a sword going into the downed body. Before getting pulled back out, with a resultant shower of red. That was when everything went red. Bloodred, and it was coming with every agonized spurt of his heart.

"Nae!"

Aidan yelled it as he vaulted the retaining wall, landing in a crouch and then running in a half-standing stance from the moment he landed, making it look a seamless movement. He had his claymore pulled and readied as he neared, but then he slowed his pace and straightened at the same time. The body on the ground wasn't Alpin. Nor was the victorious man holding his sword in the air and pumping it his uncle, Dugald.

Aidan scanned the end tents. Dugald paced outside the farthest one. Aidan turned direction and loped his way to the other, ignoring the new calls and loud cheering making the ground thump with it as they recognized him, and what that might mean.

Aidan slapped the tent flap open and looked over the seven members of Alpin's honor guard, who were all in a semicircle facing outward. One of them moved to the side, allowing him to see his brother, in a ball on the ground . . . retching and sobbing.

"Alpin?"

Aidan was on his knee and lifting his brother's head and looking him over for the wound to cause such an event. His brother moaned and exhaled a foul breath all over Aidan.

"Aidan. Forgive me. I canna' do it. I've . . . been poisoned."

Aidan grinned, felt the huge release of worry as well as a complete dispersion of the red that had hampered his vision. He was nearly giddy with it as he hugged his brother, shaking with the laughter, and making the other groan worse in his agony.

"I'm . . . dying. And . . . you laugh," Alpin complained.

"What . . . did you drink last eve?"

"'Twas na' the drink. 'Twas that Sorcha."

"Sorcha?" Aidan wrinkled his brow.

"Juliana dismissed her from your . . . bed . . . so I thought—"

"I had a woman named Sorcha?" Aidan asked.

"Long black hair. Luscious limbs."

"Ah. Aye. Her."

"She gave me something. I—"

Alpin rolled and was on his knees spewing nothing but bile, and Aidan looked up at his men.

Aidan pointed at a large, burly lad. "Find this Sorcha. And hold her."

The man had a slight smile on his mouth before he nodded and moved from the tent.

"Clan Patriarch . . . Dugald MacKetryck . . . sends another warning!"

One of Dugald's men was yelling the words from just past the center of the list. On this side of center. The crowd added to it with whistles and calls.

Aidan gestured with his head to Tavish. Then, he picked up Alpin and put him back on his cot. "Get him to Lady Reina. Nae. First get him water. Cold water. And not to drink."

"Na' to drink?" his man asked.

"Nae. To dunk his head in."

Tavish was back. "Dugald claims the Lady Juliana's hand in wedlock from Alpin MacKetryck. By forfeit."

"He canna' have her. I claim her."

"You canna' stop this, my liege. If Alpin does na' meet the challenge, then Alpin forfeits."

Never. She was wedding Dugald over Aidan's dead body. And not before.

Aidan pulled in a huge breath. Exhaled it. And then he did it again. And again. Over and over, tightening every muscle in his body as he called on the ache that was hitting him with each increased heartbeat . . . forcing the red back into his vision. And making it stay there. Then he turned, lowered his chin, and snarled the answer.

"Send word to Dugald. For my challenge."

And then he forwent the wait. His uncle would know what was happening. Aidan was right behind Tavish onto the list, lifting his claymore in his arms and pumping it over and over into the air, to gain the power of crowd noise that added to the charge of heartbeats hitting him, bringing alertness and readiness and anger. Massive anger. Everything went blood-red hued and perfectly focused.

It was as exciting and massive an emotion as it had been seven years earlier when they'd met on this list. With Lady Reina and Dame Lileth tied and bound to a stake. Aidan hadn't won in time to prevent the lighting of it, but that was the farthest it went. That was his uncle's trick, at the last moment, to cheat a win from him.

Dugald was at a run when he heard, gathering his own crowd noise with the way he answered. Aidan stayed where he was, his claymore high above his head, with his back to his uncle until he'd reached midfield before swiveling and starting his own charge.

Each step flooded him with more red emotion, darkening the view to a blood hue that his slit eyes made darker. More powerful. Harsher. A moment before impact, he slid to a knee, scraping skin on the sod, putting his claymore upward at the same time, and that hooked the hilt of Dugald's sword as he ran right past his nephew. The man's weapon went sailing right out of his useless bloodied hand, and then Aidan was up on his feet, moving to face his uncle, head lowered and bellowing. Deep. Throbbing deep. Making certain there was no mistaking his intent, by his stance and tone.

The crowd answered his bellow, making a swell of noise that barely penetrated the angry haze of red Aidan was living. He watched Dugald's frustrated search before the blade landed to the side of him, blade down, where it trembled in place. Aidan circled his uncle, giving him time to retrieve his weapon and making certain Dugald understood everything that wasn't put in words. There wasn't going to be a survivor this time.

And that was when he saw what he most prized. Fear. Soaking through the red haze, coloring everything and feeding the heartbeat that was controlling everything. There wasn't pain attached to anything. There was anger and intensity and movement and reaction. Instant reaction.

Dugald moved his vision from his nephew's for a moment to fetch his sword, and when he looked back, Aidan had moved so far to one side, his uncle had to find him again. And then Aidan was charging, gaining speed and momentum and surprise to the attack. Dugald MacKetryck was a stout man. The match to his nephew in bulk. And muscle. And weight. He didn't move easily. He was hampered by his injury and had to use his left hand. The right one was held to his side, dripping and bloodied and useless.

Aidan used a pushing motion behind each slash of his blade, staying on the attack and forcing the man to give ground, shoving and pushing with each sword move until Dugald lost his stance and started backing away. Again. Despite sticking his feet in and lowering his head and sending cursed slurs through his teeth. Tripping. Breathing hard. Tripping again.

When he went down, Aidan was right with the movement, using his uncle's falling motion to slice at his left hand, hooking the hilt of Dugald's blade again. From there, it was another flip of his wrist to send it up and into the air again.

Aidan backed off again, jogging backward ten paces. Then he put his head and shoulders down and bellowed again, raising his chin as he did so, which sent the cry to the heavens above. This time the crowd was loud enough to get through the red haze coloring everything. Thumping came through the ground as Aidan circled his uncle, waiting for the man to regain his blade again.

Circling. Pumping his blade into the air, calling on the crescendo of crowd thumping in rhythm with his motions. Reveling in it. Waiting. Taunting.

Dugald moved his vision again to gain his blade. This time when he looked back, Aidan was right in front of him, making his uncle react with a jerk that didn't come naturally to the man. And enjoying the abject fear deep in those emerald eyes. Eyes that had stolen Aidan's wedded wife. Usurped his place. Seen his father's last gasp for breath, after he'd shoved the blade into him.

Just as his nephew had seen. And witnessed. And staunched. Setting it aside as something too painful to deal with. Ponder. Think on. Aidan watched the dawning realization of it in his uncle's eyes. And gloried in the fear.

Aidan renewed his attack, lashing time and again, putting punishing force with each push of his blade over and over again, until Dugald started backing up again. Flagging. Sucking for breath. His uncle was forced to use both hands on his sword in order to meet the continual punishment of Aidan's blade as each move got faster and faster until the motion was near blurred. His uncle tripped again. Caught it. Parried another blow from Aidan. Tripped again. Going down.

This time, Aidan reached over and grabbed the sword from his uncle's hands, wet with blood and sweat. Aidan jogged back several steps, keeping his uncle in sight, and then he tossed his head into the air and held both blades high and yelled the reaction into the sky.

Massive throbs of crowd approval matched every beat of his heart, accompanying the red wash coloring everything and the loud whoosh of each heartbeat in his ears. Making a mass of sensation that filled every portion of him, making him one with the moment. The dawn was alive with it. The very air was filled with it. It was thunderous and it was massive, and it was daunting. And then it was something else . . . deathly. Aidan's senses warned him a moment before the dirk tossed at him would have hit his back.

He was on his back and rolling, keeping the swords above his head in order to keep the motion as the dirk aimed at his back passed harmlessly by. Another dirk hit the ground beside his head. Another near his leg and then another and another as his uncle violated every code of conduct by tossing dirks without honor or anything other than murderous intent.

It was the same that had done in Aidan's father.

His push-up shove from the ground was punctuated by the fanning of one sword in front of his chest at the same time. That movement deflected the next dirk, sending an arc of sunlit sparks flying from the contact of skean to sword blade. The reaction of the crowd made the air vibrate, pumping red through the entire scene, while surges of thumps went all along the rock walls, into the earth, the sky. His very existence. Joining the red-induced vision he was enjoying, encapsulating and moving through.

Aidan went into a crouch, with bouncing movements made on the balls of his feet as his thighs took the brunt force to make each parrying move. That way he made the smallest target possible. He started circling Dugald again, keeping the blood-lust fully in front of him with the thunderous beat of his heart. Each breath. Each blink of his dry punished eyes.

Dugald MacKetryck was on his feet, swiveling in a small arc, a dirk in each hand, ready to launch them. Aidan made the same maneuver, except he held swords in his hands, rather than blades. He watched his uncle sneer, giving him the time to move. Then the man tossed both dirks directly at him. Aidan was too quick for him as he moved to slam his fists against each other in front of his face. This put the sword tips down while the flat of the blades shielded his chest and throat. He heard the dirks hit through the trembling of the blades, and before they'd landed, he'd spun to the left, pulling his sword up at the same time. To make the perfect throw. For one moment in time he stayed still . . . posed, one knee to the ground with his arm cocked back. Then he launched the sword in his right hand, and even before it left his hand, he was pulling two dirks from his belt and sending them flying behind the sword.

Dugald was impaled by a sword through his chest, while the man shook in place from the two dirks spearing each eye socket. Aidan watched as his uncle sagged to his knees and then fell forward, slamming the blades further through his skull. And then Aidan put his remaining sword in the air and yelled until his throat gave out. And then he did it again.

The Red MacKetryck had won again.

Chapter 23

"It's time to prepare for your wedding."

Of course it was. Juliana looked at the rock wall before her nose and blinked it back into focus. She'd thought she'd spent every tear before falling into a fitful sleep on this mat. Sleep filled with dreams, desires, wicked entreaties. More than once she'd awakened to such a clear image of Aidan MacKetryck, it had hurt a thousand times worse to find she was still in Dame Lileth's tower room.

"Come, Lady Juliana. Your bath awaits."

Her bath. Juliana sighed heavily and rolled onto her back, looked at the crosspieces of wood supporting the roof, and waited for her eyes to dry. Nothing made sense anymore. She'd always thought life had a destination. She was alive for a purpose. A reason. She had a destiny to fulfill. And the moment she'd admitted love for Aidan, that was when she thought it the clearest. She loved him endlessly. Completely. Wholly. With every breath her body kept sending her. She'd die for him. She'd risk heaven for him. But it wasn't to be. He required her to wed another. And that changed her certainty of destiny. Was life truly just a series of nonlinked events until one died? Did nothing have significance? Not even love?

"You should try a bit of this pie. Baked fresh this morn. With fresh duck."

Juliana's shivers worsened. The slats of wood assembled above her went blurred and indistinct. She gulped and kept swallowing and blinking until the sensation passed. "I'm not hungry," she answered finally in a whisper.

"You will be. You've a long eve ahead of you." The woman snickered again.

Juliana hugged her arms about herself and watched the ceiling waver some more. She wondered if there was a potion the woman could give her to get her through the upcoming evening and then the ceremony without one sign of her heart breaking.

"Come along, dearie. I'll reheat your slice for you."

"I'm not . . . hungry," Juliana repeated.

"Starvation takes a powerful long time to kill one."

"Does it?" Juliana asked.

"Dugald MacKetryck proved it. With his first wife, Dame Fiona Finlay. Now . . . that woman lasted fortnights of time. Howling and crying and carrying on with the agony. Starvation. *Tsk. Tsk.*" Dame Lileth clicked her tongue.

"Dugald's first wife . . . starved herself? But . . . why?"

Dame Lileth thought that was very funny. She was cackling with it. "Oh nae. Na' that one. Too stubborn. All the Finlays are stubborn. Dugald starved her. All the way to her grave. He dinna' even care about starting a clan war with Finlay. They're a small clan. Weak. And Dugald was getting impatient. Seven years wed. He wanted a differing lass to wife. One that would give him bairns. Male bairns. And he had his eye on Siniag MacGorrick. She was a lovely lass. Winsome. All who met her wanted her. Dugald got her."

"So . . . he wed again?"

"I just told you Siniag was winsome. Frail. She could na' withstand his fists. Or his mating. She cried herself to weakness. The ague took her. That first winter."

Juliana blinked at the roof above her, not even noticing it was clear, focused, distinct. "So. He's not wed."

"You are a verra lucky lass."

Juliana frowned on that. "How so?"

"My sweet laird is a demon on the battlefield. His anger takes over. He is nigh invincible. 'Tis why you're na' preparing to be Dugald's fourth wife. Lucky lass."

Juliana moved into a sit and crossed her legs beneath her, while leaning against the rock behind her. "Dugald's . . . fourth wife?"

"Come. Sit at my table. Drink a bit of my mead and eat a bit of my pie."

"And if I don't . . . you won't explain?"

Dame Lileth bobbed her head and smiled at Juliana. "You're a verra sharp lass. Verra. Aidan would've done well with you at his side."

Juliana winced but had it covered over as she stood, and shook out the folds of her green linen bliaut. It was heavily creased, worn-looking, and damp in places. Used. Found lacking. Ready for the discard pile. It matched the wearer of it, she decided, walking over to the table. Dame Lileth had an oblong table, set against one wall and jutting out into the room. The end closest to the wall was devoted to all kinds of urns and vases and pots and vials. That was where it was dark and shadowed unless the torches were lit. It was a complete contrast to the side closest to the fire and the slits cut through rock to allow air and light, and if one bothered to look, a good view over the shoreline of Buchyn Loch with the rise of mountain beyond that.

The lighter, companionable side of Dame Lileth's table had an arrangement of thistles and heather garnishing it, goblets crafted of thick glazed glass, and hammered leaden platters. Juliana pulled out a stool and sat at that end.

"What happened to his third wife?" she asked once she

was seated and sipping at mead that had been darkened with molasses.

"That would be Dame Edme KilCreggar, Lady Reina's sister. Dugald was wed to her the longest. Nigh on a decade. Still . . . nae bairns. I was sent for to assist her with the creation of one. Stupid man. The barrenness was na' his woman's issue, but his. The pox does odd things to a man's abilities. I made the mistake of telling him so."

Juliana gasped. "What did he . . . do?"

"Strapped me to a stake. With Lady Reina. But you already ken what happened next . . . and how that ended."

"What about the wife, Edme?"

"She just . . . died. Lachlan could na' even find out how."

"Lachlan . . . MacGorrick?" Juliana split the name in her disgust.

"Aye."

The woman chuckled and set a sliver of her meat pie onto the platter in front of Juliana. She'd warmed it somehow atop her fire, and it gave off wonderful smells.

"He spies for . . . you?"

Dame Lileth sat on a chair facing Juliana, put her arms into a steepled position with her hands clasped, and then rested her chin atop it. "Lachlan is a man of many talents. And useful. 'Twas always best to know what the Black MacKetryck was up to . . . afore he did it."

"Smart," Juliana replied.

"So . . . do you think he'd be of more use to Arran . . . or Alpin?" she asked.

Juliana reached out and broke off a bit of her pie, chewed it, and swallowed before answering. They'd used a bit of herbs . . . perhaps garlic and sage, with their filling, making it tastier than the usual. With the addition of the mead, it made excellent fare. It seemed Highlanders knew how to feed their captives once they placed them in fancy, invisible, silver-lined cages, too.

"I would na' remove him from Dugald's service," she replied.

Dame Lileth lifted her head and grinned, showing she still possessed most of her teeth, and they were in healthy shape. "Ah lass. I forget. You're sharp, but untried. Frightened of what you might learn. You doona' ken."

Juliana stopped her sip from the tankard to look over the rim at Dame Lileth. "Know . . . what?" she asked.

"How everything changes just by your presence. As I foresaw."

"What?" Juliana asked again.

"You've been here less than a day, and already you've done what none others could. I thank you for that."

Juliana tipped a swallow into her mouth. These Highlanders truly did brew the best ales and meads, and their whiskey was probably vision-inducing as well.

"You've freed us of Dugald. He was killed this morn. In battle. At Aidan's hands. As is just and destined . . . and seven years overdue."

"Aidan . . . killed—" Juliana was choking and coughing. She shouldn't have tried to swallow when shock closed off her throat.

"Aye. Aidan. Your Aidan. I already told you the man is a devil on the field. None others will challenge him. Except Dugald . . . and then he cheated. And now he's gone. Doona' fash it. The man was black all through. 'Twas a fair match. All agree. Aside of which Aidan had to win your hand back . . . after Alpin lost it."

Juliana put the tankard down very carefully, right next to the leaded tin platter. And looked at it. Then she looked back over at the woman. Grimaced on the dry feeling in her throat. Steeled herself. "What . . . of Alpin?" she asked, and hunched her shoulders slightly not only to withstand the answer but to hide an emotion that might be relief.

The woman's features settled into lined blankness. "Alpin

lives, lass. And that was your doing as well. He was dosed up with a bit of dandelion mixed with valerian . . . or so Lady Reina informs me. By a wench named Sorcha. You recollect Sorcha?"

Juliana nodded. Her throat wasn't working. Her heart was using the space to hit her with every beat of it.

"Seems Alpin found Sorcha as lusty as his brother did. He'll regret that. The woman is vengeful. Mean-spirited. She left him prostrate. Unable to fight. Although he'll be well in time for the wedding."

The wedding . . .

Juliana looked away. At the window and then at the view past that. She didn't see any of it. "Lachlan will be of more use to Arran, then," she said finally.

"Arran?"

"Alpin will have no need of him." Juliana's voice cracked despite the effort she was exerting. She couldn't help it. "He'll have me."

If Lady Reina had been put to work on a wedding dress that would be correct attire for a bride of a MacKetryck clansman, she'd outdone herself.

The richness and artistry of it was apparent with every breath, and every heartbreak-filled moment it took to walk down the five stories of stairs from Dame Lileth's tower, Arran at the lead, the looming form of Heck at Juliana's left side, while the near albino-looking form of one of Alpin's men was on her right. He had the palest hair Juliana had ever seen. The palest blue eyes. And the leanest form. His name was Muir. Juliana remembered that from the introduction. Muir . . . MacGorrick. She'd nodded and looked away quickly, and kept the musing quiet. It appeared that not only was MacGorrick a large family in the clan, but none of them appeared to favor the others.

The silken feel of her blue-toned underdress caressed
every step, while the drape of her pure white samite bliaut
added a rustle to the stillness. The satin had been embroidered
all about the bodice and hem with silver stems and leaves, and
then they'd filled in the leaves with real golden threads. The
underskirt had been gathered from beneath, forming a billowing effect that contrasted with the smallness of her waist, as
well as allowed the underdress to peek out whenever she
moved. There was a strap attached to each wrist, one holding
to Heck's outstretched one, the other to Muir, and that lifted
the skirts elegantly from first the stone steps, and then the
rushes on the floor just outside the great hall.

"My lady?"

Heck stopped at the archway leading to the great hall. Juliana could hear the laughter and chatter and music that had
grown louder with every step they'd taken. Heck stood patiently, looked down at her. Juliana knew why. It was the
same question he'd asked when he'd arrived to escort her.
Aidan had sent his senior man. He'd been several minutes
behind Muir. And too much reminder. And that was trouble.

"You ready?"

It was said with the same concern. And it engendered the
same reaction as her eyes filled with more stupid tears. She
hadn't been able to hide them when she'd turned from con-
templation of the unseen view from Dame Lileth's tower and
seen who it was.

And she couldn't now.

She nodded slightly and kept her eyes on the space right
in front of her. On the back of Arran's *feile breacan*. She
didn't dare look up. Not with tears filling each eye and just
waiting for a wrong blink to send them down her cheeks.
Maybe when she was seated, with her hands clasped in front
of her, and Alpin at her side. Then . . . she'd look. Maybe.

The caplet atop her head pulled slightly at her tresses with
the bowing of her head. This headdress had been brought

when she was nearly finished. It was fashioned of silver and gold, interlaced and studded with all shades of pearls, some white, some ecru, some gray, and there were even black pearls smelted into the latticework by yet another metal artisan. The same pearls were attached to the ribbons leading from her caplet to thread among her hair, in a vain attempt to contain it. Lady Reina had worked her fingers through Juliana's hair, enticing it into a riot of silken curls. That shortened the length considerably from the knee-length one of yester-eve, to one that just grazed the bottom of her buttocks.

They entered the great hall, and a resultant hush started settling among the inhabitants. All of them. Throughout the room. Juliana heard the shuffle of feet, the scrape of stools, the dropping of more than one tankard, or body, and then what could be the sound of many breaths being held. Arran walked in a path that was opening while Heck and Muir continued to walk her inexorably right past the larger, raised dais that belonged to the laird of Clan MacKetryck, toward the smaller one.

That one was now assigned to Alpin.

From her side vision, Juliana noted the bottom of Aidan's platform as Muir passed in front of it, the carved wood meeting him at the waist, while it was nearly to her throat. She stumbled slightly, swallowed around a huge obstruction in her throat, and sucked her bottom lip into her mouth as she failed. Tears obliterated the rushes before her, turning the path into a wash of darkened straw atop slate flooring. Heck must have known of it, for the moment she faltered, his other hand went atop hers, helping hold her up. Juliana bowed her head farther, watched the drops peppering her bodice with such self-disgust and loathing she didn't know how she didn't perish of it.

They'd arrived, and Juliana was forever grateful for Heck's presence, as Muir MacGorrick just let her go and walked up and onto the platform. Heck put his right arm about her and lifted her with him the three steps to the dais and then he walked along the back of it, making certain she reached her assigned seat without falling into a sobbing heap on the floor. She didn't know how to thank him, and was afraid to look up to even try.

"Juliana?"

She'd known she was seated next to Alpin. The thin legs that were jittering beneath his plaid could belong to none other.

"It is na' that onerous to be wed to me," he informed her.

Juliana smiled slightly and took another shuddering breath. It wasn't onerous at all. And given time, he might even match his brother in bulk and might. As well as in other areas . . . and other pursuits.

She gulped around the obstruction in her throat, pulled in another shuddering breath. Eased it out. And then nodded. "I know that," she replied finally.

"Than act it. I'm getting dark looks from just about everyone."

"May I have a cloth . . . Alpin?" she asked.

"Here." He pulled a white linen square from his belt and handed it to her. "And I want it back."

Juliana swiveled and leaned away from him, past where Muir sat, trying to make it look a shy gesture while she wiped quickly at her eyes and then her face. She'd forgotten this side to Aidan's little brother. She felt like kissing him as his words dried tears better than anything she could have devised.

"Just because I'm wedding you, does na' mean anything. You ken?"

She nodded.

"I'm na' changing."

"Changing?" she asked, turning back forward in her chair.

"You're still too auld. And doona' take this poorly. But you're . . . large."

Juliana sucked in on her cheeks, turned her head, and looked up at him. *Large?*

"You probably even . . . sag." He dropped his eyes to her bodice, leaving her no excuse to misinterpret what he said.

"How old are you, Alpin?" she asked.

"Eighteen."

"Well, I'm seventeen. You're the one that probably sags." Juliana dropped her eyes to his groin so he'd know what she referred to.

"Why, you—"

"Haven't you heard of Elinor of Aquitaine? The greatest heiress of the ages? Seriously, Alpin . . . your education is lacking. She was thirty-one when she wed England's King Henry. And he was your age."

"Thirty-one?" He was aghast. His voice even rose.

"Yes. Thirty-one. To his eighteen. And they had a long . . . and fruitful marriage."

"Fruitful?"

"They had four sons, Alpin. Four."

"Speaking of . . . sons. And sagging. And such . . ."

Juliana had the cloth in her lap and was looking at it and then she was twisting it. She didn't know why she hadn't kept her mouth closed. Then again, she no longer felt any inclination to cry.

"I'm na' fond of red hair. Jesu'. My sons will probably have it."

"Alpin—" she began, only to get interrupted.

"Will you arrange it so your hair is hidden tonight? I mean . . . after the ceremony? For our consummation?"

"Why . . . Alpin . . . I'll try," she replied, using a soft, hesitant, virginal voice.

"Good. Then . . . perhaps . . . with the lights dimmed enough. That might work."

With the lights dimmed?

"You probably doona' ken what I speak of, but trust me. It's na' going to be easy," he informed her.

"What will you need from me, Alpin . . . dear?" she asked, stressing the last word into a breathless tone. She watched him jump slightly.

"Na' that. You'll have to keep silent."

"Silent. Very well. Anything else?" She asked with a sweet tone.

"Nae. Except—nae." He finished.

"Except . . . what?"

"Are you any good . . . with your mouth?"

Juliana's eyes went wide and it matched her slack jaw. He couldn't possibly mean . . . and she wasn't possibly doing it!

"That's it! I'd rather wed Arran!" She flung the linen at him and shoved her chair back to stand, glaring down at him. Muir was right with her, doing the exact same stand, as if to block that side.

"Arran? He's na' even a man yet!"

"Well . . . that can be cured, and there's one thing he definitely is," Juliana informed him.

"What?"

"Mannered."

"I have manners."

He'd stood now, too, and towered over her, effectively blocking that escape as well. He was definitely Aidan Mac-Ketryck's brother. The lowered chin, slit eyes, and angered look were every bit his brother. Juliana ignored it.

"It's a shame you don't show them, then," she replied.

"I doona' want to wed you," he told her.

"Then why are you?"

"Because my brother commands it. Why else?"

"Well, he can't command the consummation, Alpin."

"Are you threatening me?"

His voice had lowered and he'd put his shoulders forward

a bit, too. All reminiscent of Aidan. Juliana blinked at the solid menace he was presenting, gulped on the slightest taste of fear, and blinked again. Then she had to find her voice. It didn't come out as aggressive as she'd planned either.

"I'm not so certain I'm going to be willing, Alpin. That's what I'm saying."

He sucked in air several times, enlarging what looked to be a developing frame that would rival his brother, given enough time and work. And then he exhaled it. And then he glared at her.

"You ken something, Juliana? I believe that just might work."

She gasped. And fell back into her chair.

Chapter 24

He couldn't take much more of this.

Aidan blinked on dry eyes that had felt sand-filled since before they'd pulled him off the list and tossed him into the loch. It was being added to by the ache in his head, until it owned and punished him with every pulse beat. Then she arrived and it actually got worse. Pain thudded through his head with every pulse beat, and it just got harder and more intense and more difficult to endure.

And then Kerr and Ewan started up.

"It appears Alpin MacKetryck received Dugald's household today, with the apartments and portion to maintain it . . . and he does na' seem to be in charge of much of it. What say you, Ewan?"

"The laird kens what he's doing, Kerr. You just try and get me in more trouble. This is why you ask."

"Oh look. She argues with him. And wins. Alpin Mac-Ketryck is getting more lass than he can handle. This is what's happening."

"And I still tell you, our laird has a plan. This is part of it. I doona' fathom what it is, but the man would na' give the lass who holds his heart to his brother for nae reason. Especially that brother."

"Oh. It looks like she's going to hit him. Nae. My brother Muir prevents that. He is assisting."

"We truly should find something better to watch than Alpin's household at this banquet. The laird still hasn't found his sporran and Loch Erind is a good distance."

"Well said, Ewan. I forget."

"Look! It appears Alpin may hit her!"

Aidan swung his head in his brother's direction and wished he hadn't. Kerr and Ewan were right. Alpin was having issues with his soon-to-be lawfully wedded wife. He was standing up to her, though. And then Aidan watched as Juliana appeared to back down from whatever the threat was. Aidan didn't realize he was half out of his chair until Tavish shoved at his shoulder from his left side, startling him back to a sit.

"Your brother will na' tolerate interference, Aidan. Na' with that one."

Aidan lowered his chin and glared at him. Tavish grinned.

"He's right," Heck replied from Aidan's other side. "The lass needs to ken her master. Nae man wants a shrew to wife."

Aidan turned to his senior man and glared at him as well.

"'Tis what happens when one weds. The woman becomes his property. She obeys. Or she's beaten."

"Nae man can alter that. 'Tis a lawful wedded husband's place to chastise his wife. Right, Tavish?"

"Right."

Aidan lowered his forehead on the surface of his table and hit it into the wood several times. It didn't do much, except make the pounding between his ears even louder. More painful. More inescapable. He lifted his head a little and sighed. Long and hard. And then he swiveled his head to face the man on his left.

"How do you feel about the Campbell clan, Tavish?" he asked.

Tavish straightened. As did Stefan beyond him. And Gregor past that. And the three more clansmen beyond that.

"Campbell clan? Hmm . . . They're a large clan. Bloodthirsty. Far-flung. They cover a goodly section of the Highlands. Good allies to have."

"What kind of foe would they be?"

Tavish grinned. Widely. "Worthy," he replied.

"Heck?" Aidan swung his head to the other side and looked upward at his senior man.

"What is the question?" Heck asked, although it was obvious he'd heard it from the smile on his face, and on Arran's and Kerr's and Ewan's faces beyond as well.

"Campbell clan? How do you feel about them?"

"Begging your pardon, but I have na' had much interaction with them. I understand they're a fighting clan. Tough. Strong," Heck replied. "Why do you ask?"

"I was thinking of starting a war with them. What do you say now?"

"Well, I've tired of taking on unworthy foes. The Sassenach? Pah. The MacDonals? Pah. We're wasted on wars with their ilk."

"Those shields on yon wall do seem to be missing a Campbell one," Kerr inserted.

"Well then. Let's go get one." Aidan sat up fully. Put his arms above his head and stretched. Pulled in air that felt like it was racing through his veins, filling him with energy and resolve and thrill.

"It's a-a-about time!" Arran announced, sounding young and high-voiced amid the others.

Aidan stood. The men all about him stood as well, and then they turned to the right without a word of direction being said. He watched as Alpin's table noted it, and then the floor below him started noticing as well as movement and chatter and drinking and song slowly halted until a hush was falling over the entire gathering.

Then his men started moving, pulling claymores as they went, until they were assembled on the floor in front of Alpin's table.

"Alpin MacKetryck!" Aidan was bellowing it before he reached the floor, and gritting his teeth as the jump sent more ache flashing through his head.

"Aye?"

Alpin was on his feet. His men all were as well. The lone one ignoring him was Juliana. She was looking at her hands in her lap. Or something.

"Give over the lass!"

"W-W-What?" Alpin stuttered.

"The lass, Juliana! I claim her! Now!"

Alpin looked confused. And then relieved. And then his man said something to him, for he puffed out his chest and yelled back, "By what right?"

"Right of conquest. And victory! And title!"

His man spoke with him again. Juliana had lifted her head and was looking at him with huge blue-green eyes in a very white face. Aidan hoped she didn't faint.

"What do you offer?" Alpin asked.

"Hand over the lass, Alpin. Or I'll take her."

Aidan walked right up to the table, bent his knees until he was level with Juliana, and then met her gaze. And was lost. Completely. Perfectly. He winked, and watched her jerk. And before she'd stopped the motion, he'd leapt onto the edge of the partition, reached across the table, grabbed her by the shoulders, and pulled, bringing her back with him and onto his shoulder, with his backward drop to the floor. And then he was running for the opposite door amid a massive amount of cheering, and hooting, and tankards getting thumped onto tables.

* * *

Her belly was getting the worst of it. Aidan took a series of steps in plateaus of three at a time, with a resultant jog of her body against his. Her hair was falling all about her and bouncing with every move, and where he'd captured it beneath her, the pearls were bruising and annoying. Juliana lifted her head and watched the men trying to keep up with him. Everyone was grinning. Chattering. Pointing. Creating more confusion and havoc in her mind as they hurried after Aidan.

This couldn't be happening, but every bit of her body knew it was. Her heart sent complete happiness and giddiness into every portion of her with every single beat. Then he was running along corridor after corridor, lit with torches and not much else.

"Where . . . are we going? Aidan?"

She knew he heard her, because he started laughing, before moving even faster than before. They passed beneath an archway, and then another, and finally he slowed, his footsteps echoing all through the large room they were in. Hard wooden benches lined the walls, showing exactly what it was. Aidan came to a stop in the center of the room, and stood, breathing heavily, raising her with each of them, and then he leaned forward and brought her over his shoulder and onto the floor. He didn't let her go, though. He stood, holding her within an enclosure created by his arms and breathing all over her.

"Where . . . are we?" she whispered.

He looked down, and smiled. "My chapel," he replied.

"Your . . ." Juliana started, but his grin widened, silencing her.

"Chapel."

"Aidan . . . I—" she began.

"Am wedding with me. Right here. And right now, Juliana."

Her mouth dropped. Her heart was right behind it. "What . . . of . . . the Campbell . . . heiress?"

"What of her?"

"Aidan—"

"I'm past arguing it, Juliana," he replied.

He was still grinning down at her, and then he tightened his arms about her, turning her entire existence into heated, shuddering, sweaty arms, and a chest to match. Juliana was close to melting. His honor guard was starting to arrive, holding on to the vestibule doors while they recovered from their run, some even bending double. And then Arran crossed through them, and behind him were Alpin and his men. And then more of them, filling the area behind Aidan. Juliana ducked back behind Aidan's arm and placed her nose at the center of his chest. Breathing with him, glorying in him, feeling perfect peace for the first time in her life.

"You ready?" he asked against the caplet, which had somehow managed to stay affixed to her head.

She nodded.

He swiveled her, putting her back to him, and then moved her slightly to the side of him, and started walking. And then he moved farther from her, leaving her his arm to hold on to, while everything else on her was pulsating and vibrating to the nearness of him. And then they reached such a candlelit area just below the altar that it looked near midday.

There was a healthy-sized clergyman rushing from somewhere behind the altar, still fastening the ties on his robes while a page ran alongside, holding the heavy headpiece atop his head.

"Father!" Aidan hollered, sounding incredibly loud with the reverberation throughout the chamber.

"My laird! This is—you're early! I expected you—an hour! I've na' even finished my meal, and I . . . My laird?" The man was out of breath and stumbling through the words by the time he'd reached the altar and peered down at them.

The headpiece wasn't attached properly either, and was slightly off-center. Juliana had to look down before she giggled.

"Aye?" Aidan replied.

"Where is the groom?"

"I am the groom, Father!" Aidan yelled that reply as well and in that chamber it echoed. The crowd noise behind them swelled accordingly to a near deafening level.

The priest had to wave his arm to get enough quiet to speak. "This is highly—aye. Well and good. The laird is wedding. *Wedding!* Without proper ceremony . . . and no banns! And no notice. And I—well!"

The man was opening a very large manuscript atop the altar, bound with leather straps. The booming sound of the front binder falling was nearly as loud as Aidan's voice had been. And nearly as indefatigable. And inescapable. And resolute. And unyielding. It was everything Juliana's heart surged for, and everything her mind disputed. She should protest. There would be fighting. Clansmen would die. She should protect them . . . him. She tipped her head toward him.

"Aidan? I shouldn't wed . . . with you." Juliana whispered the words. She needn't have bothered. The altar had great acoustics and the words went up and out and projected. There was a rumble of sound following it. An angry sound. Coming from the amount of clansmen filling everywhere behind them, crowding into the available space in the narrow nave.

"Oh aye. You should. And you will. Begin the service, Father."

"Aidan—"

He grabbed her to him and planted his mouth atop hers, stopping not only the words but her breath and her heart. And then he moved his head slowly from her, keeping his eyes full on hers, and canceled every desire to say them as well. And then he looked over her shoulder and up at the altar again.

"The words, Father? And say them short. I'm in nae mood for patience."

"But . . . Aidan!" Juliana tried once more. That was projected up and out for the listening ears as well.

"I already told you, Juliana, I'll na' argue it. Father? Begin!"

Latin words started getting murmured behind her. Juliana didn't even hear them.

"But—the Campbell clan!"

The priest stopped. Everyone stopped. Aidan started chuckling and then he looked down at her and grinned.

"I am ever rash . . . Juliana. Ever. As well as reckless. But there is victorious in my birth curse as well. And never more so than now. Right now." He looked back at the priest. "Father? Continue the ceremony and doona' cease! And that's an order."

Latin words started up again.

"But . . . Aidan!"

He pulled her up at the same moment he lowered his head, and this time when he kissed her, he made certain to steal her breath and her senses and send flames in their place. And they were in the house of worship! From somewhere she heard the priest intoning words that filled the space above her, his voice a drone of irrevocability and finality . . . and eternity.

Aidan pulled back from his kiss so slowly it pulled her lip flesh with it. His mouth was still in a pout as he added to it, imprinting fire all over her with the intensity of his look. Wild. Raw. Primal. Silence enveloped them, filled with the increasing beats of her heart in her ears. She pressed her nose into his chest, tipping her forehead so she could feel each beat as his heart gave it. She didn't see him turn back to the altar. She felt it.

"I gave an order, Father. And here you are silent. What? Oh. Surname. Nae. She has none."

Yes I do! D'Aubenville! She opened her mouth to say it, but he filled the space with more words.

"She'll soon be the bride of the MacKetryck. And it will be moot. So finish," Aidan continued. "Oh. 'Tis Juliana. J-u-l-i-a-n-a." He spelled it out. "And of course she says aye! Move on with it."

"Oh . . . Aidan." The emotion in those two words easily rose to the rafters and from there filled the room.

"I said move on, Father!"

The Latin words continued unabated. Juliana blinked around the surprise. Dame Lileth hadn't lied. He truly would wed her without her consent. She went back to thrilling with the immense heartbeat at her forehead, the heavy feel of his breaths against her head, and the total comfort and security of his arms about her. Avoiding it. Accepting it. Adoring it.

The priest went over a name that started with Aidan Niall MacKetryck, lord baron of Ketryck, earl of Tryck-Crannog, laird of Clan MacKetryck, and then he continued with more titles and claims to more lands than she'd known existed, including islands of land that were just vague drawings on maps from her past.

"Aye. I agree. I do. And aye. From this day forward. And further. Aye. 'Til death. What's next?"

The priest started up again, saying Latin phrases that she'd have to concentrate to understand. She didn't want to concentrate. She didn't want to do anything other than exist. Sense. Feel. The words stopped again. Juliana wasn't listening so she didn't know why.

"Nae. I have nae such thing. I dinna' think of it. She can have one of her choosing. From my treasury. She can have them all. Would you just finish?"

A token. They'd been speaking of a token, such as a

charm, or a trinket, or a ring like the signet ring her father had once worn. That was what Aidan hadn't brought.

"Get on with it, Father, or I'll be for consummating my marriage in your church aisle. I doubt the Lord will appreciate that, although I will have definite witnesses to the event."

Juliana shut her eyes tightly to the reaction at that statement. She only wished she could block her ears to the laughter and hollering and clapping and stomping. The priest had to wait for the room to calm again before he could continue. The entire time, Juliana stayed exactly where she was, experiencing it exactly as it happened. Memorizing. Enjoying. Giggling.

There were a few more intonations and then silence.

"'Tis done? We're wed? Finally?"

"Aye," the priest replied. "You may kiss your bride."

"Kiss her? Jesu'! Begging pardon, Father . . . but I doona' dare! Tavish! Gregor! Heck! See us to my chamber! Through the guard walk! Now!"

"This is highly irregular, my laird—"

The priest sputtered the words, as if he'd just noticed it. He didn't finish.

"Wait! Wait! Oh . . . sweet Lord! Wait!"

It was Lachlan. He was screaming the words and waving something and so out of breath that he was slapping a stretched drum thing against his thigh that made an even louder noise than Aidan's yelling.

Juliana heard the growl emanating from Aidan's chest before he made it. She put her hands to him, open-palmed, and pushed. He pulled away slightly and looked down at her, and stole her senses again.

"You have to . . . answer . . . this! Dame . . . Lileth—"

Aidan's eyebrow moved up at the name, and then he tightened an arm about Juliana and turned them as a unit to face the crowded mass of clansmen and women filling the chapel floor.

"By the saints, Lachlan!" It was Kerr blocking the man's access, and then it was a sea of folk.

"Nae . . . wait! She'll have . . . my head if he's done it . . . without reading this!"

"Done what?"

"Let . . . me pass, cousin!"

Juliana reached for Aidan's chin and brought his attention back to her. And then she nodded and gestured with hers to the intruder. Aidan lifted his chin, looked above her head, and then sighed. Heavily.

"Let him through, Kerr. You, too, Ewan. All of you."

She waited with Aidan until the man made it through an aisle way they'd shifted to create that had barely enough room, and Lachlan was thin. His long coat was pulled open, showing spindly legs and samite short pants. Juliana had to stop the smile. No wonder the man preferred long coats to a kilt. He had the legs of a girl. He was also balding, as the bonnet hanging from one ear mutely testified. He spent a few moments gathering his clothing back together once he reached the area right in front of her and Aidan.

"Well!" He huffed the exclamation when he'd finished and finally bowed his head in deference.

"What do you want, Lachlan?"

"The missive. You're to read it afore wedding her to Alpin. I'm under threat!"

"From whom?" Aidan asked.

"Dame Lileth. I'm to make certain you answer this . . . or she'll have me castrated!"

There was a huge gasp over that threat. Juliana had her hand over her mouth to prevent what was going to be full amusement.

"Sweet Mother of God! Please tell me I'm in time!"

"Aye . . . and nae," Aidan replied.

Lachlan went to his knees. "She's wed . . . already?"

"That is the 'aye,'" Aidan replied.

Lachlan's shoulders started shaking. Juliana actually felt sorry for him. She nudged Aidan. Who rolled his eyes. "Lachlan MacGorrick. Stand. And hand me the note."

"I'm too late. Oh, God! Have mercy! You doona' ken!"

"Lachlan! Stand up! I dinna' wed her to Alpin!"

The man's head moved and he looked up. Juliana watched as he looked from her to Aidan and back again. And then, he was struggling to get back on his feet. And looking even sillier.

"You dinna' wed her . . . to Alpin?" he asked with scrunched eyes, as if he didn't believe it.

"That is the 'nae' part," Aidan replied.

"Oh thank God! Thank—she dinna' tell me what to do in this event."

"Hand me the missive," Aidan said.

Juliana felt him tightening everywhere she touched. He probably didn't even note that he did it. She knew why. He was preparing himself. And then he released her with his right arm and held out his hand. Lachlan put the bent and pierced and dirtied scrap of folded parchment in Aidan's hand as if it were a treasure. Aidan brought it close, so he could unfold it without releasing her. And then he held it up and started reading, moving his lips . . .

And then he threw back his head and started laughing.

The acoustics in the room echoed and reechoed it. While all about everyone had the same perplexed expression. And then Aidan stopped. Looked down at Juliana with the tenderest expression while she counted three of his heartbeats, and then he put back his head and hollered even louder than before. Juliana had to put her hands to her ears. Several of his clan had the same issue.

"What?"

"Jesu', Aidan! Tell us!"

"Have you lost your wits?"

"It is ever true, lads! Ever!"

"What is? Well?"

That was Heck. He was the closest and reaching for the missive. Aidan handed it to him, and then enfolded his wife with both arms again. Fully. And then his lips were on her caplet and he was shuddering. And then he whispered words that completely stopped her heart.

"I love you, Juliana."

"Well . . . would you look there." That was Heck. It was easy to hear him since everyone was silent and waiting.

"What?"

"For the love of God! What does it say?"

"The Campbell clan is refusing the MacKetryck laird. Their daughter's hand was promised to the Finlay clan na' two fortnights ago. That would be . . . just afore our laird sent his request! They are offering their younger daughter instead."

"Blast it all!" That was Tavish. "I was looking forward to a good fight."

"There's always a good fight, Tavish, my lad. But there's never been a wedding like this! Come all! Back to the hall! There's good Killoran ale still to be drunk and lies to be told!"

Chapter 25

"But there's the bedding ceremony!"

"Aye! The bedding ceremony!"

"And proof of consummation!"

More cheers and loud clapping and stomping added to the melee about them. Juliana watched Lachlan as he held on to his bonnet with one hand while crawling his way to one side. Heck had possession of the drum thing, though, and was using it with brute force.

"Hold on to me!"

Aidan wasn't whispering, but he might as well have been, since she barely heard him. He didn't wait for her to follow the instruction. He didn't wait to see if anyone followed Heck's enticements. He gestured with his head to more of his men, took a step forward, lifting her into his arms at the same time, and then another step, and another until he was at a run for the leap to the altar platform.

He hadn't needed to tell her to hold on—she was clinging as he raced behind his clansmen up so many spiraled stairs she got dizzy. And then they were through a door jamb and beneath a stone archway, and out atop the conjoined buildings, in the chill and mist-wrapped star-strewn heavens of the night. Juliana bounced with Aidan as he jogged along the walkway, returning greetings and cheers with little more than grunts. The closest man was Tavish. She'd have known his spare frame anywhere, even without the addition of the torch he held aloft.

Then they were stopped. Aidan huffed out a sigh of breath larger than the ones he'd used while running, but his heart didn't miss a beat from the harsh rhythm it made. There was a contingency of guards atop the walkway, looking seven to eight heads deep. Juliana pressed closer into Aidan. They looked familiar. She couldn't decide why. Then all of them went to a knee with their right hands atop the hilts of their claymores.

"As Dugald MacKetryck's former honor guard, we pledge service, my laird."

A large bearded fellow was their spokesman. Aidan grunted before shifting Juliana to his left side and then he shoved her up, holding her with one arm beneath her buttocks and her torso and hair draped atop his shoulder. It probably looked exactly like the abduction pose it was meant to.

"You're freed . . . of service. Return to . . . your homes," Aidan replied in a clipped tone that was panted through his breaths.

"We've nae homes, my laird. By command."

Aidan grunted again. Stood taller and pulled in a breath that raised her with it. "Stefan?" Aidan burst the name out.

"Aye?"

"See these men . . . to our quarters. Once they've seen me to my rooms. I've always need . . . of loyal guardsmen. As do my brothers. We'll make a contest of it. On the list. On the morrow. Nae! The next day. For now . . . move them out of my way!"

"You heard him, lads! Move! And I'll see your sorry arse on the list, Iain. You also, Grant. And you, Gawain. Think to best us, do you?"

"We've been hankering for a good fight!" That sounded like Gregor.

"Aye! A big one . . . since the Campbell war was denied us!" That was Tavish again.

The shuffling of boots and weaponry accompanied their movements. There was a bit of hooting and grumbling, and what sounded like fighting, but was instead the thumping of their fists against their own chests. Juliana saw that since Aidan had moved her back into his arms while he waited, getting more locks of hair and pearls draped about both of them. And then Aidan was moving rapidly again, only this time, he had more men behind him as well as a wall of them in front.

Men! She'd never understand them.

She knew when they moved from the chapel building onto the top of the keep by the downward slant of Aidan's steps, and then they slowed again. Stopped. She heard a chain rattling, wood groaning. Juliana twisted to watch as a trapdoor was lifted, showing a yawning aperture of black below.

"You need to put the wife down now, Aidan." Tavish grinned, showing pearly white teeth in a shadow-dark face.

Aidan looked at her. Juliana returned it. And was lost in his gaze. Just like always. Then he shook his head.

"Nae."

"We'll hold her," someone offered.

"It would only be for a moment, Aidan." That sounded like Stefan, but she didn't move from looking at Aidan to check.

Aidan's arms tightened beneath her knees and around her back. And then he looked away, releasing her from the locked gaze. Took another deep breath. "Lead on. I'll follow. And nae man holds the wife. Save me."

Tavish was shaking his head as he scrambled onto his buttocks at the top of the hole and then disappeared right through it. Aidan went to his haunches and swiveled her about so she settled atop his lap. He had one arm about her torso and the other beneath her knees, and then he gripped his hands together, locking her in place. He narrowed his eyes for a moment and shuddered, and then reopened them.

"Hold tight, Juliana!"

He didn't need to say it. Her arms were squeezed about his neck. She shut her eyes as he launched them forward into black space. She couldn't prevent the squeal that echoed eerily from the room they landed in as well as through the opening.

Aidan was laughing when he landed, going to a crouch that jolted her, before standing straight again. And then he was looking up toward the opening, which had several heads blocking it.

"Lads?"

The heads disappeared, and then the night sky did, too. Groaning accompanied the wood block's movement back into place. Tavish was already leaving the tower room before the chain sound came again, and Aidan was at his heels.

"You're mad," Juliana told him.

Aidan grinned. Nodded. Grinned wider. "I have been so named that before. Too. Tavish?"

The man tipped his head backward, but didn't stop moving. "You've earned additional portion this eve. And my thanks."

The man started them down a spiral stair, this one dark and musty. The torch sent shadow chunks of light in a skipping pattern with Tavish's pace. At the bottom, he spun to face them, walking backward for a few steps, the torch held high.

"As soon as I get through your chamber, I'll bar any from coming in. I'll call on more if needed. You doona' need witness to your consummation."

Juliana's eyes went wide. Aidan grunted again. And then nodded.

Tavish stopped speaking and stopped walking, a hand span from smacking into a door barely the size of Juliana.

Hewn from a single block of wood, it was mounted with old leather, and studded in place with iron pegs. Tavish had it opened and pushed backward, lifting the back of a tapestry with the motion. Then he was gesturing them into Aidan's chambers. He did it with a grandiose wave of his arm and a huge bow that nearly scraped his forehead against an outstretched knee . . . as if responsible for the entire chain of events.

"Your rooms, my laird and lady," he announced.

Juliana heard the bolt falling, locking the hidden door. She watched the tapestry fall back into place, completely covering it as well, before looking back at the same room, the same fire, the same view of starlit loch through the panorama of windows that she'd been removed from a mere day before.

And that was when it felt totally real.

Aidan didn't set her down. He stood in place, breathing heavily as the door to his outer chamber shut, after accepting Tavish's wink, nod, and wave. Juliana rolled her head against his chest, settling it into the indentation between his chest muscles, and looked out at what he was looking at.

The shutters were open, pulled to the inside walls of each aperture, and a moon was just peeping from atop the land on the other side of Buchyn Loch, shedding a jagged line of light onto the waves. As if she'd asked it, Aidan started walking slowly toward his windows, each step rocking her head slightly back and forth against the hard mounds of his upper chest. From such a vantage she could hear his heart beating, feel his every breath, and experience the low throb of a moan he must have voiced.

"Oh . . . Aidan."

"Juliana."

"I . . . can't believe . . . this is real."

"You're na' crying, are you? Again?"

She shook her head, and wiped at the evidence at the same time.

"What did I do . . . now?"

"Wed me."

"You dinna' wish me to?"

Juliana giggled. "I . . . it's just so . . . beautiful."

"Women cry tears over beauty?"

"And happiness," she whispered.

"Oh, Juliana, I'm near mad. Your smell. Your beauty. Your wit. Your . . . innocence. I'm afire with want and filled with need. And I was a fool to even think I could watch all that given to Alpin."

"You were a fool for not reading your missive."

He pulled in one cheek and lifted the opposing eyebrow. Juliana lurched within his arms. Then he nodded.

"Aye. That . . . I was."

He was trembling slightly, and his heart had elevated. He'd tipped his head to whisper the words against her ear, earning a froth of shiver all over her frame so distinct he had to experience it, too. His arms adjusted, rotating her body so her feet could slide to the floor and leave her standing on the consistency of clouds, while her head hadn't moved from a berth against his heart. His hands began a mesmerizing slide down each arm and then back up, down . . . up . . . trailing his index finger along the flesh. Then he spoke again, sending the words echoing through his chest wall into her ears. "I've wanted to show you this . . . since I first . . . knew you, Juliana, my love."

"Oh, Aidan." That time, she couldn't contain the sob.

"Now what have I done?"

"You . . . called me . . . by name."

She probably deserved his look of confusion.

"What would you wish to be called?" he asked.

"Ju . . . liana." She paused midname.

"I doona' understand women," Aidan replied.

"And then you called me . . . your . . . *love.*"

"That? 'Tis nae secret. Even Dame Lileth knew. And 'tis true. I do love you, Juliana. My Juliana. Beauteous Juliana . . ."

He breathed air all over her with each word . . . sending quiver after quiver in its stead, the action threatening to turn what was real into magic and delight and view-enhanced enchantment.

"You do-do-doona' feel . . . it, too?"

His voice stammered and altered through the question, sounding unsure and young and just like Arran, and Juliana wiped at more tears.

"Jesu'! Tears again?" He stiffened.

Juliana gulped. "I . . . love you, Aidan Niall . . . Mac-Ketryck. More . . . than I ever imagined. More than life . . . itself! I'd die for you. And . . . you made me want to!"

"She also told me that," he replied.

His hands moved to her upper arms before pivoting her in place, spinning and then catching her. Juliana registered the slide of her slippers against his wood floor, the grasp of hands about her upper arms, the force of man right in front of her. And then he was lifting her up against him and shuddering in place the entire time. He had his eyes closed, his nostrils flared for the quick gasps of breath he was taking, and his lips pursed. She'd never seen anything as erotic and enticing.

"Oh . . . Aidan . . ."

His lips twitched and he lowered them, halting her mid-voice while the last word was moaned into the confines of his kiss. Magic erupted, encasing her with fingers of feeling, and fantasy wove about her vision with sparkle-touched mist . . . erasing all the heartbreak and doubt as if beckoned there. Juliana stayed rooted to the spot, her arms kept from responding by the pressure of his hands on them, and sucked at his lips as he was hers. Slid her tongue along the inner edge of his lower lip, lurched against him, and then arched in shock as his tongue flicked against the inner cavern of her mouth.

Her knees sagged, melting her against him. Aidan responded with an instant move of his arms about her back, lifting her fully against him, and then he started spinning slowly, rotating them in a slow circle. Moonlight lightened where they were standing, flashing in narrow bands of light as he danced her through it. Juliana felt him stop, his free hand pulling at the caplet atop her head before he slowly and sinuously pulled the piece away and slid it all the way to the ends of her hair, lifting her farther as he went.

"Ah . . . Juliana. You doona' ken. 'Tis even worse than I thought. And better. Your beauty. Your smell. Your . . . taste."

Aidan's whispers against her lips had accompanied the motion of his hand, grazing buttocks and thighs and loins. Her jerk of reaction had him shoving strong, hot, and rigid thickness against the linen covering her thighs. And then he pushed farther, his action moving the material into the opening her thighs created as they separated to make room.

Everything ceased. Sound ceased. Breathing ceased. Time ceased.

Aidan shuddered in place while everything about him tightened and constricted and stilled. Totally. With vicious intent. And then he gave a groan that ripped their lips apart. He'd tipped his head back as well, giving her a perfect view of throat and chin . . . and all of it muscled and defined and coated with a film of moisture that beckoned. Invited. Thrilled. Dared . . .

Juliana leaned forward and licked skin and got an instant grip in response, as the arms about her back seized her to him, holding her locked to him, while he shook and quavered and shuddered in place. And then stilled. He lowered his head, pinned her motionless with the moonlight-caressed beauty of his face, and then put his lips to a pout and blew a sigh.

"That was . . . Whew." A tremor accompanied the words,

vibrating through them before it halted. "We've got to slow this, lass. Slow. You ken?"

She shook her head, got his smile, and then another sigh. He lifted her above him then, the movement releasing the shaft from between her thighs, and that caused another tremor to score his frame and another sharply indrawn breath. Juliana hovered above him, her belly atop the muscle of one shoulder, while he finished trembling and groaning and flexing. And then fingers reached and peeled the last of the pearl and silver wire ribbon–bedecked headdress from her tresses and then dropped it. Juliana heard the slight rattle of it, and then he was running his fingers through the ringlets all over her back and buttocks and the backs of her upper thighs.

And then fingers were pressing against the satin-covered flesh at the backs of her knees, grasping and kneading and massaging . . . before roaming higher along the backs of her thighs. Every touch released froths of tingles that flew over her frame again and again and with increasing momentum and effect. She felt him at her buttocks, cupped to hold her as he slowly lowered and slid her down from the perch atop his shoulder until she was pressed fully and totally against him, while the solid, firm portion of him pushed at her belly with the size and mass and power of it.

Juliana glanced at the shadow-darkened recess created by his groin before looking back to him, and Aidan was watching for it. His one eyebrow was cocked up as he moved to a finger-width distance, narrowing eyes that locked on to hers, entrapping her deeper, more fully, and more irrevocably by the bare hint of moisture she could see of the amber color.

"Juliana. Juliana. Sweet . . . sweet Juliana . . ."

What began as a groan turned into a litany of her name, gaining in depth and speed and breathlessness until it blended into a blur. The sound accompanied one hand movement up her back, sliding along her spine before reaching the curls at the back of her head to grip her and hold her and deny her the option of receiving his kiss. Passion gripped at her, owning and taking her, and making her lips the ones to devour his, sucking and lapping and tasting. Aidan's groans filled her ears, his tongue her senses, and then he was moving, trailing a kiss over her chin and to her throat . . .

Juliana put her hands on his chest muscles and pushed, and he allowed it, loosening his hands and moving them to her shoulders . . . then her back . . . and then he used them to hold her as she bowed backward until wisps of curls nearly touched the floor. Juliana started swaying then, moving her upper body back and forth and again, and he moved with her, making a graceful dance with silent music.

Aidan stilled, stopping her movements with the pressure of his fingers, and then using them to bring her back to him with as much connection as her arched position allowed. Juliana opened her mouth and gasped for each breath as he started lapping his way down her throat with a tongue laced with passion and eroticism and fervor.

Waves crested over her, keening through her entire frame before finding a berth at each breast. Juliana pulled up and out of her arch, granting him access to everything he wanted, every place he desired, every speck of flesh he craved. Her hands moved of their own accord to his shoulders, then up along his face, before shoving into the hair at his temples, gripping handfuls of the silken strands, and pulling them loose from the queue he'd trapped them in.

The satin of her bodice was shoved aside to a questing tongue that sought and reached, and then licked one of her nipples. At the first touch, Juliana reacted, flinging her head back to look with unseeing eyes at the ceiling joists, tightening her fingers in his hair, and opening her mouth for each gasp of breath as the jolt of shock was replaced almost instantly by a molten sensation . . . overtaking, encompassing, and then overriding everything else. She was flying. Falling. Soaring. And her choked squeal told of it.

Aidan licked her flesh again, gaining another squeal, greater tautness of her entire frame as she shoved farther back against his supportive arm, and tighter fingers through his hair.

"Sweet . . . Juliana. My Juliana."

The murmur was made atop flesh that immediately reacted to the wetness he'd put there. Juliana wriggled, moaned, trembled, and then shoved her breast closer to his mouth, subconsciously begging for what he denied.

Her eyes closed. She was floating. Being carried. Falling.

Cool linen touched her back, the softness embracing her back, hips, thighs, everywhere except where one of his arms still enwrapped. The limb gave a thick support for another arch and Juliana bowed into one, sinuously sliding back and forth while shoving her belly and breasts upward, and receiving nothing but air-touched wetness that accompanied his chuckle.

"Aidan . . . please?" The hoarse whisper scratched at her throat, sounding desperate and breathless and distressed, and the second time it was even more so. "Please . . . Aidan. Please?"

Juliana sensed movement, experienced the mattress beneath her shifting and swaying, felt air from a heavy sigh careening all about her, and then she heard ripping.

"Aidan?"

The form-fitting samite of her wedding dress released its grasp . . . before getting pushed into a confining wrap about her waist. She twisted and moaned and slid about the linens as he shoved the material to her knees . . . her ankles . . . feet . . . and then pushed it from her completely.

Swift spurts of tightening heralded the white satin underdress's surrender, as Aidan pulled each bit of stitching apart, one spot at a time, first down one side and then another. Night air caressed the flesh revealed, feeling wanton and sensual, and completely erotic. Juliana arched again, sending her body into a sinuous writhe of movement against bed linens at her back and nothing atop.

"Lovely . . . beauteous . . . Juliana . . ."

More sonnet-like words filled her existence, mouthed against her throat and then her breasts, while Juliana gasped for breath after breath in a baited agony of want. And then he touched her nipple again, lapping at a nub that quivered and tightened against his tongue before he put a full mouth upon it and suckled.

Juliana lurched fully, filling his mouth with more flesh as she reacted. Waterfalls of cold snowmelt poured over her body, followed by fire, then ice, and then fire again, until she couldn't contain the sensation another moment. Her mouth was open and grasping and emitting the longest, most melodic note until she ran out of air and sucked for more. Aidan responded with a chuckle, sending chill atop chill all over the nipple he'd just sweetened, before rolling her slightly in order to give the same rapture and wonder to her other breast. Juliana's arch went brutal, affixing her in a tight bow of carnal yearning and overpowering desire, and laying bare every bit of it. Aidan was with her the entire time, sucking and licking and caressing and sending her over more snowmelt waterfalls and into more wickedly hot baths, and gaining more long notes into the chamber over and over until her throat felt raw with the effort.

Aidan lifted himself from her then before he moved, the act deflating her poised position, and Juliana slowly settled into the cloud-like mattress. Then it was denting, rocking in odd spurts of movement as he shoved from it. Juliana rolled her head, catching her hair beneath it and slitting her eyes to the sight of Aidan, pulling at his kilt band until the brooch ripped fabric and the plaid moved off his shoulder and onto his arm. A thud of sound accompanied his belt hitting the floor, followed by a peppering of sound that was his dirks and weapons. And then the *feile breacan* was unwound and pushed from him. He grabbed the hem of his shirt and yanked it over his head, ripping seams in the process and stealing every bit of her available air with the sight of moonlight-kissed masculine beauty.

Shadows carved him into a mass of valleys and hills, the light roving about rivers of muscle, entwined knots of strength, and hollows of black dimness. Then he filled his chest with air, pumped out his upper body, and turned, revealing a thick engorged and masculine part that had her in a sit, staring and gasping, and then stifling all of it with the fingers she shoved into her mouth.

"Oh . . . Aidan."

The words didn't make sense against her fingers, but he heard them, or guessed what they were. Juliana couldn't even blink as he went absolutely still and stayed that way, his stance leaving moonlight to caress and delineate him.

"Aye?"

"You're . . . so . . . beautiful."

He moved before she'd finished, crushing the mattress in front of her with a hand before propelling around and behind her and into the space at the back of the enclosed bed. Juliana's gasp stuck in her throat as his arms snaked about her, pulling her against him, matching her curl-covered back with his chest, and then he was leaning and shoving and maneuvering until they were both on their sides. It had been so rapid and precise and without warning that Juliana was blinking at the moonlit mass of chamber in front of her and pushing each breath into the band of arms about her with surprise.

And then she felt the shake of him that accompanied a growling laughter sound, before stilling, his heartbeat hard and loud against her shoulders and his breathing harsh and swift along her skin. He didn't move for so long, she squirmed.

That got the arm beneath her tensed. And that got her lifted slightly from the mattress.

A whoosh of breath touched the back of her neck, and his free hand shifted, pushing hair from his path all along her . . . down her hip and along her thigh to her knee. Returning to brush her woman-place while she jumped, then sliding along her belly . . . and reaching a breast. Aidan flicked a nipple and then toyed with it while his entire frame started sliding against hers using the same sinuous motions she had.

Juliana closed her eyes and leaned backward, putting her shoulders against the hard mounds of his chest, while the backs of her upper thighs and buttocks touched and then jerked away from the mass of strength and thickness she'd craved with vicious want.

Aidan groaned, touched a kiss to her neck, and sucked on her while he stroked again along her nakedness. Juliana jerked away again. And again. And again . . . all the while his groans deepened and his attempts never lessened . . . as if daring a touch and waiting for her to take it.

Again.

"Ah . . . love."

His whisper against her ear accompanied another slide of him, and he must've known the word had too much power. It always had. Juliana stayed connected that time and waited. And existed. Breathing. Waiting.

Aidan groaned again and moved, sliding his rod along her nakedness with slowness and precision. Heat licked at her from the connection before turning into fire . . . and then going back to heat. Aidan slid his shaft along the backs of her thighs . . . and then inserted it between them . . . pulled it back out . . . ran it along the backs of her thighs again. He spread the fingers of the hand beneath her across her belly, flexing his fingers before pulling her tightly against him in order to push between her thighs again. He held in place and shook, and then pulled out again. Then back.

His free hand moved then, skimming along her skin, igniting rivulets of reaction as he reached her hip and then moved unerringly to her woman spot. Juliana's jump was caught and held in place, and then turned into a vibration of sensitivity with his first touch. It was too much sensation and in too many places!

Juliana moaned against an onslaught of touch and sensation and wonder, her breath coming quicker and faster and uglier and harsher, while her hands went to talons of grip against both his arms. She felt another push of his rod between her thighs, sending fire to match that at her core. He pulled back out, while the sensations he was creating got wilder and faster and quicker. And then he pushed back, sliding his hardness completely through her thighs and touching flesh that was in a whorl of tension and need and wantonness. Juliana heaved at the contact, even as he moved back out . . . Again . . .

The torment ratcheted higher, going stronger, more strident and more agonized, and just when she thought her heart was going to come straight out through her throat, it happened. Her heart turned into a separate entity, kicking about in her chest and rising to her throat and filling her ears with powerful beats, while the thick-ridged portion of Aidan shoved through her thighs again, stroking across the exact spot he was strumming . . .

And Juliana exploded.

Her eyes scrunched tight and she heard screaming. Wonder flowed everywhere, an entire panoply of it . . . washing through her and over her, covering her, soaking her, and sending wave after wave of wonder and exultation and glory, before the most vivid pressure joined in, entwining with the sensations of ecstasy and making Juliana pant with the fulfillment of receiving, containing, and enwrapping it.

Aidan was grunting in small breaths that matched the shoves he was making, holding her with both hands about her hips, the position tilting her forward and making her receive him in little bits of sensation that were driving her mad.

And then something changed, and he shoved fully, filling her with as much as he could reach. Then he gave a twinge, making her moan with the sensation.

"I will na' take you quick, Juliana. Na' this time. Regardless of need and ache and want! And denial! Christ! Regardless of—" He cut off his words and everything stopped as he stiffened and tightened, except for the pounding beat of his heart against the backs of her shoulders.

Juliana slit an eye open on a rumple of bed linen at her cheek. She moved her head to face him, but before she could, Aidan responded. He sucked in a breath that moved her with it, and that just made everything flex and move from where they were joined.

"Oh Lord. Doona' move."

Juliana wasn't moving. She was doing her utmost to accept and enjoy the fullness and heat without the motion her body was tormenting her with. And then he moved, sliding slightly from her only to shove right back in.

"Too . . . wondrous. Juliana . . . it's just . . ."

Hot breath touched her shoulder, instantly followed by his tongue, and that led to more whispered words accompanying his kiss. And more movement of his groin against hers. His kiss reached her ear, and Juliana hunched her shoulder, defending skin that rose in goose bumps of reaction. There was too much sensation, too much emotion, too much intensity, and it was adding and mingling and interspersing the waves from where he was starting to rhythmically rock his loins against hers . . .

Pulling out. Pushing back into place. Pulling out . . .

Aidan moved his kiss, trailing his lips to her jaw as Juliana turned her head, and then his mouth slammed against hers, mingling breath. Combining moisture. Connecting flesh.

He rolled her within his arms, putting her onto her back

with a twist that had more ecstasy attached. The moan of it
passed into the caverns of his mouth, and became more of
them as he planted a fist into the mattress at her side and
lifted, maneuvering her thigh around and about him, until she
was fully beneath him, her legs about him, and receiving
every portion of him. While the groan he gave released her
lips due to the length and volume of it. Aidan had both
hands smashed into the mattress on either side of her as he
lifted, using a rocking motion that fueled the wonder building, elevating . . . erupting.

Liquid friction surrounded her, sending flickers down her
legs, up through her belly . . . through her breasts. Juliana ran
her hands all along and over him, again and again, enjoying
every bit of the ridges of his back, the heavy contours of his
belly and chest, the heavy roping of strength in his arms. Her
caresses sent an itch onto her fingers with every stroke, every
touch, every contact, while Aidan's movements added to the
exquisite torment creating . . . building.

Heat put a moist film in place atop every bit of skin her
fingers skimmed. Breath got harsher, more strenuous . . .
quicker paced. Aidan started moving with broader strokes,
alternately filling and releasing her with heavier and thicker
and stronger movements that started such a tension in her
core that she was going mad with it. Juliana flung her head
from side to side, blowing little gasps of breath before gaining new ones. The feeling built. Expanded. Enlarged. Got
closer. Nearer . . .

Juliana quivered with it, felt a thrill centering from where
his motions were increasing, rocking and swaying the entire
bed frame in fast-paced, heavy lunges of his body into hers.
Over and over again and again, and then she sensed it . . .
grabbed at it . . . and then careened right over the edge into
such a perfect explosion of bliss, she opened her mouth to
give full vent to it.

The note of ecstasy hung in the room, even after she'd

spent her breath, giving vent to a wonder that couldn't be contained. Juliana's fingers clung to him, she lifted with him, meeting his every thrust with one of her own as he pummeled her body with an abandon that had nothing rhythmic about it. And then he stopped, pulling her up and against his body with her hold while everything on him went tense and stiff and filled with a vibration that moved her with it.

Juliana's eyes were open and watching as Aidan tossed back his head, letting out a long sobbed note that had every cord in his throat taut and every muscle in his frame rigid, while the mattress shook from the shuddering of his arms.

And then he lowered his head, opened his eyes, blinked, and tipped his head to put a kiss on her nose. "I love you, Juliana," he whispered. "Forever."

And then he had to deal with her tears of happiness again.

Epilogue

Aidan woke from the dream reminding him of where he'd hung his sporran bag and on what tree, the exact moment Juliana informed him it was time for their son to enter the world. And time for him to vacate the area, and leave the birthing and laboring to the women.

Aidan was hesitant. If he lost this wife . . . he didn't think he could handle finishing the thought. The grief. The loss. For nine months he and Juliana had been nearly inseparable. Basking in a love that grew daily. Glowing with it.

So he did what he always did.

Became rash. Reckless. Thoughtless. And quick.

It was an omen. And despite the brutal winter weather that was putting new snow atop old crusted ice, he set out for Loch Erind, with fourteen members of his own honor guard, as well as all eleven members of Arran's, since his brother insisted on accompanying him. This left Alpin in control of the castle, and the castle business, and the birthing of the laird's heir. Alpin was in luck that Dame Lileth and Lady Reina were handling it. The lad nearly keeled over when informed. And then he started arguing, until his senior honor guardsman, Iain Blaine, put a hand on the lad's shoulder, and gave the correct counsel.

It took more than two days to reach their camp spot. An afternoon to clear ground for setting up tents and well into the night before they had three huge fires going, but only moments to reach the exact tree where Aidan had hung the sporran bag before he'd dived into the loch. Exactly as his dream had reminded him.

He didn't know what it meant, or why he had to have it, but the little signet ring that barely fit on the bottom of his finger was going to his wife. She'd yet to choose her own token, although she'd gone through his entire treasury playing at which gems she'd wear and with which outfit. But she had yet to choose. And he had yet to make her.

Aidan held the amulet Dame Lileth had made for him next to the ring taken from the woodcutter and twisted them back and forth in the glow cast from his oil wick. Identical. He couldn't wait to return to Juliana and show her.

Juliana!

He moved his vision to the tent weave above him, blinked rapidly at the moisture cursing him, and then went to his knees in prayer.

The return journey was even worse, with another windswept blizzom, costing them an extra day and a half longer. They had to spend one full day and night at the Killoran compound, eating well-roasted meats and drinking full-spirited ales, while the tension and worry kept mounting within him. He shouldn't have left her. He should have been there! If she died while birthing his bairn . . .

The fire didn't hold any answers, nor did his cot, nor did the backs of his eyelids if he tried closing them. Nothing muted the worry. It was only when they finally spied Castle Ketryck's gray stone walls between the falling flakes that Aidan's heart fully started beating again, making large and heavy strokes within his chest that threatened to choke him.

The drawbridge took forever to lower. He could have crossed the near frozen moat before they finally dropped the bridge into position. And the lower bailey had never taken so long to cross! Aidan pushed his stallion to a run on churned frozen ground, and he wasn't waiting for the others before springing from the saddle onto the second step ledge of his front door.

He wasn't but three steps inside the great hall, yanking the ties of his sodden furs apart and shoving the outer layer from him, before Alpin stood from one of the benches, looking like he hadn't slept in days.

"Juliana?"

"Doona' ever do that again!" Alpin cried.

"How . . . is Juliana?"

"Groaning and screaming and crying and making it impossible to sleep. That is how your Juliana is."

"The bairn?"

"'Tis trouble. It's na' here yet . . . but wait!"

"Oh . . . Jesu'." Aidan choked on the fear, blinked around the blur of moisture in his eyes, and shook with suppressing the instant red that hovered in his vision.

"Dame Lileth says it's na' a bad sign. S-S-Some b-b-b-bairns . . . it's—"

"What, Alpin? What?"

"He canna' speak if you choke him, my laird."

Iain's bearded face and solid voice stopped the red that was starting to permeate everything. Aidan released his brother's throat and stepped back. One step. Another.

"Are na' you supposed to protect your lord?" Ewan asked his older brother.

Iain pursed his lips and looked to the ceiling as if debating the answer. "Aye," he finally answered. "That's what I was doing."

"For the love of God! Alpin! What? What did Dame Lileth say?"

"First bairns take longer. And they—"

Alpin was cut off by a newborn's cry splitting the air throughout the hall. Aidan was at a run before he reached the tower steps, and he had most of his men with him. He didn't get past the antechamber where Dame Lileth was sitting, rocking on a chair and humming. And sipping at her mug.

"Aidan Niall MacKetryck." She reprimanded him with just his name. Aidan came to a stop.

"Aye?" he replied.

"You will contain yourself afore visiting your son. And your wife."

"Juliana . . ."

"Is well."

"But Alpin said—"

"Aidan Niall MacKetryck."

She said his name again, in exactly the same reprimanding tone. Aidan pulled up to his full height and controlled the red, until it faded completely. Then he had to admit again to the blur that was wetting up his eyes. He blinked on it and waited.

"If your wife had been in danger, I would have told you so. You ken?"

He grinned. "And my son?"

"Large. Healthy. As was foretold. 'Twas a hard birth. Give Lady Reina a moment to prepare."

A moment had never taken so long! Aidan and his men paced the antechamber width, occasionally bumping into each other, for what seemed an eternity, but they all stopped and swiveled the moment they heard the door handle being turned down. And then the door opened, and Lady Reina came out carrying a MacKetryck plaid–covered bundle with two red fists waving from it that had every man there blinking rapidly and clearing their throats, while Aidan shoved through them to the front.

"Your son, my laird."

It was a good thing she didn't hand the infant to Aidan.

His legs were warning him as his knees trembled, and his arms were right behind. He leaned forward, looked at the dark-haired babe, and then went to a giddy grin as it popped a fist into its mouth and started suckling on it.

"Juliana?" he asked.

"She's ready for you now."

Aidan turned to Dame Lileth and raised his finger. "Doona' dare give any prediction until I return. You ken?"

She smiled widely then waved her fingers at him, and then she went back to enjoying her drink.

Aidan shut the door behind him and approached his bed. Reddish curls the shade of the rowan tree berry caressed the linens and fell all over the side, as if arranged that way. Juliana looked pale, and tired, and absolutely perfect. Aidan was at her side and on his knees, and he didn't even know how he got there. He'd known she was the most beautiful woman, and now he had added proof as she smiled over at him.

"Did you see him?" she whispered.

Aidan couldn't see through the film of tears in his eyes. He had to lift the bed covering and brush them aside.

"Aye," he replied finally.

"Isn't he . . . beautiful?"

He lifted an eyebrow. And nodded. He didn't trust his voice just yet.

"He . . . looks just like you," she informed him.

"Well. He does have my hair," Aidan replied.

"He has more than that, my love. You just wait."

"He's . . . perfect, Juliana. Perfect. I thank you for him." He cleared his throat, and rummaged about in his sporran. "And . . . I have something for you, Juliana. It was in my sporran bag. The one I'd thought I'd lost. This came from the woodcutter, but I think it belongs with you."

He meant to hand her the ring, but instead she got the purple stone amulet with the link to hang from a chain.

"Where did you get this?"

"Nae. Wrong one. Here. This one."

He handed her the signet ring, too, and watched her do the same comparison he had, twisting and turning them in the light thrown from the torches. They were still identical. Then, she looked across at him and stole his wits. His ability to speak. And nearly got his ability to breathe as well.

"I've never seen this one." She lifted the amulet.

"D-D-Dame Lileth made it. She said it . . . would make things clear. I doona' ken what she meant. Then. Or now."

Juliana smiled. "This is my family crest, Aidan. D'Aubenville."

Aidan blinked several times. Sat back on his haunches. Looked from the ring to the amulet and then back to his wife.

"Y-Y-Your f-f-family crest?" *Jesu'!* He was stuttering.

"I'm Lady Juliana D'Aubenville, Aidan. Fyfen Castle belongs to me. As does all the land surrounding it. My father sent me into the woods with the steward to hide. To keep me safe until the English came to retrieve my property from that horrible clan, the MacDonals."

"You-you-you . . . The L-L-L-Lady D'Aubenville?" His stuttering was more pronounced than ever. He rivaled Arran. He had to swallow again. Clear his throat again. And try again.

"Yes, Aidan. I'm the Lady D'Aubenville. And Fyfen Castle belongs to me."

He pulled himself straight, puffed out his chest, lowered his chin, and gave her a look that usually silenced most of his clan.

"I know that look," she said. "Don't try it on me, Aidan Niall."

"You doona' own Fyfen Castle, Juliana. Na' anymore. I do. By right of marriage. And lordship. And this is yet another time my rash, reckless, and thoughtless behavior has gotten me a victory. I still doona' believe it."

"What are you talking of now?"

"Doona' you see? I went reaving from the MacDonal clan. To take a bit of sheep. Maybe a wench or two. And instead . . . I won everything they had!"

And then he put his head back and bellowed before it turned into laughter.

Books by Bestselling Author
Fern Michaels

___The Jury	0-8217-7878-1	$6.99US/$9.99CAN
___Sweet Revenge	0-8217-7879-X	$6.99US/$9.99CAN
___Lethal Justice	0-8217-7880-3	$6.99US/$9.99CAN
___Free Fall	0-8217-7881-1	$6.99US/$9.99CAN
___Fool Me Once	0-8217-8071-9	$7.99US/$10.99CAN
___Vegas Rich	0-8217-8112-X	$7.99US/$10.99CAN
___Hide and Seek	1-4201-0184-6	$6.99US/$9.99CAN
___Hokus Pokus	1-4201-0185-4	$6.99US/$9.99CAN
___Fast Track	1-4201-0186-2	$6.99US/$9.99CAN
___Collateral Damage	1-4201-0187-0	$6.99US/$9.99CAN
___Final Justice	1-4201-0188-9	$6.99US/$9.99CAN
___Up Close and Personal	0-8217-7956-7	$7.99US/$9.99CAN
___Under the Radar	1-4201-0683-X	$6.99US/$9.99CAN
___Razor Sharp	1-4201-0684-8	$7.99US/$10.99CAN
___Yesterday	1-4201-1494-8	$5.99US/$6.99CAN
___Vanishing Act	1-4201-0685-6	$7.99US/$10.99CAN
___Sara's Song	1-4201-1493-X	$5.99US/$6.99CAN
___Deadly Deals	1-4201-0686-4	$7.99US/$10.99CAN
___Game Over	1-4201-0687-2	$7.99US/$10.99CAN
___Sins of Omission	1-4201-1153-1	$7.99US/$10.99CAN
___Sins of the Flesh	1-4201-1154-X	$7.99US/$10.99CAN
___Cross Roads	1-4201-1192-2	$7.99US/$10.99CAN

Available Wherever Books Are Sold!
Check out our website at **www.kensingtonbooks.com**

More by Bestselling Author
Hannah Howell